I0777920

Nun the Wiser

Bad Habit Book Club #2

Lissa Sharpe

www.smartypantsromance.com

Copyright

This book is a work of fiction. Names, characters, places, rants, facts, contrivances, and incidents are either the product of the author's questionable imagination or are used factitiously. Any resemblance to actual persons, living or dead or undead, events, locales is entirely coincidental if not somewhat disturbing/concerning.

Made in the United States of America

Print Edition

ISBN: 978-1-959097-96-9

Chapter One

I haven't eaten since breakfast, and it's almost 8:00 p.m. That's why I'm having such a hard time focusing on the conversation. I'd like to use being hungry as an excuse for why I *always* have a hard time with the chitchat portion of a night out, but the truth is, I just hate chitchat. No, I haven't watched that show with the dragons. Of course I've noticed the weather—I don't live in an underground bunker, and I have eyes, and *skin*. And frankly, I don't give a rat's ass about that sports team or movie star or musician in all the headlines.

I get that maybe my shortlist of conversational topics limits what we *can* talk about, but you know what? We don't always have to talk. There's value in comfortable silence.

All I care about right now is food. I drum my fingers on the tabletop anxiously as the others talk about that singer dating the guy with the mustache. At least, I think that's what they're still talking about. I tuned them out a few minutes ago while I checked my work email to make sure everything was still set for tomorrow morning's meeting. Having finished with that, I sigh and scan the room for the waitress. "Where are our Pizookies?" I snap impatiently.

Everyone at the table blinks at me like I've just announced my intention to become a stand-up comedian, instead of having asked a perfectly normal question about when our food is going to arrive, at a restaurant where we've come *to eat*. It's been—I glance at my watch. Oh. Only about five minutes since we put in the order. It feels longer than that.

My friend Helen Flanagan offers me a sympathetic smile, rubbing my back. Out of everyone here, I suspect she's the most likely to understand what it's like to get hangry. It's difficult to imagine Helen ever being snappish, with how persistently cheerful she is all the time, but the woman does have a temper. I call it a Loch Ness temper—rarely spotted, rumored to be only myth, but once you've seen it, you can't unsee it.

Sitting next to her is the Bounty Hunter—actual name, Thaddeus "Thad" Hughes, but I won't deign to call him that until he's proven himself worthy. I suspect he's the reason Helen has been even *more* sunshine-and-rainbows happy lately; an endless supply of orgasms from a hot, tattooed ginger will do that, I suppose. I don't mind Helen finally getting some good sex in her life. I just know that out of everyone in this friend group, I need to be the one to remind the Bounty Hunter not to break her heart. Or else. Hence, why the Bounty Hunter won't get the benefit of being called by his real name until he's proven himself worthy.

On the Bounty Hunter's other side is Grady Kelley, the ex-priest. He's a new addition to the group. Jury's still out on him. He's too handsome to be trustworthy, with that dark hair and chiseled jaw and Irish accent. He also seems to be pretty friendly with Tha—with the Bounty Hunter, so that's a strike against him. Then again, it seems that all my fears about him pursuing sweet, young Nina when I first met him were completely unfounded, so I guess that's in his favor. Maybe tonight he'll do something awful, like eat more than his share of the Pizookie, or something wonderful, like give me his portion of the Pizookie, and I'll be able to decide one way or the other if he deserves my eternal scorn.

Last but not least is the darling little fairy princess, Nina. She's the youngest of the group, but that's not the only reason she inspires my mama-bear level of protectiveness. She's so quiet and delicate, and sometimes she gets lost in her own little dream world, far away from where the rest of us can reach her. Plus there's always the random dudes trying to pick her up when she clearly has no interest in them. It makes me want to lock her away in a tower somewhere, where she'll be safe.

I guess that makes me the evil witch in this friend group. And I'm okay with that, actually. I don't mind being a badass Baba Yaga if it means keeping my friends safe. In fact, if I could cast a spell to make the earth crack open so the other half of the table (aka, those with Y chromosomes) would fall into a fiery pit of magma, that would probably make my life a lot easier.

This thought falls into the category of things I should probably not admit out loud.

"Why don't we start talking about the book?" Helen suggests, still rubbing my back soothingly, like she can sense I'm wishing I had magic powers that would kill off all the men at the table. She gets me like that. "Maybe that will distract us until the food arrives."

I'm so lulled by her soothing, distracting-Matilda-from-being-grouchy voice that it takes me a moment to process what she's saying. What the what? "What book?" I demand.

Okay, so we are technically a book club, or at least, that's how it started out when the three of us—Nina, Helen, and I—didn't know each other all that well. Once upon a time, the only thing we had in common was that we all used to be nuns. Well, technically, I was the only real nun; Helen was a sister, and Nina was a novitiate. We all met up at a support group for former sisters who were now living as laypeople. Realizing we were all about a decade younger than anyone else attending the meetings, we'd gradually started spending more and more time together on our own, just the three of us. At first, having a book to discuss at our meetups gave us something to talk about, aside from how weird it was not to spend most of our time praying and how awesome it was to be able to freely ogle gifs of our Chris of choice. (Mine was Hemsworth, Helen's was Pine, and Nina's was Evans.)

But then we started ordering Pizookies and fighting over getting our full share. And somehow that led to us doing other things together, like going to movies, doing puzzle nights, attempting to build Ikea bookshelves, apologizing for things said while attempting to build Ikea bookshelves, celebrating Galentine's Day, binging the latest season of *Love Is Blind*. Normal friend stuff.

Eventually the "book" part of book club became a thing of the past, mostly because we didn't need it anymore to have something to connect us —and, okay, if I'm being honest, because I never actually read the books. Who has time to read anyway?

So when Helen texted me about the book for the meeting tonight, I thought it was a joke. A #ThrowbackThursday, if you will, even though it's Tuesday. I didn't think we were expected to actually *read* the thing, much less talk about it. Especially because we've been doing less and less of the girl stuff together, just the three of us. Our hangouts still happen, just not as frequently. Helen has made an effort not to be the dreaded disappearing-woman-with-boyfriend, but sometimes she brings the Bounty Hunter along, or she's so busy texting him, it's like she isn't even in the room.

This is how it starts, an ugly little voice whispers in my mind every time Helen cancels last minute or forgets we made plans.

Shut up, you, I always snap back at it, but I can still feel the voice lingering, all smug and insufferable and snuggled deep into my brain.

Now at the table, Helen's still smiling, but somehow also frowning at me at the same time. I'm not sure how her face does it, but it's a very Helen look. "The book. We texted about it."

"Yeah, but that was only a week ago. No one can read a book in a week." Granted, I wouldn't have read the book even if I'd had a year to do it, but I think I'm making a valid point here, and if it will keep us from spending the next hour talking about a book I haven't—nor ever will—read, I will happily die on this hill.

I look around the table for confirmation, searching for any allies to agree with me. Nina's obviously read the book; the last I heard, her uncle isn't letting them watch television anymore, so what else is she supposed to do with her time? But Grady, the ex-priest, is looking at me like he's not sure if I'm joking or not—I get that look a lot from people who don't know me well. I'm rarely, if ever, joking, and he'll learn that soon enough.

Finally, in desperation, I look at the Bounty Hunter. Surely if he's good for anything, it will be not doing the assigned reading. Maybe we can finally bond over that. Maybe he'll finally earn being called by his actual name.

But he has his copy of the book out on the table, and I can see it's been dog-eared in places. Great, just great. Not only did he read the book, but he took *notes*.

No "Thad" for you, I chide him silently, glowering.

"Did you read any of it?" Helen doesn't sound disappointed. Instead, she sounds more like a schoolteacher who knows I'm going to fail the assignment but is trying to give me any points she can.

"The first few chapters," I lie. "I liked the part with the . . . dog."

"The dog?" Nina echoes. She frowns to herself, flipping through the first few pages. "I don't remember that part . . ."

I'm pretty sure Nina is the only person giving me the benefit of the doubt that I might have actually read part of the book. Everyone else is avoiding eye contact, like they assume I must be embarrassed and they don't want to humiliate me any further by making it obvious that they know I'm lying.

The thing is, I'm not embarrassed. I'm sick to my stomach. I'm *terrified*. My heart is racing, and my hands are shaking underneath the table.

This is how it starts—the very first step toward them ultimately deciding to leave me behind.

As they launch into their discussion of the book, I tune out the conversation, but I watch their faces. Everyone is invested in the discussion. No one is just pretending to have done the reading or acting like they enjoyed it when they didn't. They're all having a good time. They're laughing and debating and *bonding*. And I'm on the outside, looking in.

When the Pizookie finally arrives, I grip my spoon, ready to go to war over my territory. I carefully mark out everyone's fifth of the dessert. But everyone else is so into the book discussion, they're hardly paying any attention—I know because I skim off a small slice of the Bounty Hunter's portion and he doesn't even glare at me.

I finish my section of the Pizookie well before anyone else is done and then just sit back, pretending to listen to a conversation I have no part in. As I do so, I get a glimpse of the future. I can always predict the moment a friendship shifts. The moment I'm about to be left behind. Everyone else is having a good time, and they're going to want to continue to talk about the books. And that will naturally evolve into them wanting to do other things that won't interest or involve me. They'll become a new group, the four of them, and I'll have to start over, again. All on my own.

When it becomes clear the conversation is dying down, I sit up, pasting on my most eager smile. "So what's the book for next week, huh? Can't wait to read it!"

I have no idea when I'm supposed to read it, with the hundreds of pages of trial documents I'll be scouring through on top of my already overlong work hours, but I'll find a way. I'll wake up early to read before work if I have to, or read the book on the elliptical machine at the gym.

Everyone blinks at me in surprise. My enthusiasm must be dialed just a bit too high, but I don't know how to turn it down. My smile feels strained, even to myself. "This was just so much fun, I want to make sure I've read the *whole* book for next time."

"Not just the dog parts?" the Bounty Hunter returns wryly.

I don't miss the elbow Helen digs into his ribs. She smiles at me encouragingly. "Why don't *you* choose it, Matilda? Then we'll know it's something you actually want to read."

My over-the-top smile falters at that. I know almost zero books. I haven't read a whole book since high school, and even then, it was the SparkNotes version. "Um . . . what about . . . *War and Peace*?"

A little cliche for a Russian girl, I know, but hey, it's the only title that comes to mind.

Helen and Nina both duck their heads to hide their smiles. Grady blinks at me. "That book is over a thousand pages."

"Is that long?" I ask uncertainly.

"What about *The Curious Incident of the Dog in the Night-Time*?" Helen swoops in to save me. "It has some mystery elements, so Thad, you'll enjoy that part. And there's a dog for Matilda!"

Great. Now I'm going to be the dog person in the group. I don't even like dogs. They're messy and drooly and too codependent. "Can't wait to read it!" I say enthusiastically.

This will work. This can work! I'll find a way to make it work.

Chapter Two

This will never work, I realize almost immediately when I attempt to set up my brand-new e-reader on my elliptical machine. There's too much movement. I'm getting motion sickness from trying to keep my eyes on the screen while I bob up and down with the machine's movements.

It's the next night, almost 9:00 p.m., and I'm at my local gym, Weight Expectations. It's the only time of day I can fit in a workout, but I also like coming this late because I usually have my run of the place, with only a handful of other die-hard exercisers around. The staff are pretty good here, too. I only had them attempt to get me to take a Zumba class once, but my curt, "No way in hell," seemed to be all it took to get them off my back. Now I can come in and do my solitary cardio in peace.

Well, it's *usually* a peaceful experience, except for when I'm realizing that the plan I had to keep my friendships intact is almost certainly doomed to fail. After a few minutes of my eyes blurring and my stomach rolling, and realizing I'll likely need to take Dramamine if I'm going to make this work, I give up on the e-reader and switch over to my usual go-to: ear-shattering, heart-pumping club music. As I increase my pace, my mind races. *What am I going to do? Maybe if I do a good enough job reading summaries of the books, I can fake my way through the conversation at book club nights.*

But no, that won't work. Helen will figure me out with her sneaky librarian ways, and the Bounty Hunter will just look at me with that smug, *haha-I-stole-your-best-friend* look on his dumb, handsome face . . .

Then the answer quite literally walks right past me, in the form of the priest—*ex-priest*—Grady, passing by me to position himself on one of the nearby treadmills. He has his headphones on and he doesn't seem to have noticed me. Then again, he's at the gym, late at night, running on an incline like his life depends on it, so I'm willing to bet he has some other things on his mind.

As I watch him run, heavy electronica music blasts into my eardrums and the wheels in my mind turn. I don't believe in God anymore, or fate, or vision boards, or any of that other nonsense, but I'm not stupid enough to ignore the gift that's just been given to me by whatever cosmic powers might exist.

When Grady finishes his workout and goes into the men's locker room, I wait a minute before hopping off my own machine and following after him.

For a few minutes, I'd kept one eye on Grady and the other on the men's locker room entrance, so I can be pretty sure no one else is in here now. Still, I do a quick, cursory sweep with my eyes over the stalls before stepping forward and making eye contact with Grady in the mirror. He's standing at the sink, blinking at me in surprise and, if I'm not mistaken, a little alarm.

"Hey there, Matilda," he says after a moment. "You alright?"

I brace myself. "I think we should have sex."

Hear me out. It might not be the *best* idea in the entire world, but it's not the worst one either. Grady is new to the friend group. His allegiances can still be swayed. Right now he's naturally bonding with Thad—with the *Bounty Hunter*—because they're both dudes and can talk about beer and football and big boobs and whatever else it is men talk about. If the Bounty Hunter pulls Grady over to his side, and continues using the powers of his magical orgasms to lure Helen away, that leaves only Nina on my team. And while Nina is a beautiful fairy princess, she is in no way tough enough to stand her ground and keep me in the group.

But if I get Grady on my side, with the power of my cardio butt and sexy times, and also manage to keep Nina with me, that's three of us against the Bounty Hunter. And when the Bounty Hunter inevitably disappoints or hurts Helen, the three of us will be there to pick up the pieces.

Having sex with Grady is the only way.

Am I attracted to the priest? Ex-priest, whatever? Not so much. He's an objectively handsome man, but not my type. I'm into a clean-cut, clean-shaven, power-suit kind of vibe. Grady, on the other hand, has a beard and hints of a tragic past in his dark brown eyes that might be a pantie-dropper for some women, but it's not my thing. I don't have any desire to borrow someone else's wretched life story and fix all their broken pieces—maybe because I've never met a man with a darker past than mine. I just can't grow the tragic beard to make it as obvious to the world.

If only women could grow tragic leg hair, or tragic pit hair, and somehow make it both socially acceptable and sexy. Talk about a vicious double standard.

But I digress. It doesn't matter if I actually want Grady so much as if I can make Grady want me. And hello, perky boobs and a tight ass—who wouldn't want this?

Grady is just staring at me, though, so I repeat myself, in case he didn't hear me the first time. "I think we should have sex," I say again.

"Ermmm," Grady says.

"It doesn't have to be here. We can arrange another time," I hasten to add, in case that's the reason he's being so weirdly inarticulate. Frankly, he should be jumping at the chance to get with my caliber of woman, especially after so many years of celibacy.

Then, realization strikes. "Are you still a virgin?" I ask him.

I've never really been known for my tact. I figure, life is too short to hem and haw around niceties.

Grady clears his throat. "That's not . . . something we need to discuss."

"I don't mind," I tell him honestly. "I've slept with lots of guys since leaving the order. Tall, short, skinny, big dick, small dick. About time I tried a virgin."

For the record, I'm not a nymphomaniac or anything. But the thing about being a nun, taking orders, was I'd believed in it so *fully*. I gave my entire heart to it. I followed every rule to the exact letter. When I realized it was all bullshit, I wanted to reclaim some lost experience, sure. But I also wanted to commit to *not* being a nun just as completely as I'd committed to being one. Hence, the revolving door of sexual partners.

Grady doesn't say anything, just keeps staring at me, frozen in place, like he's afraid I'm going to pounce on him. "I'm not desperate," I insist, a little offended that he seems to have jumped to that conclusion—just because I backed him into a corner in the men's locker room and propositioned him for sex. Honestly! "I just thought, you're hot, I'm hot. Let's make it happen. It can be no strings attached, or whatever. We don't even have to tell anyone."

I doubt Helen or Nina would approve, so I'm more than fine with keeping it a secret. And it also means the Bounty Hunter won't get a heads up to whisk in and try to steal Grady back to his team, so, bonus for me.

Grady clears his throat again. "I, um . . . you . . . That is, you seem very . . . ?"

I resist the urge to roll my eyes. I have an early morning meeting, and if I wait for him to finish that sentence, I'm going to lose the little sleep I'm already going to manage tonight. "You don't have to decide right now, I suppose. Think about it. Get back to me."

"Will do, then. G'night!"

He all but runs from the locker room, leaving me on my own. I frown at myself in the mirror, examining my reflection. Do I have something in my teeth? Is my BO out of control or something? I lift both my arms, checking to see if I have enormous pit stains. But nothing. I look great! Skin glowing post-workout, body looking great in my sports bra and leggings. I'm tall, athletic, and toned, with chin-length dark blonde hair, big blue eyes, and full pouty lips—you know, the whole package. He should be so lucky!

"What's his problem?" I say aloud to myself.

"I have no idea," comes a deep, rumbly voice from the back stall.

Chapter Three

A man emerges from the corner stall, looking sheepish, hands raised in the air like he's surrendering a battle. "I wasn't pooping!" he announces, as if this would be my biggest worry. "I was hiding from my trainer, Abel, for a few minutes, watching TikTok, and the next thing I know, *Days of Our Lives* is happening outside the stall, so I just hung out, you know? I swear I didn't mean to eavesdrop. I just figured, I'd let you say your peace and move on your way. I was planning on running for the door if the two of you started getting it on, but I would have averted my gaze respectfully, of course."

I can't believe this is happening. I can't believe I'm having this conversation in a men's locker room with a total stranger. This is maybe one of my top five worst days *ever*, and I grew up in foster care—and saw the theatrical release of *Cats* on opening night (not my idea).

He gives me a quick and obvious once-over before meeting my gaze and nodding in approval. "For the record, that guy was lōlō. You are . . . wow. Total bombshell."

Still glaring, I take my turn to appraise him. If Grady is not my type, this guy is almost a completely different species from what I usually go for. He's tall, I'll give him that—like, *really* tall, at least half a foot taller than me, and I'm five foot ten. He is Polynesian, with a bronze skin tone, dark, long wavy hair that's been sun-bleached at the ends, and a strong jaw covered by a beard—and he's *big*. It's obvious he's strong and fit, but he isn't the chiseled, hairless GQ model–type I usually go for. He's barrel-chested with a solid belly—not fat, but not lean and muscular either. He seems totally comfortable in his skin, though, which is pretty remarkable, considering he's wearing basketball shorts and a T-shirt with actual holes in it, not just fashionable cutouts designed to show off his muscles. Oh, and he's barefoot. In a locker room that doubles as a public bathroom.

Awesome.

Still, he's not *un*attractive. And I did just get shot down, pretty obviously, and apparently with an audience. My ego needs the fluffing.

Bathroom Guy waits patiently for my appraisal to end, grinning at me when we finally make eye contact. I frown at him on principle, because who just goes around smiling like that? He must be an idiot. Likely got dropped on his head one too many times doing keg stands back during his frat days. Which I'm guessing were at least a decade and a half ago, putting him somewhere around his late thirties, if the smile lines around his eyes are any indication. He's older, but not too much older—I'd say no more than a decade over my twenty-eight (soon to be twenty-nine) years. Definitely too old to be wearing flip-flops at the gym, though.

At my frown, he grins even harder, almost like he knows what I'm thinking and finds it hilarious that I have so much disdain for him. "For the record, *I* wouldn't have to think about it, if you made me that offer."

Oh. So it's like that, is it? I preen despite myself, grateful for the validation, especially after just getting rejected by Grady.

This is probably a bad idea. Then again, despite his terrible outfit, I'm surprised to find I'm not totally opposed to the idea. He looks so strong. I bet he could pick me up, hold all my weight while I ride out all my frustration. The thought sends an unexpected ping of interest down through my lower belly. Hmm. Interesting.

I've slept with tall, short, skinny, and muscular bods. Maybe it's time for my first dad bod.

I fold my arms, looking him over again. "Do you own shoes?" I challenge.

He just laughs.

A few minutes later—after I've taken a picture of his ID and sent it to Helen and Nina, and made it known to the guy at the front desk that we're leaving together, in case he decides to murder me—we're out the door and walking the few blocks to my place. Now that I'm standing right next to him, he's even bigger than he appeared standing across the room from me. Okay, I know that's just the basic law of perspective, but he really is *big*. I'm not the only one who notices, either—a few people walking down the street do double takes as they see him passing by. I guess I won't have to worry about anyone trying to mug us on the way home. If someone came at this guy with a crowbar, it would probably just crumple in half.

I try to subtly eye him, taking stock. On the one hand, I'm not worried about his ability to throw me around a little bit. On the other, for the first time in my sexual history, I'm worried about how everything is going to fit.

Bathroom Guy catches me looking him over and grins. "I'm Kimo, by the way. Kimo Kapono."

Is it only my imagination, or does he sort of tense up when he tells me his name, like he's waiting for my reaction? I realize what the issue is right away. He's likely worried I'm going to mispronounce his name because it isn't some American, white-bread name. "Matilda Markov," I tell him, letting a little of my mostly dormant Russian accent come through to show he's in good company. By now I've spent the majority of my life in America, but they say those formative early years are really the ones that shape your speech patterns. I've gotten pretty good at tamping my accent down most of the time, though, except for when I'm angry, or tired, or hangry. Or all of the above.

Kimo's eyes light up a bit. "No way! We both have superhero names."

"Come again?"

"The double letters thing. Lois Lane. Scott Summers. Sue Storm. Pepper Potts." He gestures between us. "Kimo Kapono. Matilda Markov."

I blink at him. "I literally don't know who any of those other people are."

"Not a comic book girl? That's okay. I'll only judge you a little, ha." He elbows me jokingly in the side. I'm probably supposed to giggle, but instead I scowl at him. Why is he *elbowing* me? What am I, his frat buddy?

"So what are you into, Matilda Markov?"

I frown at him. "Into? Like a fetish?"

He laughs. "We can discuss that when we're not on the street. Geesh."

Another jokey elbow to the side. I push his arm away, and not playfully, but he laughs anyway. "No, I meant, what do you like to read or watch or whatever for fun? Anime? Horror? MMA? What's your thing?"

For some reason, this question makes me profoundly uncomfortable. "I don't really have a *thing*." That isn't precisely true, but this guy's a total stranger—like I'm going to tell him what I watch when I'm feeling sad or lonely or just need a little pick-me-up. That information is way more intimate than seeing me naked.

Luckily, he's distracted from my lack of answer when a bright flash goes off in front of us, like someone's just taken a picture. Of us? Why would someone take a picture of us on the street? It's so dark that the flash is unnaturally bright, and I blink, temporarily disoriented.

Kimo shoulders his big body in front of me, like he's blocking me from view. "Hey, come on. Not now, okay?"

By the time my vision clears, I see a man still holding up his cell phone, looking sheepish. "Sorry. That was supposed to be subtle."

Kimo softens a little, once again all affability. "No worries, brah. Just keep it to yourself, okay?"

Keep it to himself? *Brah?* I don't know which of those two things is more deserving of my attention. I already figured Kimo was some kind of aged-out frat guy, so I guess I can't hold the "brah" thing against him. But I can, and do, wonder why a stranger on the street would want to take a picture of Kimo and *keep it to himself.* I look at Kimo's profile again, searching for any sign of familiarity as we continue walking on, now with his arm around my shoulder, as if he's protecting me from any future flash photography.

"Are you famous on TikTok or something like that?" I try finally. I'm not the most pop-culture savvy person in the world, but I think I'd recognize him if he were a movie star or headlining musician. I'm busy at work, but I'm not living under a rock.

"Something like that," Kimo returns vaguely.

There are no more picture-taking incidents in the two more blocks it takes to get to my place. I lead Kimo up the stairs, letting my hips sway an extra bit to make sure he's good and ready to go by the time we make it inside. I don't have time to build up the sexy spark from scratch; I need this to be a quick, clean thirty minutes max, in and out the door. I still have some notes to review before my meeting in the morning, after all.

When I glance over my shoulder, I see my plan is working. Kimo's eyes are fixed on my ass, and he's all but licking his lips. When he catches me looking at him, he gives me a completely unabashed wink. I turn away before he can see my grin of triumph. So easy. Take *that*, ex-priest. This could have been you if you hadn't been such a dud.

Sleeping with Kimo won't solve my problem with the friend group, though. The thought makes me temporarily fumble as I reach the door, but I collect myself quickly. I'll worry about that tomorrow. Some good sex and a few hours of sleep and then I can brainstorm something else.

Once Kimo and I are inside, I instruct him to leave his shoes by the door while I go to hang up my gym bag. (He does have shoes, for the record, though they're flip-flops, and I have no idea why he wasn't wearing them in the locker room. Or why he wore them to the gym to begin with. Whatever. Not my problem.)

"Nice place," he says, picking up a picture off the mantle. It's of me in my gi, standing with my sensei. "Oh, wow, are you a black belt?"

"Yes," I say curtly, taking the picture and setting it back just where it was. He waits for me to elaborate, but I pretend not to notice. I don't want there to be any confusion about what this is between us. "You need a glass of water or something, or should we just get started?"

Kimo falters. "Um. Water would be good. Can I take a piss first?"

I don't bother to hide my judgmental nose scrunch at his phrasing. "Sure. First door in the hallway. I'll meet you in the bedroom."

My place is small, so it's not like he needs a tour to figure it out, but I don't miss Kimo's blink of surprise as I walk past him into the kitchen. I'm starting to worry he's going to be a problem—someone who's going to want to talk and connect before we get down to business. I'm hoping if I keep things moving, he'll get the picture soon enough.

When I emerge from the kitchen with two glasses of water, Kimo seems to have found his way to the bathroom, so I go into the bedroom. I debate what to do about clothing. I don't want to stay in my workout clothes since they're not the easiest, sexiest items of clothing to remove with a partner present—ugh, *spandex*—but I find lingerie to be pretty pointless with one-night stands, and being totally naked when he walks in the room feels a little aggressive, even for me.

I settle on a T-shirt and no pants. Kimo still isn't out of the bathroom yet, so I give myself a quick cowboy wash (i.e., rub down my armpits and other smelly bits with a wet wipe) and spritz myself with perfume to counterbalance any lingering BO from the gym. When Kimo still doesn't come out after all that, I run a quick brush through my hair, then set out a couple condoms next to the bed. When there's still no sign of him, I lay myself provocatively on the bed, trying out a few different positions for maximized sexiness. And when he *still* isn't out after that, I go to the bathroom and knock on the door.

"Are you shooting up in there or something?" I demand, only half-joking. Okay, not at all joking, really.

The door opens immediately and Kimo waves me in. To my surprise, he's piled all his hair on top of his head in a messy bun. "Sorry, I got distracted by the leaky shower. How long has it been doing this?"

I stare at him in dumb surprise as he kneels down next to the shower knob, examining it. "You're too worried about my leaky shower to come have sex?"

He shoots me a cheeky grin, like he finds me hilarious. "It'll just take a minute. I think I can fix it." He shuts the lid of the toilet and pats it, motioning me over. "Come on. Take a seat. Keep me company."

This is . . . not how I thought this night would be going. I check my watch. He only has twenty minutes left if I want to stay on schedule. "I can call someone to do that later."

He pauses whatever he's doing to the faucet and raises an eyebrow at me. "I know you *can*, but will you?"

Okay . . . I guess I just got called out by this random stranger I met in a men's bathroom. "Probably not, no. It's not a big deal, though, it's just a leak."

"These leaks are no joke. They can make your water bill skyrocket. Not to mention your gas bill, if the water's being heated while it's dripping. You'll thank me when it's winter."

His focus is entirely on the faucet again, so I roll my eyes at the back of his head. "What are you, some kind of handyman?"

"Not full time, or anything. But I've fixed things here and there."

Great, so he's an *unemployed* handyman. I check my watch again. "You know, we can just—"

At the same time, he asks, "You mind?" And before I can reply, he takes hold of the valve with one hand, twists it, and pulls it off the wall.

My jaw drops open. Kimo looks around in the gaping hole he's just created in my shower, grunting a little to himself. "Ah, there's your problem." He rises abruptly to his feet. "Are there any twenty-four-hour hardware stores around here?"

I just stare at him. Why would I possibly know that? "I . . . have no idea."

He pulls out his phone from his back pocket. "Here we go. Just a few blocks from here. I'll get the piece you need, be back in a jiffy, and fix it all up. Ten, fifteen minutes, tops."

"Um . . ." It's not often a man pulls a move on me that throws me so completely off my game. If he'd whipped out a sex toy or asked me to pee on him, I would have been less shocked. But what am I supposed to do with a guy who rips a hole in my shower? I can't just kick him out and have it stay that way. "Let me put on some pants," I concede reluctantly.

He looks me over, eyes lingering on my bare legs appreciatively. "No, no. Please. You stay exactly how you are. Wow. Just beautiful . . . Relax for a minute. I'll be back in a few . . ."

Chapter Four

In the ten minutes it takes for Kimo to leave and come back, I piece together what his plan is. He's like one of those sex workers who doesn't let you know they're a sex worker until you've already used their services, and then demands payment. Except in this case, he's a handyman who pretends to be interested in sex, then leaves a hole in my wall and swoops in to fix it, only to demand payment afterward. I haven't read about this scam anywhere, but I'm positive it's the new thing in scamming. I'm also determined that, no matter what, come hell or high water, I will not give that man a single dime.

When Kimo knocks, I leave the chain on the door, scowling at him through the opening. "I don't have money, you know. I'm a paralegal with student loans. I'm not going to pay hundreds of dollars for a service call I didn't even make."

He just laughs. "No offense, but I know. Your apartment is the size of a shoebox. And I told you, I'm not a handyman." He holds up the bag. "This part cost $10.92. My treat, okay? Much cheaper than dinner and a movie."

I watch him warily for a moment before reluctantly letting him in. There *is* a hole in my shower wall, after all, and if I don't let him try to fix it for $10.92, then I'll have to pay a real plumber a lot more to do the same thing. "I have you on record saying you aren't going to charge me anything," I warn him, holding up my phone to show him I've been recording our conversation.

I expect him to get defensive, tell me I'm paranoid or crazy, but he just laughs again and shakes his head like we're old friends and I'm up to my usual shenanigans. "Good to know you're into recording things. I'm going to keep that in mind for later." He winks at me as he goes into the bathroom.

I frown at his back, following close on his heels. First I'd assumed his decision to fix the shower was a way of getting out of having sex. Then I thought he was trying to hustle me. Now, he's flirting again? I don't understand what's going on. What game is he playing, anyway?

Whatever it is, he's now five minutes over his allotted time for the night. I wanted to be in bed by now, alone, watching a rerun of *Full House*. Instead, I have to babysit this "brah" from the gym to make sure he isn't breaking any more plumbing fixtures in my house. "How long is this going to take?"

"Just a few minutes." Kimo makes himself at home on my bathroom floor, fishing out the new part and examining the hole in the wall for a moment before he gets to work.

I won't even pretend to know how to describe what he's doing, but it's obvious he knows his way around a shower valve. I watch as he tinkers around for a few moments, fitting in the new piece. Then he replaces the valve, lining it up and twisting it back into place. He turns the shower on, then shuts it off again—this time with no dripping.

He grins at me, not bothering to hide how pleased he is with himself. "Told you. Simple."

I blink in surprise. I've never seen someone do something like that before. The kind of guy I usually go for is more the white-collar type who hires someone to do the handiwork around his apartment. On the rare occasion I've splurged on a repairman myself, I've just let them do their thing while I was in the other room. Seeing someone just take on a task like that, all confident and capable . . . it's kind of hot, I'm surprised to find.

"Thank you," I tell him reluctantly, gathering myself. "Do you, um . . . are you sure you don't want some money for that?"

Kimo rises to his feet, slowly, so that now he's towering above me, looking down at me. There's barely enough room for two bodies in my teeny tiny bathroom, and we're close enough I can feel his heat. I bet he runs warm; I bet being wrapped up in him would feel like curling up in an electric blanket. His bigness strikes me all at once again, making me feel, uncharacteristically, small in comparison. I'm a tall girl, and I'm slender but athletic, so I'm not used to feeling so . . . so . . . dainty. Everything about this scenario—his man bun and flip-flops and hands faintly tinged with grease—shouldn't be sexy, but somehow it is. He smirks at me like he can read all of this on my face. I swallow.

"You have me on the record saying I wouldn't charge a fee, remember?" He waggles his eyebrows at me—which again, should not be hot, but I find myself pressing my knees together in response. "Besides, I can think of some other ways you can thank me."

Ohhh. The heat that shoots through me takes me by surprise. I take in a steadying breath before tilting my head up at him. "Should we move into the bedroom?"

I'm giving him my best bedroom eyes, and I can tell from Kimo's slow, approving appraisal of my body that it's working, even though he's still smirking at me. I thought this guy was going to be a pushover, but he might just give me a run for my money, I realize, looking into his hazel eyes, sparkling with mischief.

"Nah," he says.

For a moment I just stare at him, flabbergasted. Then I blink, stepping back. "Nah?" I haven't had every man in the world falling at my feet, but never have I offered sex to a man only to have him say *nah* in return, like I was offering him a cold piece of pizza for breakfast.

"It's late," he says. "I got an early day tomorrow. I imagine you do, too, Miss Paralegal. Rain check?"

I seem to have lost the ability to speak. It takes me a full minute to stammer out a, "I don't know. We'll have to see. I have a pretty full schedule." Ha! Two can play that hard-to-get game.

He grins. "I bet you do. But I'll make it worth your time."

I want to retort something grumpy like, *You better since you've already wasted so much of it*, but before I can, he takes me by surprise and leans in. One hand fists into my T-shirt, gripping it at my waist so the material rises up a bit, giving him a glimpse of my panties in the mirror behind me. He pulls me in a bit closer so our fronts brush together. I think he's going to kiss me, but instead he sort of nuzzles at my ear and jaw for a moment before kissing my cheek, ghost-light.

"Good night, Matilda Markov." He pulls back, no longer smiling, eyes sparking at me with heat. "I'll be seeing you soon."

It isn't until about half an hour later, after I've used my rabbit to finish the job Kimo started and am curled up in bed, watching *Full House* on my laptop, that I realize his shortsightedness.

"You idiot," I grouse to myself. "You didn't even get my phone number."

Oh well. The encounter was always meant to be a brief, fleeting, ships-in-the-night kind of thing, anyway. Despite the sexual charge between us, there was no way he was going to be the Uncle Jesse to my Aunt Becky. Not that I even want that—the domesticity thing, I mean, not the John Stamos of it all, because I most definitely want that, please and thank you.

But I'm a little disappointed, though not surprised, to realize Kimo is just like so many other men—so full of potential, but ultimately nothing but empty promises.

Chapter Five

Despite the chaos of last night, this morning I'm at work right on time, coffee in hand, and looking professionally hot, if I do say so myself. Not many people could pull off shorts at work and still manage to look polished, but (a) I can thrift like nobody's business, and I always find the best diamonds in the rough; (b) Nina is an expert seamstress, and she helps me tailor my clothes to my shape like a pro, so all the lines are clean and chic and everything fits like a glove; (c) it's July and unusually muggy, even for Chicago, so no one can blame me for wanting to forego heavy trousers; and (d) I have fantastic legs, especially in these strappy heels.

Oh, and if you haven't caught on by now, I really don't go for that false modesty thing. I know all my strengths and weaknesses and I don't understand anyone who doesn't take an honest account of themselves on a regular basis. You won't ever hear me bragging about my people skills, but my calves? Excellent.

I glance at my phone on the elevator ride up to the office. I only have one message, from Brian and Connie. **Happy birthday, sweetheart! Can we take you out to dinner sometime this week?** I close it without responding. No other messages yet. It's still early in the day, though. I don't really expect to hear from my sisters until later, but it doesn't hurt to check.

My coworker Barry is waiting for me at my desk holding a balloon and a cupcake with bright pink frosting. I falter. Oh no. This is bad for a couple reasons. A few months ago I wanted to set up Helen with Barry. That was back when the Bounty Hunter had broken her heart and I was trying my best to help her get over it. I figured, Barry seemed like a nice enough guy, and if they hit it off, they wouldn't mind me third-wheeling since I was the one who set them up.

But Helen got back together with the Bounty Hunter, and it turns out, Barry? Kind of clingy. I guess he got used to all the extra attention I was giving him when I was trying to get him ready to be worthy of Helen, and now it's like he thinks I owe him something since things fell through with her. He's always lingering at my desk, offering me unsolicited shoulder rubs. And sure, I've said yes a few times, but only because I get knots in my upper back, not because he has any chance in hell of massaging his way into my pants.

That's the first reason it's bad to see Barry at my desk first thing in the morning. The second is that I'm pretty sure he's holding a birthday balloon.

Dammit! Why do jobs require you to write down your birth date, anyway? I don't need Susie from HR blabbing her mouth to every Tom, Dick, and Harry about the day I was pulled screaming into this world—not even of my own volition, mind you. I certainly don't need coworkers who are barely friends cornering me in the bathroom to ask me about my birthday plans, or forcing me into the conference room and handing me a plate of cake I probably won't eat while I'm publicly humiliated via song.

I haven't even told Nina and Helen that today's my birthday. In all our years of friendship, I've managed to dodge the question. I suspect Helen thinks it's a trauma response from being adopted. For the record, it isn't, but her believing so means she doesn't insist on making me share the information, and so I don't correct her on it. I guess the truth is, Helen and Nina are the only people I'd actually *want* to celebrate the day with, at least the only people in Chicago. But if I told them the day and they forgot about it . . .

It's better just to take the possibility off the table entirely. I'm fine celebrating alone in my pajamas with an episode of *Full House*, anyway.

. . . Except for the inevitable public display of humiliation that seems to be in the cards today. I sigh as I near Barry, folding my arms to show him I'm not impressed. "What is this?"

"Happy birthday!" Barry beams at me, offering the balloon and cupcake like he expects me to squeal and whoo. He clearly hasn't been paying attention these last six months if he thinks I'm even capable of making those kinds of noises. "The big two-nine, right?"

"Don't ask people their age. It's rude." I make no move to take the balloon, which frankly I will just release to float up to the ceiling if he tries to force it on me. The cupcake, though, I examine closely. I'm not opposed to sweets on principle, but I am very particular about my sugar consumption. If I'm going to indulge, I'm not just going to eat any crap lying around. It has to be the good stuff.

The packaging indicates it's likely from some grocery store bakery, though the sticker and price tag have been scratched off. Hmm, could be bad, could be good, depending on the bakery. I open the container to feel the consistency of the cupcake base. A little dry and stiff. Not promising. With my pinky finger, I take the tiniest smidge of the frosting and taste it. Pure confectioners' sugar, no cream cheese to enrich the flavor and tamp down the blinding sweetness.

I close the lid again and set the cupcake down on my desk. I'll definitely be throwing it away later, but I won't do it in front of Barry's face. (And people say I have no tact!) "Thanks, I guess. Even if it was totally unnecessary." I glance around at the still mostly empty cubicles. I like to be one of the first people in the office every morning, since the place can't function without me, but everyone else will be trickling in soon. "Don't make a big deal about it, okay? I'm not into the whole birthday thing."

It's like I've told Barry I don't believe in Santa. I'm sure he was envisioning leading our coworkers in singing happy birthday to me, establishing his claim as my closest office confidant, maybe even trying to get some dating rumors off the ground. His face falls a little, but he rebounds quickly. "We could do something after work? Dinner? My treat?"

"No," I say flatly, and sit down at my computer.

This should be the universal sign of dismissal, no? But Barry lingers at my cubicle. "Did you hear that Eastman's coming in today?"

Despite myself, I turn to face him—the news is that surprising. Jay Eastman is one of the partners at the firm, but he mainly deals with international law and is usually off traveling to meet clients, when he isn't being photographed having dinner with A-list actresses or supermodels. "Eastman? Why?"

Barry seems quite obviously pleased to have my full attention again. "The client we're meeting with this morning is a pretty big fish, apparently. I guess the partners want to make sure they get in his good graces so he'll put us on retainer for any future cases."

There's a trace of bitterness in Barry's voice, despite the victory of getting to be the one to share the office gossip, and I can't blame him. It must be very difficult to be a man moving in the same space as Jay Eastman. He's not only a legacy lawyer, with a father who was the mayor's legal advisor and a grandfather who founded one of the most prestigious law firms in Chicago before serving as a judge in the Illinois Supreme Court; but he also has developed a stellar reputation at a surprisingly young age—not even forty yet. Plus, he's hot. Like, movie-star hot. Like, Brad Pitt in his prime hot.

Successful, intelligent, Ivy-League educated, handsome, and clean-cut. The man is basically my vision board for the foreseeable future, except even *I* don't have the confidence to think I could nab a Jay Eastman.

Our client this morning must be a *really* big deal if they brought in Eastman for this. I was so focused on preparing our pre-trial documents that I hadn't paid too much attention to who the client himself was. I frowned, trying to scour my memory for any giveaway of why the partners would consider him to be so very special. "Is the client an actor or musician or something? Big Pharma? Silicon Valley guy? Politician?"

Barry seems excited to be able to relay this information to me. Poor little man will gobble up any crumbs I give him. I can have that effect on men. "Do you remember that story a few months ago, about the guy who was, like, the caddy or driver or something for a bunch of finance bros on vacation? They're all getting wasted, talking to each other like no one else is in the room, assuming this guy must be too stupid to understand what they're talking about. But he's been paying attention to everything and knows they're planning on shorting this chain restaurant called So Ono— kind of like what happened with GameStop a few years ago. So he figures out how to play them at their own game, gives all these Redditors a bunch of tips, and ends up becoming a multimillionaire basically overnight."

I raise my eyebrows, impressed despite myself. "Wow. Smart guy, huh?"

"That's not even the best part." Barry's eyes are shining; I'm starting to wonder if his excitement is more because he's fanboying over this client rather than getting to tell me all about it. "He has all this crazy money all of a sudden, but instead of hoarding it and buying a big house in Malibu or whatever you'd expect him to do, he starts giving it away to all these charities. They call him Kimo Hood—you know, like Robin Hood."

I feel like the wind has been knocked out of me. "*Kimo* Hood?" I repeat. It's not the most common name, after all. Chicago's a big city, but it can't possibly be *that* big.

As if on cue, the elevator door dings open, and out walks Jay Eastman, with our newest client . . . Kimo Kapono.

Chapter Six

When I see them, I do what any self-respecting, intelligent woman with a university degree and a black belt would do.

I hide under the desk.

Okay, so it's a short-lived solution to a long-term problem, but I need to buy at least a few seconds to think before Kimo spots me. What's the game plan? Do I pretend I don't recognize him? Act like we're old friends? Pull the fire alarm? No, I'm pretty sure that last one's illegal if there's not actually a fire, but the prison time might be worth it—surely Kimo's case will be over by the time I get out . . . ?

"Matilda?" I hear Barry's worried voice, hovering somewhere above me. "Are you okay? Did you lose a contact or something?"

"Stop saying my name," I whisper-hiss. "Don't look at me. Act like I'm not here."

There's no time to determine if Barry is sharp enough to follow my instructions, because the next thing I hear is Jay's smooth, confident voice, rapidly approaching my cubicle. "Barry Abrams. Let me introduce you to Kimo Kapono. Kimo, this is Barry, one of our attorneys who will be helping with your case. Barry went to UPenn and has worked with us for the past year. He's going to be a real asset to the team."

I'm convinced Jay must have a photographic memory. He always remembers every employee's name and a shortlist of pertinent information about them, no matter how low on the ladder they are or how infrequently he's interacted with them. Either that, or he spends his nights memorizing peoples' faces and tidbits about them. Some people might find that latter prospect weird or creepy, but honestly, it's what I would do if I were a partner at a prestigious firm like Eastman, Bergman & Hart.

Kimo's low, rumbly voice sends an unexpected jolt through me. "Nice to meet you, brother."

Barry mutters something inane back, but I don't really pay much attention. I still haven't decided what I should do, and my mind is racing. Maybe Barry will surprise me by having the foresight to cover for me and steer the men in another direction. He can barely function at the firm even though he's a full-fledged attorney and I'm "just" a paralegal, but hey, greater miracles have happened.

"I'd like to get the meeting started. I'm sure you have plenty of other important things you need to get to, Kimo," Jay says from somewhere above me. It sounds like he's right next to my desk now. *говно.*

"My schedule's pretty loose, actually." Kimo sounds just as affable as I remember him. He's probably still wearing flip-flops, if he's even deigned to wear shoes at all. "The kids are in day camp, so as long as we're done by three, we're golden."

The kids—that part I remember from my research. Girl, Nalani, nine, and boy, Makoa, seven. The client (Kimo, apparently) is the uncle, and is trying to get full custody of the kids even though their birth father is still alive and currently residing in Chicago.

Jay matches Kimo's tone, though his own voice is much more polished, smooth like butter. "Don't worry, we'll try to make this quick and painless for you. Barry, is the rest of the team already in the boardroom?"

Just say yes, I will Barry silently. Then I can enter late, pretend I was in the bathroom or something, or just not show up to the meeting at all. If no one saw me but Barry, and he keeps his yap shut, I can claim I have a stomach virus or something and leave. It's not something I'd usually do; even the thought of missing work for any reason, much less a *pretend* sickness, makes me want to crawl out of my skin. I haven't missed a single day of work since I started here two years ago. But, desperate times, and all that.

"Matilda's under the desk," Barry blurts.

I roll my eyes so hard back in my head that I see stars. *Barry, you idiot!* I hiss at him internally.

But because even *I* have a filter in front of my boss and a client, what I say out loud instead is, "There's my earring!" I rise awkwardly to my feet, smoothing down my dress shorts and drawing myself up to my full impressive height. In that moment, I decide on the game plan—no blushing, no stammering, no acting at all intimidated by this twist of events.

"Mr. Eastman, good to see you as always." I summon the fortitude of my inner nun-turned-paralegal and coolly appraise my almost one-night stand who now happens to be my client.

He looks different today in his suit and tie, his hair pulled up in a loose bun. His suit looks like it's well-made, and made specifically for his broad frame and height; the material is nice and it isn't cut too small, but even so, it looks like he's ready to burst out of it. Although his face is just as sunny and open as it was the night before, I can tell from his posture that he's much more at home in the shorts and T-shirt I saw him wearing at the gym.

But I don't let any of that show on my face, because as far as anyone knows, this is our first time meeting each other. Ever. I gaze at him evenly. "Mr. Kapono, a pleasure to meet you."

I expect Kimo to play along. It's in his best interest, too, not to let on that he was picking up a stranger in the gym last night—even if he *did* only work on my plumbing, and not in a dirty way.

Instead, his whole face lights up at the sight of me. "Ha, no way! Matilda Markov. That's right, you said you were a paralegal. What are the odds?"

Jay looks back and forth between us, his impeccably handsome face creasing ever so slightly with confusion. I can tell he doesn't like to be out of the loop. "The two of you know each other?"

"From the gym," I answer smoothly, before Kimo can say anything that makes me look even worse than I already do in front of my boss. This man is clearly a loose cannon. "I had no idea you were the client," I tell Kimo. I look at Jay, trying to convey to him with the sincerity of my big cobalt-blue eyes that I really did have no idea.

Jay rallies quickly. "Well, we care quite a bit about our employees' health, so I'm glad to hear you're taking advantage of that gym membership discount, Matilda." He shakes my hand, still smiling but giving me a long, meaningful look. "Nice to see you, as always."

I know that look. It's a *don't fuck this up* look. I'm usually on the giving end of that look, not the receiving end, but I recognize it well. I nod back at him, just a little, to show him he can trust me. After all, I'm his go-to paralegal whenever he's in the office, and the one who basically keeps this place running, since everyone knows lawyers can't be trusted to format a legal document to save their lives. "Thank you, Mr. Eastman."

I let myself look back at Kimo, steeling myself a little. Based on our encounter last night, I'm not sure how well he reads social cues—if he'll understand that I want to keep the nature of our almost-hookup quiet, or if he'll be broadcasting to the whole boardroom that last night in a gym locker room, I offered to deflower an ex-priest before taking another stranger home with me. Bracing myself, I hold out my hand. "Mr. Kapono, I look forward to working with you on this case."

Kimo just looks at me for one long, unnerving moment. "Hell, we're sure to win, with a ballbuster like you on my side, Mattie." He ignores my attempt to shake his hand and instead gives me a fist bump that turns into a quick side hug. I remain ramrod straight the entire time. How is this happening to me? How is this my life?

All things considered, it's not the *worst* response in the entire world . . . even though no one in my entire life has ever called me Mattie, and even though he just called me a ballbuster in front of my boss.

Aware of Jay watching me closely, and Barry eagerly lapping up all the details of the exchange so he can chatter away like the little office gossip he is, I keep my face completely impassive as I motion us all toward the boardroom. "Shall we . . . ?"

It isn't until all three men are walking ahead of me that I wipe my sweaty palms on my shorts. *Shit.* Just ahead of me, Kimo turns back around to give me a quick wink. *Double shit.*

Today's going to be a very long day.

Fortunately I'm just one of many faces in the conference room, and nowhere near the top of the pecking order, so there's no reason for me to draw any further notice once the meeting gets started. I'm just here to take notes while Jay and Kimo do all the talking. No reason to pay any attention to me whatsoever.

So why does Kimo keep looking over at me?

The first time I catch him watching me, I assume he's just looking at everyone around the room in turn. But the second time, there's a weird look on his face—almost like he's waiting for some kind of reaction from me. Maybe he's still hung up on last night? That doesn't seem right, though, because when I catch him looking at me a third time, his face is sort of gleefully expectant, like he knows someone's about to throw me a surprise party and he doesn't want to ruin the moment but also he wants to see my face when they bring the cake in.

. . . At least that's what I'm assuming happens at a surprise birthday party, based off what I've seen on television shows and observed in the wild. I've never been part of one, neither my own nor someone else's. A sudden horrifying thought strikes me, and I dart my gaze over to Barry. Is this idiot throwing me a surprise party during a client meeting?

Fortunately, Barry's expression is totally benign, and I know the man can't act since he strong-armed me into attending his community theater performance of *Fiddler on the Roof*. (Truly, the worst three hours of my life. And once again, that's coming from an orphan who grew up in the foster care system.) I frown, trying to focus on my notes, but out of the corner of my eye, I see Kimo watching me again.

He's barely suppressing a grin, and quickly looks away once he realizes he's been caught. Unfortunately, I'm not the only one who caught him this time—Jay has noticed it, too, and he gives me a long, appraising look.

Even so, he doesn't skip a beat with his next line of questioning. "So you maintain that your brother-in-law never showed any interest in having custody of the children until after you had obtained your money?"

Kimo's smile fades at that, and he finally seems more focused on the client interview than on watching me. "He's not my brother-in-law. He was my sister's boyfriend, but they never got married. And yeah, he was fine with me and my māmā taking care of the kids until he realized they'd be getting an inheritance and living expenses. Suddenly he wants parental custody, go figure."

I shift in my seat, hoping someone will ask what the children want out of this situation. It's not my place to speak up in a client interview; Jay is running the show here. But obviously, as an orphan myself, I have a bit of a chip on my shoulder with this issue. No one ever asks what the kids think, while the grown-ups argue over the paperwork.

"Do you have any documentation of Pika turning down parental custody before you received your windfall, and/or from when he began showing an interest in custody proceedings? Text messages, emails, even social media messages would be helpful."

Kimo sighs, running a hand over his face. "I'll have to go back and check. Text messages have probably been deleted, but you never know, I guess."

"I can have someone help you sort through that." Jay glances down toward my end of the table, and I see the moment he decides, *Not her,* while looking at me. "Barry, set up a time to work with Kimo once the meeting is over."

Barry beams at the attention. "Sure thing."

Great. Just great. I'm positive that task would have gone to me if Kimo hadn't been acting so weird at this meeting. I have a feeling Jay will tell me I'm off this case once Kimo leaves.

A flash across my phone screen draws my attention. I put my phone on mute for the meeting, but a silent notification pops up, telling me I have a new email. Normally I'd just ignore it, but the subject line distracts me: **Congratulations on paying off your student loans**!

What? I frown, certain this has to be some kind of spam or phishing. I'm nowhere near paying off my student loans. I'm looking at another decade, if not longer—thanks a lot, variable interest rates.

But when I glance at the notification again, I see the message appears to actually be from my lender. It's probably some kind of promotion about how I can refinance? I try to put it out of my mind and focus on the interview, but I keep glancing over at the phone. It wouldn't hurt to just check it, right? Sure, I'm in the middle of a meeting, but it will only take five seconds.

That settled, I open the email, waiting for the punchline of the joke where I had even half a moment's hope that tens of thousands of dollars of debt has just vanished.

Instead, I am gobsmacked to find the message is exactly what it seemed from the notification:

Matilda Polina Markov, congratulations on paying off your student loans! As of 7/21/2023, your loans have been paid in full. Please keep a copy of this email for your records. To see the full breakdown, visit the EduBridge website and log in to your account.

Full on ignoring the meeting now, I open a new window to log in to my account. My jaw drops open as I see my loan balance is $0. *Zero.* Yesterday it was in the high five digits, and today—nothing. Almost like it was never there. Even the loan I cosigned with my sister Alina has been paid off in full. So make that *hundreds of thousands of dollars*, wiped completely clean.

The payment seems to have been made early this morning. Definitely not by me. Even if it's some kind of autopayment error, I don't have enough money in my bank account to cover the full amount—nowhere near that.

"Oh my God." I didn't mean to say it out loud, but immediately everyone's attention is on me. Barry looks nervous that I've spoken out of turn; the other suits in the room look confused about who I am and why I'd ever be so bold as to speak when not spoken to in a client meeting; Jay looks surprised, like something like this has never happened to him before and he didn't even factor it in as a possibility.

And Kimo . . .

Kimo is grinning like he just won the lottery. No, like *I* just won the lottery, after he put the winning ticket in my hands.

I have a strong suspicion that I know where this money came from. But . . . why? We had one random encounter last night. We didn't even have sex! No foreplay, no blow job. We didn't even kiss! And I know I have a good ass, but good enough for hundreds of thousands of dollars just for a brief glimpse of it? Even I'm not that arrogant.

What I *am* is suddenly debt-free. And about to be kicked off this case, if the now-resolved look on Jay Eastman's face is anything to go by—if not out of a job altogether.

"My dog died," I blurt. I vaguely remember seeing a picture of Jay with a golden retriever on his desk when I was first hired a couple years ago. Maybe he'll be sympathetic. "He was . . . hit by an ice-cream truck. Then trampled by a high school marching band. There was a parade. The kids are obviously very traumatized." Where is this coming from? Just shut up, Matilda! "I'm so sorry to interrupt, it just came as a bit of a surprise."

Kimo covers his laugh with a cough, ducking his face to hide it. Fortunately for him, no one is paying attention to his reaction, since they're all too busy staring at me. Jay once again looks completely thrown off his game, and I can tell it's not a feeling he likes very much.

"I'm sorry to hear that, Ms. Markov. Do you need to excuse yourself?"

Translation: get the hell out of my meeting. I rise awkwardly to my feet, gathering my things. "Yes, that would probably be wise. Thank you. Sorry, again. Sorry."

I hurry out of the room, but not before casting one quick glance back at Kimo. He is grinning at me, holding two thumbs up. Yep, either he paid off my student loans, or he's an actual psychopath who hates dogs.

Either way, it's obvious I've made a huge mistake.

Chapter Seven

As I walk away from the building and down the sidewalk, I realize I have the whole day ahead of me and nothing to do. I'd planned to be in the client meeting for most of the morning, then debriefing with the team, then spending the rest of the day tracking down public records, calling up witnesses to schedule interviews, organizing our research and notes into something coherent that we could use on trial day, and doing whatever other grunt work Jay assigned to me. (As in *actual* grunt work, not a dirty euphemism. Honestly, I'd be happy to do some dirty-euphemism grunt work with Jay if he ever requested it of me, but that bridge has never been crossed, or even approached.)

The plan was that maybe, if I was very lucky, I'd get off work in time to pick up cheap sushi, watch a few episodes of *Full House*, and eat the birthday pastry I'd been planning to get from Sugar Moon during any spare fifteen minutes I could find. Then, and only then, I'd allow myself to check my personal phone for messages.

Now? The hours loom ahead of me, and I envision a day full of me anxiously checking my phone, mindlessly wandering in circles. I am not someone who does well with a lot of free time. I have no shows to catch up on. I'm too impatient for hobbies that require more than a few minutes' worth of attention. The gym is my usual go-to, but even I can't fill up an entire day working out.

And I really need today to be busy, for a variety of reasons, not the least of which is the fact that my student loans have been paid off. Paid off! Thousands of dollars of debt just—poof! Gone! Who does something like that? I can't wrap my head around it. I haven't taken any handouts in life, and truthfully, they've never even been offered. I've survived off hand-me-downs and thrift store purchases and just-expired food for so long that it's like my mind can't fully process what's happened. Even as I contemplate splurging for some nice sushi tonight, I'm calculating what corners I'll have to cut to make up for it, just in case I get a follow-up email saying it was all a mistake, I still have to pay.

I need something to do. Now.

I could always drop by the library branch where Helen works. It's only a short walk, after all. The thought buoys my spirit. Most likely I could convince Helen to come out to lunch with me, maybe even take off the rest of the day to go to the movies or get pedicures or whatever else it is that people with a lot of free time during the day do—especially if I play the whole it's-my-birthday card. I can almost perfectly picture Helen's barely contained joy at learning such a long-coveted piece of information, one that I've been hoarding like a dragon with its gold. Maybe she'll be excited enough to use her magnetic Helen charm to persuade Nina's uncle to spare her for a few hours from . . . whatever it is he has her doing at that creepy church of his, and the three of us can spend the rest of the day together. *Just* the three of us.

As the thought passes through my mind, I spot the library, now just a block ahead of me. I'm held up at the traffic light, waiting to cross, when I see a familiar ginger lurking outside the library doors.

The Bounty Hunter.

He's leaned up against the wall, waiting. I watch as Helen comes out the doors to meet him. Correction: I watch *him* as Helen comes out the doors to meet him, hoping to read some sign on his face, to find some proof that I've been right this whole time. That he's just using her. That he's not who he says he is. That he's just going to hurt her again.

What I see, instead, is a full-grown, tough-guy bounty hunter, with big muscles and scary tattoos, completely soften as he sees my best friend and pulls her into his embrace. I see him hold on to her like he's somehow managed to catch the moon and doesn't want to let it go.

I turn and walk in the other direction.

I should feel happy about this development. Helen was right. The Bounty Hunter—I guess I can use his real name now—*Thad* really loves her. He isn't going to disappear again. He isn't going to break her heart.

If I were a better person, I would be ecstatic at this realization, *relieved* that I can finally let my guard down. Instead I feel devastated, and if I'm being honest, a little betrayed. It's not that I'm secretly harboring romantic feelings for Helen, or any nonsense like that. It's just that when you've been single for a long time—in my case, for *all* time—your platonic friendships are more intense than usual. A friend like that not only fills the role of being your buddy, but also covers a lot of the significant-other stuff. They become the person who picks you up from the airport, goes out to dinner with you to celebrate a win at work, takes care of you when you're sick, helps you move heavy furniture out of your apartment, fights about what to watch on TV or order off the menu.

They become the most important person in the world to you, almost like a fill-in boyfriend or girlfriend. So when they find someone else, even if you are happy for them, it can't help but feel like you're losing something, too. It's like you've been at war together for years, deep in the trenches, relying on each other to survive, and suddenly your friend gets this wonderful reprieve, but you're still stuck on the battlefield, fighting for your life.

Hey, I'm Russian by birth. I'm allowed to be a little dramatic from time to time.

Walking aimlessly away from the library now, I feel adrift, lonelier than I've let myself feel in a very long time. There is literally no one I can turn to, no one who I'm confident would pick up the phone if I called. I am all by myself, with no one to lean on.

As the thought crosses my mind, I hear a church bell toll and look up to see a cathedral ahead of me that appears to have just opened its doors for mass.

I let out a sharp, barking laugh, rolling my eyes heavenward. "Fat chance," I mutter under my breath, then shoulder my way through the pedestrian traffic to put as much space between myself and the church as possible.

I head over to Sugar Moon and buy myself a lonely birthday sweet brioche with cream cheese frosting and strawberries on top. This is the kind of decadent snack I hoard my calories for. It's so delicious I could weep. It's so delicious that I almost forget I'll be spending my twenty-ninth birthday alone.

Well, maybe not entirely alone. Sitting down on a bench at Kosciuszko Park, I decide to splurge on that other treat I've been hoarding and pull out my personal phone. My heart catches a little in my throat as I log in and see there are no new messages.

It's still early in the day, I reason with myself. Nevertheless, I close and reopen the messages app, just to make sure I haven't accidentally missed something, only to confirm that nothing new has come through.

As I'm staring down at my phone, it begins to vibrate in my hand with an incoming call. *Stephanie* reads the name of my contact, flashing across the screen.

Unexpectedly, tears prick my eyes. I steady myself before taking the call. "Alina?"

"Hey, sis!" Unlike me, at age twenty-six, Alina no longer has any trace of her Russian accent. She was only seven when we came to the States, and aside from her dramatic dark hair and bright blue eyes, you'd never guess that she's anything but a corn-fed, all-American girl.

It takes me a moment to respond. Honestly, a part of me thought she was just butt-dialing me. I didn't want to hope that she was calling me on purpose, only to be disappointed a moment later. Recovering, I sit up straighter. "Is everything okay?" My voice comes out a bit too sharp, like I'm accusing her of something. I wince, trying to dial down my tone. "You don't usually call."

"I had to find out if that email I got about the student loans was for real. Are they actually paid off?"

Of course. I cosigned on Alina's loan, which was also paid off, so she would have been notified this morning, too, just like I was. I relax a little, relieved Alina isn't in any trouble. I know she's technically an adult now, but it's hard not to still think of her as the little kid who needed me to do everything for her, once upon a time. "It's real, all right."

"Did you win the lottery or something? If you did, I'd love some help with my car payments, haha."

I roll my eyes, but I'm smiling. "Don't be ridiculous. I would never play the lottery. What a waste of money. But if I *did* win, I'd buy you a new car. And a tree house by the lake."

I wait to see if she'll remember. We checked out *Swiss Family Robinson* once from the library and watched it three times in a row before we had to return it. Alina used to be obsessed with living in a tree house, and when we were split up into different foster homes, I used to draw her pictures of the one I'd buy for us someday when we could all be together again. Alina, Sasha, and I.

If Alina remembers, she doesn't let on. "Yeah. So how'd you pay it off? You got a new sugar daddy, or something?"

I wince at the joke, which lands too close to home, thanks to my mother's history. "That isn't funny," I snap.

Alina goes quiet for a minute, and I instantly regret my harsh tone. "Sorry," I say quickly.

"No, it was a dumb joke."

I'm eager to change the subject. "Anyway, it wasn't anything like that. I didn't strike oil or sue Amazon. It was sort of . . . an anonymous benefactor situation." A not-so-anonymous benefactor, actually, but that feels too complicated to explain, since I'm not even totally sure why Kimo would do such a thing.

"Well, whatever it was, that's awesome. Man, I don't even know what I'm gonna do with an extra hundred dollars a month."

Alina's payments were actually $250 a month, but I'll never let her know that. She had so much on her plate with finishing school and trying to get into a good dental program, then trying to keep up with her training; it didn't seem fair that she should also have to take on more part-time work to cover the bills.

"I know, right?" I answer instead. "Crazy." I pause as I wait to see if she might have anything else to add. When she doesn't, I clear my throat. "So, what else is new?"

Her voice is muffled for a second, and I hear another voice speaking up. A moment later she comes back on the line. "Actually, I have to go, sis. We'll catch up soon, okay? Love ya!"

"Okay, bye!" I barely manage before I hear the click on the other end.

I swallow back the lump in my throat, telling myself I have no right to feel hurt. I was hoping she and/or Sasha would remember to send a birthday text, and instead I got a call. What did it matter if the call was only a few minutes long and wasn't even about my birthday?

I seek consolation in the last few bites of my sweet brioche, but I barely taste it now. I ball up my trash and throw it away, not sure where I'm going next, but determined to at least get in some steps while I decide.

I've made it only a few blocks away from the park when I see a familiar figure: Kimo. He's on the other side of the street, walking in the opposite direction. He doesn't spot me, but I sure see him. He's kind of hard to miss, with his big, sturdy frame. Plus he's wearing neon green headphones and jamming out to whatever music he's listening to, either not noticing or not caring that he's getting double takes from everyone on the street.

"I can't believe I almost slept with that guy," I mutter under my breath.

An older man sitting out on his stoop overhears this and raises an eyebrow at me. I scowl back at him, waving away his judgment. "Oh, relax, you're fine."

I watch Kimo for a moment longer, frowning at his wild hair bobbing around as he dances in place at the streetlight. Then, without making the conscious decision to do so, I turn and follow after him.

Chapter Eight

I don't really know what my endgame is in following Kimo. I'm spurred on partially by curiosity, partially by boredom, partially by just not wanting to go home to an empty apartment. And, oh yeah, the fact that he just paid off all my student loans after basically one conversation and a cheek kiss. No one does something like that for someone without expecting something in return. Maybe if I follow him for a bit, I can figure out what his deal is. What weird stuff he's into. If he's planning on selling me to a sex cult. That kind of thing.

The longer I follow him, the more I convince myself this is a good idea, especially when I see he's heading toward Kosciuszko Park, where I just came from. What kind of weirdo hangs out at a park in the middle of a workday? Unless you're a stay-at-home parent with kids, or you work for the city's parks and recreation department, it's suspicious behavior, no? And okay, fine, I just came from the same park, but I was only sitting there for a few minutes to enjoy my birthday pastry. It wasn't my final destination.

I don't really have to do much to hide myself from Kimo's notice. The man is entirely lost in his own world, nodding his head and occasionally wiggling his hips in rhythm with whatever song he's listening to. Every so often he starts singing, too, off-key and seemingly oblivious to the looks he's getting from strangers, which range from amused to perplexed.

As I listen to him sing (badly), I realize I know those lyrics. Why do I know those lyrics . . . ? Oh, it's "Careless Whisper." I frown at the back of Kimo's head. Great. Now that song's going to be stuck in my head all day.

At last, Kimo slows his pace and raises his arm to wave to someone. Craning my neck, I see . . . not what I'm expecting.

A small group of octogenarians have gathered in the park. They are all faced in the same direction doing some slow, exaggerated movements that I think are Tai Chi, as someone's portable speaker blasts what is probably meant to be soothing pan flute music.

Kimo takes off his headphones and tosses them and his backpack on the ground before jogging over to join the group. I hurriedly duck behind a nearby bush, peering up over the edge so I can watch him. Kimo chats to an older woman standing off to the side for a few seconds while he removes his suit jacket and rolls up his shirt sleeves. Then he positions himself a few feet away from the others and joins right in with the slow, deliberate movements. His thick quads visibly strain against his dress pants.

. . . Who the hell is this guy? He doesn't make any sense to me, this flip-flops-at-the-gym, student-loan-paying, George-Michael-loving, friends-with-the-elderly multimillionaire. I don't buy this whole act, whatever it is. No one's this happy-go-lucky, loosey-goosey without some serious skeletons lurking in the closet and . . . oh. Yep. There he goes, kicking off his shoes to go barefoot in a public park. What a lunatic! Doesn't he know about ringworm . . . ?

That settles it. This man is either certifiably insane, or he's up to no good. Either way, I've figured out how I'm going to be spending the rest of my birthday.

I'm going to get to the bottom of Kimo Kapono, come hell or high water.

I'm not proud of what I do next. Or—you know what? No. I am *extremely* proud of what I do next. After he finishes Tai Chi, I follow Kimo from location to location for the next thirty-two minutes. I'm determined to figure out what his deal is, what nefarious schemes he might be plotting.

Minutes 1–3: Kimo leaves Kosciuszko Park, heading north. He appears to be listening to "I Wanna Dance with Somebody" by Whitney Houston, if I'm discerning the badly butchered, off-key lyrics he's singing correctly.

Minutes 4–10: Kimo stops to pet a dog tied up outside a bodega. For six minutes. I know that might not seem very long at a glance, but put on a timer. Imagine talking to a dog (that's not even your dog!) for that long. I'm too far back to hear the entire conversation, but I think it's mainly, "Good boy. You're a good boy. Yes, you are a good boy," etcetera. For *six minutes*. Insanity.

Minutes 11–15: Kimo goes into the bodega. Observing him through the window, I see him pick out a bag of chips and some chocolate milk. (Chocolate milk—what is he, five?) That takes about thirty seconds. The next few minutes are spent chatting to the owner. Are they friends, or is Kimo just chatty . . . ? Hard to tell through a window. I'm guessing Kimo isn't saying, "Good bodega man. You're a good bodega man," but you never know.

Minutes 16–30: Walking. Kimo is no longer singing for most of it, at least, since he's busy eating his chips and drinking his chocolate milk, but I can tell from the snippets of synthetic sound blaring from his headphones that he's still jamming out to '80s music. Occasionally he'll stop and play an air guitar while waiting for a light to change, so, there's that. Mostly, though, we walk, and walk, and then walk some more. I'm thankful I changed out of my work shoes and into my commuting sneakers, though I might actually kill someone for a sports bra right about now.

Minutes 31–32: Kimo at last reaches what seems to be his final destination. It's a big, warehouse-looking building with darkened windows. Shady. The logo of clashing weapons on the sign automatically has me going into a defensive stance, until I read the place's name: Dumb-Ax Throwing Club.

Ax throwing? On a Thursday morning? Watching him go inside, I spend the final minute debating whether to follow after him. I don't know how crowded it will be in there—if I can blend in, or if there will just be two guys and Kimo staring at me when I enter the room. The windows pose a similar problem. They're so dark that anyone inside will have a better view of me standing outside than I will of anything going on inside.

There's one window that isn't as darkly tinted, but it's small and high off the ground. I move toward it, wondering if I can catch even a little glimpse if I stand on my tiptoes and sort of hoist myself up onto the ledge . . .

That's what I'm attempting to do when I hear a sharp bark behind me. "Hey!"

I'm so startled that all my karate training goes straight out the window and I fall backward onto my ass.

I look up to see Kimo towering over me, his face dark and thunderous as I've never seen it before. (I mean, we've known each other for less than a day, but so far all I've experienced is pure golly-gee sunshine.) When he recognizes me, though, his expression immediately clears, and he grins like we're long-lost buddies. "Mattie! What are you doing here?"

I scramble to my feet, ignoring his offer of an outstretched hand. Once I'm standing again, I refuse to return the goofball smile he's giving me. Forget defensive. I'm in full-on offensive mode now.

"Following you. Who goes ax throwing in the middle of the day?" I demand to know.

Kimo seems completely undaunted by me coming in hot. Then again, he's like six-foot-a-billion and stacked and I'm . . . well, I'm not exactly small, but I feel downright dainty next to him. Like a chihuahua barking at a Great Dane. "The meeting got out earlier than I expected, and I have some time to kill before I need to pick up my niece and nephew from camp. My buddy runs this place so I thought, why not drop by? Plus I left a change of clothes here last time, and I couldn't wait to get out of this monkey suit."

That sounds . . . reasonable enough, I suppose. Regardless, I don't relent my severe arm-crossing pose. "What about Tai Chi in the park with all those old people?"

Kimo tilts his head, giving me a sly smile. "You *have* been following me."

Something about his tone makes me feel flustered, so I intensify my glare. "I already admitted to that, so stop dodging the question!"

Kimo rubs a hand over his mouth, like he's trying to hide a laugh. "Whenever I'm free in the mornings, I have a standing invitation from Beverly to join her Tai Chi group. I like to go as often as I can. It's really helped my posture, and I'll do whatever to get out in nature, you know? Plus, Beverly's rad. She slept with a Beatle back in the day. I can't remember which one . . . I feel like, I wanna say Greg?"

"There's no Beatle named Greg," I inform him curtly. Although, okay, now I am intrigued to find out which Beatle it was . . . but I won't let him distract me. "I don't understand you. Who goes around playing with random dogs and throwing axes and paying off a stranger's student loans?"

His expression shifts again, to something almost coy, like a little kid telling a lie and not quite able to make eye contact with his parents. "Who says that it was me who paid off your loans?"

"It was obviously you, so cut the bullshit. Why did you do it?"

Kimo considers the question a moment, then shrugs. "Why not?"

Why not. *Why not?* My brain will not compute this man. There is an error in the system. I get being suddenly rich and doing things on impulse, like buying a yacht, or flying to the Caribbean, or buying a castle in Scotland. But just randomly paying off someone's loans? Not even a family member or friend, but someone you met in a gym locker room the night before?

As if he can sense that my brain is in overdrive, Kimo puts a comforting hand on my shoulder and steers me toward the door. "Come on. Let me buy you a beer. I'll try to explain."

"It's eleven o'clock in the morning," I protest weakly. Nonetheless, I let him guide me inside.

Chapter Nine

A few minutes later, I'm sitting with a Diet Coke across the table from Kimo, who sips at his beer. "I don't usually drink so early in the morning, but going to meetings and getting dressed up makes me nervous," he informs me.

I eye him skeptically. He's hardly dressed up, compared to literally anyone else in corporate America, but from what I've seen of his wardrobe so far, I guess a button-up shirt, dress pants, and shoes that actually cover his feet does constitute a considerably more polished look. Although he's already changed out of said shoes into a pair of, you guessed it, flip-flops. And as I look on, he shucks off his dress shirt, revealing a plain white T-shirt underneath. I have a feeling he'd do the same thing with his pants if I weren't sitting here. The only other person in this ax-throwing club at eleven on a weekday morning is the guy behind the empty bar, who's shamelessly scrolling on his phone, so I doubt he'd care very much.

"You sure you don't want to split some chili cheese fries?" Kimo asks. "They have this really good nacho cheese dipping sauce."

"There is literally nothing enticing to me about anything you just said," I return briskly, folding my arms and settling back in my chair so I'm at the best angle to glare at him. "And enough stalling. Tell me why you paid off my loans."

Kimo laughs under his breath, running a hand through his hair. "Anyone ever tell you you're a real ballbuster?"

"Yes. *You.* In front of my boss, as a matter of fact." I haven't forgotten, even if he has. I forget nothing. "Now talk."

Another sigh from Kimo. He wraps his hands around his sweating beer glass, considering. "It's probably gonna sound dumb to you. Everyone always thinks coming into a bunch of money would be the best thing ever. Hell, I used to think that. But, I don't know. Even though there was nothing illegal about the way I got the money, it doesn't feel like it's mine, you know? It was starting to feel bad for my soul to keep it. So I've been trying to give it all away to good causes."

I frown at him, but now it's my processing frown, instead of my stern frown. "That doesn't sound so hard. There are plenty of people who need money."

Kimo slaps his palm down on the table. "That's what I thought! And believe me, I've given away a lot of it already. And I put aside trust funds for my niece and nephew—not too much; I don't want it to change them, make them feel entitled. Just enough so they can get through some of the early hurdles in life and be able to take some chances, go after their dreams. I paid off my māmā's mortgage, stuff like that. But . . . people get weird when you suddenly come into a lot of money. You have people—old friends, distant relatives, organizations, financial advisors—all coming out of the woodwork, trying to get a piece of you, trying to convince you they deserve it more than anyone else. It gets a bit overwhelming. I like to do my research, you know? Make sure the money's going where it's supposed to, and not going to the greedy bastards I was trying to take the money from in the first place."

Still processing, I take a long sip of my Diet Coke. That all sounds . . . reasonable so far. Not quite relatable, since I would never feel guilty about having enough money to cruise through the rest of my life, but I suppose I can see where he's coming from. "How much money are we talking?"

"When I started, or now?"

Another sip as I consider. "Now."

"Three hundred million, give or take."

I choke. Luckily it's only liquid and not a chili fry going down the wrong pipe, but still, I pound at my chest until I can breathe again. Three hundred million dollars? No wonder a few hundred thousand dollars in student loans didn't give him any pause. The amount of money he's talking about is . . . staggering. Life-changing.

Kimo winces at my reaction. "Yeah, I get that a lot. Believe me, I know. It's kind of a lot of money."

Kind of a lot of money. Right. And Taylor Swift is *kind of* famous. John Stamos is *kind of* handsome. Thank you very much, Captain Understatement.

But, if he's being careful with the money, and trying to vet where it's going, I can see why it might be hard to get rid of three hundred million dollars. Although . . .

"You didn't vet me," I accuse him. "You said you like to do your research, but you only met me once."

Kimo laughs, shaking his head. "I only had to meet you once to know you're the real deal. Totally and unapologetically yourself, no bullshit, freakishly honest."

I bristle instinctively, but he's smiling at me so guilelessly, I feel like there must be a compliment in there somewhere. "Thank you?"

"Believe me, it's a good thing. I meet so many people who just want to kiss my ass. Meeting you was . . . high tide."

The fond look he's giving me makes me feel weirdly squirmy inside. Not in a sexy way. But in a *I feel like my teacher just praised my writing and read my poem out loud to the entire class* kind of way—embarrassing but also flattering. I'm assuming that's how it would feel, anyway. I'd never do anything as dorky as write poetry.

I clear my throat, keen to move on. "How did you know I had student loans?"

"You mentioned having to pay off your loans, which is why you couldn't call a plumber."

I feel that little furrow between my eyebrows puckering into a frown again. "But *how* did you find my loans to pay them off? A random stranger shouldn't be able to access my account, even to make a payment."

"That's adorable that you think I couldn't break into your account." Kimo winks at me. "Happy birthday, by the way. Why are you spending it following me around?"

It takes me a minute to catch up. He would have seen my date of birth if he accessed my accounts, hence, the birthday wish. As to the other part . . . I shrug, not wanting to get into it. "I thought I was going to be at work all day so I didn't make any plans."

"Only now you're not stuck at work, because of me!" Kimo raises a hand to high-five me. "You're welcome!"

I leave him hanging. That's right, I'm a stone-cold bitch. "I'm pretty sure you got me kicked off the case, actually."

Kimo has the good grace to look chagrined. "Ooh. Sorry." He lowers his hand. "I'm sure I could put in a good word with Jay, get you back on the team. Especially considering the terrible tragedy with your dog this morning." He quirks a smile at me. "You're a pretty bad liar, you know that?"

Despite myself, I have to roll my lips to keep from smiling back. "Who says I was lying? Maybe I really loved . . ." I think quickly, saying the first dog name that comes to mind. "Comet. Maybe I'm devastated."

Kimo raises an eyebrow at me, not quite buying it, but not contradicting me, either. "In that case, I think we better do something to get your mind off him. Celebrate your birthday, all that."

"You can't simultaneously mourn the loss of your dog and celebrate your birthday with one activity," I inform him practically.

"In a normal dog death, sure. But with him being creamed by an ice-cream truck and trampled in a parade, we're playing by some unusual rules."

I can't help it. I smile. I quickly take a sip of my Diet Coke to cover it up, but I can tell by the pleased grin on Kimo's face that he's caught me. He stands, motioning for me to follow. "Come on. Let's throw some axes."

The hint of a smile quickly fades from my face. "What?"

"Come on," he urges me again. "It's gonna be fun . . ."

The lone employee gets us set up at one of the booths. There are nets on both sides, presumably to keep the axes from flying off, and at the far end is a wooden target for us to aim at. Our booth comes with one big ax and one tomahawk, both hanging up by the entrance. The employee offers to show us the basics, but Kimo quickly waves him off. "I got this, brother. Thanks." He takes another quick sip of his beer, then sets it on a table by the booth's entrance before getting into position. "All right, the basics are this—feet about shoulder width apart. You right- or left-handed?"

"Right," I inform him, trying to mimic what he's doing with my stance. Okay, so I wasn't exactly thrilled about the idea of throwing axes, but if I'm going to do it, I'm going to do it *right*.

"Cool. So, you're gonna pull your arms back behind your head, so you can almost reach your shoulder blades. Then step forward with your right foot and let the left kind of spring up behind to keep that momentum going forward as you bring your arms up. Release when you're about here. Keep your eye on the target and just sort of let the ax loose when it feels right."

He shows me the motion, and I do my best to mimic it, but I don't like how imprecise his directions are. *Kind of* spring forward? Release *about* here? *When it feels right?* How am I supposed to make any kind of sense of that? "What angle should my arms be at when I release? Seventy-five degrees, or more like twenty-five degrees?"

Kimo scratches the underside of his jaw. "Angle? I don't know. It's not an exact science, or anything. It's more about the feeling. Listen to your body."

My skepticism must show on my face because he laughs. "Just watch . . ."

He picks up the big ax with his right hand, using his left to pick up his beer. This time he doesn't set the beer down, just holds it in his free hand. "So you bring the arm back, then swing it forward. Use your legs for momentum. See, how I'm kind of springing forward? Then when it feels right—"

The whole time he's talking me through it, he's slowly making the motion as he's describing it, bringing the ax back then forward, back then forward. He pauses to take another sip of beer before abruptly swinging the ax back and launching it forward. It tumbles through the air before thwacking right into the center of the bullseye.

Kimo grins at me, proud as a peacock, no false humility on this one. "See? Easy."

I take a moment to process what I saw. On the one hand, I am nowhere closer to understanding how I'm possibly meant to mimic what he's doing. Despite his instructions on how to throw properly, his posture is loose, he's using only one arm, and I saw no springboarding off the left foot! Furthermore, his eyes were on mine the entire time, not the target. I'm frustrated at the seemingly impossible task he's set for me.

On the other hand . . . I'd be lying if I said that demonstration wasn't hot. *Extremely* hot, for reasons I don't totally understand. I have never been someone impressed by athletic prowess, and I certainly have never been drawn to the laid-back surfer type who sits around day drinking and singing "Hakuna Matata," or whatever. But the combination of him tossing that ax one-handed, sipping a beer, not even looking at where he was throwing, and managing to hit the target . . .

New fetish, officially unlocked.

I clear my throat, turning away to sip my Diet Coke. When I look back, the cheeky smile on Kimo's face lets me know that he's on to me. He knows I liked what I just saw, and he's not going to pretend otherwise just to make me comfortable. Humble, he is not, but I actually kind of appreciate that. As previously mentioned, false modesty has never been my thing.

But two can play this game. "Kind of warm in here," I say, shrugging off my blazer. Underneath I'm wearing a silky camisole that shows off a whole hell of a lot more skin, including my toned shoulders and arms. I also happen to know my breasts look spectacular in it.

Kimo's eyebrows rise. He's the one to clear his throat now, taking a sip of his beer. "Ready to try?"

I meet his gaze square on, holding it. "I like a challenge."

His lips quirk up in a smile, before he motions to the small tomahawk, still hanging on the wall. "You might want to start with the little guy, just while you're still learning the motions—"

I shut that idea down immediately, moving forward to retrieve the big ax from the target. My competitive streak won't allow me to practice with the girly ax, even if I *am* a beginner and have zero idea what I'm doing. "I'm more of a big ax kind of girl," I tell him over my shoulder.

As soon as the ax is actually in my hands, however, I immediately begin to rethink that position. It's much heavier than I thought it would be. I can see why he suggested using both arms. But even if I do so, I'm probably still going to look a little ridiculous trying to throw this thing around like it weighs nothing.

I bet Kimo could throw you *around like you weigh nothing*, a naughty, unhelpful little voice in my head chimes in.

I push away the visual of that, determined not to embarrass myself. Actually, if I'm being honest, I'm determined to do more than just not embarrass myself. I've never had any desire to throw an ax before, but now that the challenge has been presented to me, I'm resolved to be the best person at throwing axes that has ever lived in the history of mankind. It's not a conscious choice, it's just how my brain works. When I do something, I have to be the best at it, or what's the point?

Kimo just chuckles behind me. "You like big axes, huh? I'll keep that in mind."

Oh, so that's what we're doing now? I feel my body instantly respond to that low rumble of a laugh, him standing just off to the side and behind me—not touching me, but close enough that I can feel the heat of his body. "I know my way around a big piece of wood," I tell him matter-of-factly, before swinging the ax back and springing it forward, letting it fly loose.

My innuendo doesn't land all that well, though, considering that the ax thuds dull-side against the target and ricochets into one of the nets before dropping onto the floor.

This time there's nothing naughty or sexy about Kimo's chuckle. He's just laughing at me, at my complete ineptitude. Embarrassment floods through me—no, not quite embarrassment, more like anger. Anger at myself for doing so badly, and anger at him for witnessing it.

"It was my first try," I protest as I clomp forward to retrieve the ax. I will *not* switch to the tomahawk, so help me God. And if Kimo even suggests it, he just might become my next target practice. "And you didn't exactly give me clear instructions."

"Might help to have some beer," he suggests. "Relax a little."

"It's eleven o'clock in the morning," I snap back.

When I turn around, Kimo has set down his beer and he looks contrite, both hands up in a gesture of peace. "No, you're right. I'm sorry. Come here."

Brave man, to invite me into his personal space when I'm irritable and holding an ax. I frown at him, but he motions me closer. "Come on. I'll help you, I promise. I've been doing this for such a long time, it feels like instinct, so it's hard to explain how I'm doing what I'm doing, you know? Maybe I can show you instead."

That's right—it's *his* fault, not mine. I let him position me in front of the target. His hands press down gently on my shoulders, trying to get me to lower them. "Try to relax. This should be fun. It's not a competition."

Everything's a competition, I want to snap back, but for once, I manage to bite my tongue. His hands are big and warm on my skin, and his body presses in close to mine. I feel simultaneously soothed and alert, the tension draining out of me as a new kind of awareness awakens. One of his hands slides down to touch my hip bone, the other one still on my shoulder, as he maneuvers my body to where he wants it. "Like that. Feel how your balance moves to your center?"

Oh, I'm feeling something in my center, all right. "Yes," I agree, not wanting him to stop whatever he's doing.

He takes hold of my wrists, his arms pressed in over mine as he pulls them back, up, and over my head. I'm gripping the ax, so I'm trying to be mindful of where he's standing behind me, but I'm also aware of *him* behind me, the front of his body pressed into the back of mine, moving and flexing against me. "As you pull back, try not to just let your arms do all the work. Everything is connected. When you move here, you should be moving here"—he pushes into my back—"and here." He nudges the back of my leg with his knee. "It's all one motion."

He guides me through the movement a few more times, back and forth, back and forth. I'm sure there's something I should be learning, but it's hard to stay focused with him controlling my body like some kind of sexy puppeteer. (Another new fetish, unlocked?) I'm lost in the sensation of his big body coaxing mine to do what he wants. When I feel his warm breath at my ear, a shiver runs through me that I'm sure he must feel. "Ready?"

"R-ready," I manage to stammer.

This time when Kimo encourages me to swing my arms forward, I'm doing it on my own, though the rest of his body continues to urge on the rest of mine. I release when it feels right, and the ax arcs through the air, thunking satisfactorily into the target. Bullseye.

I shriek, gleefully spinning around to embrace him excitedly. "I did it! I'm amazing!"

Kimo chuckles. "Attagirl. I knew you had it in you."

It isn't until his arms come up around me that I fully register what I'm doing—I'm *hugging* him. As a rule, I'm not much of a hugger. I don't like having people in my personal space (with the obvious exception of sex). Bodies are smelly and awkward, and being held by someone for undetermined periods of time feels a bit like being trapped in a cage. Hugging Kimo, though, isn't *terrible*. In fact, it's downright . . . tolerable. His skin is as warm as I anticipated, his body somehow both hard and soft. He must have put on some cologne for the meeting this morning because he smells like soap and sandalwood and big strong man, and when his arms wrap me up gently and pull me in closer to his chest so I can hear the faint thrum of his heart, I feel . . .

Small. Safe. Nice.

If I'm not mistaken, he likes the feeling of being pressed up against me, too. I feel the slightest stirring against my stomach before Kimo steps back. "I'm gonna order another beer, hit the head, if you wanna keep practicing on your own for a minute."

I frown at his retreating back—because that's the only way to describe what he's doing: retreating. It's what he did last night, too. Against all odds, we seem to be vibing, but just when things start to heat up, he retreats.

This dynamic with Kimo is beyond strange. There's obviously an attraction between us, but I have no idea why he didn't go through with sleeping with me last night. I suspect he might be an idiot, or possibly crazy, or possibly both, and he's not anywhere close to my type, but I still find myself responding to his body in ways that are . . . unsettling. But, hey, I've never needed a great connection of the minds before, and a great connection of the bodies is all I'm really looking for, even if on paper he's not my ideal man.

Maybe Kimo is struggling with the same thing—he's attracted to me but knows he doesn't want anything serious. I've heard some guys can feel guilty about that kind of thing. In my own life, I've yet to experience a man feeling guilty about anything, but there's a first time for everything. Maybe all I need to do is make it clear to him that I'm not expecting anything beyond a quick encounter, and then we can both be on our separate ways. I'm not going to be on his custody case anymore anyway, so what's the harm?

Picking up Kimo's glass, I throw back the dregs of his beer for courage, then wipe my mouth with the back of my hand. "Here goes nothing," I mutter to myself before following Kimo into the men's room.

Chapter Ten

I hesitate outside the bathroom door—not because I'm having second thoughts, but because bursting into the men's room unannounced might have some very unsexy results that could prove to be a real mood killer. I hadn't really thought that one through last night with Grady, mostly because I was acting on pure desperation. But now I'm realizing that barging into bathrooms might create a huge problem. It'd be really hard to come back from catching Kimo in the middle of a number two, for example.

After a few moments of indecision, I determine the best way to know whether the bathroom is safe for me to enter for sexy times is to wait for the sound of a flush. Then I can give it a few seconds before making my entrance and, ideally, catching him washing his hands. (Please, God, let him wash his hands.)

With that decided, I press my ear to the door, listening for the sound of the flush.

Almost immediately, the door is pulled open from the other side. I lose my balance and go flailing into the room. Kimo catches me before I hit the floor, but only just barely. "Mattie? What are you doing?"

I straighten as best I can, attempting to toss the lock of hair that's fallen into my eyes back out of my face by jerking my head. I try my best to maintain eye contact with Kimo as I'm doing this, hoping for sexy, though I suspect by the perplexed look on his face that it's probably coming across a bit manic. I finally resort to using my hand, smoothing my hair back into place, before giving him my best sexy smile. "Coming to find you."

Kimo's confusion quickly morphs into understanding. His eyebrows notch up a bit. "Ohhh."

That "ohhh" doesn't sound . . . great. I'd expected him to be excited, and let's be real, a little bit grateful. I'm assuming it's not every day a woman like me throws herself at him. That "ohhh," though, sounded like more of an "oh shit" than an "oh, happy day! I'm about to get laid by a beautiful blonde!"

Maybe he's just surprised, I reason with myself. It probably takes a minute to transition from being in the *I'm going to the bathroom* mode to *I'm about to have sex* mode, right? I give him my best sultry smile, using the fact that he's still half holding me up as an opportunity to lean in and press myself up against him, wrapping my arms around his neck. "Hi."

"Hi." The long, slow swallow he gives is deeply gratifying to my ego. There, see? He's into this. I'm not just some weirdo throwing myself at him.

I wait for him to make the next move, but he just holds me, one big hand burning through my thin cami, as his eyes search mine. He's still looking more *resolved* than *turned on*, which wounds my pride a bit, but I suck it up. Closing the little bit of remaining distance between us, I stand on my tiptoes and move my mouth against his.

I'm expecting to have to coax Kimo into it, at least a little, but his response is almost immediate. His mouth meets mine eagerly, one hand coming up to grip my hair, tilting my head back so he can deepen the kiss. As his warm tongue strokes against mine, we stumble back until he guides me over to the counter. He lifts me so I'm perched on its edge, and I eagerly wrap my legs around his torso, cinching him in closer to me.

To my surprise, Kimo draws in a steadying breath as he pulls back from the kiss. He meets my gaze, offering me a lopsided smile. If I didn't know better, I'd say he was about to tell me he isn't feeling it—which I know isn't true, since just seconds ago I could feel his heart thrumming against mine, and other parts of him thrumming against me just as enthusiastically, too.

"You have a thing for bathrooms, huh?" he asks me as he strokes his warm fingers over the back of my neck.

I blink at him in surprise. That is *not* where I was expecting him to go. "Not really." I guess I can see why he might think otherwise, but honestly? I'm having to exercise incredible willpower not to think too much about just how many germs must be in here. Men are notoriously disgusting, after all, never picking up after themselves, leaving splatter on the seat . . .

Despite myself, a sudden thought crosses my mind, and I frown at him. "Why didn't you flush?"

It's Kimo's turn to blink at me, which turns into a furrowed brow of confusion. "What do you mean?"

"I was listening in the hall, waiting for the all clear. But you never flushed."

I realize how creepy that sounds only after I say it out loud. Kimo's eyebrows notch up a bit, but he doesn't comment on the fact that I just admitted to listening at the door. "I used the urinal."

I should just leave it at that. But I'm a bloodhound on the scent now, and my curiosity must be resolved. "Don't urinals flush?"

He huffs out a laugh, shaking his head a moment before meeting my gaze. "Some do. These ones are flush-less. See? No handles."

I crane my neck around him to confirm that, indeed, the urinals do not appear to flush. "Huh. What's the point of that? Won't they need to be cleaned more?"

"It's supposed to be better for the environment. Less water."

Too late, I realize this might be the single unsexiest conversation that two people have ever had in the history of human communication. I look back at Kimo, waiting half a beat before trying to lean in for another kiss, to recapture that electricity we had just a minute ago.

He pulls back, leaning his forehead against mine. "I think I'm good for now. That was nice, before. Thank you."

That was . . . *nice*? Nice is letting someone cut in line at the grocery store because they only have a few items, or seeing a flower grow unexpectedly out of a crack in the sidewalk. Nice is not making out with a hot blonde in an empty bathroom.

I'm not about to take that one lying down. "Are you into this or not?" I demand. "Because you're flip-flopping even more than your alleged gym shoes."

Kimo runs a soothing hand down my spine. "I'm into this. I just want to take it slow. Get to know each other."

Somehow, this is even more offensive than the last thing he said to me. "Why?"

"That's what you do when you're dating, right? Get to know each other."

It's my turn to let my eyebrows shoot up; I can feel them practically reaching my hairline. "You think this is dating?"

He shrugs. "Sure. Why not? I like you. You like me."

"No, I don't!" I protest, shoving against his chest to get him to back up a step. He does. "And we are not *dating*. That's absurd. We haven't even been on a date."

"So, let's go on one. What are you doing this weekend?"

I shake my head at him, more violently than I mean to. It leaves me a little dizzy, honestly. "That's not the point! We don't have anything in common. This is not some romance thing. It's just sex."

For a long beat, Kimo says nothing, just stares at me. Then he sighs, shaking his head. "Look, if this had happened a year ago, I'd be super into it. You're smoking hot, even if you are a little pushy."

A weird squawking noise that I don't even recognize erupts from my throat in protest. "*Pushy?*"

Kimo carries on without missing a beat. "But things are different now. I'm trying to be a dad for my niece and nephew, trying to be what I think a man should really be. I can't do the no-strings thing anymore. I want someone I can share my life with, be partners with. Someone who will have my back when things get tough. Someone to celebrate with when things are good. A life partner. Matching Adirondack chairs on the back deck. All of it."

My first cynical knee-jerk response is that he's just saying all this to try to get laid. Except . . . I offered him the chance to get laid, and he turned it down, because apparently he wants . . . true love?

Who even is this man?

Before I can respond, someone begins pushing open the bathroom door. "We're busy in here," I snap at them without looking over. "Come back later."

I see Kimo's face blanch. He grabs my wrist, pulling me away from the door and behind him.

I'm too surprised to protest. Much. "What are you—?" It's only once I'm behind Kimo's broad back that I see who's at the door.

Two men, dressed all in black and wearing ski masks. Both of them holding guns.

Chapter Eleven

We are ushered through the main part of the building. "Hey!" I try shouting at the guy behind the bar. "They have guns! Call 9-1-1. We're being kidnapped!"

He flinches, obviously hearing me though he pretends not to, and doubles down on wiping the invisible mess on the counter.

It takes me a minute to process what's happening. I guess I'm a little slow on the uptake, but cut me some slack—I've never been kidnapped before. This guy obviously knew two armed gunmen were coming to drag us out of the bathroom. Hell, he probably was the one to tell them we were in there, whoever *they* are. All of his intense texting from before suddenly shifts into perspective.

One of the men shoves my shoulder. "Shut up. Don't say another fucking word."

Kimo, who's been walking behind me this whole time, steps in even closer to me. "Hey, it's okay. We're gonna be cool, right, Matilda?"

Cool. *Cool?* I've never been cool in my entire life, not for a single day. I was the kid who narced on anyone who was cheating, the teenager who never got invited to any parties, the nun who tried to live every single rule to the exact letter of the law, until I couldn't anymore. There's nothing about me that's cool under the best of circumstances. So I'm not sure how

I'm supposed to stay cool with someone aiming a gun at my back right now.

As if sensing this, Kimo tells me again, softer this time, "It's okay." He raises his voice a bit, speaking to the armed men now. "You don't have to take her. I barely know her. And she isn't going to say anything, right, Mattie?"

They're here for Kimo. This piece of information slots into place, and again, it feels like it should have been obvious with him being a multimillionaire and all, and me being someone with a few thousand dollars in her bank account, but it still takes me by surprise. What can I say? Being held at gunpoint apparently makes me slow.

"I won't say anything," I agree to Kimo's prompt, even though that is a bald-faced lie. I will most definitely be calling the police the second I can reach my phone, and you'd better believe I'm, at the very least, going to get the douchebag behind the bar fired for not helping us.

Either I'm a terrible liar or the kidnappers were never going to be convinced not to bring me along, because in the next instant, one of the armed men pulls out two cloths that he uses to gag first me, then Kimo. (First *me*? That feels a bit pointed. I might protest that society always chooses to silence women first, if it weren't for the fact that I'm gagged now.)

One of the men opens the door out onto the street, peering around before nodding at the other. "All clear."

I feel someone touch me and instinctively try to jerk away, until I realize it's just Kimo, giving my hand a reassuring squeeze. Our gazes meet, and I can tell he's worried, even though he's trying to play it easy for my sake.

We're quickly ushered to a van right outside the building. Its door is wide open, waiting and ready for us, and it has dark tinted windows that are impossible to see into. Great—what a cliche, as far as kidnapping vehicles go. I don't know why I'd hoped they might be slightly more imaginative kidnappers, but an SUV would have been nice. I look frantically around the street, hoping that someone, anyone, might see us and call for help, but there's no one.

Then I'm being shoved into the van, Kimo close behind me. One of the men climbs into the back with us, and the other gets into the passenger seat. Another man is already in the driver's seat, keeping the engine running.

"Go," instructs the man in the passenger seat.

The driver obeys.

We drive. And drive. And drive. I can't see much from where I'm sitting on the floor of the van, but I'm guessing by the speed we're going that we must be on the expressway. Which means, most likely, they aren't just planning to move us from one building in town to another. I'm honestly not sure if this is good or bad news. If they're going to all the trouble to take us on what seems to be a long journey, that must mean they're planning on keeping us alive, right?

Unless they're trying to find a remote location to hide the bodies. *Our* bodies.

Panic wells up inside of me. If I wasn't still gagged, I'd likely be screaming. Instead I make this weird sort of moaning sound that I've never heard come out of my body before. It's odd enough that even the guys in the front glance back at us. They've all taken off their masks now, which also doesn't seem like a very good sign for our survival, since we'll be able to identify them and all.

The guy in the passenger seat, who I've started calling Sandy because of his sandy-brown hair, eyes me before glancing at the other kidnapper, who's sitting on the floor in the back with us. "Can you shut her up?"

The guy in the back—Freckles, because, well, *freckles*—shifts a little, looking at me uneasily. "Come on. Be quiet."

A new idea strikes me. Maybe if I make enough noise, if I get to be annoying enough, they'll pull over to the side of the road and just drop me off. It's Kimo they want anyway, not me. And if there's anything I'm confident I can be, it's a total pain in the ass. I've had several friend groups drop me over the years—why not kidnappers, too? I keep groaning, but put more volume behind it now.

I feel a little surge of hope when Freckles puts his hands over his ears to drown out the sound, until Sandy turns around again and looks me dead in the eyes. "Keep going, baby. I like listening to you moan."

That shuts me up quickly. I didn't make a conscious decision to start making that noise, but now I sure as hell make the conscious decision to stop it. Sandy looks at me a moment longer, his gaze lingering in a way that makes my skin crawl, before slowly turning back to the front.

I feel something brushing against my back. I jump, irrationally panicked that somehow Sandy, or maybe even Freckles, has found a way to reach around behind me and touch me—but of course, it's Kimo. We're sort of leaning against each other along one side of the van, and he's angled his bound hands in such a way that he can brush his fingers against mine. I suppose he's trying to offer me some comfort, but all it does is remind me that we're both tied up and helpless to do anything about it.

Kimo doesn't look like he feels helpless, though. The look he's sending Sandy gives me chills. In the short time I've known him, I've only ever seen Kimo happy, open, sunny. His positivity kind of makes you forget how big and strong he really is. But his expression now—dark, angry, even furious—is a reminder of what a force to be reckoned with he is.

Even though Kimo's the one who's tied up, Sandy's smug smile falters, then fades away. Clearing his throat, he looks away from us. After a moment he pulls out his phone and takes a call. "Yeah. So far." I see him look at us in the rearview mirror again. "He had someone with him, but we grabbed her too." He listens for a moment. "I'll let you know."

Sandy swivels around to talk to Freckles. "Ungag him. We have some questions for Kimo Hood."

Freckles leans forward and tugs the gag down off Kimo's mouth. He seems a little nervous doing it, like he's afraid Kimo's somehow going to attack him, even though he's still bound. Of the two, Freckles definitely seems like the follower, and Sandy's the leader. I guess it's hard to tell with Driver, since all he's done is drive so far. (I don't really think I need to explain that nickname, do I?)

"Your niece and nephew's camp gets out at three, yeah?" Sandy asks Kimo.

Kimo seems to consider the question for a moment, no doubt wondering if revealing this information will do anything to put the kids in harm's way. He quickly seems to realize, though, that the camp's dismissal time is something the kidnappers would be able to figure out relatively easily without any help from him. "Right."

"Any other appointments before then? Anyone expecting you?"

Kimo gives what can only be described as a shit-eating grin. "No comment."

"Let's take that as a no, then. What happens if you don't show up to pick up the kids—will the camp call someone else about it?"

Kimo stays silent.

Sandy does not look amused. "Maybe I'll just ungag your little girl-friend, then. See if I can find some new ways to make her moan."

I instinctively clutch at Kimo's fingers, still pressed in close to mine. He grips me back, a silent *I'm here with you*, even as he continues to seethe at Sandy. I can feel the tension radiating off his body.

It's probably for his family, I rationalize. All this protectiveness can't be for me; I hardly know him.

"They'll probably call the next contact listed for the kids if I'm more than fifteen minutes late," Kimo reluctantly grits out. I see a muscle in his cheek jumping. "Their bio dad first, but he'll still be at work, so then they'll probably try my mom."

Sandy nods, turning back toward the front. He pulls out his phone and begins texting. "That gives us a few hours' head start, then, before anyone starts looking for us." He flashes a quick, mean grin at us in the rearview mirror. "That's all we'll need."

We fall back into silence again after that, with only the roar of the van and the sounds of other cars on the expressway. I dart a few glances at Kimo, who seems to be lost in thought. I don't blame him. I mean, I'm currently going through it at the moment, too, but I only have myself to worry about. He has his niece and nephew to think about. They'll probably be so worried when he doesn't show up to pick them up. And then when the camp calls his mom, I can only imagine the kind of panic she'll experience when she realizes her son's gone missing . . .

"Is that a Zelda tattoo?" Kimo asks abruptly.

I frown at him, but he's not looking at me—he's looking at Freckles, who seems equally surprised by the question. On the back of his hand, I catch a glimpse of a weird-looking bird-type symbol before Freckles self-consciously holds it up against his chest, his eyes darting toward the front of the van.

"The Hylian crest, right?" Kimo persists, undeterred by Freckles's obvious reluctance to talk. "Dude, that's awesome. I played that game for about a month straight when I was going through a bad patch. Saved my life.”

Freckles glances up toward the front again, but Sandy doesn’t seem to notice or care that Kimo wants to talk about video games. Freckles shrugs, but it seems kind of forced, like he’s trying to put on a tough-guy act. “It’s all right.”

“Just all right?” Kimo shakes his head and laughs. “You can feel that way if you want, brother, but *Tears of the Kingdom* was basically a religious experience for me. I cried like a baby at the end.”

Freckles shifts. He’s still reluctant, but Kimo’s enthusiasm is obviously wearing him down. “*Majora’s Mask* was better.”

“Dude, top five of any game I’ve ever played, of all time,” Kimo agrees, shaking his head at the sheer marvel of it.

Freckles can’t resist any longer. It’s like the nerdy floodgate has been opened, and they talk, and talk, and talk. I won’t even pretend to understand half of what’s being said, but I get the vague impression there’s some kind of hero, and maybe a princess, and lots of dungeons? Doesn’t really sound like my thing, to be honest, but I’m not an idiot. I see what Kimo’s doing. He and Freckles are building some kind of geeky bond, maybe one even strong enough that if Sandy asks Freckles to shoot him and throw his body in a ditch somewhere, Freckles might hesitate. Might even say no.

Suddenly, Kimo turns to me. “You ever play, Mattie? Or are you more of a *Call of Duty* girl?”

I literally have no idea what that means, but I make a garbled response through my gag. Kimo looks back to Freckles, motioning to me. “Do you think we can ungag her? It chafes after a bit, having that thing in your mouth.”

I sit up eagerly. *Yes, please!* I try to convey with my eyes. I can talk about dorky video games, too, if it means I won’t have this cloth pulling on my jaw anymore.

Freckles eyes me dubiously. He’s gone from being open and laughing to guarded and distrustful with just that one question. “I don’t think they’d like it.” He motions toward the front of the van with a jerk of his head. “Besides, she’s kind of . . . loud.”

Loud? If I didn’t have this gag in my mouth, I’d verbally rip him a new asshole for that one.

We seem to have drawn Sandy’s attention again. I feel his eyes on me in the rearview mirror and pretend not to notice. "What's going on back there?"

"Just talking about video games," Freckles speaks up quickly. It's obvious he isn't quite on the same level as Sandy and Driver—if that weren't already clear from the fact that he's in the back with us, instead of sitting up front in a big boy seat with a seat belt. "He wanted me to ungag her, but I said no."

I roll my eyes. *Kiss ass.*

"You two feel like talking, huh?" Sandy chuckles quietly to himself. It's not a nice sound. "How about you give us some details about what you were up to in that bathroom before we burst in?"

I feel Kimo's body tense against mine, but he stays silent.

"Aww, we aren't gonna be chatty buddies, too?" Sandy shakes his head. "My feelings are hurt. Don't worry, though. I'm sure she'll catch me up on it later, when it's just the two of us."

Ew. "As if I'd touch your microdick with a ten-foot pole!" I tell him. Unfortunately, I'm gagged, so I imagine the message doesn't come through all that clearly.

Instead, Kimo speaks up. "You seem to like to joke about sexual violence, buddy. Kind of weird, I gotta say. Must make you feel big and strong, to talk that way to a woman who's tied up and helpless. But let me make clear to you right now—I'm not gonna be tied up forever. And I'm taking it very personally, the way you're talking to my friend Mattie. So I'd make some very careful decisions right now, brother, if I were you."

A long moment of tense silence follows as Sandy and Kimo stare each other down. I look back and forth between them, positive my eyebrows are up to my hairline. I guess I could quibble, since technically, when *I'm* untied, I'm pretty confident I'll be able to take care of myself just fine. (Hello, black belt!) But the fact that he's sticking up for me, this person he barely knows . . . I'm surprised. Grateful. I'm not used to people having my back this way.

Sandy seems pretty surprised, too, at having someone call him out. After a moment, he looks away, pulling out his phone and pretending to be busy texting.

We sit for a moment in silence. Freckles has gone back to looking out the window, no longer willing to talk to Kimo.

I glance over at Kimo, wishing yet again I didn't have this gag on.

Then again, I don't have any idea what I'd say. I'm not great at thanking people. It always makes me feel weirdly defensive. Maybe it's for the best I can't use my words.

Instead, I hesitate before reaching out to wrap my fingers around Kimo's index finger, giving it a gentle squeeze. He looks over at me, winking. "I got you," he tells me quietly.

Somehow, I actually believe him.

Chapter Twelve

We drive some more. Then some more. And then some more.

I'm starting to really regret not using the bathroom when I was . . . you know, propositioning someone in the men's bathroom. (Again.) *He* got to pee before we were kidnapped, but I didn't take advantage of all those available toilets, and now that Diet Coke I was sipping back at the ax-throwing gym is starting to make its presence known.

I'm still gagged, so I try to do the universal signal for needing to go to the bathroom—you know, squirming around with my lower body like a toddler does. I also try to make meaningful eye contact with Freckles, but he's pointedly not looking at me, though he does look at Kimo when all my wiggling becomes too obvious to ignore. "What's wrong with her?"

Her would prefer not to be talked about like I can't speak up for myself, but then again, I *am* still gagged. Kimo looks over at me, and my wide eyes must convey my desperate need to him, because he sighs. "I think she needs to pee."

"I do," I try to say through my gag. "Reeeally bad."

Freckles taps on the back of Sandy's seat. "I think we gotta stop."

Sandy must have been listening in, because he doesn't bother asking what's going on. "She'll have to wet her pants. We aren't stopping."

My wail of outrage is drowned out by Kimo and, surprisingly, Freckles protesting, too. "Just pull to the side of the road. We're not animals," Kimo says, as Freckles talks right over the top of him, "I'm sitting on the floor back here, too, dude. I don't wanna be in a pee puddle."

Between the three of us, we must be convincing, because Sandy finally sighs and relents. "Pull onto that side road, just up there," he instructs Driver.

We drive along the side road for a few minutes, presumably to get farther away from the expressway so we won't be spotted by any passing cars. I'd be touched by all this concern for my modesty if I wasn't positive Sandy's doing it to cover his own ass instead of mine.

The gravel road we're on is a lot bumpier, and I'm jostled heavily up against Kimo. He braces his legs into the floor, trying to steady us in place. Even Freckles is bouncing around, having to hold on to the passenger seat to keep from careening across the vehicle.

Using the distraction as an opportunity, Kimo leans in close to my ear. "Hey. If you get a chance, run for it. Try and hide if you can, then wait them out. It's me they want, not you, so they'll probably give up eventually. We aren't that far from the highway, so you can make it back and flag down help."

Wide-eyed with terror, I meet his gaze. It isn't that the thought hadn't crossed my mind, but hearing it vocalized makes it seem that much more real. Then again, if my other option is to stay tied up in the back of the van, I'd rather be hiding under a bush in the middle of rural Illinois—or Wisconsin? Indiana? Michigan? I'm not sure which way we've been traveling—and take my chances with the kindness of passing motorists. But my stomach twists in knots at the thought of leaving Kimo behind, to suffer who knows what fate. I try to reason away that sick feeling in my gut, reminding myself it'll probably be easier for him to escape if I'm not here holding him back. He seems weirdly calm about this whole kidnapping, like maybe this isn't his first rodeo.

Doing my best not to panic, I nod at him to show I understand and I'll try my best.

Finally, Driver pulls the van to the side of the road. Sandy gets out first before opening the heavy sliding door in the back and addressing Freckles. "I'll take the girl. You take our friend Kimo."

"Nope," Kimo says before I even have time to vocalize my complaints. He locks eyes with Sandy. "I promise you, I will try to escape if you take

Matilda. And I think we both know that, even tied up, I can take your friend. No offense, brother."

This last part is directed toward Freckles, who shifts but doesn't comment. Seeing as how Kimo has a good seventy-five pounds on him, and a lot of it muscle, he wisely doesn't refute the idea that Kimo could take him in a fight, especially since they seem determined to keep Kimo alive and likely won't shoot at him.

Sandy sighs—it's more like a hiss, really—clearly frustrated at not getting his way. Geesh. This guy is obsessed with me. "Fine. Dylan, you take the girl. I'll take Kimo Hood."

Dylan? I eye Freckles over. Nah. That's a terrible name for him. Dylan is the name for a rebel, a *poet*, and this guy is just . . . Freckles.

I've never tried to scooch out of a van with my hands tied behind my back and my bladder full to bursting before, but it's not the most elegant I've ever been, let's just leave it at that. When I finally manage to make it to the door, Sandy grips my upper arm tightly. "No funny business. We weren't even meant to pick you up. No one's going to care what I do with you if you don't behave."

I just glare back at him. He's lucky I have this gag on, or he'd already have a loogie on his face. Finally he lets me go, and Freckles (yep, that's the name I'm sticking with) takes me by the arm, guiding me around the other side of the van. Behind me, I can hear Kimo grunting and shuffling his way out of the vehicle, and Sandy saying something harsh to him that gets carried off by the wind.

Unlike Sandy, Freckles doesn't seem especially keen to touch me. Up close I can sense how young he is, maybe early twenties, maybe even late teens. He has that not-fully-developed build of a young man still coming into what his grown-up body will be. Maybe I should feel somewhat sympathetic to him because of that, but all I can think is how easy it would be to knock over his thin, knobby body if I rush him.

But first, I really do have to pee.

Freckles motions toward a spot in the gravel. "Go ahead. Do your thing."

He starts to turn his back to me, but I make a little whine of protest, twisting my back to remind him that my hands are tied. If it were Sandy, I have no doubt he'd offer to help me pull down my shorts (creep), but Freckles just shifts uncomfortably. Either this is his first kidnapping or he's really in the wrong profession, because he looks like he hates every part of being here.

"Fine." He reluctantly unties my hands. "Just don't do anything stupid or I'll make you regret it."

Since he's still facing me, I resist the urge to roll my eyes. The delivery could really use some work, kid. I'm not exactly shaking in my sensible walking shoes here.

With his back turned to me, I squat down to do my business. As I do so, I let my eyes roam over the tree line, just a few yards away. If I can knock over Freckles and escape into the trees, I might be able to hide, just like Kimo recommended. I can hear the not-too-distant roar of the expressway from here, so it will likely be within walking distance once I can make my way back.

Holy shit. I'm really doing this.

I discreetly pull my shorts back up and ready myself to make a break for it. First step, knock down the kid. Next, run for the trees. Then, find a place to hide. Actually, *first* first step, I take off my gag and quietly drop it to the ground. No more need for that. I work my jaw a few times, unable to resist loosening it after being clamped shut for so long.

If I were still the praying kind, I might say a quick prayer now. But I'm all I have. I've known that now for quite some time.

"You got it, dude," I mutter to myself under my breath.

Freckles's back is still turned toward me. Taking a deep breath through my nose, I center myself before launching into a spinning hook kick aimed at his buttocks.

I watch Freckles go down but don't wait to see what the aftermath will be. Instead I bolt toward the tree line, running as fast as I can go.

Chapter Thirteen

Here's the thing—yes, I was a nun, but before that, I was a coed living in downtown Chicago. I started practicing karate when I was an undergraduate, and when I showed an aptitude for martial arts, my instructor encouraged me to keep up with my training. Unlike most undergrads, I didn't spend my free time partying. Between two jobs and my own studies, I had very little free time to begin with, and without distractions like boyfriends or a social life, I was able to fully commit to my training and advance quickly. Not to brag, but my sensei said he had never met anyone so single-mindedly focused and scarily intense.

Unlike most of my classmates who were women, I wasn't training in karate because I'd felt particularly unsafe where I was. Sure, I'd had people follow me off the bus, the usual uncomfortable groping from strangers on the bus, the guy who sniffed the back of my head at the bus stop . . . come to think of it, there was a lot of bus-related sexual harassment happening, before, during, and after being a nun. Troubling. Anyway, I hadn't felt threatened during these encounters so much as annoyed. Usually a cold glare and a sharp, "Cut it out, asshole!" were enough to cow anyone from trying anything more. Someone like Nina might feel too embarrassed to call people out like that, but not me. I love a good public shaming.

No, for me, karate wasn't about physical defense as much as it was mental fortitude. I'd spent so much of my life having my control taken away. Leaving behind my babushka in Russia to come to the States for Mama's new boyfriend. Having to step up for Alina and Sasha when Mama didn't come home on the weekends, and then didn't come home at all. Being split into different foster families and homes from my sisters. I channeled all that frustration, all that rage, into disciplining my body and mind. Becoming a nun was supposed to help me escape my childhood demons, but in a lot of ways, karate did for me what prayer and fasting ultimately couldn't.

Anyway, all of that's to say, me kicking Freckles's literal and figurative ass didn't come out of nowhere. I'd been training for that moment my entire adult life; I just didn't know when and where it would come.

Do I wish that it had been Sandy instead of Freckles? Sure. Sandy's the bigger asshole by far, and I would have loved to see his look of surprise when he got his ass handed to him by a woman. It might have even made his red-pill-addled brain explode, which would have also been entertaining to watch. But do I feel bad about taking Freckles down? Absolutely not. He might be the nicer of the two kidnappers, but he's still a kidnapper. As my babushka used to say, *Что посéешь, то и пожнёшь*. What you sow, you will reap.

I make it to the trees before I hear the first shout. Freckles must have needed a moment to recover from that ass whooping I just gave him, ha! Knowing I don't have much longer now before they start looking for me, I throw myself into the dense green foliage, searching for the best place to hide.

After running mindlessly for what feels like an hour but is probably only a few minutes, I see a fallen tree. There looks to be just enough space between it and the ground where I can tuck myself and try to wait out the kidnappers. God, I wish I had my phone so I could call for help, but it's back at Dumb-Ax in my purse—or maybe in a dumpster somewhere, if that employee who sold us out was smart enough to cover his tracks.

As soon as I'm in place and my heartbeat stops roaring in my ears, I can hear Sandy, not too far away, shouting and kicking up a fuss: ". . . let her get away?"

I hear Freckles close by, too, though he's not shouting, which makes it harder to hear exactly what he's saying: ". . . didn't expect . . . freaking Buffy the Vampire Slayer . . ."

Is he talking about me? He must be. I can't help but preen at that, pleased despite myself. Vampire slayer, huh? I mean, I knew I was good, but I didn't know I was *Buffy* good . . .

"Do you even really need to find her? She has nothing to do with this. She doesn't even know where you're taking me. Maybe just leave the scary slayer out in the woods, call it good?"

Kimo. His voice comes through loud and clear, almost like he's projecting for my benefit. I hold my breath, waiting to see how the others will respond.

"I have a better idea." Sandy seems to be following Kimo's lead in enunciating clearly so he can be heard—or maybe they've just gotten closer to where I'm hiding. "Hey, Pink Ranger. If you don't come out in ten seconds, I'm gonna put a bullet in your boyfriend, here."

My eyes widen. I clap a hand over my mouth, even though I haven't made a sound. He wouldn't really do that, would he? He has to be bluffing.

"He's bluffing." Kimo seems to agree with me. He still sounds totally relaxed, like this is a typical Thursday afternoon for him. "Come on, brother. You need me alive. That's the whole point of this."

"I need you alive," Sandy agrees, "but no one ever said I can't shoot you in the kneecap. And believe me, *brother*, you'll wish you were dead once I shoot you there."

I wait for another reassurance from Kimo, but it doesn't come. Even he can't pretend to be chill about getting shot in the kneecap, I guess.

"Ten, nine, eight . . ." Sandy starts counting, loudly.

Surely he won't really shoot him . . . but what if he does? How difficult is it to recover from a knee shooting? I wish I had my phone so I could Google it.

"Seven, six, five . . ."

Won't it be better for Kimo in the long run if I'm able to escape and get help? Otherwise, who will even know where to look for him? Sure, I don't know an exact location, but I can give a general direction of where the kidnappers might be taking him.

"Four, three, two . . ."

Oh my God, I'm going to have to listen to someone get shot! I've never had to listen to that before, all Russian stereotypes aside. And all things considered, the knee seems like an awfully important body part. It's not like a thigh, which is kind of meaty and might be able to absorb a bullet without too much damage. A knee is just bone and muscle, and that's going to require reconstructive surgery, probably months of physical therapy. He might never be able to exercise in flip-flops again . . .

"One—"

"Okay, okay, okay!" I can't do it. I can't sit by and listen to that. Sandy was probably bluffing, but what if he wasn't? I may be a stone-cold bitch, but I'm also squeamish, and all that blood and screaming and whatnot is a solid pass from me.

Wriggling out from my hiding place, I hold my hands up in the air, spinning around until I find where everyone's located, only a few yards away from me. "I'm here, all right? Don't shoot anyone."

Sandy grins at me, looking pleased as punch. Ugh, how irritating. He's going to be pure hell to travel with now. Freckles looks pissy, likely because I knocked him down and made him look like an idiot in front of his kidnapper buddies. He's definitely not a fan of mine now. Well, feeling's mutual, buddy! And Kimo . . .

It's hard to tell what Kimo's feeling. He looks sort of resigned, disappointed things didn't turn out like we'd planned, but also kind of . . . warm? Is that an expression? And if so, why is he looking at *me* that way when I just screwed things up so badly?

I get my answer once we're stowed in the back of the van again. This time, at least, I don't have a gag, although my hands have been retied. "Sorry," I mumble to Kimo, not wanting to draw too much attention to myself and the fact that I don't have a cloth shoved in my mouth, in case they just forgot to re-gag me.

Kimo nudges me. "For what? You did everything I told you to. Then you saved me. Not everyone would have done the same thing in your position. That was pretty badass. You saved me, Mattie."

If this were an episode of *Full House*, this is when the treacly music would start playing. Moments like these always give me the warm gooeys when I'm watching them on TV, but experiencing them in real life is . . . awkward. I'm not used to people "expressing their emotions" to me. It makes me feel like something is crawling under my skin. "I just didn't want to hear you cry like a little girl," I tell him briskly, hoping that will discourage any more of this *emoting* he's doing.

Kimo just grins at me. "Little girls got nothing on me. I'm a screamer when I cry. Wailing. Gnashing of teeth. Full-on snot rivers running down my face."

I fight a smile. "Sounds disgusting."

"Oh, it is."

My lips tug upward as I lose the battle. We smile at each other for a moment, before I start to feel that crawly sensation again and avert my gaze. It lands on Freckles, who is glaring at me with open hostility. I seize on that. Open hostility is much easier to deal with than whatever warm, gushy nonsense Kimo is sending my way right now.

My smile morphs into something very different for Freckles, openly taunting. "Do I have something on my face, or is there some other reason you're staring at me?" So much for lying low and not drawing attention to myself and my gag-less state. I just can't help but poke the bear sometimes.

Kimo nudges me with his knee. *Play nice*, that gesture says. "Hey, man, no hard feelings. She could have taken down any one of us. Black belt in karate."

I frown at Kimo, wondering how he knows that, before I remember that he saw the picture of my black belt ceremony in my apartment. "Stalker," I mutter under my breath nonetheless.

It's a little irritating that Freckles's fragile masculinity has to be assuaged, but I guess Kimo's wise to try to keep him on our side. I do my best to look contrite. Louder, I add, "Yeah. Sorry. And if it helps, I've taken down way bigger guys than you before. More muscular, too—"

I'm genuinely trying to be helpful, but Kimo clears his throat, loudly, cutting me off. "Mattie's a little high-strung today. Her dog died this morning."

"Parade—" I start to say, but Kimo nudges me again, stopping me before I can get carried away with the elaborate lie.

To my surprise, Freckles shifts, looking genuinely troubled by this news. "I'm sorry. That really sucks." He shakes his head, as if this news has hit him like a personal blow. "Dogs are so much better than people, you know? They don't deserve that shit."

For a moment, I can only stare at him. This guy isn't at all fazed by kidnapping us, apparently, but he seems to be getting emotional about the idea of a stranger's (made-up) dog dying . . . ?

Looking at him more closely, though, I notice for the first time traces of white fur on his clothes. I send Kimo a furtive, sidelong glance. First the tattoo, now this. Kimo seems to have taken in every detail about this guy and is using it to his advantage to form some kind of emotional connection. That's some crazy Sherlock Holmes–style manipulation. I guess I should be worried that Kimo might be using that same kind of tactic on me, but I'm too busy being impressed.

I turn my focus back to Freckles, wondering if I can work the same manipulative magic. "He was a white dog. With hair, that was also white." Hopefully that will make Freckles think of his own dog and, therefore, make him more prone to feel sorry for my pretend dead pet. Let's see, what else do people like about dogs? "And he was a good boy. So slobbery and sweet. Always peed outside, like he was supposed to. Loved chasing balls."

Hey, cut me some slack. I grew up for most of my life in foster care and then became a nun. Do you think I have any experience with dogs? But whatever I'm doing seems to be working, because Freckles is nodding, and even seems a little emotional about the whole thing. "Yeah, man. I'm sorry. That's rough. What was his name?"

At least I have this part of the lie prepared. "Comet."

Freckles reacts visibly. "Like the dog from *Full House*?"

Oops. I did not expect him to be able to put that together. I recover quickly. "Yes. Yeah. It was my favorite show growing up, so as soon as I got a dog, I thought, I have to call it Comet!"

To my surprise, Freckles smiles and shakes his head. "That was my favorite show growing up, too. All the reruns on Nick at Nite? I used to fall asleep watching it."

"Me too!" This time, I don't have to lie. I sit up, eager to compare notes with a fellow cable-baby, raised by a television. "I always wished I could be a Tanner."

"Yeah." Freckles nods his agreement. "But I'd probably actually be—"

"A Gibbler," I finish for him. We laugh together companionably.

I can feel Kimo watching me and I realize that I've probably said too much on the subject now, revealed too much about myself. I clear my throat. Freckles shifts, too, glancing over at Sandy, who luckily seems to have tuned out most of this conversation. "Sorry about your dog," he says quietly.

"Sorry about . . . kicking you," I tell him. It's not totally a lie. I mean, I would definitely do it again if I had to, but now I might feel slightly bad about it afterward.

When Freckles looks away, I glance over to find Kimo watching me. I rear back, frowning defensively at him. "What?"

My voice comes out just a tad too sharp, but Kimo doesn't react, just holds his steady, calm gaze on me. "You're just an interesting lady, Matilda Markov."

There's that warm, crawly feeling again. I look away, forcing a laugh as I shake my head. "Please. You don't know the half of it . . ."

Chapter Fourteen

By the time the van finally reaches its destination, several hours after we were first abducted, it's nighttime. My legs are cramped, my back is sore, I've had to pee on the side of the road three times (never again with the benefit of my hands being untied, thanks to my shenanigans the first time), and if I never see the back of this van again, I'll be thrilled.

That is, until I see what our next mode of transportation is going to be.

"No, no, no, no, no . . ." I protest as I see the docked speedboat, with a new driver (Driver 2?) waiting at the helm.

I don't do dark water. I'm wary of any water, just generally speaking, but if it's shallow, transparent water, I can make my peace with it—at least for short periods of time during which I'm constantly watching for anything that might try to sneak its way into my space. Dark, deep water where I can't see what might be moving around underneath me, waiting to drag me down to the murky depths? No, thank you. I prefer suntanning on the firm, solid shore, where I can enjoy not getting eaten.

The fact that we've only driven roughly seven to eight hours which means we're nowhere near shark- or alligator-infested waters should bring me some comfort, but it doesn't. Are you telling me they've explored every inch of the Great Lakes and can say with one-hundred-percent certainty there isn't something big and hungry lurking underwater? I didn't think so.

"Come on, Buffy," Sandy says with mean amusement, taking me roughly by the upper arms and shoving me toward the boat. "Your royal chariot awaits."

"Go easy, man," Kimo protests. "Can't you see she's scared?"

I guess the fact that I've basically gone limp and am forcing Sandy to drag my dead weight across the dock has tipped my hand a bit with the whole fear-of-water thing. I usually keep that to myself, like my date of birth. I don't trust just anyone with my deepest, darkest fears. Who knows how that might be used against me?

Oh, God. It's my birthday, and I've been kidnapped and am being forced onto a boat, going to an unknown location across dark, mysterious waters. This is how I die.

"Get up." Sandy no longer sounds even the slightest bit amused by the situation. "Stop being so difficult, or I'm throwing you into that water."

I force myself to look down at the dark abyss. If the thought of traveling across that water in a boat is unappealing, the thought of being tossed into it with my hands tied behind my back is downright petrifying. I force myself to move, even though my legs are trembling and the rest of my body feels like it's seizing up with fear.

Once we're on the boat, none of my fears are assuaged. I hate boats. They move too much. Anything this unsteady can't be trustworthy. And I don't buy what anyone has to say about boat travel supposedly being safer than car travel. Ever heard of the *Titanic*?

Sandy drops me into a sitting position, taking a seat on the bench across from me. Freckles follows, guiding Kimo down beside me and joining Sandy on the other side. I'm aware of Kimo leaning into me, but I'm too busy staring down at the dark, fathomless water.

As the speedboat engine roars to life, I start making that odd whirring noise that I was making when we first got into the van. It's completely out of my control, by the way. Believe me, I'm not intending to rock back and forth making strange, high-pitched—but also somehow guttural—cries. Apparently this is my panic response. If fight or flight were the options, I'd choose both, but when they're taken off the table, I guess I choose creepy banshee moaning.

Apparently the others can hear it, even over the loud roar of the engine, because Sandy glares at me and opens his mouth like he's about to say something especially douchey—which for him, is an impressive feat to manage, since I thought he'd already reached the full threshold of just how much of a dick he can be.

But before he can speak, Kimo starts singing. Loudly. "Everywhere you look, everywhere you go, there's a heart, a something something onto . . ."

The whirring noise is stunned right out of me. I stare at him in open-mouthed surprise. He's singing the *Full House* theme song, or at least attempting to. It's clear *he* hasn't watched the show on a near-constant loop for the past twenty-some-odd years of his life, but come on. Everyone knows *Full House*, at least a little.

He's singing for me, obviously. Kimo, the surprisingly great observer of his fellowman, has deduced from my conversation with Freckles that I'm a pretty big *Full House* fan, though I doubt he knows the full extent of it. No one knows the full extent of it—that I *still* watch it every night to fall asleep, that I can quote whole episodes verbatim, that my sisters are saved as *Stephanie* and *Michelle* in my phone contacts and still call me DJ when they're trying to get me to do something for them. That if I ever got a real-life, non-parade-trampled dog, I would actually name him Comet, and that Uncle Jesse is and forever will be my ultimate dream man. That when Bob Saget died, it felt like I lost a member of my own family. That I cried when I watched the first episode of *Fuller House* because it felt like coming home, and because the only thing I want out of life, truly, is to have my sisters together under one roof like that again.

And, okay, sure, Kimo might be bad at remembering the words. But he's trying to offer me some comfort, trying to distract me from my fears. It's actually pretty . . . sweet.

Then he hits the verses, and it's obvious he *really* doesn't know the lyrics. "Whatever happened to something something tree? The milkman, the paperboy, uh . . ."

"The evening TV," Freckles chimes in, taking everyone by surprise—including, it seems, himself. "How did I get to living here? Somebody tell me please!"

They look at each other, neither one seeming to know where to go next. "When you're lost out there," Kimo starts up again. "And all alone . . ."

Okay, they've skipped a lot of stuff, but they're hitting the highlights. I can respect that. Despite myself, and despite the churning, dark water potentially holding unthinkable monsters and stretching for possibly thousands of feet beneath us, I smile.

That seems to energize both men, and they get even more into their duet. "Life keeps waiting to carry you home!" they sing enthusiastically.

It's actually "a light is waiting," not "life keeps waiting," but I don't want to burst their bubble, and they seem to be genuinely enjoying themselves now. "Everywhere you look! Everywhere you look—"

"Shut up!" Sandy roars over both their terrible tone-deaf singing and the sound of the speedboat. "Everybody shut up now."

I shouldn't, really, but I can't help myself. "How rude," I say in a perfect Stephanie imitation, exactly like Jodie Sweetin would say it. I mean, I've had some practice.

Kimo and Freckles both chuckle under their breaths. Sandy, of course, does not look amused. "Shut the hell up. No more singing, no more . . . quoting. Got it?"

We continue on in silence. But at least I'm not so afraid now. Oh, I'm still terrified of the water, don't get me wrong, but at least now I know I'm not alone. I lean up against Kimo, and he presses back against me. I feel the brief brush of his lips against my hairline, and I'm surprised by the gesture, the reassurance and the intimacy of it, but also its implied promise: we're in this together, for better or worse.

Chapter Fifteen

After a few minutes, we start to near an island with lights brightening the shoreline—but instead of heading in that direction, Driver 2 starts to veer away, toward a different, darker mound of an island. If it weren't for the lighthouse positioned at the tip of a thin peninsula, I wouldn't have been able to see the second island at all. It doesn't look like it's inhabited, much less hospitable.

I glance over at Kimo and see him looking uncharacteristically grim. He's remained oddly positive during this whole ordeal, and I think that's mostly been for my benefit. But even he can't read anything optimistic into them taking us to an abandoned island. Maybe the plan isn't to kill us right away, if they've kept us alive for this long. But they sure aren't planning on throwing us a surprise party, either.

Suddenly, Driver 2 cuts the engine and turns out the boat's lights. I tense, worrying they're about to throw us overboard or something—Why did they stop? In the middle of the dark water? When we're so close to shore now?—when I hear it.

Another boat's engine, approaching from not too far off.

That would explain why Driver 2 cut our engine. They don't want anyone to witness our boat going toward the spooky, uninhabited island. That might raise some alarm bells. Whatever they're planning to do to us on the island, they don't want anyone to know we're there.

Sandy pulls out his gun, aiming it toward us. "Not a peep out of either of you, you hear me? Not so much as a sneeze."

Could the other boat really hear a sneeze over the roar of their own engine? Doubtful, but now doesn't seem like the time to quibble, with a gun pointed toward me and all.

I watch the lights of the other boat as they swing in an arc. It looks like they're turning around, heading back toward the other island with all the lights and people. It feels like hope snuffing out across all that dark water.

Kimo leans into me, and at first I think he's just lending me some physical comfort, like he's been doing the whole trip—reminding me he's here with me, etc. But then his lips brush my ear, his voice low and quiet. "Time to trust me, Mattie. Follow my lead."

Follow his lead? What the hell does that mean? It probably goes without saying that I'm not much of a follower. I tried out ballroom dancing once, when I was at university, but got politely asked by the instructor to leave when I kept (helpfully!) informing my partners of everything they were doing wrong and trying to take over. For the record, they *were* doing a lot of things wrong, and I *was* better at leading, but try explaining that to the frail masculine ego . . .

Then all at once, Kimo stands and kicks his right flip-flop into Sandy's face. Sandy tumbles off the bench, his pistol shooting off into the night air, and the sound of it ricochets loudly across the water. Kimo reaches for me —Wait, when did he get his hands free? How did he do that?—and hoists me to my feet. I don't miss the slight nod he gives to Freckles before pulling me up against him. "Hey, over here! Mayday! COWABUNGA!" he shouts at the top of his lungs.

Cowabunga?

Then the next thing I know, he's wrapping his arms around me and toppling us both over the side of the boat, into the dark, churning water.

As you can imagine, I do not go quietly into that good night. I scream from the depths of my soul as we plunge into the dark abyss, the water shockingly cold in contrast to the lingering heat of the day. With my hands still bound, I can't swim properly, and even though I'm thrashing my legs frantically, it feels like all I'm doing is sinking down farther, and farther, the darkness engulfing and disorienting me. I can't breathe. *I can't breathe.*

Then I feel something wrap around my torso. I jerk away instinctively, envisioning all kinds of horrible tentacled beasties that might be grabbing at me, until my brain catches up. *Kimo.* My legs continue thrashing on instinct, but he withstands my unintentional kicks and tugs me upward. I think. I don't know which way is up, but he seems to be sure, and I go limp against him, surrendering to his certainty.

When we surface, I gasp in greedy, panicked gulps of air. Then, without further delay, I'm screaming again.

Kimo flips me so I'm on my back and starts cutting through the water, towing me under his arm. He's swimming away from the back of the speedboat as fast as he can, but his voice comes out characteristically calm. "They'll have to turn the boat back on if they want to swing around and get us," he explains. "And that's gonna let whoever's on that boat over there know we're here, so let's call them on their bluff, huh?"

I just keep screaming.

"That'll help, too," Kimo continues conversationally as he paddles us along. "Boat engines are loud, but you're a really shrill screamer, so hopefully that'll carry. Plus, that idiot fired off his gun, so hopefully between all those things—oh, heh. Yep. They're turning around."

I pause my screaming just long enough to turn my head and see that, in fact, the other boat has swung back around and is heading in our direction.

"Over here!" I'm not going to be able to stop screaming until I'm out of this water and, ideally, back on dry land, but I guess I can at least try to make my shrieking slightly more productive. "Help! We're over here!"

"Of course," Kimo continues, "now that the other boat already knows we're here, the kidnappers might decide to just go for broke and come after us. Guess it depends on how much whoever hired them to kidnap me was willing to pay. I'm guessing, based on how intricate this whole scheme was, it was probably a lot, so if you can help me swim . . ."

I'm not a great swimmer under the best of circumstances. With my hands literally tied behind my back, and floating on said back in the middle of my literal nightmare, I'm no Olympic qualifier, let's just say that. But I kick with gusto, hoping that all my regular cardio is about to pay off.

"Good, Mattie. That's real good . . ."

We're making progress, but it probably won't be enough to keep the kidnappers from reaching us before the other boat, if they put their minds to it. Behind us, I hear the kidnappers' boat roar to life.

"Shit." It's a rare admission from Kimo that the situation is anything less than ideal, and that has me frantically chopping my legs even more, trying to put as much distance between us and the kidnappers' boat as possible.

Then, over the expanse of the water, I hear the most beautiful sound in the world: "Mackinac Marine Rescue. Are you in distress?"

Marine Rescue—that means they're an official agency, not just another random boater out at night. They've probably already radioed into their headquarters on the island, which means there will be a record of us being here. The marine rescue team might even have guns. The kidnappers would have to be extremely organized and proficient to even consider taking on an official government-operated department—and, let's face it, mastermind criminals, these guys are not.

Sure enough, lifting my head from the water, I see the kidnappers' boat making a speedy exit in the opposite direction.

"Yes!" I shout, thrashing my legs frantically. "We're in distress! Help! Over here!"

Kimo treads water, raising his arms over his head to wave as a searchlight sweeps over us. "Told you to trust me," he says with a huge, shit-eating grin. "I knew everything would turn out all right . . ."

Chapter Sixteen

"All right" is a bit of an overstatement, at least until a few hours later—after we've been dredged from the water, taken to the Mackinac Island Police Station, put into borrowed dry clothing, given food and warm drinks, and questioned for several hours by the police, rehashing every single detail about the kidnapping again and again. By the time we've finished, it's almost midnight, and I'm completely exhausted after the entire ordeal. I wouldn't say we hit "fine" until they take us to a local inn and set us up in adjoining rooms. That last part was at Kimo's insistence, and I didn't fight him on it. With the kidnappers still at-large and no idea as to who was behind the crime, I feel a whole lot better having a huge, possibly crazy Hawaiian millionaire in the room next to me.

"Not as good as I feel having a black belt in the room next to me," Kimo says with a wink when I express this (slightly censored) thought to him.

I can't help but smile, though I roll my eyes so the moment doesn't get too mushy.

Mackinac Police have been more than accommodating and have stationed a few officers around the inn to make sure we can rest in peace tonight. I'm guessing they don't get a lot of kidnappings on a quaint little island like this, which literally has no cars and no public transportation, so . . . we're kind of a big deal. They even asked if we'd be willing to be interviewed by the *Mackinac Island Town Crier*, the local newspaper, in the morning before we leave. And, naturally, since Kimo has made best friends with every single cop we've spoken to since arriving, and one of those cops is married to one of the newspaper reporters, we have an interview scheduled after breakfast. Delightful.

Normally I might put up more of a fuss about this, but honestly, I'm so ready to shower the lake water off me, collapse into bed, and not move again for at least ten hours that I'd agree to just about anything.

"Fine, yes, interview, great," I say brusquely, trying to move things along. "See you in the morning."

Kimo lingers after the officers have left, motioning to the hotel phone next to my bed. "If you want to call your family, friends, whoever, tell them you're okay, I'll pay for any charges, so don't worry about that."

Oh. Right. That's what most people would want to do right away in a situation like this, I'm guessing. Kimo must be itching to call his own family, reassure them that he's okay. I honestly wonder if anyone will even notice I was missing. The thought produces an unexpected lump in my throat. I clear it away. "Great. Thanks. I'm sure everyone will have been very worried."

With that, Kimo leaves me to make his own calls. At last, I'm on my own in the hotel room. I do a quick, cursory search of the closet and under the bed to make sure there are no bad guys waiting to snatch me up, then relax once I realize I'm truly alone. Still, just to be safe, I turn on the television and flip through the channels to find the most wholesome show I can. Unfortunately, *Full House* isn't playing, but there's an old rerun of *Sister, Sister*, and that'll do. Nothing bad has ever happened to anyone while *Sister, Sister* was on.

I don't realize until I'm out of the shower that I don't have any clean clothes to change into. My lake-drenched clothes are being temporarily held as evidence by Mackinac Police, and the clothes I was given to change into at the station already feel a bit grimy after I sat in them for hours, still covered in dirty lake water. I guess I can always just sleep in the robe that came with the room . . .

As if on cue, someone knocks on the adjoining door between my room and Kimo's. I tense, but his voice follows shortly: "It's just me, Mattie. The innkeeper brought us some clean clothes."

I throw open the door to find Kimo holding up a neatly folded stack of items. "Nothing too fashionable," he warns me. "Just stuff from the gift shop down the road, but they're comfy."

I barely process the words. I've been tied up next to Kimo all day, then at his side in the police station, so I thought I was immune to his physical presence by now. But seeing him freshly showered, freshly clothed, his uniquely Kimo essence hits me all over again. It isn't that his gift-shop clothes are especially sexy. He's in gray sweatpants and a tank top, his hair pulled into a messy bun at the top of his head. And of course, he's barefoot. But something about his look is weirdly *intimate*. It's like opening the door and stepping into an alternate reality where this is a normal night and we're getting ready to Netflix and chill. Emphasis on the chill, if I have any say in it.

Kimo is staring at me, too, but that one's easier to explain. I'm in nothing but a towel, still glistening and rosy-cheeked from my shower. And, well, he's a heterosexual man.

I watch as he peruses the length of my body, swallowing slowly. He looks like he wants to push me onto the bed and tear this towel off me . . . or maybe that's just me projecting. He gives another slow swallow.

Nope. Not just me projecting.

Kimo clears his throat, dragging his eyes back up to mine. "Need anything else before we turn in?"

Two minutes ago I was ready to collapse onto my bed and never move again, maybe take up permanent residency on the mattress. Now, suddenly, my whole body is awake and alert, ready for a few rounds of naked sexy times. *A few orgasms would be nice*, I want to say, but even *I* have a bit of a filter. Sometimes. Occasionally. "Do *you* need anything else before we turn in?" I ask instead.

We stare at each other for a long moment, before Kimo abruptly clears his throat, all but shoving the clean clothes into my arms. "Well, I'm beat. Night!"

He retreats back into his room, shutting the door behind him.

I stare after him, my jaw hanging open in astonishment. That is, until I remember his rejection of me in the men's bathroom earlier today. And last night, too. Then I remember what he told me in the bathroom. That whole pesky wants-to-have-something-serious nonsense. *чертовски дно*. For the record, I, too, would like to have something serious—some *seriously* hot, no-strings-attached sex, please and thank you.

But consent is important, I have to respect his wishes, etc., etc. Dammit. I don't even have my vibrator here . . .

The laugh track to *Sister, Sister* jars me out of my funk. Right. No sex for me tonight. With a sigh, I put on the gift-shop clothing, an outfit which is pretty similar to what Kimo was wearing, except I get a pale pink *I Love Mackinac Island!* T-shirt and gray sweat-shorts. There's also a packaged toothbrush and comb with the clothing, so I furiously attack my teeth and hair, perhaps venting some of my sexual frustration into my personal hygiene.

Staring at myself in the mirror, I lament anew that I have all this pent-up energy and nowhere to channel it. The gift-shop outfit isn't anything I would have ever chosen for myself, but I look cute in it, with my fresh face and still-damp hair. The girls are looking good in the snug-fitting tee, if I do say so myself. And shorts have always been my friend, because my toned legs are my greatest weapon.

Maybe if Kimo saw me in this, he wouldn't be able to resist me, personal rules be damned. I look just the right balance of cute and sexy—and *cute* is not usually a term I'd apply to myself. I'm usually too aggressive, too intense to ever be labeled cute, but the pink T-shirt is just innocent enough to say, *I'm not a threat!* while also simultaneously saying, *But look how perky my boobs are, aren't they nice?*

Not bad for a $12.99 T-shirt. I may have to pick up a few more before we leave . . .

The question now, though, is how to get Kimo to see me in this outfit so he realizes just how irresistible I am. To be clear, I would never force anything on him, but if he sees me and decides he wants to override his own rule, who am I to say no? But we've already said good night, and I already have everything I need—clothes, toothbrush, comb. What else could I possibly use as an excuse?

I meet my own gaze in the mirror, widening my eyes for dramatic effect. "Kimo, I'm so scared. Terrified. I can't sleep."

Pfft. Terrible. Wooden, unbelievable. Nobody would buy that. I pout my lower lip, batting my eyes. "I'm so scared, Kimo. Can I sleep with you tonight?"

Hmm. That was maybe too sultry. The key is that this needs to be *innocent*, like I have no idea the effect I have on people with my deliciously sexy body. Ah, I know. I'll channel Helen. She's all sexed up now, but before the Bounty Hunter, she was totally oblivious to the men who would be ogling her ginormous breasts, pretending to need help with the library catalog system or whatnot. I try my best to summon her guilelessness: "I know it will probably repulse you to have our bodies pressed up together all night long, but would you do me the favor of letting me sleep in your bed tonight? I hope it won't be too shocking or disgusting, but I might not even wear any clothes—I'm just *so* scared!"

Okay, that probably won't work, but it was fun.

Before I can brainstorm any other ideas, I hear a knock at the door adjoining our rooms. My pulse spikes, and I rush out of the bathroom to answer it. "Kimo?"

He looks like he's been to war—or, at least at war with himself. His hair is even more messily chaotic than usual, his face set grimly. "I was wondering if maybe you have any extra soap?"

I stare at him blankly. "Soap?"

He clears his throat, nodding just a bit too forcefully. "Yes. I seem to have lost mine. And I need more. Soap. Urgently."

Oh. *Soap.* I smile at him, taking his hand and tugging him into my room. "Yes. You can have my soap. You can have all the soap you want . . ."

Obviously, *soap* is not soap. The man was already showered and dressed when he dropped off my clothes a few minutes ago. So unless he's the cleanest man alive, who uses up multiple bars while washing himself, he doesn't suddenly need more. I'm not great at social cues, but even I've picked that up. Soap is a reason to come into my room. Soap is a reason to be near me again, to maybe lower his defenses, change his mind.

I guide him into the bathroom, searching for the extra packet that came with my room. After a moment of searching, I find it, and hold it up to show him in the reflection of the mirror. "Here you go. It's all yours." There may or may not be some suggestion laced in that statement.

Any subtext turns out to be unnecessary, though, because when I meet Kimo's gaze in the mirror, I see he's standing right behind me, smoldering intently at me. My breath catches in my throat. I watch his eyes move down to my breasts, swallowing as my nipples harden visibly under the thin fabric. Our eyes meet again.

"Is that all you wanted?" I ask breathlessly.

Bracing his hands on the counter on either side of me, caging me in, he presses into me from behind with a low growl. His erection is already firm and hard against my lower back. "Not all I want," he grits out.

"Don't tease me," I warn him sternly. "If you're going to run away again, you should just leave now."

"No running," he promises, rubbing himself slowly against me and making that low, growly sound again. "I'm in no hurry at all."

It's just what I want to hear, but I find myself frowning at him nonetheless. "Earlier today, you said you didn't want a no-strings thing."

As soon as the words are out of my mouth, I curse myself. *Лох!* Why am I trying to talk him out of this? Luckily, though, Kimo just shakes his head and continues to grind up against me. "Those rules don't apply after a kidnapping. What happens on the island stays on the island . . ."

That sounds promising. I bite back a triumphant smile, moving toward the bedroom. "Well, then let's get started—"

He grips my hips, guiding me back into place in front of the mirror, so the front of me is pressed up against the edge of the counter. "Not so fast, legs. I know how much you like bathrooms . . ."

I watch our reflections, my breath catching as he dips his head to kiss my neck, my jaw, my ear. His hands rub up and down my sides, keeping things PG with where he's touching me; what *isn't* PG is what his tongue and lips are doing to my ear, swirling and sucking in a way that is positively indecent. My breath catches in my throat. Heat spikes down my lower belly.

The thing I love about sex is it's a dance. I may not always know what other people expect out of me in conversations, or how to play the role of a sister, a friend. But in sex, you follow your partner's lead. If they're moving forward, you're moving back. If you change position, they shift to match you. The rules are so much more clear-cut.

So if Kimo is going to tease me, I have to tease him right back. I begin a slow rub of my ass against his crotch, unable to hide my smile at his little grunt of pleasure. His eyes lock on mine for a moment in the mirror before sliding downward. My smile widens.

"Are you looking at these?" I tease, thrusting out my breasts a bit. This shirt, I'm telling you—they look like a million bucks! Hell, even I'm staring at them, and they're mine. "Do you want to see them . . . ?"

I take the hem of my shirt and slowly, tauntingly, begin to raise it, bit by bit. Kimo's eyes burn into mine through the mirror's reflection. He gives a little caveman grunt and bites—not too hard, but not too soft either —down on my earlobe.

At last, with one final tug, the girls are free. Kimo gives a low rumble of approval from deep in his chest that almost sounds like a growl. I wait eagerly for him to touch them, but it's *his* turn to tease me now. His hands trail slowly from my sides, agonizingly slowly up my belly, then linger underneath the swell of my breasts until I whine and protest. Chuckling low in his throat, Kimo finally engulfs my tits in his big, strong hands, stroking, massaging them, his thumbs sending lightning bolts through my hardened nipples.

As if this sensation weren't intense enough, he lowers his mouth back to my neck again, licking, sucking, biting, while his hands knead my breasts. And if *those* sensations combined weren't enough, the erotic picture that it makes in the reflection of the mirror has my core already aching, my thighs beginning to tremble with want. When one of his hands releases my breast, I almost command him to put it back, until I watch it snake down my torso to cup my pussy and begin stroking me there through the fabric of my shorts.

"Oh, God," I groan, my head sinking back against him. I can't take it anymore—the sight of us, the things he's doing to me with his hands. He's stopped kissing my neck, at least, but I can see *he's* looking in the mirror now, watching what he's doing to me, and that has me almost frantically writhing against his fingers. I'm shocked to find I'm almost there already. I need him inside me, I need, I need—

"*Fuck*," Kimo says abruptly, and it's not a sexy *fuck, this is so hot*, but an *oh shit, we have a problem* fuck.

"What is it?" I ask, my voice shaky with want.

"We don't have a condom."

Chapter Seventeen

A h, yes. The gift shop provided us with dry clothes, the hotel gave us some basic toiletries, but no one thought to supply us with a handy box of condoms. Rude. They are *not* going to like the Yelp review I leave after this.

The logical, rational part of me knows it's time to pump the brakes, immediately; but the horny, needy part of me wants to beg him to lean me over the counter and fuck me from behind anyway.

"Noooooooo," I whine, which I feel is a fair compromise, all things considered. "You don't have any with you?"

"I left my wallet back at Dumb-Ax." I can sense how agonized he is by the rough, clipped way he says the words. He sounds almost *angry*, like he needs someone to punish, and—

Whoa, Matilda. Rein it in, girl. "Me, too," I half sob. And I left my phone. And my favorite blazer. But none of those things matter so much as that emergency condom I always keep stashed inside my purse.

I lower my gaze back to the mirror. For one long, drawn-out moment, our eyes meet in the reflection. I'm still holding up my shirt, flashing him my tits like it's Mardi Gras. He's still cupping my pussy. But we're both completely still, staring, the moment charged with want.

"Whelp," Kimo says abruptly, "plan B."

And before I know what's happening, he's flipped me around, slung me over his shoulder with one arm, and started carrying me toward the bedroom.

He tosses me onto the bed, like my weight is nothing to his superior dad-bod strength, like I'm a sack of flour and he's some kind of naughty baker. An odd but intriguing image of him in an apron—and nothing but an apron—springs to my mind and has me practically salivating. Okay, *completely* salivating. I prop myself up on my elbows, watching him closely to see what he'll do next.

He's eying me like I'm a tasty snack. I half expect him to lick his lips, and—oh, wait, there he goes, actually licking his lips. This move should look ridiculously cartoonish, but I remember what that tongue was just doing to me a moment before and shiver with anticipation. He arches an eyebrow at me, and his expression is pure filth. "Take off your clothes."

That order makes me instinctively bristle, even as it simultaneously sends a little ping of excitement straight to my core. I arch an eyebrow back at him. "You first."

It's not that I don't want to get naked. I *desperately* want to get naked. I want to do all the naked things together. But I'm used to calling the shots, leading the dance, so to speak. And I want to set the tone, straightaway—so there won't be any confusion—that *I'm* the boss.

If Kimo takes umbrage at being ordered around, he doesn't show it. He straightens, giving me a *hold-my-beer* smirk, then starts twitching his hips. "Ugh, ugh," he sings under his breath, setting his own rhythm as he slowly begins to lift his shirt, never breaking eye contact with me. "Boom chicka boom boom . . ."

I blink at him. Is he doing his own bad '70s porno music now . . . ? But somehow butchering the lyrics? "I think you mean bow chicka wow wow."

He ignores my feedback, untangling himself from his tank and tossing it over his shoulder. As expected by his shape in clothing, his chest is big and broad with a light smattering of hair, his torso like a barrel. He's not fat, but he doesn't have a ripped six-pack either; to my surprise, I find the whole spectacle powerfully erotic, even as it's over-the-top ridiculous. His utter self-confidence, how much fun he's having, how much he's feeling himself, is a complete turn-on.

I can't help it—I laugh. I'm horny and totally aroused and laughing, and that is a complete and total first for me.

Pivoting so his back is to me, Kimo continues moving his hips as he starts tugging down his sweatpants and briefs. At the first glimpse of his perfect crescent moon of an ass peeking out, my laugh instantly dies in my throat, and my mouth runs dry.

Then his pants are down, and he's kicking them off his feet, revealing his backside in all its glory. And I mean *glory*. His back is broad and thick, muscles rippling underneath his skin. His legs, too, are long and strong and well-defined. And his ass . . . my God, his ass. I've never seen something so round and juicy. I have to fight the urge to lunge at him and sink my teeth into it.

I'm so absorbed by his backside that I don't even notice when he starts to turn around, until all at once he's facing me again, completely and unabashedly naked. My eyes instantly hone in on his cock.

"Oh my God," I blurt, unable to help myself. I'm sure my eyes must be cartoonishly wide as I take in the sight of his huge, half-erect cock.

He must like me staring at it, because it quickly goes from half to fully erect. When I drag my gaze up to his, Kimo is smirking at me. No false modesty—a motto we share in common, apparently.

Taking his smirk as a challenge, I rise up on to my knees. He won't get a dance from me, but let's be real—what man actually needs an erotic dance if he's about to see a naked chick? I tug off my shirt with no preamble, tossing it aside. Then, just to be petty, I turn my back to him doing the same slow tease of revealing my ass bit by bit.

Or at least, I'm trying to. I barely make it halfway before Kimo pushes me down onto my belly, impatiently tugging off my shorts and panties and dropping them to the floor. Then he peppers my bare back with kisses, as his strong hands massage my ass and his big cock bumps up against the backs of my legs, a friendly reminder that it's there.

Not that I could forget. Oh, God. Why don't we have a condom . . . !
"Maybe the gift shop is still open?" I gasp out desperately.

His voice is a low murmur across my skin. "Nope. Everything closes at, like, eight around here. They had to call the owner back from his house just to open it up and get us some clothes."

"Did you get his phone number? We could call him again!"

Kimo laughs softly, warm breath dancing over my skin and sending goose bumps across my shoulders. "That would be a no."

I will not give up! There has to be a solution. "Maybe the hotel has some?"

This time, Kimo's laugh is not soft, but a full chortle. "Did you see the lady who checked us in here? You really think she has condoms?"

I did, in fact, see her. Her name is Bea, she looks like she's about 140 years old, and she has knitted lace doilies across every available surface in the lobby. She might actually die from shock if we called down to ask for a condom—preferably more than one, if she has them.

It might actually be worth the risk to try.

Kimo moves away suddenly, and I hear the bed squeak as he gets off it. "Put it out of your mind, baby. We're still gonna enjoy ourselves tonight, I promise."

Baby? That feels kind of . . . intimate, coming from someone I've known for less than forty-eight hours and will probably never see again after tomorrow. But, whatever, a man can't really be held accountable for what he says pre-ejaculation anyway.

The next second, it really is put out of my mind—or rather, *pulled*, as Kimo suddenly takes hold of my legs and drags me toward the edge of the bed. I'm still belly-down on the mattress, but my ass is hanging precariously close to tumbling to the floor. "What are you doing?" I bark out, more harshly than I intend.

"Spread your legs, honey. Let me worship that sweet pussy with my mouth."

I feel another spike of heat low in my abdomen at his words, even as a spike of panic shoots through the rest of me. "Uh, no. It's okay. Why don't I just give you a blow job?"

"Hmm. Maybe later." I feel him getting into position under me, bracing my thighs with his shoulders, but he pauses before fully committing. "You okay with this?"

It's fine, I reason with myself. "It's fine," I say aloud, maybe just a tad too forcefully. "Just, ah, I don't have my vibrator, so I probably won't finish. Unless—and listen carefully to this. Actually, you might want to write it down . . ."

I proceed to give Kimo the exact play-by-play and precise order of operations he'll need to follow to get me to come, down to the exact amount of pressure at each step and when it should be applied.

When I finish, Kimo is silent. "Did you get all that?" I ask him.

His response is a light smack to my bottom—not quite a slap, mind you, but no gentle tap, either. "Listen, baby. You can be in charge everywhere else. Hell, I'll love it when you give me orders. But here, now, with my face in your pussy, I'm the boss. Capisce?"

I should tell him to take a hike. But my general horniness, or the fact that he just said *capisce* like golden-era Uncle Jesse, has me shutting up and spreading my legs.

It's probably good he can't see my face, with the inevitable disappointment I'm bound to feel written across it. But because I can't see him or track what he's doing, I gasp in genuine surprise when I feel his fingers trailing over the skin of my thighs, teasing me with light brushes that get closer and closer to my core. Just when I think he's going to touch me there, where I most need him, his hands pull back, gripping me by my thighs and pushing them even wider.

"Mmm." I feel his words on my skin, at my center, his mouth closer than I thought it was. "Look at you . . ."

The first stroke of his tongue is bolder than I anticipated, and I gasp, instinctively jerking up off the mattress. He responds by tightening his grip on my thighs. His shoulders push up under my legs, lifting up my lower half. I hear his grunt of satisfaction as he finds just the right angle and begins to lap at me—the pressure less forceful now, but still with dogged intensity. His tongue alternates between rough and soft, soothing and torturing, but always determined to explore every part of me.

It's clear he's listened to absolutely none of my instructions, but I'm still whimpering and moaning like he's somehow managed to jump straight to step 7. I'm embarrassed, actually, at the sounds I'm making, the sounds I thought only happened when women were faking it, trying to make their partners feel better. I grip the sheets and press my face into the mattress, trying to muffle myself, but Kimo doesn't seem to like that. After a grunt and another light tap to my bottom, he tightens his grip on both my thighs and buries his face into my pussy. The moans of appreciation he makes reverberate through the softest, most responsive parts of me. His tongue swirls around my clit a few times before his lips enclose it, and he begins sucking, sucking, sucking . . .

"Oh my God," I blurt out as my thighs begin shaking, and then I'm catapulted over the edge without warning, without mercy. I shudder and cry out, too overcome to try to muffle the sound. For a moment, I can't breathe, and for a moment, I don't actually care.

"Holy shit," I say when I'm able to catch my breath and form coherent thought again.

I angle my head back to look at Kimo and find him smirking at me shamelessly, waggling his eyebrows, before he boldly, lasciviously, licks his full, soft lips.

As soon as the intense euphoria wears off, some post-orgasm anxiety starts to kick in. I understand what to do when I'm engaging in the physical part of sex, the dance with clear-cut rules and expectations. It's afterward that I feel a little lost, especially when we're on an uneven playing field. If my partner and I have both climaxed, well, fair is fair, have a nice life. If he's the only one who's climaxed, I have no problem telling him he owes me and better make things right, but it's always a real mood killer when the guy acts like it's a chore. But when only *I've* orgasmed . . . well, come to think of it, that's never happened before. I'm in uncharted waters. Hence, the anxiety.

"You want a blow job?" I ask him brusquely over my shoulder, determined to get any weirdness out of the way. I won't make him demand it, like I've had to do sometimes.

Kimo rises to his feet and seems to consider my offer for a moment, as he leisurely smooths his hands over my lower back, my ass. This motion is calm and deliberate, not frantic and horndog-ish, like I might expect it to be from a man who's at full mast. "No, thanks."

I blink at him in astonishment. I have never, in all my life, known a man to turn down a blow job. And believe me, I made up for lost time after I left my order. Noticing how he's still rubbing up and down my backside, another idea strikes me. "You want to jack off on my ass? Or I can roll over if you prefer my boobs."

He sighs. "Nah."

Again with the *nah*! I've never been so infuriated by a word before. "We don't have any lube, if you're angling for anal, so don't think for a minute—"

Before I can finish that thought, Kimo cuts me off. "I think I'd like to just hold you, if you're down for that."

I can't help the dismayed look I give him. "Hold my what?"

He laughs. "Hold *you*, doofus. You know, cuddle. You down?"

No. Absolutely not. Normally there'd be no way in hell that I'd curl up in bed for a spoonfest—not that, frankly, it's something that's been offered to me much before. But . . . I've orgasmed. He hasn't. That leaves us unbalanced, and I don't like to feel like I owe anyone anything. That things aren't fair between us.

"Okay," I agree reluctantly, not even bothering to disguise my trepidation.

Kimo winks at me. "It's gonna be fine, Mattie. I promise. Nothing weird."

Ha. Easy for him to say.

He gathers my clothes for me, presenting them as gallantly as if they were a bouquet of flowers. "Milady." Once I've taken them, he motions back toward his adjoining room. "Be right back. I'm just gonna brush my teeth . . ."

I dress quickly and go into my own bathroom to get ready for bed. When I return, all the lights have been turned off except for the one on the nightstand. Kimo is lying on the bed, underneath the covers, a conspicuous spot saved for me.

Woodenly, I make my way over to him, trying not to make any physical contact as I slide into the bed, promptly turning my back so I don't have to face him. Either willfully or unintentionally, he ignores my cues and wraps an arm around my waist, tugging me closer to him so we are properly spooning. The feeling of his warm body pressed against mine is . . . not terrible, I have to admit, even though it is weird. I notice his hard-on is gone, so either he took care of things in his room, or he's been picturing fungus or something.

He yawns into my hair. "I'm beat. You want to watch TV for a bit, or are you ready to go to bed?"

"I'm ready to sleep." No need to prolong this awkwardness. Plus, between the intense adrenaline rush of being kidnapped and escaping being kidnapped, followed by hours in a police station, followed by one of the most intense orgasms I've ever had . . . I'm exhausted.

"Mmm. G'night." Kimo switches off the light, then promptly goes back to cuddling me again.

I lie awake for a long time, just staring straight ahead into the dark.

There's no way I can sleep like this, in this foreign bed in this unfamiliar room, smushed up against a big radiator of a man . . .

But the next thing I know I'm drifting back into consciousness just long enough to see that the clock on the nightstand reads past two in the morning, and Kimo's arm is still looped around me. His soft, rumbly breathing quickly lulls me back to sleep.

Chapter Eighteen

I wake to the sun streaming into my face and Kimo still snoring softly at my back. One of his heavy arms drapes over my midsection, pinning me to the bed. I feel like that should have kept me awake, but honestly, it was the best night's sleep I've had in a really long time.

It must have been all the kidnapping, I reason with myself. *That's why I slept so well.* The life-and-death threat of danger looming over my head, those high peaks of adrenaline, and suddenly crashing down . . . Or that other high peak I experienced last night. Or some combination of the two.

Yep. Let's go with that.

Whatever the case may be, I know I need to get out of here. If I don't do post-sex cuddles, I really don't do morning afters. Of course, I don't know just how exactly I'm supposed to get out of here. Last night the police officers gave us the rundown of this place—apparently there are no cars on the whole island, which probably means no taxis either, so I have no idea how I'm supposed to get to the airport. (Sidenote: There had better be an airport. If a boat is the only way off this godforsaken island, I may have to stay here forever.) I don't have my phone, so I can't even Google an escape route. And even if I could, I don't have my wallet, so unless the airline accepts IOUs, I'm pretty stranded.

Okay, plan B. Maybe I can't escape, but surely there's a way I can keep this from becoming an awkward morning after. Maybe Kimo will let me even the scales this morning by letting me give him a blow job. Then things won't have that stilted, strained morning-after feeling, because it won't be *after*, it will still be *during*, and there will be no sleeping before we part ways.

But Kimo changing his mind on that front seems unlikely this morning, since he wouldn't even let me do it in the heat of the moment last night. I could try to jump straight into morning sex, but since we still don't have a condom, we'll just get stuck in limbo again. Unless . . .

Surely I can find a condom, now that it's morning! There has to be a convenience store open somewhere, for all the sundry needs people might have on this island, sexual or otherwise.

There is the pesky detail that I still don't have my wallet, but I'll cross that bridge when I come to it. If the shop owners in this town are anything like the police officers, they'll be over-the-top with their hospitality. Last night the marine rescue officer practically begged us to come stay in his home; it was only at Kimo's gentle but firm insistence that we ended up getting a hotel room. And even then, the officer ended up paying for us, trusting that Kimo will pay him back as soon as he has access to his money again. If Kimo hadn't cut things off there, we might have left the island with the man's wallet, the title to his house, maybe even his firstborn grandchild.

But maybe the officer's kindness was due more to Kimo's easy charm than the officer's innate generosity. After all, this is the same man who befriended one of our kidnappers, just by chatting with him about a video game. Hell, he convinced me to sleep in the same bed as him last night, just by asking. I'm not sure which was the more impressive feat, honestly.

Without Kimo there to play Mr. Nice Guy, I'm not sure I can persuade anyone to give me a condom without money. Unless the clerk happens to be a perv, and will take a boob flash as payment. Here's hoping! Otherwise I guess I'll just have to be . . . nice? Friendly?

Hey, it's worth a try.

I manage to wriggle my way out from underneath Kimo without waking him—or maybe he's just a sleep-through-an-earthquake kind of guy. Either way, I make it out of bed and sneak across the room, wondering if my shoes have dried out from the night before.

They haven't, but I see something I missed earlier in the pile of goodies from the gift shop: a pair of flip-flops. Great. I hold them up for inspection, frowning. Generally, I don't trust a shoe made out of plastic, but I guess beggars can't be choosers. And anyway, maybe wearing them will enable me to channel my inner Kimo and help me turn on the charm!

I'm, unfortunately, still in my tiny Mackinac Island sleep shorts and tight T-shirt that makes my boobs look like a million dollars. Paired with the flip-flops and no makeup, I definitely look like I'm making the walk of shame home from a wild night of debauchery. Not totally wrong, I suppose. And anyway, I don't know anyone on this island, so why should I care?

Out in the lobby, I find the oldest woman alive, Bea, sitting at reception and crocheting. At the sight of me, she blinks through her coke bottle glasses, as if she's not entirely sure whether I'm a real living person or someone coming to guide her to the afterlife. "Oh, hello, dear. Do you need anything?"

I think about just asking her directly where I can find condoms, but I remember my earlier fear about the shock of it killing her, and I don't want that on my conscience. Besides which, leaving a dead body in my wake will only prolong my time on this island. "Are there any stores open? Someplace I can walk to from here?"

"I'm not sure when Doud's opens." Bea sets down her crocheting and shuffles over to her desktop computer. She presses a button and it whirrs to life. After a long minute of waiting, she presses another button, then begins the slow one-finger-pecking typing of a person who was raised when telegraphs were still the fastest form of communication.

I, too, will be approximately 140 years old by the time she finishes looking this up. "Never mind. I'll just walk there myself and see. Which direction?"

Bea points a shaky finger straight out the doorway. "But be careful!" she calls after me. "I saw some strange men in dark clothing outside."

Probably the grim reapers, coming to collect on their overdue payment, I think unkindly, not pausing in my stride.

It isn't until I'm already outside that I wonder if Bea might be referencing the kidnappers—who, so far as I know, are still at-large.

Luckily for me, I quickly realize "the strange men" are not, in fact, the kidnappers. Nor are they grim reapers.

They're photographers—and as I step out into the bright morning light, they all turn on me like I'm a crust of bread and they're a flock of seagulls, and then I'm hit with a barrage of shouted questions and clicking cameras.

"Are you the mystery woman?" one of them calls to me. It's impossible to tell which one, since they all look vaguely similar, and since their faces are mostly obscured behind their cameras or microphones. There are a few film crews present, too.

I raise a hand to block the sun, which is shining directly into my eyes. "What?"

"The one who got kidnapped with Kimo Kapono."

"What's your relationship to him?"

"Are you his assistant?"

"Are you his girlfriend?"

Before I can orient myself, much less answer, a strong arm engulfs my shoulders. Kimo. He swiftly guides me back toward the entrance of the hotel. "Lay off, guys. Not cool. You wanna talk to me, you talk to me. Don't bother my . . ."

Kimo seems uncertain of what to call me, so he just doesn't call me anything, but I can tell by the roar of questions that follows us through the door that his silence has been noted.

Behind the lobby desk, Bea continues to crochet placidly, seemingly unconcerned by the mob of reporters outside. I cast a wary glance over my shoulder. "How do we know they won't follow us in?"

"Because I told them I'd sue their asses six ways from Sunday if they come into my place of business," Bea says calmly, not even looking up from her project. "Can't make them leave the public street, though."

"Come on." Kimo places a hand on the small of my back, guiding me toward the room. "I'll call Jay, see if he can find a way to get us out of here incognito."

Jay? As in . . . Jay. My boss. Glancing over at Kimo, I notice for the first time that he's shirtless, his sweatpants low on his hips, like he just rolled out of bed and tugged them on, which is likely what happened. And I'm dressed like . . . like Morning-After Barbie. A bunch of reporters just took our picture, looking like we definitely just had sex, and now Kimo's going to call my boss and pull him into the whole mess.

I groan, covering my face with my hands. "I'm so fired."

"Nah." Kimo pats my shoulder reassuringly. "Jay's cool. Let me handle him."

It should be reassuring. After all, I've had a front-row seat to just how well Kimo "handles" people. But Jay isn't a normal person. Jay is a cutthroat, top-of-his-game lawyer who's going to be pissed that I've gotten so involved with a client. No matter what he says to placate Kimo, I'll be edged quietly out of the company within a week, if not fired altogether.

Kimo must sense my concern, because he pats me on the shoulder again. "I got this, Mattie. Have a little faith."

I answer by groaning again into my hands.

Chapter Nineteen

After a very awkward hotel breakfast and interview with Rhonda, the reporter from the *Mackinac Island Town Crier* who's married to the police officer who became best friends with Kimo last night and who, therefore, gets the only official interview, we're on our way home.

Luckily, the journey back to Chicago is far less traumatizing than the journey to Mackinac Island was. By that, I mean Kimo is kind enough to charter us a private flight so we don't have to take a boat again. Oh, and we aren't being held at gunpoint in the back of a smelly van, so there's also that.

Despite the fact that we're the only two passengers on the plane and could easily spread out, Kimo takes the seat right next to mine. I pretend not to notice this, and instead spend most of the flight fretting over the inevitable news headlines about Kimo Kapono's new "gal pal" while he tries, unsuccessfully, to get me to relax. "I'll relax when I'm dead!" I snap at him at one point. He just laughs, shaking his head at my antics, like I'm some kind of . . . Kimmy Gibbler, put on this plane for his amusement.

Kimo purchased a burner phone so he could contact his friend who owns Dumb-Ax Throwing and try to get hold of our actual phones and wallets and whatnot. "Make sure he knows his employee sold us out to the kidnappers," I insist, looking over his shoulder as he texts. "Better yet, make sure *the police* know! That has to be aiding and abetting or something, right?"

Kimo looks uncertain. "He might have been held at gunpoint, just like us. What was he supposed to do, get himself shot?"

I stare at him, gobsmacked at his naivety. "Kimo, he's the one who told the kidnappers we were there. Remember all that texting he was doing and all the weird, shady looks he was giving us?"

Kimo looks like he very much does not remember any of that. He rubs a hand over his face. "To be honest, I was a little distracted by the beautiful blonde who kept finding reasons to rub her ass against my crotch."

His comment sends an unexpected jolt of heat through me, as I remember the crotch in question, and Kimo revealing it to me last night in his full, naked glory. I haven't had a chance to fully explore that crotch yet, and that's a debt I need to repay, and soon. Very soon, hopefully.

But he's trying to distract me, and I don't want him to know that it's working, so I make a show of rolling my eyes. "Don't be naive—you're a multimillionaire now. You need to be aware of your surroundings if you don't want to be an easy target."

Kimo sighs, looking unconvinced. "How would he have even known to text the kidnappers? That doesn't make any sense."

This poor, sweet idiot. He's lucky he's so rich and handsome. "Have you been to Dumb-Ax before?" At his nod, I persist, "Do you go there regularly? So regularly that people watching you and trying to keep tabs on your whereabouts would know it was only a matter of time before you popped in there again? Making it easy for them to plan ahead by bribing one of the staff members to let them know when you showed up so they could catch you unawares?"

Kimo just stares at me for a moment, then clears his throat. "I'll make a call . . ."

Satisfied, I settle back against the seat. Someone has to watch out for Kimo. It's obvious he's much too trusting. Luckily, that's not a problem that I have.

When Kimo finishes his call, I convince him to let me use the phone to check my work email. At least I haven't gotten any messages from Jay, hinting at an impending firing. Then again, I haven't heard from Jay at all. It's been complete radio silence. Either he's busy at one of his CrossFit sessions, or he and the other partners are busy conferring about the best way to get rid of me.

"Hey," Kimo interrupts my downward spiral, his voice gentle. "Everything's gonna be okay, Mattie. *Relax.*"

That's easy for him to say, Mr. Multimillionaire, *I'll-hire-a-private-plane-on-a-whim* guy. It's hard to relax when you're living paycheck to paycheck and worrying about your job. While I appreciate Kimo paying off my student loans, and that will definitely help my financial situation, it doesn't eliminate the deficit in my bank account caused by my low salary combined with the high cost of living. And this is compounded by the fact that I'm not only responsible for my own financial needs; I need some extra cushion so that if Sasha's car breaks down again or Alina can't make rent, I can be there for them. That's what being a big sister means.

Some of this stress must read on my face, because Kimo sighs and snatches the burner phone from me. "Hey!" I protest, making a grab for it.

"Nah, nah, nah." Kimo puts it in his pocket for safekeeping. "You need a break from this. And maybe just a break, period. Here, gimme your shoulders." He angles me so my back is to him.

Facing away from him, I roll my eyes. I've been around the block—I know what a shoulder rub leads to. First the amateur masseuse will dip as low as he can go on my back while still being able to reasonably argue that he isn't just trying to touch my ass. Then he'll start rubbing my sides and, whoops, an accidental boob grab, how did that happen?

Not that I didn't enjoy last night. I enjoyed it a lot. But men using sex as a way to "distract" me from my stress is not as effective a strategy as they'd like to believe.

But after a few minutes, with Kimo humming what sounds like the greatest hits of Bryan Adams under his breath, I realize he actually has stayed strictly in the shoulder and neck region. And, admittedly, I do have quite a few knots there that need to be loosened. I suck in a breath as he finds a particularly sore spot. "Poor Mattie," he commiserates. "You carry the weight of the world on your shoulders, huh?"

I consider the words. "The weight of my world, at least." I'm not some do-gooder, out to save the planet or the children or whatnot. But I learned a long time ago that no one else is going to care what happens to me and my sisters. If I don't take care of us, who will?

"I knew it when I first saw you. Tough outer shell, but deep down, you get mālama."

I frown at the foreign word. "Is that some new kind of STD? Because I get checked regularly, I'm totally clean."

Kimo laughs under his breath. "No, it's a Hawaiian philosophy. It means you take care—of the planet, or your community, or your family. Ideally, all of the above."

I try to wrap my head around the concept. I don't know about the planet . . . but if you consider Nina and Helen my community, I guess I do try to make sure those naive, beautiful idiots don't get taken advantage of by the world. And Alina and Sasha are my only family, so of course I look after them.

Still, it feels awkward to try to claim that I'm some kind of righteous do-gooder. I shrug under the warm weight of his hands. "I dunno. Maybe that's true."

"You're a champion. You kicked a grown man's ass and then came out of hiding to make sure they wouldn't hurt me. I see you, Mattie. You'd fight tigers for the people you love."

I . . . guess that's true. Preferably metaphorical tigers, but if push really came to shove, I'd take on a jungle cat if I needed to. But only for the people I really love. And the downside of that is, sometimes I turn into the tiger without meaning to, because I love too hard, and I don't always know when my claws are coming out.

I don't say any of that out loud, though, because . . . feelings. #Uncomfortable. But Kimo seems to get it anyway because he gives my shoulders a quick squeeze. "Who takes care of you, though?"

"I . . ." The question hits me hard, knocking the wind out of me for a second. I rally as quickly as I can, not wanting to let on how much it's thrown me. "Me. I take care of me."

There's a challenge in my voice. I'm ready to fight him if he tries to tell me that isn't enough, because it's gotten me this far.

To my surprise, Kimo sounds thoughtful as he responds, "That's part of mālama, too. Taking care of yourself. Mālama pono. But sometimes, it's nice to let other people help out. It goes both ways, you know?"

I don't say anything to that, because . . . what is there to say? Of course it would be nice to have someone who looked after me. To be able to let my guard down, to trust that someone else might have my back as much as I'd have theirs.

Unfortunately, life experience has taught me otherwise.

***

Once we've safely landed in Chicago, I try to think of the best way to broach the subject of money with Kimo. I still don't have my wallet, which I'll hopefully be able to recover at some point from Dumb-Ax Throwing or the police, whoever has it at this point. Without it, getting back to my place will be tricky. Kimo's taken care of me this far, I'm assuming because he feels guilty that I was kidnapped along with him, but I doubt he's going to want me to stick around forever. He probably has important multimillion-aire things to take care of.

My concern turns out to be a moot point, since as soon as we step off the plane, Kimo motions toward the airport with his thumb. "You wanna get something to eat while we wait for the car? It shouldn't take long to get here, but we have enough time to grab something to go." He rubs his stomach thoughtfully. "I could go for a burrito."

"We?" I echo stupidly. We as in . . . *we*? Both of us?

Luckily, Kimo is distracted from my blurted question as a thought seems to strike him. "Shoot. Still don't have my wallet. I keep forgetting that. Maybe the driver will spot us some cash and let us stop somewhere on the way back?"

I have no doubt, if anyone can sweet talk a total stranger into buying them food, it's Kimo. Fighting a smile at the thought, I try to keep my focus on the big picture. "So, you don't mind dropping me back at my place?"

Kimo blinks at me for a moment, like the question doesn't fully register, then shakes his head. "Mattie. Come on. You think I'm gonna leave you stranded at the airport?"

He says it so easily, like I should obviously take for granted that the guy who gave me an orgasm last night is going to make sure I'm taken care of in other ways, too. Ha. That's cute. Maybe in Hawai'i they do things differently, but in the rest of the world, I'm lucky to even get that first orgasm, much less breakfast or cab fare home.

Still shaking his head, Kimo wraps his arm around me and guides me toward the parking lot. "Come on, tiger. Let's get you home."

The hired car hasn't arrived yet, so Kimo and I wait at the curb. I'm obviously not expecting to run into anyone I know at Chicago O'Hare the morning after getting kidnapped, so I'm surprised when I hear a familiar voice calling my name. "Matilda?"

Turning, it takes me a moment to fully register who it is. My face blanches as I take her in. "Dominika?"

Dominika Kroft is just as ferociously glamorous as I remember her being, decked out in a designer dress and low heels, along with her usual chic jewelry—no tracksuits and sneakers for this woman, even in a busy airport terminal. Her blonde hair is swept back from her face, the only concession to the fact that she's traveling, and her intense blue eyes sweep over me once before settling on my face.

There's a tense beat where neither of us quite knows what to do. Then we hug—or rather, she hugs me. I just kind of awkwardly pat her back. "It's been a long time," Dominika reminds me. Not that I'd forgotten, of course. "How have you been?"

"Fine, fine," I say, much too brusquely for anyone to even remotely buy it. Dominika knows me too well, anyway—or at least, she *knew* me too well, once upon a time. I'm also keenly aware of Kimo watching us, and all of this is making me feel like an awkward cardboard cutout of a human being. "Busy. You?"

"Things have been good. Luca is married now, you may have heard. His wife, Anna, is expecting." Dominika waits a beat before adding, with her usual bluntness, "Did you get my email?"

I know exactly which email she means, but still, I feign ignorance, scratching the back of my head. "Um, I'm not sure? When did you send it?"

The look Dominika gives me lets me know she's onto my tricks. "A few years ago now." She shakes her head, just a little. "Anyway, I better go. I have a flight to catch. It was nice to see you. I hope you're well." She looks at Kimo briefly, giving him a quick nod, before looking back at me. "There's no expiration date on that email, by the way. If you happen to go back and find it."

"Oh." I swallow nervously, trying to smile. "I'll check my spam folder. You never know."

I watch her walk away, keenly aware of Kimo's eyes on me. "An old friend," I say to him brusquely, hoping we can leave it at that.

Kimo keeps his face carefully neutral. I can tell it's an act because his eyebrows don't entirely cooperate with how nonchalant he's pretending to be. They keep twitching. "I gathered that."

We remain silent. I tense, bracing myself for him to press me on it. When he doesn't, I can't quite help myself from blurting, "From when I was at university. She was my mentor, assigned to me since I was considered an 'at-risk' student." Most likely due to me being in and out of the foster care system, but I didn't want to go into that right now. "I guess they figured, I was born in Russia, and she's Russian. A successful Russian businesswoman, at that, so maybe she could keep me from becoming another dropout."

Kimo just nods, listening.

"I was my usual charming self." I say this with a self-deprecatory eye roll, because I know better than anyone just how "charming" I can be. "But she was good for me. She called me on my bullshit, told me when I was being too pushy, helped me figure out how to do the perfect red lipstick. She became like an older sister to me."

The words stick in my throat. I blink, waving a hand in front of me, as if to scatter the thick fog of emotions away. "Anyway. We drifted apart. It happens." Something in Kimo's open, interested expression makes it impossible to lie to him. I can tell he's feeling sorry for me, and I need to set the record straight. I'm not the injured party here. "Well, not so much drifted apart as I kind of panicked and imploded things."

His face creases into something like a frown—an expression that looks extremely foreign on his usually sunny face. "Imploded things how?"

"I tried to sleep with her brother. Luca. The one who's married now with a baby on the way, apparently. He wasn't married then, for the record, or even in a relationship."

Kimo's eyebrows notch up a bit before he can catch them. "Were you into him?"

A short bark of laughter escapes my throat. "No! That's the worst part. I mean, objectively, he's a handsome man, smart, charming when he wants to be, but it wasn't about him at all."

Another furrow of the brow. "Were you into *her*, then?"

If only it were that simple. "No. Not in that way, anyway. I didn't want to sleep with Dominika, I just . . .” Saying it out loud to someone else brings into focus how stupid the entire thing was. “I guess I figured sooner or later we’d drift apart. That’s what happens with people. She’d get a job across the country or get married and start a family, and we’d talk less and less. One day we’d be strangers.”

That lump is back in my throat. This time for Dominika, but also not. My sadness is deeper than that, and older, too. I still miss Dominika all the time, but she was an aftereffect, not the cause.

When I look back at Kimo, something like understanding glimmers in his eyes. I think he’s gotten me all wrong, until he opens his mouth. “You thought you could keep her close if you kept him close.”

My mouth runs dry. “Something like that.”

Now I’m thinking about the first time *we* met—Kimo overhearing me proposition Grady in the gym locker room. I can tell by the look on his face that he’s thinking about it, too, maybe putting some things together.

“Anyway.” I put a curt finality into my tone, signaling the conversation is over. “Where’s this car? I thought you said it would only be a few minutes . . .”

Kimo lets me have it—this abrupt exit from the conversation—though I can feel in his silence, his sidelong glances, that he’s weighing me out.

Chapter Twenty

The car arrives not long after. I'm surprised when Kimo doesn't ask the driver to spot him some cash, as he suggested earlier, but instead gives him an address. Leaning back in the seat, he gives me a wink. "I got a better idea. Trust me . . ."

A few minutes later, we pull up in front of a small, cute restaurant not too far from the airport. So Ono. With its turquoise-blue walls, surfboard-and-seashell aesthetic, and the ukelele covers of pop songs playing from the corner jukebox, it seems like the kind of place that would be more at home in a beach town than in the Chicago suburbs.

I, of course, know the importance of this restaurant. It's the national fast-food chain that Kimo rallied the internet behind to keep from going bankrupt. If the crowded tables and line of customers almost to the door are any indication, Kimo's intervention did more than just keep the restaurant's stock value from plummeting. The place looks rejuvenated and thriving.

What I don't know is if Kimo will tell me about his role in keeping So Ono alive. I check his face as we go inside, but he's keeping his expression neutral. "I have some friends here," he tells me vaguely.

Hmm. Not going to brag about single-handedly saving this place from ruin. Interesting.

When the middle-aged Polynesian man behind the counter spots Kimo, his face breaks into a broad grin. "Kimo Hood! Get over here!"

"Good to see you, Uncle." Kimo meets him halfway across the room and they embrace.

"Did you come here for a kau kau?" the man asks. "It's free for life for Kimo Hood—though it looks like you've been putting that offer to good use, brah." He pats Kimo's belly good-naturedly.

Kimo's grin turns sheepish as he glances over at me, though I suspect it has more to do with this man calling him "Kimo Hood" than for the remark about his belly. As I saw firsthand last night, Kimo has absolutely zero self-consciousness about his body . . . his big, sexy, manly body . . .

Nope. Stay focused, Matilda.

"This is my friend, Mattie." Kimo pauses as the older man and I shake hands. "Can you spot her a meal and I'll pay you back later?"

"Pssh." The man waves away Kimo's request. "Your money's no good here. Sit down. I'll bring you both a plate of loco moco . . ."

A few minutes later, the dish of meat, rice, gravy, and fried egg is set down in front of us. I didn't realize how hungry I was until the food arrives. I scarf mine down, only thinking to be embarrassed by my voraciousness afterward, when I see that Kimo's finished his plate and eaten half of the macadamia nut pancakes the manager brought out for us to share.

We say thank you and Kimo gives the man another hug before promising to visit again soon, then we're back in the car and making our way downtown.

Somehow, despite the large, hearty lunch, I'm still very aware of the unfinished business Kimo and I have. Namely, the sex we started last night but were unable to finish. Surely he's pieced together by now that I'm the type of woman who has a Costco-sized package of condoms back at her place. We could have safe sex until the end of time and still have a handful of condoms leftover. I understand now why he was so attentive on the plane, why I got that freebie shoulder massage with no strings attached, why he's treating me to lunch and escorting me home: He still wants to have that hot, no-strings-attached sex with me, as promised. That's all.

I'm relieved that all of his niceness now makes sense. Relieved, and definitely not disappointed.

To my surprise, there's an unfamiliar man waiting for us outside my apartment door when we arrive. He's older and looks gruff, with a tough, no-nonsense air about him as he beelines toward us. I shrink back instinctively because—hello, kidnapped twenty-four hours ago! But Kimo approaches him with his hand extended, as if they're buddies already. "Hey, Stan, right? I'm Kimo Kapono. This is Matilda Markov."

The man nods to each of us in turn, as if he was expecting us. Which is weird, because I wasn't expecting him . . . I look up at Kimo, and he gives me a sheepish smile, like he knows what he's about to tell me is something I'm not going to like. "I asked Jay to set some security detail up. I thought it wouldn't hurt for you to have, just for a while, until those kidnappers get caught and we find out who was behind the whole thing."

This was so not the kind of protection I was hoping to put to good use back at my place. I glower, first at Kimo, then at Stan, then back at Kimo again, since technically Stan's just doing his job—and also, he's kind of scary. "I don't want some guy following me around. No offense."

"Who'd be offended by that?" Stan mutters under his breath in a thick Boston accent.

"Well, he's not just 'some guy,'" Kimo informs me. "He works for Cipher Security—they're, like, the best of the best, according to Jay." He gestures toward Stan. "Plus this guy used to be, like, the bodyguard for Abram Harris, so . . ." Kimo raises his eyebrows to show how impressed he is.

Stan clears his throat, looking a little embarrassed by Kimo listing out his credentials. "I'll also be doing a lot more than following you around, Ms. Markov. I'll be monitoring who comes in and out of the building, keeping an eye out for anyone else who might be following you—"

No matter how impressive this guy is, I still don't need someone watching my every move. "Unless you're planning to help me fold laundry, I'm not super interested," I inform him curtly.

Stan arches an eyebrow at me. "Not really in my job description, lady."

My knee-jerk response is to snap at him, but I realize that, once again, my ire is being misplaced on the guy just hired to do a job. So I glare back at Kimo instead. "I don't need a babysitter. Those guys weren't even after me, they were after *you*."

"Yeah, but now you're on their radar." Kimo puts his hand on both my shoulders, lightly running his palms up and down my arms. "Now they know how I—"

But he cuts himself off before he can finish the sentence. I frown at him, opening my mouth to call him out on that weird pause, before rethinking it. What *was* he going to say? I'm not sure I'm ready to hear it. "What about you?" I challenge. "Are you going to hire a Kevin Costner to follow *you* around and keep you safe?"

Check out my movie reference! And Helen says I don't know any pop culture after the '90s—likely because I was raised by cable reruns of shows and movies from that decade. Pfft. I say, who needs to know any pop culture after the '90s?

Kimo's expression shifts to something sheepish. He scratches the back of his head. "Uh, no?"

I fold my arms, intensifying my glare. I was just trying to call him out on his bullshit before, but now that he's actually admitted it, I realize how colossally stupid he's being. "And why not? You were just the target of a kidnapping! From the sound of it, it wasn't even the first one. One of these times you're not going to be able to sweet talk your way out of things!"

"I'll think about it," Kimo says vaguely, which I know is code for, *I want to get this Russian beda off my back.*

I want to protest more about his lack of caution, but I realize it's not really my place. We're barely more than strangers, despite spending a bizarre few days together. Now it's my turn to uncomfortably scratch the back of my head. I guess this is where we part ways, maybe exchange a few awkward texts checking up on each other over the next few days, until we eventually let things peter out. Unless . . .

I eye the security guy, who's thankfully stepped farther down the hall and out of earshot, I guess to give us some privacy. Even so, I lower my voice to make sure he can't overhear. "I don't suppose you want to . . . ?" I motion toward my door with my thumb, raising my eyebrows meaning-fully. Then, in case Kimo misses my meaning (subtlety was never my thing), I add, "I have lots of condoms inside."

Kimo huffs out a laugh. "Believe me, I wish I could, but I should get home. My niece and nephew are pretty worried about me. And my māmā is about ready to murder me for getting kidnapped again. I think I better get back, smooth some things over."

Kidnapped *again*? My eyebrows arch at the confirmation of what I already suspected—that Kimo has been kidnapped before, maybe even more than once. The knowledge makes me nervous for him, especially now that I know he hasn't hired any security, and he basically just shrugged off my suggestion that he do so.

But . . . it's not my place. It's not my place! I bite my tongue and force a smile, just in case he thinks I'm offended that he isn't coming inside. Which I'm not—well, not much. I know the pecking order of things. "Of course. Get back to your family."

Kimo observes me carefully, his face creased with concern. "Do you have someone you can call? Any family nearby or . . . ?"

"Oh, yeah. Lots of people!" I say this as brightly as possible, even though I'm not convinced it's true. There's always Nina and Helen, but Helen might be at work, or busy with Thad, and sometimes Nina's uncle is really strict about letting her out of the house if it isn't for work or church. I'm sure someone will come by eventually. And anyway, I might decide I'd rather put on one of my box sets of *Full House* and spend the rest of the day in bed. "I'll be fine."

Seeing he's still unconvinced, I shoo him toward the elevator. "Go on, go. Go! I'll be fine. Go see your family."

Kimo lets me sort of sweep him toward the elevator with my hands, though he lingers as he waits for it to arrive on my floor. "We're going to see each other again, Mattie."

"Sure we will," I say in that same overly bright, too-forceful tone.

Kimo stops me, cupping a hand to the side of my face. He looks intently into my eyes, and for a second, I forget to breathe. "You can't get rid of me that easily."

I think for a moment that he might kiss me. I think for a moment that I might want him to.

But a kiss that doesn't lead to sex . . . why bother? At least, that's always been my motto. Anyway, it's a moot point, since he doesn't even try. No lean in for a kiss. Nothing.

The elevator door dings open, making me jump. I self-consciously step away from Kimo as he steps into the elevator and turns back to give me a wink. "Take care, Matilda Markov. I'll be seeing you, *soon*."

Chapter Twenty-One

After Kimo leaves, Stan returns my purse to me, along with my favorite blazer and my phone, which were recovered after the police took in the Dumb-Ax Throwing employee for questioning. Once I'm in my apartment, showered and wearing a fresh change of clothes, I check my phone—which has been charging next to my bed—and find I have dozens upon dozens of missed calls and messages.

Whoa! Any hope I had that the story might have flown under the radar is blown to smithereens. Most of the messages are from Nina and Helen. I see one from Brian and Connie, which I scroll past without reading. Alina's sent a message, and even Sasha has reached out, which is unusual for a non-holiday or birthday. I roll my eyes affectionately at my absentee youngest sister. She's such a Michelle. Or rather, maybe such a Mary-Kate and/or Ashley, who notably never returned for the spin-off, *Fuller House*, even though they were begged repeatedly to show up for a cameo.

Whoa, is that your boyfriend? Alina asks. She sends along a few fire emojis and a few of the money with wings.

U alive? Sasha wants to know.

My heart warms at the exchange. I hadn't realized my sisters would be so concerned. And, okay, it isn't effusive, over-the-top care, but come on, we're not gushy Americans. We keep our hearts buried under layers and layers, in the tiny center of our Matryoshka-doll selves.

Alive, I text back. **And, not my boyfriend.** I fire off a few eggplant emojis with it, though, to show we aren't entirely platonic buddies either.

Helen and Nina are, predictably, more vocal with their concern. **Are you all right????** Helen wants to know. **What happened? Are you back?**

What do you need? asks Nina, tagging on a few hearts.

These were sent earlier this morning, but presumably the offer is still on the table. *If they're busy*, I reason with myself, *I'm sure they'll let me know.*

I'm back.

Long story.

Just some company.

You don't need to bring anything.

Even as I send the text, I know they'll bring something. Probably too many food-based somethings that I'll never be able to finish on my own. *And probably too many somebodies, too*, I muse morosely, before correcting myself. No, no. I reluctantly approve of Thad now, after seeing him in that unguarded moment with Helen. Of course, I reserve the right to change my mind and despise him with the fire of a thousand suns if he ever hurts Helen again, but that's a given any time someone is dating your close friend. In the meantime, I'll do my best to be cordial.

Helen and Nina both chime in within minutes that they're on their way, which surprises me. I guess one perk of getting kidnapped is your friends won't be too busy to come hang out in the middle of the day. While I wait for them to arrive, I face what I've been delaying and check my unread messages from Jay.

Hope you're okay. It sounds like quite an ordeal you've been through. That must have been the HR department talking; it doesn't sound like Jay at all. **When you feel up to it, I need to have a word with you. Preferably Monday if you can manage**.

Oh, *дерьмо*. I'm definitely getting fired.

As expected, when Helen and Nina show up, it's with arms overflowing with junk food and Thad and Grady in tow. As soon as Helen sets down her bags, she engulfs me in a tight embrace. I put up some protest, because otherwise they might think something was wrong with me, but honestly, it feels good to be fussed over a little—especially when Nina joins in on the other side, making a Matilda sandwich out of me.

"You got kidnapped!" Helen exclaims after a moment, pulling back to examine me worriedly. "Why aren't you in the hospital?"

"Because there's nothing wrong with me." I eye the loaf of French bread sticking out of one of the bags. "Nothing some bread won't cure, anyway."

I don't normally splurge on complex carbohydrates, but hey, kidnapped! If not now, then when?

I brace myself to try to make nice with Thad, who I suppose I might have been a tiny bit rude to in the past, but he's preoccupied with sizing up Stan, who let them in the door. "Who do you work with?"

Stan, in turn, sizes up Thad, looking none too impressed. I like him already. "Cipher Security."

Helen perks up at that. "Ooh, my friends own that!" She tilts her head, correcting herself. "Acquaintances? Friends? Acquainta-friends?"

Stan frowns, looking like he would very much like to know more about *that* statement, but Thad intercepts, still clearly not convinced. "Did you notice the fire exit on the east wall?"

"Hanging low to the ground, could make for possible street-level entry," Stan returns without skipping a beat. "We've reached out to the landlord about it, but in the meantime, I've made sure the window is locked so it can't be opened from the outside. I've also seen the out-of-order security camera at the north entrance. The landlord says it'll be fixed by Monday—and believe me, I'm gonna make sure he sticks by that. Fucking safety hazard for everyone in the building."

Despite himself, Thad looks impressed. "Fair enough. Just wanted to make sure *you* were aware."

"What's wrong with him?" I mutter to Helen, confused by Thad's weirdly territorial behavior. "Is he trying to get a job as a security officer or something?"

Helen looks at me like I'm a naive little doofus—a look I know well, since I'm usually the one giving it. "He's worried about you, dummy. He wants to make sure you're safe."

I instinctively frown. No. She can't be right. He can't be . . . concerned. About me? We're not even that close.

But as I peer over at Thad's phone and see he's trying to discreetly do a background check on Stan, I realize it must be true. Thad is concerned about my well-being. An unexpected surge of warmth fills my chest. I know he's probably only doing this because Helen asked him to make sure I'd be safe, not because he particularly cares for *me* as a person, but still. It's . . . nice. I attempt to give him my friendliest smile when he finally meets my gaze. "Hello, Thaddeus."

Thad blinks at me in surprise, clearly taken aback by my attempt at playing nice. Hmm. I guess I'll have to work on that a bit. Recovering, he offers me an awkward smile in return, but not before shooting a quick glance in Helen's direction and seeing her look of encouragement. "Hey, Matilda. I'm glad you're okay."

Well, we aren't exactly exchanging friendship bracelets, but it's a start. Bracing myself, I turn to face the only person I haven't greeted yet. "Hello, Grady." Then, guessing it's better to address the elephant in the room, get it out of the way, I add, "Sorry I propositioned you for sex the other day."

Nina chokes on the water she was sipping. Helen and Thad both do a double take at me. Ah, so . . . he didn't tell them. For some reason, I assumed he would've. I guess this could have just been a private conversation between him and me, but too little too late. It's already out in the open.

Grady flushes a little but holds my gaze, nodding. "That's alright, then. No harm done."

I extend my hand to him. "Friends?"

"Friends." He gives my hand a firm, warm shake. It's solemn between us for a moment, until his eyes sparkle, and that's all the warning I get. "As in, Chandler and Phoebe–style friends. Not Ross and Rachel friends, yeah?"

Helen and Nina both laugh, seeming more surprised than amused. I grin at Grady, pleased to be in on the joke. "I know that reference! And, deal." I shudder. "If I ever give up Paris for a man, please shoot me . . ."

After that, we find ways to fill the day. We play cards and board games. We go for walks. We snack, and we watch TV. Not every single person participates in every activity, but no matter what I do, the unwritten rule seems to be that I shouldn't be left alone, with the rare exception of using the bathroom. Even then, I'm not totally convinced someone isn't outside the door listening in, just in case someone tries to snatch me through the third-story window. (Ridiculous.) It should all feel incredibly stifling, but it doesn't. It feels . . . safe.

It's only when the men have gone off to get supplies to make dinner that I notice the overnight bags by the door. "What are those?" I ask in confusion.

Helen and Nina exchange a guilty look. "We thought you might want us to stay with you, just while you adjust to being back," Nina explains. "But no pressure! We'll give you space if you need it."

Helen doesn't look as convinced of this, but I can tell she's trying to respect my wishes and not smother me. "Mm-hmm. But if you *don't* need it, we are ready to stay here for as long as you need us!"

For the second time today, I feel overwhelmed by a warm feeling spreading in my chest. It's a good feeling, but it also makes me feel awkward, like I don't quite know where to look. "One night shouldn't hurt. If it will make *you two* feel better."

"It will," Helen answers quickly, before I can take it back. And with that, it's decided.

When there's a break in the games, I sneak into my bedroom to check my work email on my laptop. I haven't gotten anything else from Jay, which might be a good sign. Or a very bad sign. *Дерьмо.* I suppose I'll just have to wait until our meeting on Monday.

I move to shut the laptop when another thought strikes me. Without second-guessing myself, I type Kimo's name in my search bar.

Thousands upon thousands of results come up. I look at some of the headlines and scroll through pictures of him for longer than I'd care to admit, analyzing his relationship to any woman who happens to be in the frame with him. Relative? Assistant? Friend? Lover? He strikes me as the type of person who makes connections easily, based on what I've observed. What might feel like an unusually close bond to me is probably just his normal daily interaction with a stranger.

I'll be seeing you, soon.

"*Идиот,*" I reprimand myself sharply.

I mean to go back to my friends, but instead I find myself searching for one last thing: Kimo Kapono Kidnapped.

There are fewer results this time, but still too many for one person. As I suspected from Kimo's behavior during our kidnapping, and as he later confirmed, this was not his first time. Reading between the headlines, it seems like he's been kidnapped at least twice before—perhaps another side effect of being so open and friendly and trusting with strangers.

"He's the one who needs the bodyguard, not me," I mutter to myself. I want to be irritated at Kimo, but instead I find myself feeling something even more troubling.

I'm . . . *worried*.

"*Идиот*," I tell myself again, finally shutting my laptop.

Chapter Twenty-Two

Dinner is even less eventful than the lazy, feckless day. The gumbo Thad made is good, I'll give that to him. We talk. We eat. After anticipating that I'd be all alone for the day, I'm grateful for the company. Afterward, when Grady has gone home and Nina and I are cleaning up the kitchen, Helen sends Thad off like he's going to war, instead of a five-minute bus ride away.

I give Nina a look. I'm surprised when I see her return my eye roll, even if she is giggling while she does it. There's some hidden sass under that quiet exterior. She reminds me a bit of my sister Sasha in that way. Sasha was always the quiet one, the one you thought you could push around, until she'd finally snap and do something really terrible, like put gum in your hair while you were sleeping. (Alina found this out the hard way, unfortunately.)

"Ten bucks says they're texting all night," I mutter as I hand her a dish to dry.

"Twenty bucks says he ends up sleeping in the hallway," Nina returns with a sly smile.

I bark out a surprised laugh. Helen is all happy blushes as she re-enters the kitchen. "What's so funny?" she asks as she starts to put away the clean dishes.

Nina and I exchange another conspiratorial glance. "Nothing," we say together.

To my surprise and chagrin, after we've changed into pajamas and are getting set up to watch a movie together, Helen seems less interested in sending lovey-dovey texts to her boyfriend and more interested in perusing my DVD collection. Okay, let's be honest, my *Full House* collection. "Matilda, do you actually own every season of *Full House*?" She gives me a puzzled look. "Why?"

"Uhhh . . ." Somehow in all our years of friendship, I've managed to keep my *Full House* obsession under wraps. I know Nina and Helen wouldn't care, per se, but it feels too exposing to share this vulnerable thing with them. "It was a gag gift. From my coworkers."

"All eight seasons?" Helen isn't calling me out, exactly, but I can tell she's confused. I guess that would be a pretty extreme gag gift. One season, sure, but eight?

Thinking quickly, I blurt out the first thing that comes to mind. "It's because I got really drunk at a holiday party once and admitted that the first time I masturbated, it was to John Stamos."

Silence.

It's not a total lie, but it's definitely not something I meant to say. That happens sometimes: my mouth works faster than my brain. Still, I refuse to be ashamed, so I raise my chin and an eyebrow and look around the room, daring anyone to call me out.

Helen blinks at me. "Well . . . sure. What woman of a certain age didn't grow up with a huge crush on Uncle Jesse?"

"Have mercy," Nina agrees.

The remark is unexpected coming from her, in her quiet little voice, and the timing is just so spot on that all three of us dissolve into cackling laughter. We're laughing more than the situation really calls for, honestly, but it's been a long few days and the joke lands just right, and it's good to be here with my friends.

A few minutes into the movie we finally decided on (after some healthy debate), Helen nudges me with her knee. "So, who was the guy you were kidnapped with?"

Her tone suggests she's already drawn some conclusions about who *she* thinks he is, but I refuse to take the bait. "What guy?"

She frowns at me, clearly not buying my obtuseness. "Just how many men have you been kidnapped with?"

I don't know what to say to that, so I pretend to be really invested in what's happening onscreen. "Shh. No talking during the movie."

To my surprise, Nina holds up the remote and pauses it. Traitor! I gape at her in protest. "Nina!"

But she just shrugs. "What? He's cute." Her eyes widen a little. "And *big*."

I ponder that statement for a moment, lost in memory. "Yeah, his dick was on the larger side." Too late, I realize that likely isn't what she meant. "And also his stature," I add.

It's Helen's turn to gape at me now. "You two had sex? How? When you were tied up in the back of the van?"

"In the hotel, after we were rescued. And anyway, it wasn't sex. Not penetrative sex, anyway." I wave my hand, as if to dissolve the conversation. "Who wants popcorn?"

To my dismay, I see Helen and Nina exchange a conspiratorial glance, much like the one I shared with Nina earlier in the kitchen. Betrayal! Nina's lucky she's so little and cute, or she would be getting my stink eye right about now. "Is she blushing?" Helen asks Nina, her tone sounding teasing, but also like she can't really believe what she's seeing.

I cover my face with my hands. "I am not blushing! I'm not a schoolgirl or a Jane Austen heroine."

More gently, Nina asks, "Do you like him?"

"No!" I shout, more aggressively than I meant to, and I see both my friends visibly recoil. Taking in a deep breath, I temper my tone. "No. We fooled around a little. That's all. It didn't mean anything. Anyway, I'll probably never see him again."

Another look exchanged between Nina and Helen. "Stop that!" I snap at them irritably. "I can still see you."

"Do *you* want to see him again?" Helen prods. There's nothing teasing in her tone anymore. She looks almost . . . hopeful? But also like she's treading carefully, so as not to spook me off—like I'm a wild animal she's trying to coax into eating out of her hand. (Knowing Helen, she probably does regularly feed woodland animals while she sings about love in the forest.)

Helen's question makes me feel squirmy inside. I shrug. "No. I don't know. If he were to reach out, I'd probably meet up with him—but only so we could have sex."

Even as I say the words, I don't know if they're true. What would I say if Kimo asked me to go see a movie, or throw axes again? Preferably not anywhere with an employee who'd sell us out to kidnappers, but still. The fact that I don't know the answer is in and of itself . . . alarming.

"It doesn't matter anyway," I say, waving my hand again. "He hasn't texted me all day."

"Have *you* texted him?" Nina asks.

Damn her sensible questions! "Of course not."

"How did the two of you leave things?" Helen leans forward, clearly invested. "Did he say he wanted to see you again?"

I cast my mind back to our parting, trying to recall the details exactly. "He said, 'I'll see you around.'" I check their reactions.

Another glance is exchanged between Nina and Helen, this time far more muted. "Oh," Nina says noncommittally.

Their lack of response deflates something in me, until I remember something else. "No, wait, it was—'I'll be seeing you, *soon*.'" I try to give the words the same emphasis Kimo did, standing there by the elevator doors, gazing into my eyes.

"Ohhh," Helen and Nina say together.

I look back and forth between them. "Is that good? What does that mean?"

Helen smiles, nodding a little to herself. "I think you should text him."

I scoff, but it's mainly to cover the fact that the suggestion has my armpits breaking out in sweat. Not dainty little droplets, either—Niagara Falls–levels of moisture. "And say what? I think we should have the penetrative sex we didn't get to back on the island?"

"Definitely not that." Helen takes a moment to ponder. "Maybe just check in with him? Tell him you want to make sure he's okay after everything that happened, and see if he keeps the conversation going."

"Send him a gif!" Nina suggests. "Everybody likes gifs."

Nina notoriously overuses gifs, often ones that don't make any sense, but she's so sweet, no one has the heart to tell her. I honestly can't see myself sending off either of their suggestions. It's what Helen might say, or what Nina might send, but it's not . . . me.

Pulling out my phone, I hesitate a moment, then type out my message and send it off before I can second-guess myself. Even so, my heart is pounding, and I have to wipe my hands on my pajamas.

"What did you say?" Nina wants to know.

I show her and Helen the message: **U still alive? Not kidnapped again on the way home?**

Helen worries over it. She's the writer of the group, so I can tell she's afraid it isn't just right. "It's . . . direct, but it doesn't really open the conversation. What if he doesn't know what to say back, beyond yes or no—"

Nina shakes her head, cutting her off. "No, it sounds like Matilda. It's just right."

I put the phone on silent so I don't have to stress all night whether or not he writes back. Despite Helen's protests, I'm determined not to check it again, and I don't, until I'm by myself a little while later, brushing my teeth in the bathroom.

My heart lurches when I see that Kimo's responded. **Still alive, home safe. Just tucked up in bed, thinking about my vampire slayer.**

He sends me a gif of Buffy roundhouse kicking a vampire in the face.

I grin so hard it hurts. For a few minutes, I dither over what to write back, before finally turning off my phone without saying anything. It was nice to hear from him. But I already know I'll be disappointed if I write back and he doesn't respond. It's probably better to just cut off the conversation now and see if he starts it up again later. Not that I'll be waiting, or anything.

Chapter Twenty-Three

It's Monday. I've had the weekend to recover from my kidnapping, and I'm wearing my best dress—an outlet-purchased Ann Taylor belted sheath—and matching heels for my meeting with Jay Eastman. Hey, if I'm going to get fired for fraternizing with a client and lying about a dead dog, I'm going to do it looking great.

"Matilda, please. Come in." Jay stands as I enter his office, shaking my hand and motioning for me to take a seat. If I weren't so nervous, I might appreciate his faint but expensive-smelling cologne—Bleu de Chanel, if I'm not mistaken. The man might be about to fire me, but he has great taste in scents. "Do you want anything to drink? Water? I can send Everett for a coffee."

"No, I'm fine." Better to just get this over with. I carefully cross my legs, folding my hands in my lap. I'm cool, calm, and collected. No sign of weakness. But just in case, I'm keeping my arms firmly down since I can't be confident I don't have pit stains. "Thank you for seeing me. I wanted to apologize, first and foremost, for having to leave the meeting early the other day. Fortunately, everything is resolved on that front. Comet is in a better place now."

Hey, you never know. Maybe an apology will be all it takes to get me out of this mess . . . ?

Jay seats himself, but to my surprise, chooses a chair close to mine instead of going back to the other side of his desk. He gives me a look, laughing a little under his breath. "I think we're pretty far past that now, don't you?"

I shift before I can catch myself; so much for not letting any nerves show through. "You're probably wondering about me being kidnapped with our client."

"Yeah," Jay says bluntly. He folds his hands in his lap, waiting.

I shift again. Dammit. "That obviously wasn't something we planned. We had bumped into each other, randomly, and the next thing I knew, I was —randomly—in the back of a van."

Jay nods, watching me intently. "Kimo told me how you tried to rescue him."

I stare at him for just a beat too long. I'm not great on my feet, obviously. And I'm also trying to stay focused on this conversation, here and now, but my brain keeps snagging on the fact that Kimo thought to contact Jay and put in a good word for me, maybe even ensure I didn't lose my job. "I . . . I did do that. Yes. I tried to rescue him. I'd do the same thing for any client. Any person, really." Okay, that might be overstating it a bit, but as long as I'm going to fib, I might as well go all in with the lie, right?

Jay studies me, shaking his head. "It's an incredibly brave thing to do. I've had employees go above and beyond for clients before, but I gotta tell you, this just might take the cake."

Whaaat? This sounds almost like . . . I'm not being fired? I blink at him for several seconds before managing to formulate a response. "I just really care a lot about the firm."

"I can tell." The hint of a smile tugs at Jay's lips. "I've noticed your work ethic for a while, Matilda. And I've been very impressed by the work you've done with past clients. I have to admit, I thought maybe we'd hit a snag with that meeting last week, but to know you'd go so far out of your way to help a client, well . . . I think maybe we've been sleeping on you for just a bit too long."

Any other day, my brain would be short-circuiting about Jay Eastman making any reference to sleeping on, in, or around me—because *hello, gorgeous, rich, handsome boss*—but weirdly it does nothing to me now. I'm probably just flustered about the meeting. "Thank you," I manage finally. "That's very nice to hear."

"I'd like to first make sure that you have any counseling that you might need to process the . . . event that occurred this past week. Our insurance covers a number of well-reputed therapists, and I'm sure HR would be happy to recommend someone to you."

Ha! Therapy. I try my best not to openly scoff at the idea. Sitting and talking about my feelings and childhood traumas—that would be more traumatic than any kidnapping. I don't say any of this, though, of course. "I appreciate the offer."

Jay meets my gaze cannily, as if he understands me perfectly but still needs to give the HR spiel. "If you need to take some personal days, that's fine as well. As soon as you're ready, though, I'd love to get you back to work."

My eyebrows notch up. "On the Kapono case?"

"Kimo insists that you're the best person for the job. And considering the lengths you were willing to go to protect him, I don't know that I can argue with that." Jay levels me with a stern gaze that, again, would have probably made its way into my erotic fantasies if I weren't so thrown by this whole meeting and all its twists and turns. "Provided those headlines were inaccurate—you aren't actually Kimo's girlfriend, are you?"

"No," I say quickly, definitively. And it's true! No promises have been made between Kimo and me. I don't even know if anything will happen between us in the future. I suppose we might still sleep together at some point, but that doesn't mean we belong to each other in any way. Maybe I feel strangely bonded to him, but I'm guessing that's from the trauma of being kidnapped together. I might think about him, often, but it's only because I'm worried about him and his case. So being on the case and helping him win custody of his niece and nephew is probably the best thing to fix that, right?

Jay's own raised eyebrow tells me he's not totally convinced. "Listen, I know how easy it is to mix business with pleasure. But I don't want anything interfering with the case. No fights, no love spats—"

"Definitely not his girlfriend," I say, more firmly this time. "That won't be a problem."

And it won't be. I might be socially awkward at times and a bit obtuse when it comes to emotions, but aside from that weird blip last week, I've always been nothing but professional in the office. I don't see why this time should prove any different.

Jay nods, finally seeming convinced. "Good. In that case, I'd love to have you back on the team."

My poker face is good, but even I can't hide just how relieved I am to hear this. I thought I was getting fired today! Instead, I'm basically being lauded by my boss for being amazing. See the power of a perfectly chosen outfit?

I smooth down my skirt, readying to rise to my feet. "Thank you so much, Mr. Eastman. I'd love to jump back into work, take my mind off things."

"A woman after my own heart. And please, call me Jay." Before I can stand, Jay touches my knee. It's just the briefest skim of a touch, but it takes me completely by surprise. I wasn't confident Jay even knew who I was before today; we'd never spoken this long one-on-one. He is not known around the office for being touchy-feely, and he's certainly never been touchy-feely with me. This knee graze, however minor, seems . . . in-tentional? "Before I let you go, I wanted to also mention that I'd love for you to be my guest at the upcoming Over the Rainbow Gala. It's next weekend—I know that's short notice, but I'd be thrilled if you could make it."

This time, my brain does actually short-circuit for a moment. Of course I know about the Over the Rainbow Gala—it's one of the firm's biggest charitable events. All of their biggest clients are invited, along with celebri-ties, local politicians, the who's who of Chicago. As a lowly paralegal, I've never scored an actual invite, and the tickets are far too pricey for me to splash out on, just to go for funsies.

That isn't what's making this difficult for me to process, though. The way the entire meeting has played out—Jay making sure I'm not dating Kimo, then touching my leg, then inviting me to be his special guest. And that intense look he's giving me with his smoldering movie-star eyes . . . Is he interested in me? Romantically? A week ago, I would have laughed at the idea; he's basically the model for my perfect man, but I was never delu-sional enough to think I could actually land *him*, just someone like him—the diluted, less-impressive version.

But I'm getting ahead of myself, aren't I? He's probably just being friendly, wanting to make sure that I've recovered from my ordeal of being kidnapped for a client and that I don't hold any resentment toward the firm for it. "That would be lovely. Thank you," I stammer out finally.

We stand. Jay smiles at me, gesturing toward the door. As I start that way, I feel his hand touch the small of my back. I'm glad he can't see my face, since I'm sure my eyes are cartoonishly wide. Oh, Mylanta! What is happening?

"I'm sure Barry will be able to catch you up on what we've been working on," Jay says. "Though I'd also be happy to go over anything you need."

It's all perfectly professional, and if his hand weren't still on my back, I'd never think twice about it. But there's no two ways about it—he's *lingering*.

Damn this dress! I look too good today and it's confusing everything. It's confusing *me*. I don't know how to feel about this, honestly. If it were a week ago, I'd be plotting what underwear I should wear to seduce him, but things are different now, right? At least they feel like they are, even if nothing has actually changed.

As we step out into the hall, I'm taken aback by the sight of Kimo coming toward us—almost as if my brain summoned him out of thin air. Though, of course, it makes sense he'd be here, since he is Jay's client and all. Still, I haven't seen him since Friday, and my heart does a weird, nervous lurch at the sight of his open, handsome face, and the grin he gives me as he approaches. "Mattie!"

Instinctively, I step away from Jay. His hand dropped before we left his office, but still, I feel like I can't let Kimo see me standing too close to him. It doesn't make any sense. I'm not making any sense. Kimo's not my boyfriend and I'm not his girlfriend, and even if my boss just kind of hit on me, which I'm not sure he did, it wouldn't matter because nobody belongs to anybody. I am a free agent! I can do what I want.

"I have to pee!" I blurt, all but running to the bathroom, and keenly aware of both men watching me as I go.

Chapter Twenty-Four

I take my time in the bathroom, in no rush to get back and face the confusion of what I left behind. Luckily, by the time I return, Jay's been informed that Pika Kalili—Kimo's deceased sister's ex-boyfriend who's suing him for custody—is in the building and on his way up, and everyone is all business now, including Kimo and Jay.

"Do you need me to take notes on this?" I ask Jay. I know I just got put back on the team, but I'm eager to jump back into work—and I'm also curious to see who we're up against.

Jay considers me a moment. "I have Barry prepped to take notes, but if you would start putting together the pre-trial memorandum, we can coordinate after the meeting's over."

He touches my shoulder, then slides his hand down my arm, lingering at my elbow for a moment before releasing me. It's the briefest of interactions, but it's definitely far beyond the kind of touching I'd expect from my boss at work. I can't help but glance over at Kimo to see if he noticed.

He did. He blinks at me, then shakes his head a little as the elevator door dings open, and Pika and his team enter the office.

Pika is a Polynesian man close in age to Kimo, somewhere in his late thirties or early forties, but at least half a foot shorter, with a frame that's hard to decipher under his oversized button-up shirt and baggy trousers.

He's wearing colorful, expensive-looking sneakers and sunglasses—even inside the building.

I decide to wait to sneak off to my desk, so as not to draw attention to myself as introductions are made. When clients are here, I'm meant to be just a fly on the wall—no, even less noticeable than that. A thumbtack on the wall. Observing, but not observed.

So I quietly observe a lot of things. I observe that Jay is polite and deferential to the opposing attorney. They seem to be familiar with each other, but more than that, I know it's one of Jay's strategies—to be Mr. Nice Guy until suddenly, he isn't. I see that Kimo has actually dressed up for today's meeting, and that he looks uncomfortable and nervous in his dress slacks and button-up shirt that's just a bit too snug around his barrel chest.

And I notice, now that he's pushed his sunglasses up, that Pika keeps looking over at me.

This is not a *come hither* kind of look. I mean, I've been doing my squats, but even I know I'm not so hot that all the eligible men in the room (and Barry) can't resist me. No, Pika's eyes keep darting over to me, almost like he can't stop himself from looking. And I notice that whenever our eyes do meet, his narrow a bit, as if we're mortal enemies, though I'm positive I've never met this man before in my life. And honestly, there's no reason to single out a paralegal for vitriol like this. I like my job and I'm good at it, but we're glorified document formatters. If the case goes wrong for Pika, it will be because of Jay, not because of me.

As the clients and lawyers move toward the conference room, I hang back to let them go by; Pika briefly makes eye contact with me, sneering—yes, *sneering*—as he passes. "Hey, it's Hilary Swank."

Hilary Swank? I frown at him, perplexed. I've been compared to celebrities here and there, but never Hilary Swank. I'm blonde with dark blue eyes, for starters, not brunette with brown eyes. I guess we're both slender with athletic builds, but other than that, I don't see a resemblance at all.

He's probably just trying to throw me off my game, for reasons only known to him. Kimo did suggest he's kind of an asshole. Shrugging it off, I watch the group through the conference room window as they all take their seats. I don't want to linger too long, but I can't help but seek out Kimo. He meets my gaze briefly through the window, and I give him a quick nod to let him know not to be nervous. He's in good hands with Jay. Everything is going to be fine.

After my forced time off work, I'm eager to throw myself back into things, and I start drafting the pre-trial memorandum with all the notes we have so far. I'm tucked back in my cubicle, so I miss when the meeting adjourns and everyone leaves. On the one hand, that's good since I won't have to run into weird Pika again, but on the other hand, I don't get a chance to say anything to Kimo, and he doesn't make a point to come over and talk to me.

Whatever. It's fine. I'm sure he has a lot on his plate right now with the custody case and all. And the only reason I feel even a tiny bit disappointed, I reason with myself, is because I thought that maybe we'd finally have sex tonight. I have that huge box of condoms next to my bed, just ready and waiting. But it's probably not a good idea, anyway, to sleep with the client. Then again, I'm not his lawyer, so who cares . . . ?

Aggravated at myself for getting so distracted by the whole Kimo thing, I put in my earbuds, turn on some angry techno music, and throw myself back into work.

By the time I surface again, it's nighttime. Jay was meant to meet with me about the memorandum, but he ended up getting called out of the office, so nothing's resolved there, either. Great. Just great.

I don't check my phone until I'm out of the building. When I do, I'm pleasantly surprised to see I have a missed call and a voicemail from Kimo. *He's probably just calling to tell me he can't afford any distractions during the case*, I reason, bracing myself as I click on the message.

"Hey, Mattie. It's me. Uh, Kimo. I guess you probably have my number saved by now. Or, uh, I hope you do. Anyway, I know things are busy right now for you, being back at work, but I was wondering how you feel about pancakes. Specifically, pancakes for dinner? I know the best pancake place in town. Tomorrow night?"

I'm fighting a smile, but it breaks free anyway. Pancakes, for dinner? It's just so . . . Kimo. *Is this a date?* That thought gives me some pause. Do I want it to be a date? If I'm being honest with myself, I'm happy about the thought of spending more time with Kimo, but I don't want to put too much pressure on things. Maybe it's a sort of pancakes-and-chill situation? Is that a new Gen-Z thing?

I text my only Gen-Z friend, Nina. **Is pancakes code for something sexual? Or is it a thing now to have pancakes before sex?**

If not, it should be. Pancakes before sex sounds awesome.

I guess I don't fully consider *who* I'm texting, though, because Nina sends back a gif of someone awkwardly shrugging. Right. She's not exactly tapped into the Gen-Z sex scene. Or any generation's sex scene, from what I can tell. Though come to think of it, Nina doesn't really divulge a whole lot about herself. For all I know, she's hosting weekly sex parties and just never talks about it.

Why do you want to know about pancakes? Helen asks. Oh, right. I must have accidentally pulled up the group chat instead of messaging Nina directly.

I hesitate, not wanting them to make a big thing about it, but simultaneously really wanting them to make a big thing about it, somehow? This is all so confusing. And dammit, I'm smiling again! **Kimo invited me to get pancakes tomorrow night**.

Nina sends a gif of a pinata exploding into confetti.

It's not a big deal, I send, as I receive a text from Helen: **I don't think pancakes are a sex thing . . . I think they're a LOOOOOVE thing!!!**

Shut up, I type back, then temporarily mute the thread so I don't get any more notifications tonight.

Helen is getting carried away. I know this isn't *love*. I like Kimo, sure. I think he likes me. I'm looking forward to having sex with him, but I don't expect it to turn into anything more. We're too different. When we inevitably part ways, I won't have any hard feelings. I'll probably be relieved.

But it already feels like a lie I'm telling myself. It already feels strange, after less than a week of knowing someone, not to be near him anymore, not to see his grin or hear his laugh. I already worry I'll be devastated when he's ready to move on.

Chapter Twenty-Five

"Here?" I ask Kimo dubiously, looking at the brick building in front of us.

Kimo seems uncharacteristically nervous as he continues to gesture, Vanna White–style, at the brownstone. "Did I forget to mention that the best pancakes in town happen to be made in my kitchen? By me?"

I fold my arms, determined not to be charmed. "That most definitely was not mentioned."

Under normal circumstances, I'd be thrilled if a guy brought me back to his place to cook for me. I still may not know what "pancakes" is code for in dating terms, but I know what "cooking back at my place" is code for, and from my (limited) experience, almost no cooking actually happens.

But the situation with Kimo isn't a normal circumstance. I happen to be very well-acquainted with the fact that he's in a custody dispute over two young children who are currently living with him full-time. So unless he plans to keep them locked in their bedrooms, chances are very good that we're going to be having pancakes *with* those two children.

It's not that I don't like kids. I tolerate well-behaved children who keep their hands to themselves and don't shout or scream or cry. Or bite. If I remember correctly from the trial documents, Makoa is seven and Nalani is nine, so I'm guessing they're out of the biting-and-crying phase. At least, I think? It's been a long time since I was looking after Sasha and Alina at those ages, so it's kind of hard to remember. It does make sense, though, why Kimo suggested pancakes. Children of any age love sugar—I remember that much.

"Are the children having pancakes with us?" I ask bluntly, deciding to cut to the chase.

Kimo runs a sheepish hand over his face. "Yeah. They sort of need to eat three times a day. At least. It's pretty obnoxious."

I don't begrudge them for eating. What I don't understand is why he wants *me* to be eating with them. "And you want me here because . . . ?"

Kimo reaches for me, hooking his index fingers through the belt loops of my jeans and tugging me half a step closer. His eyes rove over my face and he smiles to himself, like he can't help his reaction to me. I will not find it endearing. I will not! "I wanted to have dinner with you, but I want to make sure I'm spending good quality time with Makoa and Nalani, too. So . . . two birds, one stone." He tugs me just a little bit closer. "Besides, they wanted to meet you."

"Me?" I narrow my eyes at him. "Why?"

"I told them how you karate chopped one of the kidnappers in the butt. You're their new hero."

I shift, surprised—and honestly, a little pleased—at this turn of events. It's sort of cool to be known for beating up kidnappers. "Me? Really?"

"Yeah." He releases my jeans and wraps an arm around my shoulders, drawing me toward the door. "You and JoJo Siwa."

"Who?"

Kimo laughs under his breath and shakes his head. "Oh, boy. Get ready to find out . . ."

I let him guide me inside, where I hear giggling long before I see any children. The evidence of them is all over, though. Toys tucked away into various shelves and bins around the room, art supplies scattered across the coffee table, stickers on the wall. I'm surprised, too, to see how modestly Kimo lives, even if this property is just a short-term rental they're using during the custody trial. Knowing his net worth, I expected to walk into a lifestyles-of-the-rich-and-famous type of house; instead, it's nice but more on the comfy, cozy side. Then I remember what he told me, about not wanting to change his lifestyle too much after making his money. I guess

I'd just chalked that comment up to being the kind of thing a guy says when he's trying to get into a stranger's pants, but maybe his modesty actually goes beyond his flip-flops-and-board-shorts wardrobe.

Before I can think about it much longer, two small humans pop up from behind the couch. "Boo!"

I'm genuinely startled—I'm not used to people jumping out and screaming at me—but it seems to be par for the course for Kimo. He lets out an obviously staged scream, clutching at his chest and then dropping dramatically to the floor, like he's passed out. I worry that might be too morbid for the children, but they shriek in delight and rush over to tackle his carcass. "He's dead! He's dead!" they chant triumphantly, pounding on his broad back.

Huh. Okay. I guess it's not *too* morbid for the kids.

Then the girl—Nalani—notices me, and she straightens up. For a moment, I'm worried she's going to tackle me to the floor, too, but she's suddenly all shy, like she wasn't just using her uncle's limb like a club to beat him over the head two seconds before. "I'm Nalani. You're pretty."

"Oh." Frankly, I'd probably be less flustered if she tried to beat me with my own arm, too. "Thank you." I should probably return a compliment with a compliment, right? That's true even with children. "I . . . like your necklace."

Nalani is wearing a shell attached to a pearl chain around her neck. She twists it shyly. "'Anakala made it for me."

"'Anakala?" I repeat, unsure of the word.

"It means uncle." Kimo speaks up from the floor, still face-down in the carpet. "I found the shell at the beach near our house on the Big Island."

"It had a snail inside of it," Makoa tells me gleefully, still perched atop Kimo's back. "But we didn't know until it *died*, and 'Anakala had to scoop it out with a chopstick!"

Wow. Okay, so these kids really are into death. It's kind of surprising, considering that their mother recently passed . . . but maybe it's their way of coping with it, by trying to normalize it or something?

"Oh," I say, when I realize both of them are watching me for my reaction. When they continue to blink at me, I realize they're waiting for something more. I search for something comparable. "One time I found a dead mouse inside of my toaster."

A beat. Then Makoa and Nalani look at each other before running into the kitchen shrieking in delight. "Check the toaster! Check the toaster!"

I stare after them, stunned in the wake of their chaos. Kimo looks up at me, grinning. "I have a feeling I know what they're going to be doing every morning for the next week."

We're interrupted by another voice coming from the kitchen—a woman's voice, sounding distinctly irritated. "What are you doing on my kitchen counter? Leave that toaster alone!"

If I'd paused to consider it, I probably would have realized that the children wouldn't have been left here alone while Kimo picked me up from work and walked me back to his place. But beyond my own nerves at the unexpected situation, I hadn't really thought about it much.

Now I do, and I piece it together quickly. With wide eyes, I stare at Kimo, willing myself to be wrong. "Please tell me that's a babysitter."

Kimo offers me another sheepish grin. "That would be Anela Kapono. My mother."

Mrs. Kapono is a short woman, with a round frame and an open, pretty face. She has white-gray hair and wears a beautiful bright pink floral-print muumuu and house slippers. Everything about her looks soft and welcoming, like one of those little teddy bear creatures from that *Star Wars* movie. So in theory, she should seem completely approachable and adorable.

She is not. She is absolutely terrifying.

As soon as Kimo leads me into the kitchen, she sizes me up, making no effort to hide the fact that she is not impressed by what she sees. She purses her lips, folding her arms.

"Māmā," Kimo says, and if I'm not mistaken, there's a hint of warning in his tone—a reminder to *play nice*. "This is Matilda Markov. Matilda, my mother."

Oh, God. Oh, God. I do not do mothers. I have hookup buddies and flings and one-night stands specifically to avoid mothers. My own didn't want me; how am I possibly supposed to convince someone else's to take me on?

If Kimo had told me she was going to be here, I never would have come. But I guess I'm here now, and although I might be socially inept, I'm not ever intentionally an asshole, so I have to make the best of things. I thrust out my hand, willing my voice not to crack like a teenage boy going through puberty. "Mrs. Kapono. Nice to meet you."

Immediately by the way her nose wrinkles, I can tell I've somehow already said the wrong thing. "You can call her Aunty Anela," Kimo supplies quickly.

"Aunty Kapono," she corrects, then reluctantly takes my hand, shaking it limply. "So this is the haole girlfriend, huh?"

"Māmā," Kimo says, not quite angry, but scolding, like she's a naughty dog who's chewed up his flip-flops again.

If I had time to think about it, I'd guess he's reprimanding her for the *haole* comment. I'm not sure what that word means, but it does not sound complimentary. Instead, what my brain sticks on is the word that follows it, and I think his irritation must be caused by that.

"I'm not the girlfriend," I blurt out quickly. I want to show him, and her, that I'm not expecting anything to come out of this. I know my place in everything. "I'm just a . . . friend," I finish awkwardly. Because I probably shouldn't say fuck buddy in front of his mom, right?

I didn't think Aunty Kapono's eyebrow could go any higher than it already was, but it does. She gives Kimo a long, meaningful look. "You hear that, Kimo? Just a friend."

I'm confused now . . . Is she mad that I might be the girlfriend, or mad that I don't want to be? Or both?

Kimo gives my shoulders a quick squeeze. "Okay, let's make pancakes. Where did my keikis run off to?" He raises his voice to be heard. "Remember, anyone who doesn't help make the pancakes doesn't get to help eat them!"

The pantry door flies open and both children come spilling out, a chaotic tumble of laughing and shouting and arguing about who gets to crack the eggs. Despite the chaos, I brighten at the possibility of being put to work. At least I'll know what to do with myself if I have a task to fulfill. "What can I do to help?"

"Sorry, Mattie, I can't let you help. Then you might learn what the secret ingredient is." Kimo winks at me, before leaning in to whisper, "It's chocolate chips." He gives my shoulders another squeeze, then motions me toward the dining room. "Why don't you sit and have a little talk with Māmā? Give the two of you a chance to get to know each other better."

I glance over at Aunty Kapono, who looks just about as thrilled by this suggestion as I feel.

"Uhhh," I stall, before Kimo all but shoves me into the other room with his mom.

Chapter Twenty-Six

For a long time, Aunty Kapono and I just stare at each other across the dining room table. I'm smiling nervously. She is not. There is no hint of anything warm or welcoming on her face. The grandfather clock in the corner of the room ticks loudly, punctuating the uneasy silence between us. I can faintly hear the children shrieking with laughter in the kitchen, and Kimo doing a loud, silly voice to egg them on. I would give my right arm to be in that room right now.

"So how did you and my son meet?" Aunty Kapono breaks the silence.

She strikes me as the kind of person who wants complete and total honesty. But I don't know if I can be *that* honest. "At the gym," I say finally, diplomatically.

"What do you do for a living?"

I sit up a bit straighter. This is actually something in my favor, I think. "I'm a paralegal. I'm working on the custody case for Kimo. It's kind of a funny coincidence."

Aunty Kapono doesn't seem to find it all that funny. Her mouth remains a flat line. "Not smart enough to be a lawyer, huh?"

Her boldness knocks the wind out of me. I'm used to being the most direct person in the room. To have it turned back on me makes me feel like I'm trying to Rollerblade with my arms tied behind my back. "Well, I, uh, I don't know about that. But I didn't want to go into more debt."

"More debt?" Aunty Kapono's eyebrows inch up again.

I reach for the glass of water in front of me, wrapping my hands around it to steady myself. I wish it were a glass of wine. Or better yet, vodka. "I supported myself through school, and my two sisters. I had to take out some loans," I explain.

Aunty Kapono's flat expression reveals nothing. "Where were your parents?"

Oh, so we're jumping straight into that, huh? I gulp. "My father died, back in Russia, where I'm originally from." *Honesty.* She'll want direct honesty, I know. I brace myself. "My mother brought us here to America because she had a new boyfriend who sponsored her fiancée visa. But after we got here, he decided he didn't want children. So one day they left us."

I'm not trying to play the sympathy card, really. I've made peace with what happened a long time ago—well, no, that's not quite right. I would never describe myself as being at peace. But the wound has healed over, and I have enough self-control not to pick at it.

Still, I can see something shift in Aunty Kapono's face. She isn't smiling, or open, but she isn't quite glaring anymore, either. She's frowning, but that frown no longer seems directed at me. "How old were you?"

"Ten." I wave my hand. "But it was fine. We were put into the foster care system. And we're all university graduates now, so." I shift again. There's a lot left unspoken in that *so*. Like how I took on Alina's debt to make sure she could get a well-paying job. Sasha's adoptive parents helped her with university, but I still loaned her money for textbooks and other fun things she might not have gotten to do otherwise, like her study abroad trip to France. Fun things *I* didn't get to do during my own university experience, since I was busy juggling two part-time jobs, and regularly donating plasma, so they could have an easier time in school than I ever did. But we all made it, we all have university degrees and jobs now, and we didn't fall prey to what happens to so many kids put into the system like we were.

So.

"Congratulations." Aunty Kapono says it almost begrudgingly, still valiantly holding on to her suspicion of me, though for the first time I see a crack in her armor. A woman doesn't get so many laugh and smile lines from always being this tough. If I were any other person sitting across from her at the table, telling her this story, she'd be all warmth and kindness. It's only because I was brought here by her son that she's being so tough.

I know it because I recognize it. I respect it. I'm the same way with Alina and Sasha, Helen and Nina. Anyone who means something to me. Someone has to prove they want what's best for them first, before they get the benefit of the doubt from me. Some things are too precious to just hope the best for. For people like Aunty Kapono and me, it's not our own hearts we're protecting; it's everyone else's.

I relax a little now with this new understanding of her standoffishness. I'm not sure what I'm feeling for Kimo yet, but there's no doubt in my mind what I feel for Aunty Kapono. She's tough and fierce, a mother with the heart of a warrior. It's complete love at first sight.

She settles back in her chair, not willing to give up her protective stance quite yet. "How many boyfriends have you had?"

"None," I say honestly. I'm almost enjoying this, now that I understand where she's coming from.

"None?" Aunty Kapono does not like that answer. "What's wrong with you?"

I bark out a laugh. "What's wrong with men?" I counter. "I can provide for myself, take care of my needs, and if I get lonely, I'll get a cat. What does a man bring to my life?"

Again, I can see Aunty Kapono fighting against her begrudging respect for me. "Still . . . none? What are you, a virgin?"

"No. Are you?"

The words slip out of my mouth without my thinking. Seeing Aunty Kapono's eyes narrow in warning, I realize immediately I've taken it a step too far. "Sorry," I say quickly, and hurry to add, "In high school, I was too scary, I think. At university, I was too busy. Then I became a nun for a couple years."

Aunty Kapono stares at me. "A nun? What do you mean?"

"Like, a nun." I mimic clasping my hands in prayer. "You know, wimple. Lived in a monastery. The works." I puff up a little, prepared to wow her. "I was a Poor Clare."

"A poor what?"

Her question deflates me a little. I forget not everyone is keyed into the world of nuns. "They're the most austere nuns," I explain. "They have very small communities, with only a few members. It's a pretty big deal to get in."

Aunty Kapono does not look wowed. "And yet, here you are, not dating my son." She folds her arms again, sizing me up. "Was being a nun too tough for you?"

Two can play this game. I fold my arms back at her. "Nothing's too tough for me. I thrive under pressure."

Let her take that as she will. If Aunty Kapono thinks she's going to scare me away from Kimo by not smiling and asking for brutal honesty, she has another think coming.

"Hmm," is all she says, pursing her lips.

"I joined the community because I liked the order and structure of religious life. And I used to have a close relationship with God, though not anymore. I left because one of my sisters at the monastery ended up getting deported. The church could have intervened, but they didn't, and I didn't think that was fair." I level Aunty Kapono with my gaze, so she'll see how sincere I'm being. "I care a lot about things being fair. I didn't think it was fair of the church, and I didn't think it was fair of God, so I left."

"Hmm," Aunty Kapono says again. This *hmm*, however, is harder to read than the one before. It isn't exactly friendly, but she's no longer frowning.

Deciding to go all in with my brutal-honesty strategy, I shrug. "Besides, who wants to go their whole life without sex?"

Kimo and the kids whirlwind into the dining room, a flurry of plates and silverware and pancakes. "Who's ready to eat?" Kimo asks.

As Makoa and Nalani both try to outshout each other with their "Me!"s, Kimo makes eye contact with me, then his mother, then again with me. "How are we doing in here?"

"Just great," I reply. It's an honest answer, but I'd be lying if I didn't say it wasn't in part for Aunty Kapono's benefit. *You don't scare me, Aunty,* I silently tell her across the table. Then I smile at the huge stack of pancakes. "Yum."

"Māmā?" Kimo asks as the older woman continues to stare me down.

At last, Aunty Kapono shifts. "Well, she's honest. I'll give her that much . . ."

Dinner is pure chaos. Syrup gets spilled. Makoa ends up with chocolate all over his mouth and hands. Nalani interrupts the grown-ups any time we start to have a conversation. Aunty Kapono threatens to get out her wooden spoon if the kids don't behave, but I can tell by the way they respond to her that it's never actually been used. They adore their gruff dragon protector, but not as much as they adore Kimo. He's almost as much of a kid as they are, blowing bubbles in his milk and spearing his strawberries on his fingertips just to make them laugh.

I'm used to eating dinner by myself, in complete silence, unless I'm watching an episode of *Full House*. Sometimes I'll just eat over the kitchen sink so I don't have to wash any dishes. My life has been a total lack of chaos for as long as I can remember. I guess some aspects of being a Poor Clare lingered with me—I like order, and I like silence.

I should be miserable at this wild circus of a table, but I'm not. My heart feels too big for my chest as I quietly observe the Kapono family just being a family. I watch Kimo teasing Nalani about the boy she likes at camp and threatening to hose Makoa off in the backyard if he doesn't use his napkin and coaxing Aunty Kapono into begrudging smiles with his antics, and I think to myself, *This is the kind of man who would never make a mother leave her children behind. This is the kind of man who would fight tigers to keep his family together.*

Oh no, I think, as I meet Kimo's gaze across the table in a rare quiet moment before the next round of tumult starts.

Oh no.

Chapter Twenty-Seven

Kimo holds my hand as he walks me home, even though I insist I can make it back just fine on my own. "Maybe I'm the one who needs protection, karate kid," he teases me.

The reference triggers something in my brain, but it's gone before I can latch onto it, and then I'm distracted by the whole hand-holding thing. His big hand enveloping mine, his warm skin, the light squeezes he's giving me to remind me he's there. Hand-holding is fine, right? It doesn't have to mean anything. Friends hold hands all the time. Maybe fuck buddies do, too, although never a fuck buddy that I've had before.

"I wish I could say that was an unusually crazy night at the Kapono household," Kimo tells me. "But it's not. Actually, back on the Big Island, it's even wilder than that most of the time. Three of the seven houses on my street are owned by relatives, and we eat together almost every day. Sometimes the neighbors pop in, too. Sometimes my cousins bring their football teammates. So, yeah, it's a bit of a free-for-all."

"It's nice," I tell him honestly. "That sounds . . . nice."

We walk in silence for a moment. Kimo swings our hands idly and does that thing where he runs his thumb over the back of my hand. Somehow that gesture feels more intimate than anything we did back in that hotel room on Mackinac Island. "We're only here in Chicago for the court case," he explains to me after a moment. "Once it's resolved, we'll go back to the Big Island."

My heart seizes in my chest. I knew this would be coming at some point. This is where he starts hinting about how things will only be temporary, letting me know that I shouldn't get my heart set on anything. Usually that isn't a problem for me. But I'm starting to worry it might be this time. Still, I force myself to nod and try to smile. "You miss it?"

"Oh, yeah." Kimo shakes his head, lost in some memory. "We live about a two-minute walk from the beach, so when you fall asleep at night, and when you wake up in the morning, you can hear the ocean humming outside your window. I like to get up really early and go out to the water first thing. Sometimes I swim or surf. Sometimes I meditate or do Tai Chi. I just like having a little quiet time to say hello to the day, just by myself, you know?"

I try to picture it, but I can't. There's nothing in my experience that gets anywhere close to that. I've always lived in a city, surrounded by people. "A two-minute walk?" I echo. "You didn't splurge on a house right on the beach, Kimo Hood?"

He groans at the nickname, but answers my question nonetheless. "Nah. We thought about it, but it would mean leaving the neighborhood, and we've been there forever. It's nice to be someplace where no one cares about my money, but they'll still remind me about the time I ditched school to go skinny-dipping and got my clothes stolen, so I had to walk home naked with nothing but a shell over my junk." He raises an eyebrow at me. "It made the local paper."

I smile despite myself. He has a way of doing that, of making me open up even when I want to stay closed. "I'm sure your mother loved that."

"She got it framed and made me hang it in my room, to remind me what happens to young men who bring shame to their families."

We laugh together. Kimo rubs his thumb over the back of my hand again. My heart squeezes painfully. I wish he wouldn't do that if he's planning on leaving in a few weeks.

Oblivious, Kimo continues on, "My mom is really tight with my neighbors, especially since my dad left. They really stepped up. My next-door neighbor is the guy I consider to be my real father—he's the one who had to deal with my rebellious years and my party phase. I'll owe that guy forever for keeping me from throwing my life away."

I look up at him in surprise. "Your father left?"

"Yeah. When I was thirteen."

For a moment, I feel like I can't breathe. It would be easy to just not say anything, to let the moment pass. But I'm surprised at how much I *want* to tell him. I've already mentioned it to Aunty Kapono, so it's likely he'll hear about it anyway, but somehow it still feels terrifying to say it now, in this moment, to him. Not only because it will show him my vulnerability, this soft spot in me, but also because it will be this thing that bonds us, that deepens *this*, whatever *this* is, when I know it can only be something temporary.

"My mom left." I carefully avoid his gaze as I say this. "When I was ten."

Kimo doesn't say anything for a moment, doesn't stop holding my hand or stop walking, but I feel the shift in the air. I feel him treading carefully, searching for the right thing to say. "Man, grown-ups suck sometimes."

"Yes," I agree curtly. Too curtly. I feel myself pulling back, but surprisingly, I don't want to. I want to stay connected to him, but I don't know how. "Not you, though," I blurt out. "You're not leaving Nalani and Makoa."

"I couldn't." Kimo shakes his head. "Not after what my dad did to me. Even if things go wrong, even if I lose the court case, I'll move wherever Pika goes, stay nearby so I can always be there if they need me."

"That's really nice," I say, or start to say before a blinding flash takes me by surprise.

Kimo pulls me behind him, though his voice is still affable as he calls out into the dark. "Hey, brother, no pictures, please. Just out for a walk."

I glance behind me and see a few others have pulled out their phones to record us. I look to him, uncertain how to proceed. "Kimo . . . ?"

He glances back, seeing the growing crowd, and swears under his breath. "How's your cardio these days, Mattie?"

"My cardio is always excellent," I reply honestly.

Threading his fingers through mine, he tugs me into a run.

We sprint down several city blocks, hand in hand. I'm determined not to let him outpace me, though it's difficult with his height advantage. Still, I manage to hold my own. I'm not sure who starts laughing first, but soon we're both howling as we barrel down the sidewalk at full speed. It's not the most incognito way to make an escape, but if anyone's trying to follow us, they're going to have a pretty hard time keeping up.

When we're a safe enough distance away, Kimo finally tugs me to a stop. He pulls me into an alleyway, pushing me up against the wall. He looks around us with exaggerated diligence. "Hold on. I need to protect you with my body in case anyone's following us."

He crowds me up against the bricks with his big, strong body, trying his best not to smile. I fight my smile, too. "I thought I was the one who was supposed to protect you?"

"That was obviously just for show. I'm a big, strong masculine type who can protect his lady."

His lady? Hearing that sends a weird thrill through me. I press myself up against him, batting my eyelashes. "That was so terrifying. My weak feminine sensibilities are too fragile to handle it. Please protect me, big, strong masculine type."

Grunting alpha-male style, Kimo tilts my chin up and looks deep into my eyes. "Is it weird this is actually really turning me on?"

"Kiss me," I tell him.

He does.

I haven't spent much time kissing just for the sake of kissing. Kissing was always the prelude to something else, the first step you take so you can get to the thing you really want to do, like eating your vegetables so you can eat your dessert.

Kissing Kimo doesn't feel like the prelude to the next thing, though. Kissing Kimo feels like the main event. I'm caged in by his strong arms, the heat of his body pressing me into the bricks. His mouth is somehow both soft and firm, exploratory but sure, as if he knows exactly how to kiss me to turn my knees to jelly and my brain to mush. We are no longer in an alley in the middle of the city. We are alone in a vacuum, where nothing exists but us.

When we break apart, I'm breathless, trembling with want. The look in Kimo's eyes tells me he feels exactly the same way. "How far?" he wants to know.

"Six blocks," I tell him.

Twining his hand through mine, he tugs me back onto the sidewalk and sets a brisk pace.

Chapter Twenty-Eight

After saying a quick hello to Stan in the lobby, we head upstairs. I brace myself to be thrown around my apartment, in the best possible way, the second we step through the door. We are out of the public eye now, just the two of us, with a big box full of condoms in my bedroom. The night is ours.

Instead, I'm surprised when Kimo makes a beeline for my bookshelf. The term *bookshelf* is a little misleading, since there are zero books on there—it's more like a "stuff-shelf"—but he takes his time looking at everything, like it's the site of an ancient civilization and he's piecing together truths about their society based on these artifacts.

"These are your sisters?" he asks me finally, picking up a framed picture.

It's an old one of the three of us, the last time we were all together. Alina had just graduated from high school, so I'd picked up extra shifts at both of my part-time jobs and bought us all tickets to go to Santa's Village, a Christmas-themed amusement park about an hour outside of Chicago. It was an ill-planned adventure on pretty much every level. I'd hoped it would be just the three of us, finally together again, but Alina invited along her best friend without telling me and spent most of the day talking to her. I'd thought Sasha would love the Christmas theme since she'd loved the holiday so much as a little girl, but at fourteen, she was surly and irritated about anything that reminded her of her childhood. It was the same trip where Alina announced to me that she'd be rooming with her friend at the University of Chicago instead of with me, like we'd been planning, and then Sasha informed us her adoptive family was moving to Oregon. That picture was the last time the three of us were together in person, and it was taken only after lots of cajoling that turned into aggressive scolding on my part.

Seeing that picture in Kimo's hands now, my stomach seizes up, but I force myself to smile. At least I don't snatch the frame out of his hands, so —progress! "Yes. Sasha and Alina. Taken about . . . eight or nine years ago, I guess?"

"They live close by?" Kimo's voice is careful, and I get the sense that he's treading lightly, aware this is a sensitive topic. "You see them a lot?"

"Um." I think the last time I saw Alina was about a year ago? I've FaceTimed with Sasha occasionally, but the last time I saw her in person was probably . . . at least three years ago now? She still lives on the West Coast and doesn't seem to have any plans to change that. But saying all of that out loud feels like admitting I failed—failed at being the sister they needed me to be, failed at keeping our family together. "Fairly often," I lie.

Kimo sets the frame back down, and I hold back a sigh of relief, hoping we'll move on to something else. "You have other family nearby?" he asks instead.

I'm not sure where all of this is going, or why he's so interested in my family all of a sudden. I fold my arms, feeling defensive. "No." But two lies in under two minutes is my threshold, apparently, so I correct myself. "Not biological family. My adoptive parents live close enough, I guess."

His face brightens almost hopefully at that. Am I really such a transparent loser, that he's this worried about me? "Oh, yeah? Are you close?"

"No," I say bluntly this time. There's no sadness around this topic, just irritation, so I cling onto it. I'm much more comfortable in this emotional zone. "They're just two people who let me live with them for a couple years. Kind of like adult roommates."

Kimo's brow furrows. "But they adopted you," he points out.

I huff out a laugh. "When I was seventeen. What did I need parents for then? Why couldn't they have found me when I still needed them?"

When I make myself meet Kimo's gaze, his face is all sympathy. "Kind of seems like that's not their fault," he points out to me kindly.

How dare he be so logical about the whole thing? I glare at him. "You don't get it, okay? It's . . . complicated."

And that much is true, at least. Logically I can reason that Brian and Connie were nice people, that they had always done their best by me and had supported me in whatever ways they could in the short amount of time we had together. Sympathetically, I can even understand that it probably wasn't their dream to get placed with a surly teenaged foster daughter who wanted nothing to do with them, when all they'd wanted was a child to help complete their family.

But illogically, irrationally, I've always resented them for everything they offered me. Kindness and love, when I'd already suffered too much rejection to be open to it. Parents, when I felt too jaded and grown-up to need them. A family, when it was already too late.

Kimo closes the distance between us, running his hands up and down my still-folded arms. "You're right. I don't get your situation. But I do get complicated." He sighs, as if bracing himself. "You know my dad left. Well, before he took off, our thing was working on cars together. I don't know how much I actually helped him, but every weekend, we'd be out in the garage, tinkering around with whatever new piece of junk he was trying to salvage, jamming out to '80s music."

I remember following him through the park and hearing "Careless Whisper" blasting through his headphones. "'80s music?" I prompt him, curious to hear more despite myself. I know he's just trying to soften me up, get my walls to come down, to *bond* with me, and dammit, it's working.

"The greatest era of music," Kimo confirms. "Music isn't really music unless it makes you feel it in your gut. Unless you have to stop whatever you're doing just to close your eyes and sing along."

A smile tugs at my mouth, despite my best efforts to fight it. "I don't think there's literally any kind of music that does that to me."

"You must've been listening to the wrong stuff. Don't worry—I'll make you a playlist." Kimo nods to himself as if it's a done deal, and surprisingly, I trust that he'll actually remember to do it. "Anyway, when my dad left, I couldn't listen to that stuff anymore. Too many painful memories. I'd change the radio when that music came on, leave a party if someone started playing it. It was very dramatic. But, you know, I was in my emo phase."

Now there's no stopping it—my smile breaks free. "Just how emo was this emo phase?"

"Black combat boots, dog collar, haircut like a bearded collie, dance sequence in *Spider-Man 3*–level emo," he confirms with a shudder. "And before you ask, I've destroyed all the photographic evidence, though I suspect my mother has a safe box somewhere to use for blackmail purposes someday."

I laugh, and Kimo grins before continuing. "Anyway, one day I'm stuck in the dentist's chair getting a tooth filled, and they're playing a classic radio station. Michael Bolton comes on, but I obviously can't run out of the room. So I have to just sit there and listen to 'When a Man Loves a Woman.' And you know what I realized?"

"What?" I ask obligingly, though I suspect I already know where this is going.

Kimo grips my upper arms and gives my body a gentle, enthusiastic shake. "That song's amazing! That guy really pours his heart out, you know? Anyway, Bolton turned out to be the gateway drug. Next thing I know, I'm listening to Journey, and Foreigner, and frickin' George Michael, and I realize . . . my dad took away a lot from me when he left. But those memories are mine, and me refusing to listen to the music I used to love just gives him the power to take that from me, too. I'm not punishing him by keeping that music out of my life—I'm punishing myself. And that's hammajang."

"Hammajang?" I repeat, smiling around the unfamiliar word.

Another gentle shake. "That's messed up!" Kimo shakes his head at me, rueful. "Look, I'm not trying to tell you what to feel. But I guess I'm just saying, don't shut out the people who want to be there for you to punish the people who weren't."

Hmm. That's certainly . . . something to consider. But I'll have to parse through all that on my own, and I'm feeling too open and exposed again, so I focus on something lower stakes in what he just said. "I think I'm going to need to get a Hawaiian dictionary to understand all these words you and your family are always throwing around. What was it your mother called me? Halo?"

"So you noticed that, huh?" Kimo runs a sheepish hand over his face. "It was haole. It basically means you're someone not from Hawai'i. A mainlander."

I can tell from his grimace that this is not meant to be a compliment. At my widened eyes, he hurries to tag on, "Honestly, Māmā has a bit of a chip on her shoulder about dating haoles, but it's not personal. It's because my dad was a white guy and left us to go back to Denver. I think she figures most non-Islanders will eventually want to leave again and won't stick around."

I want to be offended, but again, I understand where Aunty Kapono is coming from too well to hold too much of a grudge. "Does that make you haole, too, since your dad was white?"

"Hapa," he corrects me. "It means mixed, basically."

I study his features carefully, noticing he does have a slightly different look than his mother and even his niece and nephew. "You took your mom's last name?" I guess.

He shrugs. "She's the one who raised me. And I know she can be a pain, but she means well. And it isn't personal."

I consider this. "So she's tried to scare off all your other haole girls, too? It isn't just me?"

Kimo's face unexpectedly softens as he looks at me. "There's never been anyone else like you, Mattie."

I'm having that weird sensation again, where my heart feels like it's trying to burst out of my chest, like my body is suddenly too small to contain it. I don't know what to do with my arms. It's so much, so fast; I don't know what to do with someone offering me so much softness. I blink up at Kimo, and abruptly ask, "Do you wanna have sex?"

He huffs out a laugh, giving me a sideways look, like he knows exactly what I'm up to. "Later." He takes a step back from me, like he needs the physical space, then crosses back over to the bookshelf. "First I wanna watch *Full House*."

Oh no. This is worse than conversations about love and family, somehow. I might as well be naked on an operating table, with my legs spread wide and my body cut open, that's how exposed I feel. "Why?" I bark out defensively.

"You have all the seasons. Multiple copies of them," he points out. "You bonded with one of our kidnappers about a dog in here I barely remember from the reruns I used to watch when I was a kid. This is obviously a thing for you. I want to get it." He selects a season at random and holds it out to me.

"Why?" I demand again, not quite able to stop the shake in my voice.

Kimo holds my gaze, unafraid, unflinching. "I want to get you."

I could spontaneously burst into flames or into tears—those feel like the only two options if he says something like that to me again. Instead, I take the season he's holding out and pop the first disc into the DVD player —because, yes, I know that streaming is a thing, but I'm always worried they'll take the show down and then I won't be able to find it. I like having my own set.

When I turn back around, Kimo has shamelessly made himself at home on the couch, his bare feet up on the coffee table, one of my blankets across his lap. He pats the spot next to him, leaving me no option to sit farther down the sofa and keep some space between us.

I sit next to him, ramrod straight, but let him draw me up against his warm body. I'm not the passive type of girl who lets anyone tell me what to do, so I'm not sure why I'm letting him get away with all of this. Maybe it's possible that I . . . want him to succeed in his obvious efforts to knock down my walls? It must be, since this is no gentle demolition. He's shown up with twenty wrecking balls and is pummeling down all my defenses.

As the familiar music of the opening credits begins to play, I let myself relax against him, just a little. He's done so much of the work that I feel like I need to offer him something, just to show him I want him to be here, sitting next to me on this couch. I may not know what to do, or what happens next, but I want him here. "I learned how to speak English watching this show," I tell him quietly as the cheerful laugh track permeates the background.

Kimo doesn't say anything, but I can tell he's listening intently, from the way his body tightens, just a little; and I can tell it means a lot to him that I'm sharing something personal, by the way he's holding his breath.

"It was always on," I continue. "On some channel, at some time of day. And they were always so happy. Even though . . . even though they lost their mom, too. They all took care of each other. And everything gets resolved in the end, every time. I needed that. I really needed it."

Before and after my mom left. Through the different temporary foster homes, and the group homes, and while I was living with the Bergmans. During those lonely hours at university, when I was too busy studying and working my various jobs to make real friends. After leaving the Poor Clares, when I no longer had any sense of purpose or family, until I met

Helen and then Nina. And now, when I spend almost every night by myself, surrounded by my fake family.

As if he understands, Kimo puts his arm around my shoulder and squeezes it before drawing me even closer to him. My head comes to rest on his chest, and I can hear his heart beating.

"I get that," he murmurs into the top of my head. Or maybe, it's "I got you."

Either way, it's the safest I've felt in . . . ever. Either way, I think I might believe him.

Chapter Twenty-Nine

When I wake in the morning, the *Full House* DVD menu is playing on a loop in the background. This isn't an unusual circumstance for me—it definitely isn't the first time I've fallen asleep on the couch, comfort-watching this show—but what is unfamiliar is the warm, lightly snoring pillow underneath me.

Kimo. The reality of him, here with me, fills me with a giddy, dizzying level of joy, followed almost immediately by a sharp spike of outrage. This son of a bitch convinced me to sleep platonically with him again, and we still haven't had sex! My outrage ebbs quickly, though, when I look down to see his face softened in sleep, mouth hanging open. He's left a little puddle of drool on my throw pillow, and that really shouldn't be adorable, but somehow it is. When I glance at the door and see his flip-flops lined up next to my heels, it makes my heart go all fuzzy.

Oh, God. This is bad.

Or . . . is it? There's never really been a reason for my set no-dating stance, beyond finding most peoples' personalities repulsive and my inherent distrust of men. But I like Kimo's personality. I like his cheerfulness, his lack of shame, his generosity, his fierce love for his family. He is the best parts of Uncle Jesse mixed with the best parts of Uncle Joey. He is a real-life sitcom character, in the most positive way possible. I think he might actually be a good person.

Before I can process this realization too much further, though, Kimo's eyes flutter open. He looks disoriented for a moment, until his gaze lands on mine, and a lazy, happy smile stretches across his face. "Good morning, beautiful."

"Hi." I don't know what I'm supposed to do in this situation. Should I climb off him? I'm probably crushing him, with the way I'm sprawled out across him.

But when I try to push up, he wraps his arms around me, pulling me back down. "Hey. Not so fast. Let me wake up slowly with my Mattie blanket keeping me warm."

"Oh. Okay." Even though I'm pleased by the sentiment, I can feel my body going stiff with awkwardness and uncertainty, until Kimo starts smoothing his hands down over my back and shoulders, and my body can't help but relax at his warm, sure touch.

"Mmm," he mumbles happily. "How do you not have morning breath? And how are you so pretty first thing?"

"I waited until you fell asleep and got up to brush my teeth and wash my face," I admit, honest to a fault as always.

Too late I realize what I'm admitting to him—that he was already sleeping, and I could have used that as an opportunity to go to my bedroom and sleep on my own, but instead I chose to come back here. To him.

"So pretty," he says, tilting my chin up so he can look into my eyes.

Our faces are so near each other. I can tell he didn't get up in the night to brush his teeth, but his breath isn't bad, just a bit musky. I like even that about him. I don't recognize this side of myself. I'm usually so critical of everyone, about everything, so quick to find a flaw. But he could probably belch in my face right now and I'd still think he hung the moon.

"Do you want to come to book club with me on Friday night?" I blurt out without thinking.

Usually we meet on Tuesdays, which would have been last night, but Helen had something going on at the library this week, so we postponed. I don't know why I suddenly invited him, honestly. I instantly regret it.

"It's okay if you can't," I say quickly, pushing up and off him before he can grab me and stop me again. "It's not a big deal. I don't even like books, so . . . I get it if it's not your thing. Anyway, I have to pee."

I race out of the room, shutting myself in the bathroom and squatting down on the floor in a sort of standing fetal position. Oh, God. What have I just done?

Not two seconds later, I hear a knock on the door. Still huddling on the floor, I reach up to pull it open. Looking up, I see Kimo grinning happily as he reaches down to help me to my feet. He cups my face, his thumb brushing the worry lines from my brow, then moving once over my lower lip. "I'd love to come to book club. Even though I also don't read much. If you're there, I want to be there."

I swallow heavily, unable to help my grin of raw, hopeful relief. "Really?"

"Absolutely."

I give him the time and place, then check my phone to get the name of the book: "*The Curious Incident of the Dog in the Night-Time* by Mark Haddon," I read from Helen's reminder text. I can't believe how excited I am about a book, now that I know he'll be there with me when we discuss it.

Kimo writes the title down, but shakes his head. "I don't know if I can finish a book in two days. I'm more of a comic book guy myself, you know? But I'll give it the old college try—or what I imagine the college try was like, since I didn't go."

I wave off his concern. "Don't worry about reading the book. I never do. I can send you a good summary site so we can fake it together."

"I might try the audiobook—so I can get stuff done while I listen."

"The audiobook?" I raise a skeptical eyebrow at him. "Isn't that just someone *reading* a book to you—how is that any better?"

Kimo laughs, chucking my chin affectionately, like I'm the most adorable anti-reading gremlin he can imagine. "Nah, they're way better than that. The narrators do all the voices and sometimes there's even music and stuff to set the scene. It's like a movie, but for your brain instead of your eyes."

That doesn't sound too bad, actually. I like movies, on the rare occasions when I actually get to sit down and watch them—as long as they aren't too slow, or have subtitles or anything, because again, *reading*. "That doesn't sound so bad," I admit.

Kimo has to leave so he can help get the kids off to camp, which does sound kind of bad—Kimo leaving, that is, not the children bonding and having fun with their peers. I walk him to the door, and we just sort of stand there, smiling at each other and holding hands. "Today and tomorrow are kind of crazy for me," he tells me.

"Yeah, me too," I agree with a sigh, remembering how much there is for me to catch up on back at work.

"But I'll see you Friday night," he promises. "I've never been so fucking excited to talk about a book in my entire life." He leans in conspiratorially toward me, like he's telling me a secret he doesn't want anyone to overhear. "'Cause you'll be there, just in case you missed that."

My cheeks feel all weird, like they're unusually warm and kind of tingly. And I can't stop smiling. My mouth actually hurts, but in a good way. "I, too, am also feeling very excited for that." That came out much stupider than I intended.

Kimo grins anyway. "To see me, right? That's what you're excited for?"

My smile, impossibly, pulls even wider. "Yes, you doofus. To see you."

Kimo nods a sort of *hey, did you hear that* greeting to Stan out in the hallway, then grins at me before turning toward the elevator. He raises a fist in the air, holding it there. "Whoo—book club!" At the elevator, he winks at me. "See you Friday, beautiful."

I'm pretty useless for the next couple days. Luckily, even though I have a lot to do, most of it doesn't require too much brain power. I'm filing, transcribing notes, and setting up the calendar for the upcoming weeks, those kind of things.

My mind is on Kimo the whole time, though, and on my building anticipation to see him again on Friday night. Wanting to feel close to him, I decide to do something I've never done before.

I download the audiobook from the library.

And you know what? He was right! Audiobooks are amazing! I can listen to it as I do the mundane tasks at my job, and as I walk to and from work, and as I cook and clean, and even while I work out at the gym. "Did you know how many audiobooks you can get for free from the library?" I gush to the guy on the elliptical machine next to me, who looks like he could not care less. Whatever—his problem, not mine!

If this is what reading a physical book is like for Helen and Nina, I'm no longer surprised they like doing it so much. I don't know if it's the narrator or the story or the fact that I can multitask, but I can't remember the last time I was so enthralled with a book. By the time I reach the last hour of the audio, I'm not even doing anything else, just *listening*, waiting to see what happens next.

I can't wait to share this with Kimo. I can't wait to talk about our favorite parts and to see if he was as surprised as I was when we found out about *the thing* that only the people who've read the book know about. I can't wait to see his funny flip-flop walk and the grin he gets on his face when he sets eyes on me across a crowded room.

Friday night can't come soon enough.

Chapter Thirty

I t's Friday night! I'm at Lou Malnati's Pizzeria, and the rest of the group is here—everyone but Kimo. My eyes keep darting toward the door. I want to catch the exact moment he comes in. I want to see the exact look on his face when he sees me.

In the meantime, my leg is jackhammering so hard underneath the table that I could probably dig a hole to China if I were wearing my spike heels. Noting my nervous energy, Helen reaches out and puts a comforting hand on my arm. "Hey, it's still a few minutes before seven."

"He'll be here any second, I'm sure of it," Nina chimes in.

Of course I told the two of them via text about inviting Kimo. Helen had to talk me down from texting Kimo and canceling this morning—not because I'm not excited, but because I'm so anxious I'm afraid I might puke all over him when he walks in the door. Or worse—do something hopelessly embarrassing, like blurt out that I love him. Which I don't. That would be crazy.

I *like* him, though. A lot. A *lot*. Somehow, that feels even crazier.

Nina met me at my apartment to help me get ready. Even though she's one of the frumpiest dressers I've ever met—and that includes Helen's extra-extra-large turtleneck phase—Nina has surprisingly good taste in clothes. I wonder why she doesn't apply it more to herself. Tonight she's wearing a thick, plain gray wool skirt that reaches down to the ground, and a beige cardigan buttoned all the way up to the top, despite the fact that it's summer and almost as hot inside the crowded restaurant as it is outside. Regardless, I've seen Grady and Thad taking turns warding off a couple helpless men who wander up to the table, staring at her with that same dazed expression we all recognize now.

"Who'll be here any second?" Grady asks, leaning forward to take a sip of his coffee. Yes, you read that right—coffee at seven at night. I don't know if I've ever seen Grady not drinking coffee, regardless of the time. He's either desensitized to the caffeine, or he's moonlighting as a late-night phone-sex operator. I can't really think of any other scenarios that might apply.

Helen looks to me for permission to tell him, and I shrug. What do I care? Kimo will be here any second, anyway. The cat's about to be out of the bag. "Matilda invited a friend of hers tonight. A *male* friend."

To my surprise, Thad raises an eyebrow—which is a strong reaction coming from his generally stoic self. I would have thought Helen would have told him already, given the expected *women don't keep secrets from their boyfriends* clause in every friendship. "As in . . . a date?" he asks.

I roll my eyes, but it's more out of nerves than real annoyance. "Yes, he's a gentleman caller of mine, here to court me with my many chaperones. Don't let him take any liberties!" Actually, scratch that. Please let him take some liberties. A girl can only cuddle for so many nights.

Thad and Grady exchange a meaningful look. They try to be sly about it, but they're men, so it's about as subtle as a Hallmark Christmas movie. "Is it . . . serious?" Grady asks, sounding as though he's attempting to tread carefully.

I consider the question. "We haven't had penetrative sex yet. But we've done other stuff." I realize almost immediately by the way both men's eyes widen that this isn't what Grady meant by "serious." I guess I'm also not the queen of subtlety. I force a smile. "And . . . I like him. Sort of. We'll see. Jury's still out."

Liar, liar, pants on fire. I take an anxious sip of my water, then check my watch. Five minutes after seven. Kimo's officially late. I check my phone, but there are no missed calls, no messages.

"He probably got caught up in traffic," Helen quickly reassures me, giving my arm a squeeze. "I'm sure he'll be here any minute . . ."

Another five minutes crawl by, then another fifteen after that, and still no sign of Kimo. Nina eventually persuades me to try calling him, but I get sent to voicemail after the second ring. Which means . . . he saw my call and rejected it, right? His phone isn't just set to Do Not Disturb.

Thad excuses himself while Helen and Nina try to run through all the plausible, excusable scenarios of why Kimo might be late. Grady just sips his coffee, looking increasingly more uncomfortable with each minute that ticks by.

And I . . . feel numb. I barely hear Nina and Helen talking at me, coming up with increasingly more ridiculous theories. All I can think is, I knew it. I knew not to get my hopes up. I knew not to trust him. I knew not to hope for . . . him. For us.

For anything.

Thad rejoins us a moment later, and he's got his scary bounty hunter face on. "He isn't at any of the local hospitals. I have a friend at the downtown police station who'll let me know if anyone matching his description gets booked there tonight."

"Wasn't he kidnapped recently?" Grady asks, sounding almost hopeful. "Maybe it happened again?"

I bark out a bitter laugh. "I think if a kidnapping is our best-case scenario, we know where we stand."

Pushing to my feet, I grab my purse and march toward the door. Before I can leave, I'm caught by Helen and Nina, who have rushed after me. "We'll come with you," Nina suggests.

It's a nice gesture. On some level, I can recognize that. But I'm too hurt, and too embarrassed, to want anyone's pity. "No. I want to be alone."

That's how I've survived so far, isn't it?

Late that night, I have a missed call from Kimo, and a voicemail. I listen to it with a roiling stomach.

"I'm so sorry, Mattie. Something came up at the last minute. Please believe me when I say it couldn't wait. I want to explain everything, please. Call me."

I won't, though. It's not that I don't believe him, precisely. Maybe he has a good excuse, maybe he doesn't. It doesn't really matter anymore. Tonight was a cold dose of reality. I've done this before—put my trust in people, hoped that this time things would be different, that they could be different. But the moment you put your happiness in someone else's hands is the moment you set yourself up for crushing disappointment. It's a rerun even more familiar to me than all those episodes of *Full House*.

And the story always turns out the same. Always.

Chapter Thirty-One

I ignore Kimo's calls and texts all weekend. I make myself scarce at my apartment in case he drops by, and I go to a different gym location to work out so we don't bump into each other at the other one.

So far as I'm concerned, it's all over. I tried it out, and it didn't work. I'll learn from my mistakes, just like I always do. There are people you can't cut out of your lives no matter how many times they let you down, like your sisters, but random flip-flopped men you meet in men's locker rooms and happen to get kidnapped with? Nope. Those kinds of people get exactly one chance, and he's used his up.

That's the policy I've had to live by. I've been adrift at sea my entire life, clinging to my life raft, and if I let go, that's it. I'm lost. There's no way I can keep treading water without it.

And yes, this specific metaphor terrifies me, but that's the point. I need to be scared. I got too complacent. I let down my guard.

Never again.

Of course, that might end up making things awkward at work for as long as we still have Kimo's case, but only if *he* makes it a problem. I'm a professional. And I'm a stone-cold bitch. I can handle it.

The moment I see Kimo through the window in Jay's office on Monday morning, I immediately second-guess myself. My heart starts pounding.

My palms become slick with sweat. For a moment, it feels like I've forgotten how to walk, and I stumble a bit before correcting myself.

You're fine, I snap at myself, irritated at that show of weakness. *Pull yourself together, Matilda Polina Markov!*

Despite this, I can't keep my eyes from darting back to Kimo. He's seen me now, and our eyes lock together for a moment. He says something quickly to Jay, and I know he's making his excuses so he can come out and talk to me. I hurry to my desk, determined to be desperately busy by the time he finds me.

Even technology is against me today, though. When I make it to my computer, I see that a software update has just started with approximately twelve minutes left. "*черт побери!*" I mutter under my breath.

"Mattie?"

At the sound of Kimo's voice, my entire body reacts. It's like it's forgotten that I need to be impervious to him because I can no longer trust him. My heart stutters, my mouth runs dry, and I pivot toward him without meaning to.

Our eyes meet. Kimo's hazel eyes are teddy-bear soft. It looks like he might have dressed up to come see me. He's still wearing those stupid flip-flops, but he's in nice dress slacks and a button-up shirt. That might have meant something to me, if I hadn't turned off all emotions toward him completely.

"Can we talk?" he asks quietly.

I look pointedly back toward Jay's office. "Don't you have a meeting?"

"I just had something to sign." He leans in toward me, lowering his voice even further. "It could have waited, but I wanted to see you."

"Well, I'm busy," I snap, almost before he's had a chance to finish.

Kimo looks pointedly at the update timer on my computer screen, which still clearly shows the desktop is completely useless at the moment. I ignore it, and him, sitting down in my chair and pretending to rifle through one of my drawers for something *very* important that has to be found right this moment.

"Mattie, please. Just give me five minutes. We can grab a quick cup of coffee, I'll explain everything—"

"Barry!" I call loudly through the thin partition separating our cubicles. "Mr. Kapono wants coffee. Can you show him to the break room?" I lock eyes with Kimo, unflinching. "I'm busy."

Barry's head pops over the partition. He's so quick that it's obvious he was listening in. "Sure thing. Right this way, Mr. Kapono . . ."

An obviously reluctant Kimo lets Barry lead him back toward the break room, and I don't check to see if he looks back at me, no matter how much I'm tempted to do so. Because that would be weak.

Fortunately, my computer is functioning again by the time they return, and I really am busy answering emails. As I sense someone approaching, I tense and look up. To my surprise, it's Barry, not Kimo.

Barry looks . . . weird. It takes me a minute to place what's happened. His forehead is wrinkled with concern, and his face has gone all soft and furrowed, like he's just gotten out of seeing a really sappy Christmas movie and he feels moved by the spirit of kindness. It's such a specific look that I know instantly what's happened.

He's been Kimo'd.

"Hey. So, I was just talking to Kimo."

I roll my eyes. "I'll bet you were."

Barry either doesn't get my sarcasm, or he just chooses to ignore it. "He's awfully sorry about what happened. But there's a good explanation for it. For the record, I can confirm that Jay called him in, and he was here at the building—"

I glance behind me to see Kimo standing a few cubicles back, obviously listening in. When he sees me looking, he ducks behind a partition.

"Oh, for God's sake!" I rise to my feet, folding my arms to show just how unamused I am by this whole spectacle. What is this, seventh grade? Sending his buddy in to see if I still like him? What's next—a note where I'm supposed to circle yes or no to the school dance? This is my place of work—and more to the point, this is my *heart*. Not some juvenile game.

I direct my words toward where Kimo is hiding. "It's water under the bridge. It's fine." It's not fine, obviously, but I don't want him to *know* how not fine it is for me. "No hard feelings. We can all be great work colleagues now, and nothing else, and that's *fine*."

I march down toward Jay's office, fully aware that Kimo is following me. "Mattie, wait. Just talk to me—"

Rapping sharply on Jay's door, I let myself in at his call. He's sitting at his desk, typing at his computer with an intense, furrowed brow, but his face smooths out into a smile when he sees me. "Matilda, good morning. Can I help you with something?"

"The gala's this weekend, right?" Jay doesn't know that Kimo's standing just a few feet away, listening to this conversation, but I do, and I play this moment for all it's worth. "I wanted to ask you about the dress code. I've bought a new dress, but I'm worried it's too provocative."

I haven't bought any such dress, but I will as soon as I'm off work. Even if I have to splurge and put it on one of my credit cards—what do I care? I don't have student loan payments anymore.

Jay straightens up, clearing his throat. "Just how provocative are we talking?"

He's pitched his voice low, but I'm hoping his voice will still carry out to Kimo. I answer him with a flirtatious smile, leaning up against the door. "Well, the thigh slit cuts up to here . . ." I slowly drag a finger up my leg, stopping only when I see Jay's eyebrow start to rise. "And it's very low-cut. I don't think I'll be able to wear a bra with it." I widen my eyes a bit, affecting an innocent look, which is negated by the smile tugging at my lips. "I might not even be able to wear panties with it, come to think of it."

This is a super risky game. If I was wrong about Jay's interest in me, or he thinks I've crossed a line, I could actually lose my job. Two weeks ago, that would have been my top concern. Now I'm surprised to find that I don't give a flying fuck. My heart is on the warpath, and apparently I'm adopting a scorched-earth policy.

Jay clears his throat. "I think that sounds . . . just fine." He shifts in his seat, holding my gaze. "You'll find we have a much more lenient policy at our gala than during normal work hours. Anything goes."

Two weeks ago, I would have been thrilled by Jay's response. Now all I really care about is whether Kimo heard our exchange or not.

"I'm looking forward to it," I tell him before pushing away from the door.

As I walk back to my cubicle, I look for Kimo but feel my heart stutter a little bit when I see he's already gone.

Chapter Thirty-Two

After work, I scour every store that won't completely bankrupt me and pick out three dresses that vaguely resemble what I described to Jay, even though there isn't one that's totally right—and only after being reassured by the salespeople at each store, more than once, that they will honor the return policy as long as the dress hasn't been worn and I have a copy of the receipt. (This might be my dramatic meltdown, but there's still no way I'm paying for three dresses at full price!)

I need that moment, the one that's in every cheesy movie, the scene I always mercilessly mock but deep down, in my secret heart of hearts, I want for myself: I need to walk in the room and have everyone stop and stare at me. Not because I've fallen down the stairs or said something awkward, but because I look irresistible.

And if one particular person happens to see it when that happens, that would be . . . tolerable.

I only need one dress to make it happen, but which dress? None of them feels exactly right. So I send out an SOS to Helen and Nina, calling in a best friend emergency, code red, this is not a drill.

Whatever else Nina and Helen might have had going on on a random Monday night, they drop it to meet me at home. I realize I've been calling on them to do that an awful lot lately—what with being kidnapped, then stood up, and now this—and they keep showing up. I've spent so long expecting people to let me down that maybe I haven't been so good at recognizing when people don't. Maybe men have proven themselves to be as untrustworthy as I always believed, but my friends? They have my back. I see that now. They've taken Kimo standing me up as personally as I would have if it had happened to one of them, and for that, I truly love them.

I might not show it, though, in the way I immediately start barking out orders once they arrive. "Which dress?" I demand in a tone I know is too harsh for the occasion, despite my best attempts to modulate it. "I need to be drop-dead gorgeous. I need his heart to shrivel up like a raisin when he sees me."

"Got it," Helen says, nodding briskly. "Try them each on."

So I do. I like the shade of the first one—a midnight blue that makes my eye color pop—but the cut is too tasteful. I look like I'm going to the opera or . . . well, a gala, but not the kind of gala where I may or may not be wearing underwear.

The second option is flame red, and I have the perfect shade of lipstick to pair with it, but the silhouette doesn't show off my assets the way I want it to—it's low-cut and high-slitted, but the fabric hangs too loose, so it's just giving a subtle peek, and I don't want subtle. I want va-va-voom.

The last dress is hot pink and is basically a glorified tube sock, so my assets are fully on display, but I'm afraid I've veered from sexy Barbie into cheap dollar-store knockoff doll.

"You look great in all of them," Helen reassures me. "Kimo—" She stops at the look I give her, immediately correcting, "He Who Shall Not Be Named will lose his mind at the sight of you in any of them."

I shake my head, frustrated. "That isn't enough, though. I need to be a showstopper. I need to be . . . Julia Roberts in the red dress in *Pretty Woman*, but sluttier."

Nina, who has been quietly and thoughtfully observing me in each dress, finally speaks up: "I can do that."

Helen and I exchange a surprised glance. Luckily, Nina is too busy examining the fabric of the dresses to notice. No offense to Nina, but the word *sexy* is not exactly what comes to mind when I look at her. She's a petite fairy angel, who is delicately and devastatingly beautiful, but I've seen nuns who show off more skin. Literally.

"I'm talking sex bomb," I explain to her. "I want to show off lots of skin—like more than just my clavicle."

Nina looks up from the red dress and fixes me with a surprisingly steely gaze. "I can do that," she repeats firmly, nodding a little at her own proclamation. I'm not sure if it's to drive home the point to me or herself. "I'll need to work on it here, though. My uncle won't let me take this out of the house if he catches me with it."

Helen and I exchange another glance. This isn't the first time Nina's said something about her uncle that's set off alarms, and Helen and I have had lots of discussions about when and if we should say something about it. Well, mostly Helen has discussed while I've raged about what a controlling creep he is, but for now I've agreed to hold the peace unless Nina tells us something too distressing for me to keep it to myself—

"Stop making faces over my head," Nina tells us calmly, still examining the fabric. After a moment, she holds up the midnight-blue dress. "This one, I think. The silhouette will be the easiest to fix, and the color looks amazing on you."

Nina makes me put the dress back on so she can measure and pin it how she likes. I'm beyond grateful for everything she's doing, but I know we only have a few days until the gala, and I'm still a little worried that Nina doesn't fully understand the "knock his socks off" memo. "You know I mean Hollywood sexy and not Utah sexy," I pester her.

"I know," Nina reassures me. "It's going to be perfect. Trust me."

The next night after work, Thad helps Nina bring over her sewing machine, and after that, she's busily working away whenever she can. I even give her a spare key so she can come and go on her own schedule. Hour after hour, Nina toils away, confidently cutting and pinning and sewing. She's made me swear, on pain of death, not to touch the dress when she isn't there, and she so rarely gets so stern with me that I have no choice but to comply.

Luckily work keeps me busy enough that I'm not spending every waking moment thinking about the gala, or . . . *him*—only, like, sixty-two percent of my waking moments—and time passes quickly. Saturday morning, I wake up to find that Nina has let herself in early and is putting the finishing touches on the dress.

Even though it's early, we call Helen over to see me try it on, because she also made me swear on pain of death to let her be there when the dress makes its debut. Still in her pajamas, Helen arrives with coffee, and sits next to Nina, handing her one of the cups, though she slaps away my hand when I try to take one too. "Not until we see the dress," she orders.

I know the second I put the dress on that all my worrying has been for nothing.

When I walk out, Helen gasps theatrically and Nina sighs, her body sagging into the couch as she nods to herself.

Nina has reshaped the midnight-blue fabric so the silhouette is very similar to the red *Pretty Woman* dress, with the same off-the-shoulder sleeves and scooping sweetheart neckline. *This* neckline scoops even the tiniest bit lower and drapes in such a way that it looks like it could slip off at any moment, though it's actually tightly fastened to my bodice and fully supporting the girls. The material hugs my torso and hips, but flares out with a full skirt sweeping to the floor—that part looks a lot like the original dress, but with a daring cut on both sides, almost all the way up to my hips. You can't really see it when I'm standing still, but when I'm walking, those cuts will titillatingly showcase my legs—my number one asset, or so I've been told.

"It's perfect," I say.

"It's perfect," they agree.

Forget a revenge dress. This is a war dress, and I'm out to take no prisoners tonight.

Chapter Thirty-Three

The Over the Rainbow Gala is just as beautiful as I'd always imagined it would be. True to its name, everything, from the lighting to the flowers and table settings, is tastefully decorated in various colors of the rainbow. The ballroom is spacious, with a grand staircase descending from the lobby to the main floor. Mirrors line the walls at the top of the room, reflecting the light and colors and movement from the ballroom in a way that feels truly magical.

I'm a pretty confident person, overall. I'd probably rate pretty high on a scale of self-esteem, especially when it comes to my looks. My genetics have graced me with a slim, athletic build, and I eat well and exercise regularly to maintain it. I've never had to wallow in much doubt over whether someone finds me attractive; I usually assume they do, until proven otherwise.

So I'm not questioning whether or not I look good in the dress, because I know I do—that isn't why I'm nervous as I'm let into the gala and ushered toward the grand staircase.

I'm nervous because, as I pause at the top of the stairs, I belatedly realize I'm finally having my movie moment. Okay, so not everyone in the room stops to stare at me, but I see lots of faces craning up. Naturally. After Nina's careful ministrations, the dress is a knockout, and I look fantastic in it.

But scanning quickly through all the faces in the room, I realize with a sinking heart that it was never about seeing everyone in the room fall silent and turn to look at me. There's really only one face I want to see looking up at me, only one person whose opinion I care about, and he isn't here.

"Matilda." Jay breaks away from whoever he was just speaking with—wait, was that Nico Moretti??—and comes over to join me as I reach the bottom of the stairs. I watch him do a full body scan, see how his eyes linger briefly in a few key places, and I feel . . . nothing.

On paper, Jay is my perfect man: handsome, clean-cut, well-educated, cultured, successful, ambitious, and financially secure. I would never have to feel unsafe with Jay—I know, from having read the tabloids, that even when things don't work out with his romantic partners, he has a reputation for being a perfect gentleman. And if things did work out, I'd be set up for life. I would never have to struggle or worry or work again.

But I would never have to be vulnerable, either, and for the first time in my life, this feels like a lack. I would never stay up late watching *Full House* episodes with Jay Eastman, or fall asleep on the couch with him because we stayed up too late talking. He would never fix my shower for me because he noticed it was leaking, or send me silly selfies throughout the day, just to make me laugh.

He's perfect on paper in every way. Except, he isn't Kimo.

Jay is good at reading people, so it probably shouldn't come as a surprise that he seems to immediately clock that something has changed tonight from my flirtation earlier in the week. To his credit, he shifts gears right away, standing a respectful distance away and giving me a nod in greeting, like he might to any colleague. "You look lovely tonight," he tells me kindly.

"Thank you." I hope my voice doesn't sound as miserable as I feel. It was a mistake, all of it—coming here tonight, flirting with Jay, and doing it in front of Kimo. He probably wrote me off after that, and he was probably right to do so. I really ought to have learned my lesson by now—most people come and go in your life, and it's all too easy to push them away.

I force a smile at Jay. "It's a great turnout. I'm sure you'll raise all the money you were hoping to."

"We already have," Jay informs me. "Kimo wrote me a check the first day I told him about the gala and matched the amount we were hoping to raise. But I figured, everything was already paid for, the space was already reserved, and maybe people would be moved by Kimo's show of generosity to give more."

This new information makes my lungs feel like they're full of lead, each breath painful and difficult—and not just because of the tightly fitted bodice I'm wearing. That's so like Kimo. He won't be happy until he's given all his money away. Kimo Hood, indeed. I blink, struggling to compose myself. "That's . . . wonderful. I just realized, I don't even know what the charity is?"

"The Adoption Center of Illinois."

Unexpectedly, tears flood my eyes. I blink and nod, doing my best to hold them in. "That's really nice," I manage finally.

"Kimo's very generous," Jay agrees. "And we're lucky the donation's already gone through, what with"—he gives me a meaningful look—"the new development."

I frown at him, not liking how ominous that just sounded. "What new development?" I've been happily foisting anything to do with Kimo's case off to Barry this week, just to avoid seeing his name. I knew something major happened with it last weekend, when Kimo ditched book club, but like the self-denying, immovable bitch that I can sometimes be, I wouldn't even let myself get anywhere near it. I didn't want to know if there was a good explanation for Kimo not showing up that night, because—I realize now—I was more interested in punishing him, and me, too, for allowing myself to be so vulnerable.

Jay looks surprised by my ignorance. "The settlement offer from Pika. Where he'll grant all custody rights to Kimo if he signs over all of his remaining assets from the So Ono stocks."

I feel as though I've just taken a spinning kick to the solar plexus. I grip Jay's arm, unable to catch my breath. "He's not going to do it, is he?"

Jay's brow furrows. My reaction is, obviously, much stronger than what it should be for someone who's just a paralegal on the case—and whose relationship with Kimo is actually as minimal as I've tried to make it out to be. He searches my gaze for a moment, before blinking back into his professional persona. "You know I can't discuss that without my client."

He doesn't have to, though. That's lawyer speak for *yes*. Still gripping his arm tightly, I cast my eyes wildly about the room, trying to speed-brainstorm a solution, some way to keep Kimo from signing everything away—when my gaze catches at the top of the stairs.

Kimo has just arrived. If I thought my entrance caused a commotion, it's nothing to a six-four, broad-framed Polynesian man in a maroon-and-black velvet tux. His wild hair has been tamed back into a more respectable bun, his facial hair trimmed, and he's even wearing loafers instead of flip-flops.

He looks incredible—out of his element, and endearingly not entirely comfortable, but still incredible. I watch as he pauses at the top of the stairs, his eyes searching the crowd for someone. For me, I realize, as our gazes lock together.

He holds eye contact with me his entire walk down the grand staircase, and I can't breathe the entire time. It isn't until he reaches us that Kimo finally glances away, nodding to Jay. "Jay. Good to see you, brother."

Jay says something pleasant back, but I don't really hear it. My heartbeat is roaring in my ears. I'm the one who can't look away from Kimo now, my eyes shamelessly glued to his face.

I see him glance down at my hand, and it's only then that I realize I'm still gripping Jay's arm, out of the shock from hearing about the settlement. I release Jay none too gently, half flinging his arm away from me, not wanting there to be any confusion about what is—or isn't—happening between us.

"Ow," Jay mutters under his breath.

Then Kimo's eyes lock with mine again, and I'm not aware of anything, or anyone, else in the room. There could be a fire, or an avalanche, or a spontaneous group performance of the Macarena, and I'm pretty sure it wouldn't register with me at all.

"I know it's rude to interrupt," Kimo says finally, "but can I have this dance?"

I want to tell him he can have so much more than that—he can have everything if he wants it. That I understand now why he had to miss book club—that the settlement offer must have come in and that it needed to be discussed right away, that his niece and nephew are children and he's their guardian and they always will have to come first, and I'm not only fine with that, but I admire that about him, maybe even more than any of his other amazing qualities. That I made a mistake taunting him by flirting with Jay, that I was being immature and spiteful and trying to protect myself, like I've always had to. But none of that matters right now so much as me needing to keep him from making an even bigger mistake by signing everything away to Pika.

"Yes," is what I say instead.

Then Kimo wraps his warm hand around mine and pulls me to the dance floor.

Chapter Thirty-Four

Once we step onto the dance floor with the other couples, Kimo pulls me in close, one hand gripping mine, the other touching the bare skin of my back where the bodice of the dress scoops low. I guess I should say that I assume other couples are out there dancing —I'm only aware of Kimo and myself, so close that our chests are brushing, his eyes locked on mine so all I can see is *him*, and all I can hear is my own heart pounding in my ears.

"You look unreal in that dress," he tells me finally, after a long, protracted moment of us just gazing into one another's eyes.

I don't know how he's had time to notice my dress, frankly, since it feels like he hasn't taken his eyes off mine, but I gulp anyway. "You look pretty fantastic, yourself."

"Thank you." After a moment, and a long, slow swallow, Kimo clears his throat. "I have something I need to say to you."

I blink in surprise, then nod. I'm grateful, honestly, for a reprieve from my own tangled thoughts and my inability to articulate them out loud. "Go for it. Please."

Another beat passes, and then Kimo sighs through his nose, shaking his head a little. "I'm super pissed off at you."

That was so not what I expected him to say right now. It throws me off, and I stumble a little over my too-high, too-pointy heels. Kimo holds on to me, keeping me upright until I can find my balance again. "I got you," he murmurs quietly.

It would be a sweet moment, if I weren't so irritated at him now. "You're pissed at *me*?" I repeat, feeling my outrage mount with each word.

Kimo makes a low sound, shushing me. "I'm not finished yet. Let me say my piece and then you can have your turn."

Frankly, I'm too flabbergasted to object, so I just clamp my mouth shut, glaring as I dare him to continue.

"I'm mad at you for throwing this away over a simple misunderstanding. I had a good reason for missing book club, if you'd just hear me out."

"I know all about that now," I blurt out, unable to help myself. I don't want to have to stand here and listen to his—very legitimate—excuse for not attending a weekly get-together with my friends that he could easily join another time. I already know I made a mistake.

He raises an eyebrow at me, searching my face for a moment, then continues. "I know I should have gotten in contact sooner, and that one's on me. I take responsibility for that. But Makoa and Nalani are my children now. If you can't understand that sometimes I'll need to put them first—"

"I understand that," I interrupt him again, swallowing hard. "And I'm not angry with you for that. I agree with you. Your children should come first."

God knows I wish my own mother had felt that way. That's the kind of love a parent should have for their children. It's the kind of love I'd hope to have, if I ever . . .

I shake the thought quickly from my mind and see Kimo frowning in confusion. "Then why were you mad at me?"

Floundering, I search for the reason, only to find there isn't one anymore, not really. Maybe there never was one. Maybe it was never about being upset with him, but more about protecting myself. It's been so long since I could trust anyone else to do that for me. I don't quite know how to let go of the reins.

"I don't know," I say helplessly, but it's too uncomfortable sitting in that vulnerable position, so I switch tack quickly. "But I *am* upset at you now, for a different reason."

The look Kimo gives me can best be described as exasperated. "What," he says, not asks, his voice flat.

I barrel on anyway, refusing to back down. It seems very important, somehow, not to concede any ground on this. "You say you want to put your kids first—so then why are you handing over all of your assets to Pika?"

Kimo sighs, releasing his hold on me long enough to rub the bridge of his nose. "It isn't that simple—"

"It is that simple!" I insist. "You can't give that asshole what he wants. It isn't right. It isn't fair!"

"What do I care about fair?" Kimo shrugs his broad shoulders. "This way I don't have to drag the kids through a custody case. We get Pika out of our lives for good. And it's just money. I'll make more, or I won't. I'll be a caddy again, or a handyman, or whatever it takes to keep us afloat."

"And what about when the kids want to go to university?" I challenge him. "Or your mom needs medical expenses covered? Or your house needs a new roof? It won't be 'just money' then."

Kimo shakes his head. "Why are you so hung up on the money— because you want some kind of rich, fancy kahu who'll buy you nice things and take you nice places?"

It feels like I've been slapped in the face, hard.

"Isn't that why you went after Jay the second you dropped me?" Kimo challenges, doubling down. "Or is it true love with the guy who barely knew your name a couple weeks ago?"

Up to this point, I'll admit freely, some of my anger has been performative. I've been wrong-footed, and I don't like that feeling, so I tried to find ways to make Kimo the bad guy in all this. I really don't want him to give his money to Pika, but that could have been a civilized conversation, if I were a less volatile person.

Right now, though? This feeling? Is not performative anger. I'm furious. Blindly, seething-with-rage furious. I draw myself up to my full height, and thanks to the heels I'm wearing, I'm not too far off from Kimo's towering size.

"Listen to me, *Засранец*," I bite out at him. "I never once asked you for your money. I'm just fine with my life of working and watching DVDs and going to book club with my friends. I don't need anyone—not you or Jay Eastman or anyone else—to pay my way."

I take a moment, letting that sink in, before I continue. "You can tell yourself whatever you want about my advice, but I'm not wrong. You think it'll be hard for the kids to go through a custody case? What happens when they find out their birth father sold them for their inheritance? And I'm sure you don't mind hard work, but I promise you, it's different when you have other people you're taking care of and not just yourself. You have to work that much harder, and sacrifice that much more, and still try to be everything else they need you to be." I swallow, thinking of Sasha and Alina. "And you'll more than likely fail. Despite all your best efforts."

Kimo stares at me like he wants to hold on to his anger yet can't help but hear the truth in my voice. "People do it all the time. There are lots of single parents with low-income jobs who survive just fine."

"Yeah, they do," I agree. "But sometimes that's all they can do—survive. Don't you want more for your children? Don't you want more for yourself?"

I can tell I've thrown Kimo for a loop, and despite my other faults, I've always known when it's time to make an exit. "It's your choice. It really has nothing to do with me anymore, does it?"

And with that, I make a beeline for the stairs.

Chapter Thirty-Five

I don't know where I'm going, really, except that I have to get away from Kimo. If that's what he really thinks of me—that I'm just some gold digger after his money—then there really isn't anything more to say.

. . . Although, if I'm being honest with myself, I suspect that was just something he said out of anger. I suppose I can't really fault people for the things they say when they're upset. God knows I've never been one to hold my tongue when I feel like I'm backed into a corner.

I aimlessly push my way through the building, trying to give myself some space to think. I don't want this to be the end with Kimo. But I also don't know how to dig myself out of this hole with him. I don't know how to stop defending myself, how to be vulnerable with someone and just say, *I'm sorry. I was wrong.*

Somehow I find my way to the empty third floor of the building. There are only darkened offices up here, and though I can hear faint traces of music floating up from the gala below, it is otherwise mostly silent. I walk to one of the windows and realize that I'm looking down into the ballroom. What looked like mirrors from downstairs are actually one-way windows, allowing me to covertly see what's happening in the ballroom. Like a masochist, I search for Kimo in the crowd, only to find that he's conspicuously missing. He must have gone home.

"Mattie."

Startled, I jump and whirl around to see that Kimo followed me upstairs. He holds up his hands as if in surrender, gauging my face carefully before venturing forward. "I'm sorry," he says. "That was really out of line, what I said about the money. There's no part of me that thinks that's really true."

Even though I suspected as much, I'm relieved to hear him say it. I nod in acknowledgement. "Thank you."

He sighs, running a hand through his hair, which is no longer so neatly pulled back. I like it better this way, I think—rumpled and a little bit wild, just like him. "I just want it to be done, you know? I wake up sick every morning thinking about what happens if those kids get taken away from me. Pika offered me this out, and . . . I'm scared of what happens if I don't just take it."

I'm the one to venture a step closer to him now, responding to the fear and vulnerability I hear in his voice. I can't help it. Even if things are over between us, even if he doesn't want to be with me anymore, I'll never be able to hear Kimo sound afraid and not do everything I can to try to fix it. "I understand. But I'll help you. The whole team will. And you have Jay. He's the best out there, he really is."

Kimo's face shutters at that. He gives me a wry, searching look. "Yeah, Jay's great," he says flatly. "He'll probably be wondering where you've run off to."

Something swells in me as I recognize Kimo's obvious jealousy. A very small, very petty part of me wants to egg him on a bit, see just how jealous he can be, but I decide to take the high road. Be honest. "There's nothing going on with Jay. He knows that, too. I just said all of that stuff to make you jealous."

I hold Kimo's gaze, watching for his response. He takes another step closer to me, deliberately eying me up and down. "So all of that talk about you not wearing any underwear . . . was just for show?"

Well, full honesty, right? "Actually, I'm really not wearing any underwear," I admit. "But that was never for Jay. It was partially because you really can't wear anything under this dress. But mainly, it was for you."

Kimo lets out a little growly noise, taking another step forward and closing the distance between us. My whole body lights up with anticipation. I understand, suddenly, why all the heroines in Helen's romance novels always have heaving bosoms: it's partially because of the restrictive bodices, true, but it's also nervousness, excitement—the feeling like you've just run up ten flights of stairs even though you're standing completely still. Just waiting for him to touch me.

Kimo holds that intense eye contact for a moment longer before deliberately sliding his gaze down my neckline, to the top of my bodice, where my heaving bosom—modest as it is—is on the verge of spilling over. He hooks his index finger into the front of the bodice, his knuckle grazing over the swell of my breast, making my breath catch in my throat, before he pulls the front of my dress forward as far as it will go and peers down at the gap left between the fabric and my skin. "No bra," he confirms, his voice low and growly.

His other hand starts a slow path up my thigh, disappearing underneath the slit in the skirt. The pads of his fingers brush over my core. "No panties."

I moan and buck against him, needing more, *now*. "Kimo . . ."

To my dismay, he removes both his hands from me, pressing them up against the windowpane and pushing against it hard.

It's my turn to growl, in dismay. "*ублюдок*. If you trick me into just falling asleep with you again tonight, so help me God . . ."

Kimo just keeps pushing up against the glass, even making a fist and pounding it. "Trust me, baby, sleeping is the last thing on my mind right now. But I need to test the structural integrity of this window."

This man is trying to kill me. "Now? *Why?*"

Finally, seeming satisfied, he gives the glass one last rap with his knuckles. "To make sure we can do this." And with no warning, he picks me up by my thighs and lifts me, my back pressed to the glass.

I gasp, first in surprise, then pleasure, as Kimo leans in to kiss me. I'm half propped up on a small ledge built into the window frame, so for once I'm just a little bit taller than him, though his bigness still engulfs me as he presses his body up against mine. I feel him hard and erect through his suit pants, rubbing slowly but eagerly against my bare thigh as his tongue explores my mouth.

After a moment, he pulls back, resting his forehead against mine. "I hope this isn't too presumptuous, since we were just in a fight and all, but for the record, I did bring condoms with me."

I laugh breathlessly, nuzzling my nose against his. "That's okay. So did I."

He pulls back enough that he can look into my eyes, and his expression is so genuinely perplexed that I giggle—a sound that, frankly, I didn't know I could make, it's so girly and sweet. "Where?" he demands.

I'd asked Nina to sew a little pocket into the front of my bodice to hold some cash and a condom. I didn't tell *her* that's what it was for, of course, since I wouldn't want to accidentally give her an aneurism; but given my past luck with Kimo, I never want to leave home without protection again.

I don't explain all that to him, though—where would be the fun? "Come and find it," I challenge him.

Kimo grunt-growls again and then kisses me until my head is spinning. Still using one hand to help keep me propped on the little ledge, he touches my gown's low-cut back with the other. "How attached are you to this dress?"

For my own sake? Not all that much. But considering how long Nina worked on it, I'd feel bad letting him tear it to shreds, no matter how much I might want him to. Plus, there's the whole issue of how to get home without any clothing. "Very," I warn him.

He sighs and leans his forehead against mine for a moment before regrouping. "Okay . . ." He fumbles around the back of the dress. "Is there a zipper?"

I can't help but giggle again, he sounds so genuinely frustrated, not at all like my usually easygoing Kimo. "Yes, it's hidden underneath some ruching, and there's a clasp at the top . . ."

I reach back to help him, and between the two of us, we manage to find the hidden clasp. If I didn't already know how comfortable and safe I feel with Kimo, it would have been glaringly obvious in this exchange. A one-night stand fumbling around to get my clothes off would have been a huge turn-off; with Kimo, it feels unbearably endearing, not to mention hilarious.

Although, not quite so hilarious anymore as he eases the dress off me, gently letting it drop to the floor. I'm in nothing but my heels and a good faux-pearl necklace, my bare ass pressed up against a window overlooking a ballroom filled with people, including my boss, nothing but Kimo holding me up.

"Fuck, Mattie," he breathes, taking me in. "You're so beautiful, I can't stand it."

I pull him closer, needing to feel him up against me, needing his mouth on mine. There is nothing slow about this kiss, only eager. Every brush of his hand on my skin feels perfect, just right, but also somehow not enough, because it immediately leaves me wanting more, more—an unquenchable thirst that feels like it will never be satiated.

When his free hand moves to my pussy again, I moan in protest and shake my head. "No, not that." I'll never be able to come pressed up against a window, so there's no point wasting his time. "I want you inside me, now." That much is true, at least. I'm desperate for his cock, desperate to feel him inside me.

Kimo tsks me, keeping his hand in place. "What did I tell you, huh? You can be the boss everywhere but here, babe." He sweeps a daring thumb over my labia, eliciting a shocked gasp from me. "I'm the boss here, yeah?"

He must take my moan as confirmation because his fingers slide their way down to my clit. They circle and rub and thrum there, all while Kimo watches my face intently to follow my response.

I close my eyes and let my head fall back against the glass. I'm not going to come. I know I'm not, so I won't stress about it, I'll just enjoy the feeling for what it is, and in a few minutes he'll move on . . .

And it does feel good. It's a feeling I know won't go anywhere further from just touching alone, but my core feels pleasantly aware, then after a few moments, throbbing with need.

When I feel Kimo's body shift a moment later, I think he's already giving up, and I eagerly await the next part, when he'll thrust his cock into me. Instead, I'm surprised when I feel Kimo maneuvering himself so he can simultaneously prop me up and dip his fingers in and out of me, still lightly circling my clit with his thumb.

My startled gaze meets his. I watch his lips tug into a smirk, then look back into his eyes.

It isn't even just the mechanics of what he's doing, even though it is impressive. (How is he multitasking so efficiently?) It's the look in his hazel eyes as he's watching me, like this part isn't the appetizer—it's the meal. Like he's in no hurry whatsoever, just content to do this for as long as it takes—

The orgasm crashes over me, taking me unawares. One minute I'm in the middle of a coherent thought, and the next my thighs are clenching and that sharp, intense euphoria shudders through me. I come loudly, too caught off guard to censor myself, my gaze still locked on his.

I shudder once, then again. That was . . . that was . . .

"Incredible," Kimo murmurs, leaning forward to kiss me softly. He removes his fingers from inside me but they continue to ever so lightly dance over my center. The sensation down there is still so strong that any more pressure might hurt, but what he's doing is just enough to stretch out the pleasure for as long as it can last.

He kisses me, slowly, savoring. His warm, lightly callused hands begin to smooth over my bare skin, starting with the not-as-intimate bits—legs, belly, back, arms, neck. Any lingering tension in my body melts away as I melt into him. I run my fingers along his scalp, and his responding growl sends heat pulsing through my center. It's weirdly hot being naked while he's still fully dressed, the soft material of his suit pressing against my skin, but all at once I need to touch him, explore him, need him to be as close to me as possible.

"Take off your clothes," I entreat him, surprising myself with how breathy and needful I sound.

Kimo happily complies, setting me on my feet. Still feeling a bit shaky after the unexpected orgasm, I lean back up against the glass, closing my eyes again. I hear the rustle of Kimo's clothing, the tear of the condom wrapper. That gets my attention, and when I open my eyes, I see the glorious length of him, sheathed and ready.

I'm ready, too, wanting—needing—to see him as undone as I feel. But I guess I shouldn't be surprised when he lifts me up and kisses me again, holding me at just the right position so that he's nudging at my entrance but not sliding in quite yet.

"Kimo, please." I'm not above shamelessly begging him, or even more shamelessly rubbing my pussy against him. "Please. I need you."

Another low, throaty growl. I never thought I'd be so into this whole caveman/werewolf thing, but it's driving me absolutely wild. "You need me, baby?" he asks, reaching a hand up to cup one of my breasts, rolling my nipple between his fingers.

My answering moan seems to be a satisfying enough answer. He enters me slowly, for the first time, gently easing his way in until he fills me up.

Our eyes meet, hold. I'm used to barely making eye contact with my partners, both of us almost pretending the other person isn't there. Kimo doesn't look away, and his expression won't let me look away, either. He's usually so happy-go-lucky, so affable, but right now his face is dark and intense and hungry. He looks and sounds and smells like pure sex—his glistening, naked body and his low grunts of pleasure and the scent of sweat mingling with his cologne. I move my body in the rhythm he's set, seeking my own pleasure, but also wanting to increase his. I want to blow his mind. I don't want him to ever come again without thinking about me.

Pressing my breasts into his chest, I lean in for a kiss, taking his lower lip between my teeth and giving it a none-too-gentle tug. When I meet his feral gaze again, I deliberately squeeze my core around his cock, rocking my pelvis up and down, up and down.

"Fuck." There's nothing slow or gentle now about the way Kimo's moving. He thrusts into me fast and hard, knocking me back into the window. His hands grip my ass, guiding me in tandem with his movements as he fills me up completely, again and again. I'm an athletic girl, but my strength is nothing compared to his. All I can do is cling on for dear life as he rides me hard, a force of nature. The glass is cold and hard against me, but I'm hardly aware of it. The only sensation I can feel is the heat pooling once again between my thighs, the impossible pleasure.

"Oh, fuck," I cry out in surprise half a second before I come for a second time, tightening and squeezing around him again and again.

That seems to be all it takes for Kimo before he gives a final jerk and then implodes inside of me. It's my turn to support him as he half collapses against me, still on his feet but momentarily incoherent with pleasure.

It takes a moment for us both to catch our breaths. When he comes back to himself, his mouth seeks out mine—slow and sweet, a promise.

"Whoa," he says under his breath, letting out a shaky laugh of surprise.

"Whoa," I agree, reaching up to cradle his head against me.

Chapter Thirty-Six

After we're clean and dressed again, but still enjoying our privacy together on the empty third floor, I keep catching Kimo looking at me. He's not checking out my ass, or staring at my boobs. He's looking at my face, and he's got a goofy grin stuck to his.

"What?" I ask defensively, reaching up to rub away any wayward lipstick or smudged mascara. I checked myself over in the bathroom, but fluorescent lighting is nobody's friend. "Is there something on my face?" At his widening grin, I narrow my eyes at him. "If you don't tell me, I'm going to curse you with an ancient Russian curse."

I don't know any ancient Russian curses, for the record. I left the country when I was eight and haven't been back, thank God. But Kimo doesn't need to know that, and I've always found it to be an especially effective threat.

Kimo surprises me by taking my face in his hands, and that roving thumb of his strokes softly over my cheek. "I think I'm falling in love with you."

That shuts me up. I goggle at him.

"It's probably crazy fast," Kimo continues on, undeterred by my silence. "My māmā told me not to fall too fast, or at least not to open up my stupid mouth too soon if I did."

I can't help but smile a little at that, even though my head is still whirring from the reverberations of that word. Love. Love? How could that be possible? That isn't the kind of thing that happens to someone like me.

Kimo seems to take courage from my smile. "But I can't ignore my gut, and my gut is telling me it's you. You're it for me. I knew it from the moment you karate chopped that guy in the butt. No—actually, I think it was the moment you came out of hiding in that roadside forest, even if you could have gotten away. I liked you before that, don't get me wrong—it's not every day you meet a woman who's propositioning someone in a men's bathroom. I already knew you were honest and tough, but that was the moment I knew you were brave and kind, too. All Russian curses aside."

That is . . . a lot of information. I don't quite know where to start, so I choose perhaps the least important part to focus on. "Then why wouldn't you sleep with me until now, if you were so into me?"

Kimo half laughs, half groans. "I figured you might not want to buy the cow if you were getting the milk for free. So I thought I should hold off on the good stuff to give you time to fall for me, too." He raises his hands quickly, backpedaling. "Not saying you have to be in the same place that I am yet. But you like me at least a little bit now, don't you, Mattie?"

His expression is somehow both terrified and hopeful. And mine is probably . . . flabbergasted. I don't know what to say to that. To *any* of that. What are you supposed to say, when someone tells you they love you? This has never happened to me before. I'm the person someone tolerates until I kind of grow on them, and then they keep me around. I'm not the woman someone falls so hard for that they have to try to stop themselves from falling even harder.

There must be something wrong with him, is my immediate, knee-jerk response, the kind of thing I'd usually think to protect myself. But I immediately reject that. I think of Kimo's generosity, his openness, his affability. There's nothing wrong with him. He's perfect.

Much too good for me. That one sounds more logical. I swallow heavily, searching his face. Maybe he likes me now because I'm different from the types of chill, easygoing women he probably usually dates, but what if the novelty wears off? What if he sees the thing in me that everyone else sees—the thing that makes me disposable?

He brushes his thumb over my cheek again. "Come back to me, Mattie. Where'd you go?"

"You don't have to tell me that stuff just because we had sex," I blurt out finally. "You don't owe me anything. I won't hold you to anything."

Kimo winces, like I've wounded him, but he doesn't let go of me. "Don't do that, Mattie."

I feel a rising panic inside of me. "Do what?"

"Try to push me away. I'm not asking for anything in return from you, just because I'm telling you that I love you."

My eyebrows shoot up. "You're in love with me *now*? I thought you were just falling in love with me."

"Yeah, that was a bluff. I'm in love with you." Kimo tries his best to smile. "And that isn't something I'm saying to try to trick you, or trap you, or force you into saying or doing something you don't want to. I just love you, that's all. I can't help it."

That panicked feeling in my chest has turned into something throbbing and almost painful. If he weren't holding on to me, I might just turn and run deeper into the darkened building. Instead, I do my best to glare at him. "Don't do that."

"Do what?"

"Look at me with that stupid-handsome face!"

He frowns at me. "My face is stupid?"

I shake my head, irritated at his inability to read my mind. "No. It's stupid how handsome you are."

The frown softens into a smile. "Aww, baby."

"And that!" I jab my index finger at him. "You call me baby." It's the type of endearment that, coming from anyone else might sound cheesy or sexist, but from him just sounds . . . right. Even if it shouldn't.

"So?" He caresses me with that thumb yet again. It's the sweetest, scariest thing I've ever experienced.

"You say it like you mean it," I accuse him. "You say it in a way that makes me want to believe you."

Now he is all softness, in his eyes and his smile, his hands stroking my face. "Then believe me." He kisses me, slow and sweet this time, with none of the frantic passion from before, but somehow my heart is galloping even harder this time. When he's done, he nuzzles my nose, then rests his forehead against mine. "You're it for me, Mattie. I feel it in my gut."

I continue to search his expression, even with his face so close to mine, his eyes closed. Maybe that's the only reason why I can say what I do. "I . . . I think I love you, too."

As if he senses my skittishness, Kimo keeps his eyes closed. He remains perfectly still, except for the grin that he can't quite seem to hold back.

I smile, too, because I have to smile when I see him smile—it's impossible not to. Despite this, my heart continues to race. "Please don't hurt me."

I don't like to show that kind of weakness to anyone. It makes me want to crawl out of my skin. It makes me want to run and hide, this feeling, this rawness. But I need him to know, this isn't some game to me. I'm not someone who can be played with, not like this.

He opens his eyes again, holding mine. "I got you," he says quietly.

Chapter Thirty-Seven

Thank God it's the weekend, because Kimo and I don't get out of bed the next day. Except for when we're in the shower. Or on the floor. Or on the couch. Or on the kitchen counter. Or up against the front door. And then on the floor again.

But we can't just stay in bed for the whole week, of course. I still have to go to work on Monday morning, but Kimo gets up with me to make me breakfast, then hurries home so he can take the kids to camp. We text throughout the day, some of it silly, and some of it flirty, and some of it sexy, and some of it just plain stupid.

Exhibit A: **Hi**, he writes around lunchtime. That's it. Just hi. But it makes me smile so hard it feels like my cheeks are going to burst. **Hi**, I write back, and send him a picture of me eating a cup of ramen soup at my desk. **Beautiful**, he responds, with two heart emojis.

Riveting stuff, I know. But it actually . . . is? I would be mercilessly mocking anyone else if I saw this kind of behavior from them, but when it happens to you . . . when you meet that person who gives you butterflies, not just because they're handsome and sexy and can swing you around like you're a sack of potatoes, but just because you see their name pop up on your screen, and they make you laugh so hard you can't breathe, and you feel like tomorrow is actually going to be a good day, and all you need to do is just say something, anything to them so they know you're still there and thinking about them . . . are there really any words that can capture that? Maybe *hi* is as close as it can really get.

Wednesday I actually manage to finish my work early, so I go with Kimo to pick up the kids from camp. It is pure chaos—hundreds of kids pouring out of the building and at least a dozen identical SUVs parked in a row and everyone passive-aggressively honking at each other to scoot forward. When Nalani and Makoa find us in the crowd, they both fight to be heard over the other to tell a story about people I've never heard of and that, frankly, doesn't make any sense, just so they can be the center of attention for a moment. As we're about to leave, Makoa realizes he's forgotten his lunch box back at the school gym, and I see Kimo get genuinely irritated for the first time as we all have to circle back around. He keeps shooting me apologetic looks like he thinks I'm going to be annoyed.

I'm not. I have to hide my smile of pure joy. I can see how the grind of it could wear on you, day in and day out. But the way that Nalani and Makoa run up to us, and Nalani slips her hand so guilelessly into mine, and Makoa hands me his thermos like, of course, I'm just here to carry it for him . . . I can't remember the last time I felt like I was such a part of something.

***

We fall into an easy routine after that. Texting when we're away from each other during the day, making eyes across the conference table from each other when Kimo has to come into the office. On the days when I'm finished early enough, I go with Kimo to pick up the kids from camp, and when I'm not, I go over to the house and hang out with Nalani and Makoa while Kimo makes us dinner.

Luckily, the children and I have found a common language to share. Remembering how much the kids liked death, I dig up an old book of mine that I managed to keep with me throughout my childhood in the system. When I show Nalani and Makoa the cover, with the old haggard woman with her eagle eyes and wizened, decaying flesh, their eyes widen and they look at me in wonder.

"Come, children," I instruct them briskly, sitting down on the living room floor and motioning for them to join me. "Let me tell you some stories about Baba Yaga . . ."

Aunty Kapono joins us sometimes, pretending to work on her quilting in the corner of the room, though I catch her frowning at me every time the tales start to get dark. Naturally, that's the part the children like best, and if it comes down to catering to their whims or hers, I've decided I'm going to go with theirs. They're much easier to win over.

As I read one story about Baba Yaga trying to trick her new daughter-in-law into a terrible death, I meet Aunty Kapono's eyes across the room. She raises a brow at me, unimpressed. "A little on the nose, don't you think?" she challenges me.

"As true today as it ever was!" I say brightly, as if I've misunderstood her meaning.

Aunty Kapono just shakes her head and goes back to her quilting.

Eating dinner is always a raucous, chaotic event. Between Makoa complaining about first not getting enough ketchup, then too much ketchup, on whatever it is that we happen to be eating, or Nalani constantly getting up from the table to try to show us the latest baton-twirling routine she's learned, or the children fighting over who gets to sit next to whatever adult they've decided is their favorite for the day (sometimes it's even me!), there's never a dull moment. Any attempts that Kimo and I have to converse with one another are usually interrupted, either by the children or by his mother. Sometimes we manage to hold hands under the table, but not if Makoa's underneath pretending to be a dog, or Nalani decides that *she* wants to be the one holding her uncle's hand. She likes me overall, I think, but sometimes she wants to put me in my place, remind me that she's his first, best girl.

Sometimes I wonder if his mother isn't doing the same thing.

"I still think you should have settled with Pika," Aunty Kapono brings up one night at the table, shaking her head. It's clear, from the look she's giving me across the table, who she blames for this decision.

I suppose she's not entirely wrong. Kimo had seemed set on taking the deal before I intervened, but I wouldn't have stood in his way if that was what he really wanted. After our conversation at the gala, though, he ultimately decided to tell Jay to reject the offer. We're due to go forward with the case in just a couple weeks.

Kimo clears his throat. "Māmā, let's talk about that later." He looks meaningfully at the two kids, who have gone unusually silent at the sound of their father's name.

Aunty Kapono shrugs. "We could have been done with it all by now. On our way home instead of just playing house here."

There's no ambiguity this time. It's clear that statement is being directed completely at *me*. I swallow the chicken katsu that's in my mouth, even though it suddenly feels like I'm trying to force a small boulder down my throat. Of course, that's the natural next step of this. Once Kimo has full custody of the kids, they'll want to go back to the Big Island. He's never made a big secret of that, but he's also never clarified what that will mean for us, and I've been too afraid to ask.

Is that all we're doing together now, just playing house? Am I just filling in the role of girlfriend while he's still in Chicago?

"I like it here," Nalani says.

Kimo squeezes my hand under the table, catching my eye and giving me a wink. "So do I."

I try my best to smile back, but I notice he doesn't clarify whether that means they'll be staying longer, or if he's just making the best of things while he's forced to be here. The latter seems like a very Kimo thing to do.

Abruptly, Makoa bursts into tears.

It's so out of the blue that it takes everyone a minute to respond. Then Kimo's out of his chair and kneeling at his nephew's side, trying to coax him into lifting his face off the table. "Come on, little kāne. What's wrong?"

"I don't want to stay here!" Makoa moans. "And I don't want to live with Pika. Whenever we go there he just sits on his phone and ignores us. He gets mad at us if we try to play and tells us to shut up."

Kimo makes eye contact with me across the table. I feel the first stab of worry, wondering if Aunty Kapono is right, and if I made a mistake persuading Kimo to turn down that deal. Pika is their blood father, after all, and he doesn't have a criminal record or a drug addiction or anything else that might automatically rule him out from getting custody. Just because he's been a negligent father up until now doesn't mean the judge won't see things his way.

I look over to find Aunty Kapono watching me, too. From the way she's pursing her lips, I'm guessing she's thinking along the same lines.

"Hey." Kimo gathers Makoa into his arms, then gestures for Nalani to come over, too. "You don't worry about that, okay? I'm taking care of that. No matter what happens, we're 'ohana, you hear? Tūtū and I aren't going anywhere without you . . ."

A family that sticks together no matter what. *It's a nice thought*, I muse to myself, as Kimo walks me home that night. It's another part of our routine. On work nights, when the kids have to get up for camp the next morning, Kimo just walks me back to my place, though when Friday rolls around, he stays over. Then we go back to his house and spend Saturday with the kids to give Aunty Kapono a break. I've looked ahead and it's supposed to be cloudy, so we're going to play board games and then have a movie night. Kimo's reassured me I don't need to let the kids win, so I'm planning on bringing my A game.

When we get to my place, we say a quick hello to Stan, who promptly makes himself scarce. Now that Kimo's started spending more time at my place, Stan hasn't been around as much, or at least his presence hasn't been quite so obvious. I suppose Kimo is supposed to be my protector now, even though I'm a) a black belt and b) obviously much tougher than he is any day of the week. But I don't find this decision too hard, because I also like our privacy, and honestly, it's nice to have someone looking after me for a change.

Once we're alone, Kimo kisses me until I'm dizzy, then rests his forehead against mine. "You make it so hard to leave you," he murmurs.

My heart twists at the words. That's never been *my* experience. I seem to be exceptionally easy to leave. I close my eyes and lean into him. "Tell me what it's like at your house on the Big Island."

If Kimo thinks the abrupt topic change is strange, he doesn't let on. "We've got more space there than here. The house isn't much bigger, but we have a huge yard and a big porch. We'll do barbecues out there or just hang out and shoot the shit with neighbors when the weather's good."

"You have a lot of family that lives around you, right?" I prompt him, wanting to hear more.

"Oh, yeah. They come over at all hours. Hardly ever knock. Kind of like that Kimmy girl from your show."

I laugh, and he does too, his thumbs making lazy circles where he's holding my hips. For a moment, we're both silent.

"I have some girlfriends who didn't much like that," Kimo says after a moment. "Everyone always up in our business."

It's stupid, I know, to get jealous about people he loved before he even met me, but I instantly hate these women—the ones who got to sit with Kimo on that porch and watch the sunset, who got to hold his hand on the beach and see his face first thing in the morning, who got to be surrounded by all that love but who had the gall to find it annoying. "Oh," I say finally, because I don't trust myself to say anything else without sounding like a crazy person.

Take me back there, I want to beg him. *Let me soak up all that sun and love, and I swear I'll never complain, not once.*

But he doesn't ask me, and I don't say anything, and after a moment he sighs and pulls away, cupping my chin before stepping back. "I should get home."

"Yep." Irrationally, I want to cry, but I make myself smile, and blink rapidly so the tears can't form. "Let me know when you're back safe?"

Kimo gives me one last quick kiss before heading toward the elevator. He sighs like it's a terrible effort to walk away. "I'll find you in my dreams tonight, beautiful," he promises, winking just before the elevator doors close.

Chapter Thirty-Eight

few nights later, I clomp back down that same hallway, barely bothering to acknowledge Stan at his post. I'm too irritated by the intense smell wafting through the corridor. It isn't a bad smell —in fact, it's a really, really good smell—but I wish people would have the decency to keep their cooking to themselves, or at least to crack a window if they're going to be using garlic.

It's been a day. Nothing especially bad happened, but it's just been long and unrelenting. I forgot to set my alarm for this morning, so since I'd been up late texting with Kimo, I slept in way too late and missed an all-staff meeting. In my haste to get ready, I forgot that my black sandals cut into my feet the last time I wore them, and son of a bitch, those monsters did the same thing to me today. The AC at the office was on the fritz by the end of the day, and my deodorant did its best, but I'm still pretty confident I smell somewhere between stinky cheese and old socks. Oh, and despite the broken AC, I still had to stay late to make up for some stuff I missed in the morning, and then I realized I had to stay on even *later* because I'd done some things wrong when I got to the office in a panic at sleeping in. Suffice it to say, I missed picking up Nalani and Makoa, missed hanging out while Kimo cooks, missed dinner. Oh, and missed lunch, too, come to think of it. And breakfast. No wonder I feel like I might murder someone for a baguette.

To top it all off, I'm feeling extra irritable because . . . maybe it's stupid, but I kind of thought I wouldn't be like this anymore now that I've found Kimo. You know, Grouchy Matilda—or, let's be honest with the name: Bitchy Matilda. I thought that maybe, I don't know, I'd been cured by love or whatever. (Hey, don't judge me—this is all new to me!) Turns out the potential for mega-bitch still lurks under my skin, just waiting for its chance to be freed from its ancient curse and wreak havoc on the city.

I pause when I reach my door, frowning as I see it's ajar. I'm not frowning out of concern for my safety, because I just saw Stan keeping his usual careful but distant surveillance outside, and I can hear Journey floating out into the corridor, so I know it isn't an intruder. Well, it is an intruder, but it's *my* intruder.

Kimo. And whatever that delicious smell is, it's coming from inside my apartment.

No, I'm frowning because I know what I get like when I'm in one of these moods. I need to burrow under a blanket and put *Full House* on a loop and eat an entire box of cereal. I need space to turn into that feral creature for a while so I can emerge again on the other side like a normal human being. I'm afraid I won't be able to pull things together for Kimo, and he's going to get a glimpse of that side of me that seems to repel everyone else.

If I had anywhere else to go, somewhere I could just be on my own, I probably would retreat. Instead I sigh and push open the door.

Kimo's used what looks like every single pot and pan in the kitchen. "Open Arms" is playing at an ungodly volume, and he's singing along, eyes closed, his messy bun bobbing precariously on the top of his head.

Under normal circumstances, I'd find this spectacle pretty adorable. Now, though, all I can think about is how long it's going to take to clean my kitchen.

Somehow he senses my approach, even with his eyes closed and the music blaring. "Hey, baby!" He sounds so genuinely excited to see me that it should soften me a little. Instead, I feel myself going rigid. He comes forward to hug me but draws himself up short. "Whoa. What's wrong?"

"Nothing," I say quickly. "I'm fine."

I guess it's less convincing when you say it through gritted teeth, because Kimo arches some major eyebrow at me. "You sure?"

Do not shout, Matilda. Don't be a bitch. Don't scare him off. "Yes, fine," I say again. I tell myself to try to smile, but my face is incapable of the lie at the moment.

Kimo gauges me, then claps his hands together. "Right. Sit down. Eat. I'll get you your food then draw up a bath for you . . ."

A second later, I'm alone at the table with a heaping bowl of spaghetti bolognese in front of me. True to his word, Kimo is in the other room, running a bath, though I can still hear him singing off-key to himself. The song is so badly butchered I can't make heads or tails of what it's supposed to be.

Even though I didn't want Kimo here, I'm also kind of irritated that he left me alone at the table. "Whatever," I mutter out loud to myself, heaping a healthy helping of spaghetti onto my fork.

This is the best goddam thing I've ever tasted. All those flavors I'd been smelling in the hallway have blended together perfectly. I let out a moan that is, frankly, indecent, then shovel the entire bowl into my mouth faster than is safe or sane. When I see there's also garlic bread on the table, I don't miss a beat; snatching for it, I inhale half the loaf in just under a minute.

Belly full, I feel some of the earlier rage subsiding. Now the bone-deep weariness is beginning to set in. As if on cue, Kimo appears. "Bath's ready." He eyes the table quickly, and if he thinks it's bizarre how much I've managed to eat in such a short amount of time, he wisely doesn't say anything.

In the bathroom, I tense again, expecting him to try to make this a sexy moment somehow—to offer to soap up my boobs or some other asinine thing that might actually make me bite off his head right now. Instead he disappears then reappears a moment later with a glass of wine. "Enjoy. Take your time, okay? There's no rush."

Then, he's gone.

I'm surprised, but also relieved. I need some time to just unwind. When I slip into the bath, I find he's left it at just the perfect temperature, and the first sip of wine helps me feel more centered and calm. This is nice. This is . . . really nice.

For just a moment, I let myself imagine this is a normal weekday night. I'm tired from work, but I get to come home to Kimo, and he takes care of me when I'm having a rough day. No one's ever looked after me this way. Maybe it could always be like this between us—not that I'd be in a bad mood every night, but when I am, Kimo would step up to make sure I'm okay, and I'd do the same for him when he needed me. We could take care of each other.

But it would all fade over time, wouldn't it? I remember how my mother's boyfriends were in the beginning—flowers and romance and compliments—and just how quickly all of that wore off. Not that I'm likely to find out one way or another with Kimo. He'll probably be gone long before the shine begins to dim.

Almost an hour later, when I finally emerge from the bathroom in my robe, I'm surprised to find the entire kitchen is spotless—maybe even cleaner than it was before he started cooking. Kimo's hanging out on the couch, wearing sweatpants and a tank top and watching something on TV. When he sees me approach, he turns it off. "Hey. Wanna watch *Full House*?"

This man has pulled out all the stops. I want to just enjoy it—I tell myself, *Just enjoy it, you idiot!*—but a part of me is still waiting for him to disappoint me. I hone in on the sight of him so dressed down. "Are you staying the night?"

I actually don't know what I want the answer to be. If he says yes, he's presumptuous; if he says no, he's abandoning me. Even recognizing it, I can't shake the weird, cagey tension I'm feeling.

"I don't have to," he reassures me quickly. "But Nalani's spending the night at a friend's, and Māmā says she's fine with Makoa on her own. So I can stay, if you want."

I can tell he's trying to sound light about the whole thing, like it doesn't really matter either way, like there's no pressure. After a moment's reflection, I shrug. "Stay. But maybe let's keep it low-key tonight, okay?"

"Sure thing. Come here, baby . . ."

I get into my usual position as little spoon, engulfed in the safe warmth of his big body. Kimo starts up where we left off last time, and for a while, we just watch together in silence, except for when he laughs at something happening onscreen. I've seen the show too many times to still find any of the bits genuinely funny, but I delight in his amusement and enjoyment at the characters' antics.

After a couple episodes, I feel something nudging against my lower back. *Of course*, I think to myself with a good-natured roll of my eyes, but then I realize it's his knuckles. "You want a massage? I can feel your shoulders are still all tense."

Okay. Come on, now. I might be new to this whole relationship thing, but even my fuck buddies would play this game sometimes. "Right," I drawl sarcastically. "A massage. We both know what that's code for."

Kimo scoffs behind me as if genuinely offended. "Hey, I take my massages seriously. No funny business. And that goes both ways. Don't start begging me for sex in a few minutes once you start feeling all loose and good."

Despite myself, I huff out a laugh.

I raise my eyebrows knowingly as Kimo tugs my robe open and down over my shoulders, exposing the naked expanse of my back to him. True to his word, though, Kimo really does just focus on the massage. He's really good at it, seeming to intuit where I need him to be and just how hard to make the pressure.

And sure enough . . . after my back and shoulders start to feel all loose and good, other parts of my anatomy start to want the same treatment. Dammit. I know that was his plan all along, but God help me, it's working.

I start to move my bottom back and forth, deliberately rubbing it up against his groin. Kimo pauses his ministrations on my back. When he speaks, his voice is stern. "Excuse me, ma'am. That's against our policy here at this parlor."

Fighting a laugh, I adopt the same overly officious tone. "Apologies. I didn't realize I was rubbing my ass against your cock. It won't happen again."

"Make sure it doesn't."

He begins to massage me again. I wait for just the perfect moment before I let out a deep moan of pleasure.

"Ma'am. Come on, now. That's very inappropriate."

"Sorry," I play along, rubbing myself back against him once again. "It just felt *so* good."

To my surprise, he sits up and away from me. For one startled second, I think he's really going to leave—until I glance over and see he's taking off his clothes. Yep, briefs, everything. He's completely naked now.

I burst out laughing. Kimo fixes me with a faux-stern look. "Come on, lady. Keep it professional."

"You're the one taking off your clothes!" I protest.

"I'm just trying a new massage method. To show you the benefits of skin-to-skin. Stop being so inappropriate, or I'm going to have to punish you."

Whoa. Now *that* shoots my slow-warming lust straight up to sizzling. "Punish me how?"

Kimo moves to lie back down again behind me, but pauses so he can whisper in my ear. "I'm taking away your loyalty card."

Giggling again, I allow him to pull me back down so I'm lying in front of him. The massage continues just like before, only now I'm keenly aware of him being naked behind me. And also keenly aware that I need him to notch those G-rated touches up pretty quickly, now that my libido's been fully awakened.

But Kimo seems committed to playing his role, and he stays strictly out of my bathing suit zone. Damn him! He's really trying to make me beg for it. Which I'm not against in principle, but since I just know he's waiting for me to give in, I need to make *him* be the one to give in. I know, it doesn't make much sense, but that's my brain, folks. After a moment of scheming, I start wriggling around to get his attention.

His hands, which have been massaging my upper arms, still. "Ma'am? You aren't getting frisky on me again, are you? Because then I might have to call in my manager."

"I was just thinking . . . for skin-to-skin to work, wouldn't I also have to be naked?"

Kimo ponders this a moment. "All right," he says finally. "But no funny business."

I sit up, eagerly shucking off the rest of my robe so I'm naked as a jaybird. When I lie down again, I move back until my bare skin is in contact with Kimo's, feeling a shiver run through me.

"You feeling those benefits yet?" he murmurs in my ear.

His hands finally move down from my shoulders, and he begins applying the same firm but gentle pressure to my lower back, then down to my buttocks. He gives a low grumble of appreciation, rubbing me, smoothing his hands over my curves.

I don't hold back my sigh of pleasure. "I'm not sure," I say after a moment. "What are the benefits of skin-to-skin supposed to be?"

There's a long enough stall that I realize Kimo doesn't actually know. I stifle a laugh. "Well . . . uh, it's meant to relax you. Make you feel safe. Make you feel taken care of."

I'm pretty sure we're not talking about skin-to-skin anymore. I bite back my smile, pretending to consider it. "I *am* feeling those things. I think it's working."

"Good, good. Because there's another experimental treatment I'd like to try on you."

My heart rate spikes in anticipation. "Oh? Will it cost extra, because I'm kind of on a budget?"

"Don't worry, ma'am. This one's on the house. It's called advanced tongue therapy."

I don't quite catch the giggle before it escapes my throat. "Ooh. Sounds French."

A moment later, I feel him sitting up, angling me so I'm on my back and facing him. At the sight of his gentle, handsome face, I forget the game for a moment and reach up to touch his cheek.

"Ma'am," he tells me faux-sternly. "That's the kind of unseemly behavior that's going to get you kicked out of this place."

I laugh. I didn't know it was possible to feel this way—happy and safe and giddy, but also so, so turned on. I thought those different emotions always had to come separately, and that one would always be off-limits to me. I am so, so happy I was wrong.

"Sorry," I tell him, giving him my best innocent eyes. "I'll be good."

"Good. Now lie back so I can try out this advanced tongue therapy on your boobs. Don't get any ideas. This is strictly professional."

Grinning, I do as he orders. My mirth shifts quickly into something far more intense as his mouth closes over my left breast, his tongue swirling over my nipple until I'm crying out, back arching off the sofa. He moves to the next breast and does the same, until I'm a whimpering, keening mess.

He grins at me, shamelessly pleased with himself. "What do you think of the new technique? It's supposed to make you feel super horny."

I huff out a laugh. "That's not very professional."

"It's still being workshopped."

"Hmm." I spread my legs wide, an invitation. "Well, it worked. I feel super horny."

Kimo keeps a straight face, though his eyes flick down. "Interesting. I'll have to give my feedback to corporate . . ."

He really isn't going to give up this game, is he? It's time to expedite this process a bit. "You'd better lodge a complaint with headquarters, while you're at it. I think it's negligent to get a client all hot and bothered and not finish the job."

Kimo pretends to consider this. "So you're saying . . . you want a deep, deep tissue massage."

"I'm saying you better fuck me senseless, or I'm taking this whole parlor down."

He shakes his head, as if deeply put out. "Anything for the company . . ."

And, after grabbing a condom from the small tin by the couch (hey, this isn't our first time winding up here), he makes good on his promise.

Chapter Thirty-Nine

I keep Kimo away from the next couple book clubs. It's not that I don't trust him, it's more like . . . I don't want to jinx anything. Things are going so well between us now. And I don't want my friends to feel awkward around him, or him to feel awkward around my friends, because of what happened the last time I invited him.

I'm also waiting for Helen to rub it in my face. I was *not* nice when Thad broke up with her a few months ago. But I guess, if I have *any* defense, it's that I truly didn't know what this feeling was—this vulnerability that comes from love, like you're a dandelion, one puff away from being scattered into pieces. There are no walls. No protective coverings. All you can do is stand out in the open on your own, hoping the other person won't choose to destroy you.

Feeling like I do now, I realize the agony that I put Helen through back then. Even if my intention truly was to help her, in my own bulldozer-ish way, I should have just supported her. Like I'd hope she'd support me.

I show up at the library one day, bearing a strawberry pavlova from Sugar Moon Bakery. "Here," I say, dumping the box unceremoniously onto Helen's desk.

She looks at the treat box with big, happy eyes. "Yummy! To what do I owe this pleasure?" Then she eyes me up and down, squinting. "You look . . . different. What's different about you?"

I blush—I actually *blush*, like some Victorian schoolmarm who's accidentally shown off her ankle. "Who can say?" Desperate to distract her, I gesture toward the doors to the main entrance. "Have you felt that temperature outside? It sure is . . . temperate."

Tilting her head, Helen continues to study me. "Are you . . . ?" Her eyes widen a little as it clicks. "Are you *relaxed*?"

I think of last night, the bath, the massage, the . . . after the massage. Then this morning, when Kimo made me laugh by drawing a smiley face in syrup on my French toast.

"What? Maybe. I don't know." I push the box closer to her. "Shut up and eat your pastry."

Helen's still smiling at me, though she looks puzzled. "What's going on with you?"

"I'm dating Kimo again!" The words burst out of me, just a little too loud. I'm aware of several patrons in the library turning to stare at me. I ignore them. "I know, I'm a hypocrite. I'm doing the thing I was so mean and judgy of when you did it with Thad. Even though, to be fair, Kimo actually had a legitimate excuse." At Helen's raised eyebrow, I rush on. "And I'm sorry, is what I'm really trying to say. I shouldn't have done that. That was . . . awful."

Helen takes a moment to process all my verbal diarrhea. "You're dating Kimo again?"

"Yes. And I'm a bitch. That pretty much sums it up."

She gives me a scolding frown. "You're not a . . ." Helen isn't much of a swearer, though she's gotten more adept at it since she began dating Thad. I still wouldn't say she's *great* at it, though. It always sounds a little bit like a kid trying to sound grown-up. ". . . a *bitch*," she finishes. "Even then, I knew you weren't trying to be mean. You were just being honest. In a kind of mean way."

I can't help but crack a smile at that, even if I still feel sick to my stomach. That's so Helen. Always trying to see the best in people—still aware of their faults, but trying to paint them in the best light possible. "I guess that sums it up," I agree.

For a moment, Helen is silent, still processing. She sighs, reaching for the pastry box. "You know what, though? I kind of get it."

"You do?"

She takes a plastic knife from her desk drawer and uses it to cut the pastry down the middle, then offers me one of the halves. "I wish you could have said it more tactfully, but now that I'm on the other end, I understand. I want you to be happy, but I saw how devastated you were when Kimo hurt you, even if he didn't mean it. And I don't want that for you. I want you to have everything you want out of life."

The words take me unawares, and it feels like a bit of a punch to the gut. "You . . . do?"

Helen frowns at me through her bite of pastry. She covers her mouth so she can still talk. "Of course I do, you big dork. I love you."

It's the second confession of love I've had in so many weeks. It means just as much to me as the first one did. "I . . . love you, too. And I want *you* to be happy. And I'm glad Thad gives you that."

"Aww." Now Helen's eyes are the ones shining with tears. "You said his actual name!"

I take a more conservative bite of my own pastry, chewing and swallowing before answering to give myself time to think. "I suppose he and I can coexist peacefully now."

"He'll be so relieved. He's totally scared of you, you know."

"He is?" I'm oddly pleased by that. We may have a truce between us now, but I want Thad to always remember who's top dog. "Good." I nod to myself resolutely. "He should be."

With Helen's blessing, I invite Kimo to the next book club. This time, though, I make sure we arrive together. I don't want there to be any more derailments on his journey there.

Instead of our usual spot, the book club is meeting up at an Irish pub called Galway Bay, since we read *Brooklyn* this time around, and Helen wanted a more thematic setting. When we walk into the crowded, lively bar, I see everyone else is already there.

My stomach does a nervous swoop. That takes me by surprise—how utterly terrified I am about Kimo meeting everybody. I know the weight of those expectations when someone you care about has met somebody new, and the burden of those hopes once they've been broken. I want everything to go perfectly.

When I look over at Kimo, he looks uncharacteristically nervous. I guess that shouldn't come as a surprise, come to think of it. He tried on six shirts before settling on the one he did. His jeans have only a few holes in them, and just at the knee so it looks somewhat fashionable. He's still wearing flip-flops, but they're really nice ones.

I squeeze his hand to draw his attention, then smile up at him. "I got you," I murmur, winking at him.

He grins.

Helen waves us over. I know she's prepped everybody after what I told her about Kimo's custody case and the reason he missed the last meeting, and that she's taken it upon herself to make sure everything runs smoothly tonight.

Whatever apprehensions she might still feel about Kimo, she is nothing but warm smiles as she greets him. "Hi! You must be Kimo. It's so nice to meet you. I'm Helen."

"Oh, hey!" Kimo either doesn't notice her offer of a handshake or just decides to sidestep it for a hug. "Mattie's told me so much about you."

Mattie? Helen mouths over his shoulder, her expression somehow both shocked and delighted.

Oh my God. I'm never going to live that one down. Somehow, though, I'm beaming. "And this is Nina."

The size difference between these two couldn't be more comical than if we were planning on taking the show on vaudeville. Kimo's head is nearly brushing the ceiling, and Nina's head just barely reaches up to his pectorals.

"Nina!" Kimo goes in for another hug. Nina expects it more than Helen did, but she still goes a little limp as he engulfs her, her eyes wide with mild alarm. "Whoa. You're like a little doll."

"Thank you?" she stammers once he sets her back on her feet.

I move to the next person in line. "Then that's Thad."

"Thad, nice to meet you, brah." As Kimo moves in to hug him, Thad holds up his hands firmly, giving Kimo a look that makes him take half a step back, even though he's bigger and taller than the other man. "Okay, then."

"And . . ." I clear my throat, trying not to be weird. "You remember Grady. From the gym."

"Howzit?" Undeterred by Thad's standoffishness, Kimo goes in for a final hug, which he gets this time. He pulls back and grins at Grady like they're old friends. "How you been?"

Grady steps away from the hug. He and Thad exchange what can only be described as *a look*. "Kimo, come chat with us," Thad says. It does not sound like a suggestion.

Shrugging at me, Kimo ambles off after him and Grady.

I frown, taking a seat and glancing over at Helen and Nina before following the three men with my eyes. "What's going on?"

"Thad wants to have the talk with Kimo," Helen explains.

I wave her off. "Oh, Kimo definitely doesn't need that." I can't help the smile that plays at my lips as I toy with the charm at the end of my necklace. "He knows what he's doing . . ."

"Not *that* talk." Helen flicks some of her water at me. "The, you know, *hurt her and we'll kill you* speech."

Warmth floods my chest. "Really?" I twist in my chair so I can see them better. "They'd do that for me?"

"Of course," Nina speaks up. "They're your friends."

She makes it sound so simple.

Although, I guess it really isn't as hard as I've made it out to be for myself.

Smiling, touched by the entire thing, I turn back to face the others. "Well, that's nice, but unnecessary. Just wait. I'll give it five minutes before they're both best friends with Kimo. It's his superpower."

We watch them. Sure enough, after a minute or two of talking, I see Grady's defensive posture start to soften. Thad holds out longer, but after another minute or so, I see him begrudgingly laugh, rubbing a hand over his neck. In the next minute, they're all laughing openly, and Kimo claps both men on the shoulders as they make their way over to the dartboard.

"Oh!" Helen looks after them, bemused. "I guess they're playing darts now."

I beam after them, proud of my man and his ability to befriend literally anybody. "He's good with people."

"I see that." Helen exchanges a glance with Nina that isn't as subtle as she thinks it is. "And is he good with you?"

"The sex is fantastic, if that's what you're asking."

Helen chokes a little on her water, and Nina looks like she's about to spontaneously combust. "Oh my," she murmurs.

"That's . . . nice." Helen clears her throat. "But what about everything else? How does he treat you?"

"He's . . ." I search for the right words.

The nicest man I ever met. He looks at me like he's so lucky to know me. And I feel the same way about him. I can't believe I'm the one who gets to be with him.

". . . tall," is what I say instead.

For a moment, we're all silent. To my surprise, Nina is the first one to start giggling. "The way he treats you is *tall?*"

Helen joins in, and soon I'm laughing, too, even if it's at me as much as with me. "I'm not good with feelings!" I protest, flicking my water back at them, since apparently that's a thing we do now.

We haven't totally subsided laughing by the time Kimo rejoins us. It isn't even really that funny anymore, but we keep egging each other on to the point where I've almost forgotten why we started laughing to begin with.

"Hey," Kimo says, pausing only long enough to give me a quick peck on the cheek. He motions with his thumb back toward Thad and Grady. "So I've been talking with the boys. When the hell were you a nun?"

Nina, Helen, and I exchange a glance, then promptly burst into cackles of laughter.

Chapter Forty

The next night, I'm the nervous one as we make our way back to Dumb-Ax Throwing. And no, it's not just because that's where Kimo and I got kidnapped, although that certainly doesn't help.

"We're erasing the bad memories and making some new ones," Kimo reminds me as he pulls me through the door. "Besides, you gotta meet Akona."

Akona is the owner of Dumb-Ax Throwing, and is apparently an old school friend of Kimo's. Even though the warehouse is much more crowded at night—filled with groups of friends and couples on date nights—Akona comes right around the counter to greet us, throwing his arms around Kimo like they're long-lost brothers. "Pono!"

Pono? That's new. I look at Kimo, wondering if he'll give me an explanation for the nickname, but he just gives me an embarrassed shrug. Huh. Interesting.

"And you must be Matilda." Akona pulls me into a big, tight hug. If it weren't already obvious that he's Kimo's old friend, I'd know it from that embrace. He's just like Kimo, hugging everyone like they're family.

"Nice to meet you," I manage, though it's mostly muffled into his shirtfront.

After a bone-crushing moment, I'm finally released. Akona shakes his head at me. "I am so sorry about what happened here. That employee has been fired, of course, and he's being prosecuted for accessory to kidnapping." Then he winks at Kimo, all seriousness dissipating. "But looks like it turned out pretty good for you, huh, hoaaloha?"

Kimo just grins at me, wrapping an arm around my shoulders and pulling me close. "Yeah, she's a babe, huh? Smart, too. And tough as nails."

I flush, not liking all of this attention on me. "And what about Kimo? I hear you're the guy who can give me all the dirt on him."

"Oh, yeah." Akona doubles over laughing, then corrects himself, punching Kimo affectionately on the arm. "Nah, this here's a real one. That's why we all called him Pono back at school."

There's that word again. "Because it's short for his last name?" I guess.

"Yeah, that. And it means . . ." He looks to Kimo, searching for the right words. "Righteousness? Harmony? Someone or something that's right with the world, I guess." Akona claps Kimo's shoulder. "That's this guy. He's a good one."

I've never seen Kimo look so embarrassed. It might be the sweetest thing I've ever seen. For a moment, he avoids eye contact, but then he finally looks over at me and I grin, needling him just a little bit. "Pono. That sounds about right to me."

Kimo grabs me in an affectionate headlock, peppering my face with kisses that I only pretend to squirm away from. "You all set up for us?" he asks Akona.

"Yeah, brah. I got you in a private booth in the back. I'll let you know when the others show up." Akona reaches out to shake my hand enthusiastically. "Matilda, it was very nice to meet you . . ."

Kimo leads me to the back booth, which is separated from the others and has been roped off for some privacy. We'll still be able to throw axes here, but there's also a table that's reserved just for us, along with a menu for food.

"Do you remember what they like?" Kimo asks, looking it over. "We can order some stuff ahead. Have it ready."

I try to scan the menu, but my eyes don't really register anything as my mind races over what's about to happen. Maybe they'll yell at me. Maybe they won't show up. I'd deserve either response. My palms are sweaty, making the menu slippery, and I hope Kimo doesn't notice how badly my hands are shaking. "They're pretty easygoing. I don't think they'll care too much one way or the other."

"Hey." Kimo pries the menu from my hands and sets it back on the table, then takes my face in his hands. "It's gonna be okay. If they're assholes, we'll throw an ax at them and make a quick escape. I'm a millionaire. We'll totally get away with it."

I do my best to smile, but I know it won't come to that. They won't be assholes. What they will be is . . . much more complicated than that.

Then I spot them, being led toward us through the crowd by Akona. I instinctively grip Kimo's hand, which is still holding the side of my face. "They're here."

Brian and Connie—my adoptive parents.

* * *

The first few minutes are awkward—the kind of awkward that even Kimo can't totally diffuse, despite his best efforts. Ten minutes later, he and Brian have decided to meet for a beer at an Irish pub sometime, since Brian took a DNA test and found out he's thirty-two percent Irish and Kimo is apparently sixteen percent Irish, go figure.

Despite this, and aside from the usual perfunctory greetings, Brian and Connie haven't said much to me directly. To be fair, I haven't said much to them, either, because I just don't know what to say. And they're probably afraid if they pay me too much attention, I might suddenly become a flight risk. I guess I can't blame them for that. Before today, it'd been almost eight years since the last time I saw them in person. Despite some inevitable aging—more gray hairs and lines around the eyes—they look the same. Both are white and in their sixties, Brian with thinning brown hair and glasses, his pants a little too high, and his shirt tucked in a little too tight in a way I used to find annoying when I was a teenager but now find endearing. Connie's hair has gone full gray, but her round face makes her look younger than her years.

"I admire the work you're doing in Hawai'i," Connie tells Kimo after a moment. "I read that piece about you in *The Atlantic*."

Kimo nods his appreciation. "Thank you. There's still a long way to go, but at least it's a start."

"What work are you doing in Hawai'i?" I ask, confused. I've always taken Kimo for being a gentleman of leisure, aside from hanging out with his kids and learning all the words to '80s power ballads.

I guess I should have pieced together that this isn't his normal life, here in Chicago. He's just here for the court case. Once that's done . . .

No. Nope. Not focusing on that tonight. Kimo gives me his patented sheepish look, which I'm starting to realize is a good indicator that he's done something nice for somebody and doesn't want anyone to know about it. "Ahh, I've bought up quite a bit of property on the Big Island, and I'm working on buying some more."

That . . . doesn't sound like Kimo. He hasn't even moved out of his old neighborhood—why is he buying up so much real estate?

Connie supplies the rest for me, once it becomes clear that Kimo isn't going to. "He's buying back properties from vacation rental companies that have jacked up the price of living there so that locals can't even afford to buy homes. Then he's selling back to locals at a loss so they can afford to stay in the same neighborhoods they've lived in for years."

Kimo is studying his beer, looking more embarrassed than I've ever seen him. I watch him until, finally, he darts a glance up at me. "Pono," I tell him, reaching out to squeeze his hand. He grins back at me.

When I look at Connie, she's smiling at us wistfully, like she's lost in a memory. She blinks, pulling herself out of it. "I knew as soon as I saw that picture of you with Matilda that you'd be good for her."

"That picture?" I wince, imagining I know which one she means.

"From Mackinac Island."

"Oh, God," I mutter under my breath. Of course—she's referencing the paparazzi picture from outside the hotel. Somehow I've managed to willfully block out of my memory that the image of me in those short shorts and that tight pink T-shirt is plastered all over the internet.

Brian is watching me now, too, looking worried. "Are the stories true? Were you really kidnapped?"

Their concern feels unearned. I don't know what I've done to deserve it. I squirm in my seat. "It was only for a few hours. And it was my first time being kidnapped—Kimo gets kidnapped all the time."

Connie raises her eyebrows in alarm. "Really?"

"Not all the time," Kimo hedges, giving me a look.

I give it right back to him. "Has it happened more than once?" He doesn't say anything. "More than twice?"

"Three times," he admits finally, "including the time with you." At the matching expressions of horror on Brian's and Connie's faces, he quickly clarifies, "Between 'stealing' all that money from those hedge fund brahs and buying up all the rental property I can on the Big Island, I've made a few enemies. Mostly it's just people trying to scare me out of rocking the boat." He winks at me. "But don't worry. I don't scare too easy."

Despite his attempts to put us all at ease, I do worry. It's hard to imagine cheerful, personable Kimo having any enemies, but three times is too many times to get kidnapped.

To my surprise, Brian laughs. "I know that must be true, if you're dating our Matilda."

The words hang in the air. I stare at Brian in surprise. Connie stares at Brian in surprise. Brian seems to have surprised himself by what just came out of his mouth.

Kimo laughs.

That seems to crack the ice, because soon I'm laughing, too, and Connie and Brian join in. "Are you trying to say I'm difficult?" I attempt to sound offended, but I'm not. I know I am. I just didn't know I'd ever get Brian and Connie to admit it.

"Determined," Connie says. "You know what you want, and what you don't want."

She's still smiling, but there's a hint of pain laced in her expression, too. Brian reaches out to take her hand.

I swallow down what feels like shards of glass. As long as we're being honest, I might as well say what I should have said a long time ago. "I'm sorry for how I was back then. I thought there was no way you could really want me. You'd probably been hoping for a cute little kid, and instead you got an angry teenager."

Kimo takes my hand under the table, squeezing it. We've talked about this together, but I've never said it out loud to my adoptive parents before. Taking in a deep breath, I continue, "You were always nice to me—you didn't deserve how sullen and moody I was all the time. I guess I didn't want to get too attached because . . . I was sure you would change your minds as soon as you got what you really wanted."

"Oh, honey." Connie hesitates before reaching out to take my hand. "I won't lie—it definitely wasn't what we expected. But it didn't take us long to fall in love with you. Totally and completely."

"Braces and acne and all," Brian adds, gently teasing.

Kimo clears his throat. "I'm gonna need to see pictures of that phase, please. For blackmail purposes."

"Over my dead body." I'm not entirely joking, either.

Swallowing, I look back to Connie, who is watching me hopefully. "I know I can't make up for the past. I know I did everything I could to push you two away. But I was hoping we could be in touch again. More than just texts on birthdays and holidays. I mean, I don't expect you to treat me like a real daughter—"

"Matilda," Connie interrupts, shaking her head at me. "Don't talk yourself out of it again. You'll always be as much of our daughter as you want to be. It was always, *always*, up to you. We'll be here for you, whenever you need us."

Brian puts his hand on top of ours, squeezing.

Finding myself unable to speak, I grasp their hands and nod instead. Hopefully that will be enough.

After a moment, Brian clears his throat. "Well, thank God that's why you brought us here. I thought it was maybe to chop us up with all these axes."

"That was plan B," Kimo deadpans. He stands, clapping a hand on Brian's shoulder. "Come on, Uncle. Let me show you how to throw one of these things . . ."

Chapter Forty-One

My apology tour has felt good so far. There are some wounds that I know will take more than just a conversation, like with my sisters. So far I've managed to clear the air with Helen, Brian, and Connie. But there's someone else who deserves an apology from me, too. So that night, after Kimo's already fallen asleep, I sneak out of bed. Grabbing my laptop, I take it into the living room.

It takes me a minute or two to find Dominika's email. It's from several years ago, so I have to do some sifting. My heart starts pounding as I see her email address, and I click on the message, even though I've read it more than once before:

Matilda, I've been thinking about you a lot these past few weeks. I know it's been a long time since we've talked, but old friends are like that, I suppose. You can go years without speaking and then pick up the conversation again like it happened only moments before.

I know that isn't quite our situation. We didn't just drift apart. We were severed. No, to be honest—*you* severed us, Дружище. I forgave you a long time ago for trying to sleep with Luca. What took me longer was forgiving you for leaving without saying goodbye. But even that anger has faded now. I just want to talk to my friend again.

I'm here, when you're ready.
-Dominika

My palms are sweating as I read it through again. I feel sick to my stomach. It's too late, probably. That door has likely long been closed. But if I don't write out what I'm feeling now, I never will. Kimo has knocked down these walls, but I'm afraid of what happens when he returns to Hawai'i and they go back up again. Maybe if I let a few people inside, then at least I won't have to be alone once they do.

I'm sorry, I type out quickly, before I can second-guess myself. **I'm so sorry, Dominika. I miss you, too.**

I hit send before I can talk myself out of it. Once it's done, I'm afraid I'll be sick to my stomach, but instead I find . . . I'm relieved. It's out of my hands now. If Dominika never answers, I won't blame her, but if she does . . . I'll be so grateful to get a second chance.

I try to crawl back into bed as gently as possible, but Kimo still stirs, grunting as he reaches for me. "You okay?"

"Yeah. Just forgot something I had to do." I'll tell him more about it once we're properly awake; I don't want to disturb his sleep now.

Sleep seems to be the last thing on his mind, though, as he pulls me close. As he kisses me long and slow, I feel him stirring against me.

"*Kimo.*" I can't help but laugh. "It's two o'clock in the morning."

"Hey, you're the one who woke me up. Shouldn't have done that if you didn't want to wake up the kraken, too."

I groan. "Please don't call your cock the kraken . . ."

"What other name could capture its raw power and charisma?"

He kisses me through my reluctant laughter, until my body is stirred into awareness, too, pulled under by the tide of my attraction, my affection, my want for this man.

Pulling away, Kimo nudges my nose with his own. "Should I grab a condom?"

I think about it for a moment. "No."

He nods, planting a kiss to the tip of my nose. "Okay. Wanna just cuddle?"

I wet my lips. "No, I mean . . . we don't need a condom, do we? I was tested a few weeks ago, and I'm clean. I haven't slept with anyone else since then. And I'm on birth control."

"I'm clean, too," Kimo reassures me. "I got a full physical right before coming here to Chicago. And there hasn't been anyone since then."

Unable to hide my smile of pleasure at that information, I pull him back to me. "I want you close," I murmur to him. "As close as you can get."

Kimo tucks me into his arms.

There's nothing fancy about it this time. Nothing frantic. Nothing out of the ordinary. It's slow and measured. It's all about connecting. We're face-to-face, eyes locked almost the whole time. I fight the old instinct to close my eyes, to protect myself from the intimacy of this moment. I want him close, after all. As close as we can get.

Afterward, Kimo kisses me, long and slow again. "I love you, baby."

"I love you, too," I tell him, honestly, stroking his hair the way I know he likes.

It takes everything in me not to weep. I'm so, so happy. I don't know what I'm going to do when it all goes away.

Chapter Forty-Two

"Don't stick that in your mouth!" I shout.

Makoa pauses with a butter knife full of peanut butter halfway to his mouth. We're standing in Kimo's kitchen, making peanut butter and jelly sandwiches, which I thought would be easy enough to do with two children, but . . . it is not. When Kimo called about an hour ago, with effusive apologies for being late, I was already at his house, so it seemed just basic manners to offer to help the kids with dinner.

Kimo's pause spoke volumes. "Are you . . . sure?"

I was a little affronted by his lack of faith, honestly. "It will be fine. We'll keep it simple." At Kimo's continued pause, I remind him, "I basically raised my younger sisters when we were kids. I think I can handle watching two children just fine now that I'm an adult."

"I can pick something up on the way home. Why don't the three of you just relax and watch TV?"

"Kimo," I snapped. "We're making dinner. It's settled. Now just hurry and get here."

I hadn't even wanted to make dinner with the kids. I should have just let him pick up the fast food. When I've made dinner with them and Kimo before, it was fun, but I'm not much of a cook on my own, and I'm used to working on quiet, highly organized tasks I do independently.

There is nothing quiet or organized about the state of the kitchen right now. I thought peanut butter and jelly would be simple, but Nalani wants the creamy peanut butter and Makoa wants the chunky, and Makoa needs his crusts cut off but Nalani wants *her* sandwich cut in a triangle, not in two rectangles—and that's not even mentioning all the varieties of jellies in the fridge, and the children fighting over who gets the last of the strawberry.

Still, I shouldn't have shouted at Makoa. Even though he *was* attempting to put a knife in his mouth—the same butter knife we've been using on all the sandwiches, mind you.

But the volume I used to shout is too much, I realize it right away by the wide-eyed looks Makoa and Nalani are giving me. I do my best to soften my tone with a smile, because I can be fun and easygoing and flexible! "You don't want to spoil your dinner . . ." I search for some term of endearment that won't sound too baby-ish. Makoa is very sensitive about being treated like a baby. "You . . . silly goose!"

Aunty Kapono pops her head into the kitchen. She seemed more than fine with letting me take on the task of making dinner with the children on my own. *Thrilled*, even. Like Kimo, she seems to think I'm bound to fail. "Everything okay in here?" She gives me a look that lets me know there's no way she will be convinced things are *okay.*

"Great!" I will sail right past *okay* and into *great*. Why not? Things are fine in here. Everything is under control! "Aren't we having fun, kids?"

To my relief, the kids agree with this readily. "Yeah!"

Either they intuitively sense that I need them to be on my side for this, or they somehow find it fun to have a frazzled Russian lady shouting at them. Either way, I plaster my most reassuring smile on my face and give Aunty Kapono a thumbs-up. "Awesome!"

The "awesome" was too much; I sense it right away. Aunty Kapono frowns at me distrustfully but goes back to her show in the other room.

I turn back to the kids, feeling a surge of camaraderie with them after they didn't blow my cover with Aunty Kapono. "Okay, we have our sandwiches. Should we go eat?"

Makoa frowns. "What about drinks?"

"And side dishes?" Nalani asks. "We're not just going to eat *sandwiches* for dinner, are we?"

I do my best to keep smiling, though I can feel my expression getting a bit manic. "No. Right. Of course. We'll have drinks. And side dishes. Obviously."

"What kind?" Makoa wants to know.

What do kids drink? "Juice?" I try. That seems to work fine, since Nalani goes straight to the fridge to grab a few pouches. My shoulders relax a little. That wasn't so hard.

"What about the side dishes?" she presses again when she comes back out.

I flounder. "Fruit?"

Makoa makes a face at me. "I want chips!"

"Sure, great, chips," I agree.

Nalani and Makoa exchange a glance I intuitively don't like. "And Oreos," Nalani adds.

I frown. I'm not an idiot—I know she's pressing her luck, but just how much, is the question. If it would be normal for them to have an Oreo with dinner, I don't want to be the kind of ogre that says no just because I don't know what I'm doing. I fold my arms. "Does your uncle let you have Oreos with dinner?"

Another glance exchanged. "Sometimes," Nalani hedges.

I narrow my eyes at her. "One Oreo each," I agree finally. I feel like I'm probably being taken for a ride, but one cookie can't hurt that much, and hey, if it earns me a few brownie points with the kids, what's the harm?

"And ice cream!" Makoa tags on.

I give him my sternest face. "Don't push your luck."

Both kids scramble to the pantry to get their add-ons. By the time we're sitting down to eat, I'm already exhausted from the effort it took to produce even the simplest of meals. How does Kimo do this every single day?

Thinking of Kimo, I check my phone. It's been an hour since he last checked in with me, and I haven't heard anything else from him. I wonder what could be holding him up for so long? **Everything ok?** I text him before taking my seat with the kids.

But I don't hear anything back—not while we're eating, not after we've cleaned up, not even after Aunty Kapono has strong-armed the kids into bathing and putting on their pajamas.

I try calling him, to no avail. The call isn't declined, just rings out several times until it goes to voicemail. "Let me know you're okay as soon as you get this—please?" I don't bother to hide the anxiety in my voice, my stomach roiling as I hang up the phone.

Turning, I see Aunty Kapono standing in the doorway to the kitchen, watching me with a frown. "Still no answer?"

I can tell she doesn't like being on the same side as me in all of this. But I'm too worried about Kimo to care. "No. Have you tried calling him?"

"A few times," she allows, but she shrugs. "Maybe something came up." The look on her face suggests she doesn't believe it, though.

Reluctantly, she pulls out her phone. "I can look up his location."

"Great!" I move to stand behind her, trying to peer over her shoulder, but the glare she gives me has me retreating a few paces back. "Just, uh, tell me what you find . . ."

After glowering at me one more time for infringing on her space, Aunty Kapono gets lost in looking at whatever's on her screen. Her frown is not encouraging. "His phone is by the dockyard, near Calumet River."

My stomach sinks. "Why would Kimo be there? Something's not right."

"Maybe he had something to do there." Aunty Kapono sounds like she's trying to convince herself as much as she's trying to convince me. "Or he's just passing through."

"Refresh it in a few minutes," I suggest. "See if he's still there."

We wait in silence for a few tense minutes. I'm glad the kids are upstairs in their rooms, oblivious to what's going on. When Aunty Kapono refreshes the location, I can see by the look on her face that it isn't good. "Still there."

I begin pacing the room, biting my thumbnail worriedly, as my mind races over the possibilities. *No, don't go there, Matilda.* I need to be practical, think through solutions, things we can actually do. But it's easier said than done. When I think of what could have happened to Kimo, all the people out there who have a vendetta against him . . . There are people out there who want to *hurt* him, who have already tried kidnapping him. Maybe this time they won't just stop at that. Maybe . . .

"We need to call the police," I snap, not sure where my anger is directed—at myself, or maybe the situation in general? And a little bit at Kimo, too, if I'm being honest. If anything has happened to him, I'll never forgive him. And I know that doesn't make sense, but that's how I feel.

"And what will that help?" Aunty Kapono challenges. "I've seen all those cop shows. They won't do anything about a grown man going missing until at least forty-eight hours have passed."

She's right. *черт возьми.* Still, I protest, "Well, we have to do something!"

"*We,*" Aunty Kapono gestures back and forth between us, "don't have to do anything. I'm his mother. I'll take care of it. You're '*not the girl-friend,*' remember?"

I've been trying my best these past couple weeks to get Aunty Kapono on my side. I like her. I respect her. I want her to like and accept me, too, so I've been treading carefully, giving her my brightest smiles, putting forward my most easygoing personality, being on my very best behavior.

But you know what? Not tonight. "Of course I have to do something!" I explode at her. There's no hiding behind any artifice tonight. I'm too scared and worried to care what she thinks of me. "Kimo's been kidnapped three times already. The last time they were trying to take us to some abandoned island. If it's the same people, they aren't just taking him somewhere to talk. They might be trying to hurt him or, God, even worse. We have to do something!"

I see in her weary expression that Aunty Kapono is just as worried as I am. "What, though?" she asks, and I can hear her helplessness.

"I don't know!" I start pacing again. "But we have to do something."

A sudden idea strikes me, and before I can second-guess myself, I whip out my phone, dialing a number I haven't had to use until now. "It's Matilda. I need your help . . ."

Thad shows up even quicker than I'd hoped, and he's brought reinforcements with him—Helen and Nina and Grady, of course, but also some people I don't recognize.

"Celia and Joaquim are private detectives—the non-asshole variety," he introduces us briskly. "Woodruff is former CIA. And you know Stan."

I blink in surprise at the sight of Stan, my sometimes bodyguard. Apparently he and Thad are friends now.

Under any other circumstance, I'd want to know more details: How did this happen? What do they do together? Do they engage in law enforcement–adjacent activities, or do they just go to lunch together? But for now all I can think about is finding Kimo. "What do you need from us?" I ask.

Woodruff takes Aunty Kapono's phone so he can try to narrow down Kimo's last locations before his phone went dormant. Celia and Joaquim go over Kimo's daily activities with Aunty Kapono to retrace his steps. Nina and Helen go upstairs to look after Nalani and Makoa, making sure they stay calm and oblivious to what's going on downstairs. Grady makes a pot of coffee, which for the first time feels appropriate at this time of night.

Thad takes me out on the front stoop to ask me some questions away from everyone else. "When was the last time you heard from him?"

"It was about 5:00, 5:15." I anxiously pull up my call log, eager to help in any way I can. "5:17, to be exact."

"Do you know where he was?"

I shake my head in frustration. "No. Just that he was going to be running late. Maybe he was meeting with Jay? I can try texting him to see—"

"Mattie!"

I look up at the sound of the voice shouting my name, heart pounding with fear and hope at the sound of the nickname that no one else in the entire world would be allowed to call me. "Kimo?" I look around wildly, searching for him.

Then I spot him—Kimo, running down the sidewalk toward the house. In the dark, it takes me a moment to fully process what I'm seeing. Kimo is barefoot, his clothes torn and dirty, his hands tied behind his back. Still, he's running toward me as fast as he can. "Mattie!"

"Oh my God!" I hurry down the steps to get to him, Thad close on my heels. He helps steady Kimo as he makes it to the front path, stumbling in his haste and falling forward, nearly landing on his knees before Thad catches him.

I grab the front of Kimo's shirt as Thad helps steady him on his feet—not because Thad needs my help, or because I could possibly lift Kimo on my own, but because I need to be touching him, reassuring myself he's here, here's okay. I can feel his heart thrumming wildly beneath his shirt. I want to bury my face against it, sob out all of my worry and fear and relief, but instead I just keep gripping his shirtfront, searching his face to reassure myself I'm not imagining things, he's really back, and he's all right.

All the while, Kimo doesn't take his eyes off me. He is panting, struggling to catch his breath. "I didn't stand you up . . . or forget to call."

"Kimo . . ." It breaks my heart that this was the thing he was most concerned about, even as he was being held captive somewhere. Then I notice the gash on the side of his forehead, weeping out blood. Looking down, I see blood crusting his bare feet, too. "You're hurt!" I say stupidly. Somebody hurt him, intentionally, maliciously. This beautiful man with his beautiful heart, and someone beat him over the head and tied him up like an animal.

I look to Thad helplessly, at a complete loss of what to do. Pure adrenaline has driven me through this whole night until now, and suddenly Kimo is here in front of me and bleeding, and I don't know what to do.

"It's okay, Matilda," Thad reassures me, his voice calm and steady. "Get out your phone and call 9-1-1."

With trembling hands, I do.

Chapter Forty-Three

A couple hours later, Kimo's been stitched up and is resting comfortably in a hospital bed. He took a hard hit to the head when the kidnappers grabbed him, but the doctor reassures us that he's probably fine; they just want to hold him overnight to make sure.

Stan stayed behind with Helen, Nina, and Grady to keep an eye on the kids. Aunty Kapono, Thad, and I are crowded into the room now with Kimo, listening as he reissues his statement one last time to the police.

The nurse pokes her head in as the officers leave. "He's going to need to rest now. Five more minutes, and then any non-relatives will have to leave."

Once she's gone, Thad gives Kimo a grim look. "Sorry to make you keep repeating the same stuff over and over, but can you remember anything at all about the kidnappers that might be helpful? Any small detail?"

"They jumped me from behind and knocked me out. When I woke up, I could hear them talking in the other room, but I never saw anyone's face. It was only pure luck that one of the windows wasn't properly latched, so I was able to get away."

Kimo squeezes my hand, and I squeeze it back fiercely. The thought that someone would do that to him, that someone intended him real harm, makes me feel sick to my stomach, weak and helpless in ways I didn't know were possible.

"I'm pretty sure they weren't the same guys as the last time." Kimo winks at me. "I think the karate kid here must have scared them off."

I know he's just trying to get me to relax and stop worrying, but his jokey tone rubs me the wrong way. He just got kidnapped, *again*, and he's treating it like it's some kind of game. "The karate kid was a boy," I snap irritably.

"Not in *The Next Karate Kid*," Kimo corrects me lightly, clearly trying to tease me out of my bad mood. "Classic. I had such a big crush on Hilary Swank after that movie."

"Hilary Swank?" I feel like I heard her name somewhere recently. Then I sit up in my seat, eyes widening. "Hilary Swank!"

Mistaking my meaning, Kimo squeezes my hand again. "Relax, babe. That was a long time ago. Now I only have eyes for you."

I ignore him, fixing my eyes on Thad. "The first time I met Pika, he was really weird and singled me out at the office for no reason. He called me Hilary Swank."

Aunty Kapono scoffs. "You don't look anything like Hilary Swank."

"I know! That's the point. I had no idea why he would call me that . . . except now I know she was the karate kid. And who else, besides Kimo and the kidnappers, knew I kicked that kidnapper guy in the butt?"

"You think Pika hired them?" Aunty Kapono sounds like she doesn't quite know what to feel—torn between scoffing at the idea, because it comes from me, and hoping it could be true, since it would put an end to the custody case.

"It's possible, isn't it?" I look to Thad for confirmation.

Kimo clears his throat. "As much as I think that butthead's capable of it, I *did* tell the kids about your awesome karate moves. Maybe they told Pika during one of their visits?"

I guess that makes sense. But something in my gut is telling me I'm not wrong. It was the *way* Pika said it to me, like I was some thorn in his side, not a random woman his children had mentioned in a passing, funny anecdote. "It's worth looking into," I insist stubbornly.

Thad pulls out his phone. "Let me see if Stan can meet me. I think it's time we paid Pika a little visit . . ."

He ducks out into the hall, and I can hear him conversing with Stan on the phone—Stan's distinctive Boston accent coming through loud and clear —before his voice fades away. Kimo sighs. "Well, I don't wanna get my hopes up, but that would be convenient if it were true. Then we won't have to go to trial, and I won't get kidnapped anymore. I'm pretty sick of it, honestly."

There's that overly jokey tone again. It makes my stomach boil with rage. I snatch my hand out of his, rising to my feet. "It isn't funny," I bark at him. "Do you have any idea how worried we were?"

Kimo's face softens. He reaches for me. "I'm okay, though. Just a little bump on the coconut."

"*This* time," I remind him. "But one of these days you're not going to be able to buddy up with your kidnappers, or find a random, open window. What happens if you get seriously hurt? Killed? Who takes care of the kids then?"

Kimo doesn't have a glib answer for that. He looks to his mother appealingly, but she's uncharacteristically silent, watching this all play out.

"From now on, *you* need to hire a security detail. You need to have people keeping an eye on the house and the kids and *you*. You need to get some kind of alarm device so you can alert people, quickly, if you're in danger. I don't know—maybe Stan will know more about what options there are. And you need to check in with us more regularly, at least until we know who kidnapped you. We need to know where you are throughout the day so if you go missing, we can pinpoint your location more quickly."

"I . . ." Kimo takes in a deep breath through his nose, then sighs. "Okay. That all sounds reasonable. Anything you want to add, Māmā?"

Aunty Kapono shakes her head slowly. "No, I think Matilda's plan is good."

I blink at her in surprise. Did she just . . . agree with me? And call me by my name?

Before I can process it fully, the nurse sticks her head back in the room. "Time to rest, Mr. Kapono. You can have one person stay with you, but we don't allow non-family members after visiting hours."

I swallow, bracing myself to go. Leaving Kimo right now feels like I'm peeling off my fingernails one by one, but I know that Aunty Kapono will be all too happy to remind me that I'm not family. Not even "the girlfriend."

"I'll go," Aunty Kapono surprises me by saying. "I need to get back to the kids. You stay with your husband, Matilda." She gives me a pointed look, as if to say, *Be cool and go with it so the nurse doesn't call our bluff.*

I watch her leave, dumbfounded. What just happened . . . ? The nurse pops out again, after instructing us to get some rest, so I turn back to Kimo. It strikes me for the first time that he probably wanted his mother to stay here, that I'm just getting in the way. "Do you want me to ask your mom to come back?"

"Shut up and get over here." Kimo shifts a bit, making space for me on the bed. "I need my girl."

I comply all too eagerly, crawling into the comfort of his arms. The bed is too small for us to sleep comfortably together, but for at least a few minutes, I need to be near him, touching him, reassuring myself that he's all right. Once I'm settled in, my head resting on Kimo's chest, listening to his heart beat, I'm surprised by the sudden deluge of tears that overcomes me.

I weep in silence for a few moments, until Kimo notices and tilts my head up to face him. His face creases with concern. "Baby. What's wrong?"

My whole body is shaking. I can't catch the sob that escapes my throat. I don't want to say it—I don't want him to know how much it will hurt when he leaves—but I can't help myself. "I can't bear the thought of losing you," I manage finally through my tears.

Kimo cradles my face, catching my tears with the pad of his thumb. "I'm here, honey. I got you."

He cradles my head to his chest again, and I listen to his heart beat as he strokes my hair. It's nice, and sweet, and thoughtful, just like Kimo.

But I can't help but notice he doesn't tell me I won't lose him. I can't help but hear how he doesn't promise he'll stay.

Chapter Forty-Four

They discharge Kimo early in the morning. I think it might have something to do with me shadowing the doctor, asking intricate, detailed questions about home care for Kimo's stitches and what I should be on the lookout for in terms of head trauma and when he'll be able to get back to strenuous activity like exercising and sex and are there any painkillers he shouldn't use and should he avoid alcohol and for how long . . . ? And so on and so forth. All perfectly reasonable questions, I think you'll agree, but the next thing I know, the nurse is all but shooing us out of the room. "He's fine. Home rest will be the best thing for him. *Go home.*"

Luckily, Kimo is just as eager to get out of there. "I feel fine!" he reassures me when I worry, out loud, that he might be leaving prematurely.

I notice, though, that he isn't above playing up the severity of his injury when it serves him. After the elevator door closes on us, and we're alone together, he groans and leans his weight on me. "Oh, man. I feel a little unsteady. Can I hold on to you?"

My nerves are instantly on high alert. "Are you okay? Should we go find the doctor?"

Kimo leans heavily on me, pushing me back against the wall. One hand snakes down to cup my ass. "Just need something to hold on to for a moment," he murmurs into my shoulder. His other hand slides down to cup my other butt cheek.

I roll my eyes, smiling despite myself. "Feel better?" I deadpan.

"Mmm. My strength does appear to be returning, but I better hold on a minute just to be sure." His head dips down a bit further so he's nuzzling my breasts. "This could be the cure. Let me keep doing this to find out . . ."

"Kimo!" Laughing, I shove him away from me, though not too hard.

By the time we're in the parking lot, Kimo sees he has some missed calls from Jay, most likely due to the bad reception inside the hospital. Kimo calls him back right away, and I watch anxiously as Kimo paces up and down the rows of cars, deep in conversation.

When he returns to me, he looks dazed. "Pika confessed. Thad and Stan confronted him with phone records and some kind of CCTV footage they found, and he confessed. Not just to them—he made an actual statement to the police and everything."

My eyes widen. I was right . . . ? Even though I was the one to suggest it, I guess I didn't believe it could all be that easy, since my mouth drops open with genuine shock. "To the kidnappings?" I clarify, just to make sure I haven't misunderstood.

"He was behind all of them, except for the first one," Kimo confirms. "I guess that's what gave him the idea to stage fake kidnappings to try to get me to sign over my money. He's being detained, and the custody case is being dismissed. Jay thinks Pika might be able to work out some kind of plea bargain if he signs away his parental rights and agrees not to sue for custody again, but he'll be in touch once he's spoken with Pika's lawyer."

"Kimo! That's amazing." I pull him into a tight embrace, as all the while my mind races. It's all so much, so fast. Pika won't be able to hurt Kimo anymore. The kidnappings will stop. Nalani and Makoa will be safe and happy and in Kimo's custody.

Kimo will be free to go back to Hawai'i.

I can't focus on that part now, though. I'm too genuinely thrilled for him, for the kids, for Aunty Kapono. This is everything they've wanted. Now their family can be safe and together. "I'm so happy for you," I tell him sincerely.

Kimo remains silent. It takes me a moment to process that he's crying. He laughs self-consciously, rubbing at his eyes with the back of his hands, when I pull back to look at him. "What a big baby, huh?"

"Kimo." The rush of tenderness I feel for this man nearly knocks me off my feet. He's such a good man. I've been so lucky to get to know him. "Come here."

I embrace him, holding him tight as he battles through the powerful emotions. Excitement. Relief. But also, the terror that comes when you get the thing you've always wanted and can't quite believe it's real. That's a feeling I understand all too well. I'll hold him for as long as he needs me.

. . . until I feel one cheeky hand sliding down to squeeze my butt again. "Kimo!" I snap at him, though I'm laughing.

"Sorry. Feeling unsteady again."

I push away from him. "Come on, naughty boy. Let's get you home . . ."

On the way home, we brainstorm how best to tell the kids. Kimo doesn't want to scare them by telling them that their dad might be going to prison, and he doesn't want to sour them against Pika by telling them he was behind the kidnappings. Someday, if Pika rehabilitates and grows up, he might want to have a real relationship with his kids, and Kimo doesn't want to turn him into an evil bogeyman. When the kids are a bit older and can understand it better, he'll tell them the whole truth. For now, he decides, he'll explain that Pika made a mistake and needs some time to make it right, so for the time being they'll need to stay with Kimo.

The kids cheer when they hear the news they'll be staying with Kimo. Aunty Kapono bursts into tears. I watch Kimo wrap her up in his arms, and then he pulls the kids over so they're all huddled together, and I feel like my heart is too big for my chest. I am so, so happy for them.

I also know I don't belong here for this moment. The only question is how to tactfully excuse myself.

"We need to celebrate!" Kimo enthuses after a moment. "What should we do?"

"Chuck E. Cheese!" the kids shout in near unison.

Despite my worry about overstepping my boundaries, I have to laugh at their enthusiasm. I remember how much Alina and Sasha loved it there when we were kids. I guess some things never change. I suppose I must have loved it at some point, too, though it's hard for me to remember what it was like being a kid; it passed me by so quickly.

"I should go," I speak up before any half-hearted invitations can be extended—or worse, before Kimo pulls me aside and tells me this is a family thing and he'll call me later. "I have so much work to catch up on."

Kimo looks personally affronted by this news. "Mattie, you have to come." He levels me with a faux-stern look. "Don't make me play the kidnapping card."

"Come!" Nalani begs me, pulling on my hand, and Makoa shouts at the top of his lungs, "Let's go!!!" which isn't directed specifically at me, but still feels like I'm being included in his enthusiasm.

I can't help the quick glance I dart at Aunty Kapono as I brace myself for her snide comment. To my surprise, she smiles at me. "Tell your work it can wait. I can speak to your boss if you need me to."

"She will, too," Kimo mutters to me. "Don't call her on her bluff."

I'm so stunned by Aunty Kapono's kind words, her *smile*, I say nothing. For a moment, I actually wonder if she's plotting to poison my pizza, but I decide it isn't likely. Not *impossible*, but not likely. "O-okay," I stammer finally. "I'll come."

"Wonderful." Aunty Kapono shoos Kimo toward the stairs. "You, go wash off all those hospital germs and put on some proper clothes. Kids, go find your shoes—matching ones!"

Everyone disperses, leaving me alone with Aunty Kapono. She's still smiling at me, but it feels like a trap. I gulp.

"Come sit a moment and chat with me." The way Aunty Kapono says it, it's not a request. I woodenly follow her, taking the seat she motions me toward, but sitting on the edge of the chair, in case I need to make a quick escape.

For a long moment, she just regards me. I regard her, too, but with nowhere near her level of calm. I'm afraid if my eyes get any wider they're going to pop out of my head.

"Do you love my son?" she asks me finally.

I wish this couch would swallow me whole. I've barely been able to admit this to Kimo. I've barely been able to admit this to myself. Am I going to have to admit this to everyone in Kimo's family, too?

But because Aunty Kapono's expression tells me she both suffers no fools and takes no prisoners, I sigh and squirm uncomfortably. "Yeeeees?"

It's probably the least convincing way that anyone has ever confessed to loving someone. I clear my throat and try again. "Yes. I . . . care a great deal for him." Not wanting her to misread me like she did before with the "not the girlfriend" comment, I realize I'll need to show more enthusiasm. "I love him, okay? I love him!"

"Why?"

Oh, God. Some of the sisters in my order had warned me that I would be punished for breaking my vows, but I didn't know it would be *this* awful. "Because he's . . . good. He's a terrible dresser and a terrible singer, but a good cook. He makes me laugh. He makes me feel . . . safe." I press my eyes shut, unable to look at her as I say the next part. "He's only been in my life a short time, but I already don't know what I'll do without him."

Silence. I crack open an eye to see Aunty Kapono smiling at me again. *This* is the Aunty Kapono I suspected was there from day one. She is all warmth and kindness, and for the first time, I see what Kimo inherited from her. "I owe you an apology, Matilda. Kimo . . . his heart is so big. He trusts so easily. He's had people take advantage of that, even before the money, but you can imagine it only got worse afterward. I couldn't bear to see his heart broken again. But when I saw the way you rallied people to find him, how you forced him to finally get that security detail I've been nagging at him to get for over a year . . . I couldn't be blind to it anymore. I know you really care. And I'm sorry I didn't see that before."

To my surprise, she leans forward and hugs me. I reciprocate, but I'm so surprised, I'm sure my body is stiff as a board. This is going to take some getting used to.

Still, I smile hopefully at her as she pulls back, beaming at me as she squeezes my face. "So pretty. And tall. You're going to give my son beautiful babies, aren't you?"

A shocked, choking sound escapes my throat. Boy, she doesn't mess around, does she? Yesterday she hated my guts, and now she can't wait for me to start producing grandchildren. "Uhhh . . ."

As with before, though, Aunty Kapono's statement didn't seem to be a question so much as a proclamation. "And don't worry about your job. You'll be able to get one easy in Hilo. I know everyone there is to know."

At the h-word, something heavy and leaden sinks in my stomach. "Oh, well, I'm not sure that, uh . . ."

"We'll need to get back before Labor Day, before the kids start school, so you might want to give your notice soon."

I force myself to say the words. "Kimo hasn't asked me to go."

For one, stupid moment, I hope that Aunty Kapono will have some logical explanation to offer, that she'll wave away Kimo's behavior, tell me of course it's as serious for him as it is for me. But the look of surprise on her face is all the confirmation I need that what Kimo and I have is about to be over.

"Oh," she says uncertainly, frowning to herself. Then she blinks, and forces a smile at me. "Well, we can figure all that out later. Where are those kids . . . ?"

She rises to her feet and hustles out of the room—eager, I'm sure, to get away from the awkwardness of having basically confirmed to me that Kimo is planning on breaking up with me before he goes back to Hawai'i.

For a moment, I just sit on the couch, listening to Aunty Kapono scold the kids for getting distracted by something in the backyard, and to Kimo singing off-key in the upstairs shower. *Kimo.* I should have known. I should have known that someone who could love so easily couldn't be trusted to love for long.

The thing is, I don't even blame him. I'm not angry at him for breaking my heart. I'm surprised to find I don't even regret it. It was so, so perfect, even if it wasn't meant to be mine.

But I also can't just wait for the Band-Aid to be peeled off slowly. Kimo will try to be kind about it, I know, try to soften the blow, but that will be the thing that kills me—clinging to the rock of hope, as the waves keep bashing me up against it.

I let myself out quietly. When I'm a few blocks away and no longer able to keep myself from sobbing, I call the only person I'm confident will be there for me, no matter what.

"What is it?" Helen asks when she hears my sobs. "What's wrong?"

"I'm sorry to keep needing you for things—" I start, but she cuts me off swiftly.

"Don't be ridiculous, Matilda. I'm here. What do you need?"

Chapter Forty-Five

Tonight there's no Grady or Thad. It's just me, Helen, and Nina—the original nunsters. Which is good, because I've cried so hard and rubbed my makeup so vigorously that I'm sure my face looks like a chimney sweep's from Victorian England. I'm in the fetal position on my couch, hugging a throw pillow to my chest, and I can't stop sobbing. Even *Full House* is no help. I made it as far as popping in the DVD before I broke into another debilitating round of tears, and now the home screen is playing over and over on a loop in the background, the sappy cheerfulness punctuating my grief like a neon '90s dagger.

The last wall has finally been knocked down and there is nothing left to hold me up. I'm broken.

I'm only half aware of Helen and Nina fretting over me. ". . . do you think it's Kimo?" Nina wants to know, in a whisper.

"If it is, I'll kill him," Helen vows, also in a whisper, then quickly amends, "Or maybe just wrack up his late fines so high that he'll never be able to step into another library again."

"I can still hear you, even if you're whispering," I manage to croak at them, making both of them jump in surprise. "And don't blame Kimo. It isn't him. It's me. It's always me."

Above my head, I see them exchange a bemused glance. "What do you mean?" Helen asks finally, reaching down to stroke away some of the hair that's matted to my face with tears. Probably snot, too.

Sniffling, I sit up, wiping a forearm over my face. "It's okay. I know there's something wrong with me. I'm unlovable. I hold people too far at a distance. I say all the wrong things. I'm mean for no reason sometimes. Sometimes I'm hungry, but sometimes I'm just *mean*. My own sisters don't want to be around me. I try to pretend that they're just busy with their lives, but I've known the truth for a while now. It's not that they can't make time—they just don't *want* to make time, for me. I can't hold on to any friends for more than a few years. Even my own mother didn't want to keep me. Every time I try to hold on to something, I end up holding on too tight and breaking it, but I don't know how to stop myself. There's something wrong with me, too wrong to fix, and no one will ever . . ."

By now I'm sobbing again, so hard that I can barely speak coherently, huge hiccuping gasps interrupting my words. Nina and Helen have flanked me on either side of the couch, and as if by mutual agreement, they both cocoon me in a hug at almost exactly the same moment.

"We love you, Matilda," Nina says, quietly but firmly. "You're passionate, not mean."

"Sometimes you're mean," Helen corrects. It sounds like she's crying, too. "But . . . we all are sometimes. Nobody's perfect. That doesn't mean we don't deserve love. And we *love* you, Matilda."

I cover my face again. "You're just saying that because I'm crying."

"No, we're not!" Nina insists. "No one checks up on me more than you do. No offense, Helen, but I don't know if I would have kept coming to book club if it weren't for you, Matilda. Helen was always so nice and polite about her invitations—it would have been so easy to just stop showing up. But I remember back in the beginning when I missed one meetup, you texted me fourteen times in four days to make sure I would be there the next time. I had no choice but to come! And I'm so glad I did."

I don't know whether to laugh or cry some more at this story. "So I bullied you into being my friend?"

"You knew what was best for me," Nina corrects. "And you made sure that I did, too."

"You take care of the group," Helen agrees, gently forcing me to uncover my face again. "You're everybody's protector. You're our fierce mama bear, and we would be lost without you."

I look back and forth between them. "Really?"

Helen squeezes my arm. "Really. Now . . ." She pauses long enough to pick up the remote and mute the television, putting an end to the ceaseless *Full House* theme song loop. "Tell us what happened, exactly . . ."

When I finish my story, Helen and Nina exchange a glance that they probably think is subtle. It isn't. "What?" I snap at them out of habit. Then, remembering that I'm supposed to be nicer now, I try to soften my tone. A little. It's more in the delivery, really. "What's that look for?"

"Kimo's never said he *doesn't* want you to come to Hawai'i, right?" Nina asks me gently.

I shake my head, already anticipating that point. "He doesn't have to. Believe me, I know the signs of being left behind."

"You thought we were going to leave you behind when we brought Thad and Grady into the group," Helen reminds me, "But we weren't ever going to do that."

"You weren't?"

"Matilda!" Helen sounds genuinely offended. "Never. I know bringing in Thad and Grady changes the dynamic, but there's safety in numbers, you know? The three of us lasted on our own for so long, just us against the world, but now we don't need to do that. We have Thad to scare off anyone who might mean us harm—"

"—and to keep you happy with lots of orgasms," I remind her.

Helen's face flushes pink. "And that, yes, and we have Grady to . . . talk in an Irish accent and make us lots of coffee."

"Every group needs one of those," Nina says with a smile.

I can't smile, not yet. My heart is still aching. It's the kind of ache I feel like I'll be carrying with me for the rest of my life. I feel like all the fight has gone out of me, all the bark and all the bite.

"The point being," Helen continues, "that we were never going to ice you out. You don't just get rid of the people you love. I'm so, so sorry that's happened to you in the past. But that says more about the people who did that to you than it does about you."

Nina nods her earnest agreement. "We're not going anywhere." She takes in a deep breath, steeling herself. "And as your friend, I think you need to have a real conversation with Kimo. Not just run away."

I shake my head reflexively—a quick, almost violent jerk. "He's probably relieved that I've given him an out."

"Have you checked your phone since you left?" Helen asks.

I stare at my phone, which I've put on silent and turned upside down on the table. It is so much more than a phone, all of a sudden. If I flip it over and see no missed calls, no texts, I'll know I have my answer. And even though I suspect I already know the truth, having that final confirmation might break me all over again. "I'm too scared."

"I'll look." Helen picks up the phone. Her face is impassive for a moment, then she smiles ruefully at me. "Fifteen missed calls in under two hours."

Nina laughs, too. "He's even more Matilda than you are. I only got fourteen texts in a few days when you couldn't find me."

"Give that to me!" I open the home screen and see he's texted, too, and left voicemails—lots of voicemails:

"Hey, Mattie, where'd you run off to? Everything okay?"

"Listen, I don't know what Māmā said to you, but she says she's sorry. Can we talk?"

"Mattie, I'm trying to give you space here, but can you just let me know you're okay?"

"Shit. Māmā told me what you talked about. Shit. Shit. Can we talk?"

"Please talk to me, Mattie, I need to explain . . ."

Hearing the urgency, the desperation in his tone only increasing with each missed call, something shifts inside of me. I recognize that emotion, that violent intensity of feeling, that need to do anything to keep the other person around, and in your life. I look to Helen and Nina with wide, wondering eyes. "I think he really loves me."

Nina and Helen are both crying and laughing on either side of me as they watch this all play out. "I think he really does," Helen agrees, and Nina nods happily, wiping at her eyes.

Then we hear it—Bon Jovi's "Always," booming from outside.

Helen, Nina, and I exchange a glance. "Kimo," I say, unable to stop the grin that stretches my mouth.

I race over to the window, with Nina and Helen close behind me. Sure enough, Kimo is down there, two portable speakers on the ground next to him, and a variety of potted plants around him.

Potted plants? I look to Helen and Nina in confusion. Is this a romantic gesture I'm unaware of? But they both look confused, too.

Kimo tries to shout something up at me, but I can't make it out. Frowning, I push open the window. "What?"

"I know the potted plants look less romantic, but they're more environmentally sustainable!" he calls up to me. "I hope that's okay."

That . . . really isn't what I thought he was going to lead with. But I guess it is very Kimo. "Why did you bring them here?" I call down to him.

"What?" he calls back.

The speakers must be deafening next to him; I can barely hear him over them, and I'm on the third floor. I cup my hands over my mouth. "Turn down the music!"

It takes him a moment to piece it together, but then he gives me a thumbs-up and turns down the volume. Even so, a few passersby stop on the street to watch whatever it is he's doing. Someone holds up their phone and takes a picture.

Kimo doesn't notice any of it, though. He only has eyes for me. His face looks crestfallen. "Have you been crying, baby?"

"No." But that's obviously a lie, even with three stories separating us. I sniff. "Maybe."

"You gotta believe me, Mattie. I was going to ask you to come with me. That's been the plan for a while now—almost from the first time I met you. Definitely since we realized we didn't have condoms on Mackinac Island."

The onlookers glance up at me at this overly confessional bit of information. Maybe I should be embarrassed, but I can't help but smile at Kimo's revelation. Screw those strangers and what they might be thinking. "Really?"

"Really. I just didn't want to scare you off since it's all been happening so crazy fast. But when you meet the person you were meant to love, your heart doesn't need time to catch up. Your brain might not get it, but your heart, your gut, the rest of you knows it. I know it, Mattie. I want you with me for the rest of my life. Hawai'i is home, but it won't be home without you."

Then, to my complete and utter shock, he drops down to one knee. "I was gonna get a ring, but I don't know your ring size. We've only known each other a few weeks, you know? But I know you're brave, you're strong, you're beautiful. You're a tiger fighter, but I want to be the one to fight tigers for you now, honey. Will you marry me?"

Helen and Nina gasp. I'm too shocked to even make that much noise. I don't know how to hold this feeling inside of me, my stomach swirling with nerves and adrenaline, and my head rushing from the shock, and my heart trying to burst out of my chest with the joy I'm feeling at his words. He loves me. He wants to marry me. He wants us to build a home, a family, together. It's a dream that's been building in me since the Over the Rainbow Gala, when I saw him walking down those stairs toward me—no, earlier than that, I realize. Since he started singing the *Full House* theme song to me on that boat so I wouldn't be so afraid.

I always thought pure and total happiness would be something bright and loud, but I realize now it is breathtakingly quiet.

Before I can form a response, I see a shoe hurtling through the air from the floor above me, clipping Kimo's forehead. He staggers back. "Keep it down!" someone shouts from upstairs.

I make it outside in record time, grasping Kimo by the face so I can examine the damage. Luckily the shoe struck him on the side opposite from his recent head injury, but it was still too close for comfort. A spot on his left temple is reddened and raised, and it looks like a bump is already forming.

The idiot doesn't even seem to notice—he's too busy giving me a gushy, happy smile. "Mattie," he says, reaching up to stroke the side of my face.

There will be time for that later. I turn my glare up to the window where the shoe thrower lives. "You better lawyer up, asshole! I know people. You're gonna be paying off a settlement for the rest of your life."

Kimo huffs a laugh behind me. "Mattie, it's cool. He already apologized. He didn't mean to hit me, just scare me off. I think I woke his baby up."

I should have known the assaulter would have already been Kimo'd in the few seconds it took me to get down here. But remembering that shoe arcing through the air, clobbering my man, I'm not so easily placated. "Your child will be paying off that settlement, too!" I warn.

"Mattie." Kimo guides my gaze back to him, holding both sides of my face now and looking deep into my eyes. "Was there something else you wanted to say to me, or did you just want to threaten one of your neighbors and all of his descendants?"

The fire instantly drains out of me, like someone has reached up and shut off a valve. I would go to war for Kimo if he needed me to. But that isn't what he needs from me now. What he needs from me is far more terrifying than putting my life on the line.

It's my heart that's on the line now.

My eyes dart across his hazel gaze. I see amusement there, patience. I see a man who sees *me* in return, not just my body or my face, but my warts, my flaws, my *soul*, and against all odds, finds me endearing. No, more than endearing—enchanting. I see someone who is too good to be true, and yet he is the realest person I know. Pono. Good one. The best one. My Kimo.

"Yes," I tell him.

Kimo furrows his brow. "Yes, you just want to threaten your neighbor . . . ?"

I shake my head, unable to help the grin of pure joy that's splitting across my face. "Yes, I'll marry you."

Kimo lets out a cheer that is somehow both high-pitched and guttural, as well as being completely unlike anything I've ever heard. As he crushes me in his arms and swings me around, I hear Helen and Nina cheering from upstairs and several passersby applauding us on the street. From a fourth-floor window comes the sound of a crying baby and a long, belabored sigh.

I'm too thrilled to care about that karmic revenge—well, I'm too thrilled to *only* care about that karmic revenge. When Kimo sets me down, he gives me a not entirely PG-rated kiss that is captured on several strangers' phones as they happily snap pictures and take videos. I'm sure some tabloid will be writing about this tomorrow. Oh, well. At least this time I'm wearing a bra.

Seeming to become aware of the onlookers, Kimo pulls me close to murmur in my ear, a moment just for us. "Sorry I don't have a ring. I'll get you whatever you want—just name it."

I smile even harder and pull him even closer. "I don't care about the ring. I just want you." After a moment, I tag on, "But that being said, I wouldn't turn down an Edwardian-era, marquise-cut diamond . . ."

Chapter Forty-Six

Turns out, there are so many details to consider when upending your life for the man that you love. I have to break my lease, cancel all my utilities, forward my mail, pack all my things, locate a copy of my amended birth certificate with my order of adoption (with the help of Brian and Connie), and turn in my two weeks' notice to Jay.

"I don't know what we're going to do without you," Jay tells me with one of his rare, brisk hugs. We've gone back to being completely professional with each other, mutually agreeing to forget that a few weeks ago I was taunting him about not wearing any underwear. That honestly feels like a whole lifetime ago now. It feels like that all happened to a different person.

I'm Happy Matilda now. I smile more, and I am generally more patient, and I hardly ever tell off total strangers, unless they really deserve it.

"Are you getting another paralegal job in Hawai'i?" Barry wants to know.

Jay and I exchange a glance and then both burst out laughing. I laugh until I'm weeping. "No," I tell a bemused Barry. "I'm marrying a multimillionaire. I won't be working for pennies to make other people look good anymore."

I can make light of it now, but it's more complicated than that, in all honesty. I feel weird about giving up my job, since I've been working at least one job, usually multiple jobs, since I was eighteen. But after many long discussions—and my insistence on a prenup to show to the world I'm marrying this man for his looks instead of his money—Kimo comes up with a compromise.

"I'll have Jay draft a prenup under one condition," he tells me seriously. "I want you to choose a charitable cause, any cause, and create a foundation for it, then run it."

"Me?" I blink at him, flabbergasted. "I don't know how to do that."

"You basically ran Eastman, Bergman & Hart. And everyone there will vouch that your talents were wasted by formatting documents and sending emails. If you put your mind to it, you can end world hunger, or whatever it is you decide you want to do."

I don't know about all that, but I do know what cause I want to get behind: the foster care system. I'll start small on the Big Island and see what kind of difference we can make there. It might not change the whole world, but maybe it can help one family like mine.

It's a daunting task to take on when I think of how badly I failed my own sisters. When I text them to tell them about my engagement, I'm surprised when Alina calls me right away.

She wants to know everything about Kimo. "I looked him up online. Isn't he rich? Like, *rich* rich?"

Something about the question curdles my stomach. She hasn't asked me anything else about him—not if he's kind, not if he's good to me, not if we're happy. But I reason with myself that his wealth *is* the most Google-able thing about him. "He's doing well for himself. But he's actually trying to give most of it away to good causes."

"I read about that, too. Any chance he'll want to *give* me a house on the water? I'm a good cause, haha!"

The way she says it, it doesn't really sound like she's joking, more like she's fishing. And it makes me feel sick to my stomach. The more I think about it, the more I realize that every significant interaction I've had with Alina since I was about sixteen has only occurred when I could do something for her—usually something to do with money. Could I give her money for a prom dress, even if it meant taking on extra jobs and missing my own prom so she could go? Could I help support her throughout her schooling? Could I cosign her student loan? She lives two hours away from me now, but I haven't seen her in over a year, and the last time was only for a quick coffee and so I could give her a gift I'd gotten for her graduation from dental school.

Sasha waits over a week to respond to my engagement announcement, then writes a quick, unpunctuated **congrats**. That's it.

Kimo comforts me as I confide the whole thing to him. "I just feel like I've let them down so badly," I tell him as he gently strokes my back. "They needed me to keep our family together, and I just couldn't."

Two months ago, I couldn't have fathomed being this vulnerable with anybody. Now it feels like a gift to put myself into Kimo's hands, to show him all the best and worst parts of me, and trust that he'll love them all unconditionally.

To my surprise, "Hmm," is all Kimo says in response.

Frowning, I lift my head from his chest to look at him. "Hmm?" I repeat.

Kimo looks torn. "Do you want me to just listen, or do you want me to give my honest opinion?"

Does he know who he's talking to? "Honesty, always!"

"I think maybe it's time to set some boundaries with your sisters. I get it—it's difficult with family, and you want to be there for them. But they need to be there for you, too. You can't just be their ATM or someone they get to use as a punching bag because you couldn't work miracles when you were kids."

I stare at him, aghast. What he's saying makes sense on an intellectual level, but in my gut . . . it feels like a betrayal. I can't admit that my sisters aren't there for me because then I really did fail at keeping our family together.

I swallow heavily. "My sisters are my only family. I can't just cut them off."

"No one said you have to cut them off. But they can't treat you like they do and still expect you to drop everything for them whenever they need you. They're both grown-ups now." Kimo pulls me close again. "And who says they're your only family? Family isn't just the people we were born to. It's the people we choose, and the people who choose us."

I guess . . . I guess he's not entirely wrong. The Kaponos—not just Kimo, but Nalani and Makoa and Aunty Kapono, too—they've taken me in and made me completely their own. Dominika and I have been emailing again and we're planning on having dinner before I move. Brian and Connie and I have been getting breakfast every week and catching up. And of course, I have Helen and Nina. Grady and Thad.

I've known for a long time now I was a Gibbler, not a Tanner. I wasn't born into the perfect sitcom family. My life is weird and complicated. My personality is abrasive and not everyone's cup of tea. But just like Kimmy, I found a family I wanted to be a part of, and I forced my way in. I wore them down until they finally realized they had no choice but to keep me.

I lost two sisters when my family was torn apart so many years ago. It felt like my life was ending. It felt like something I could never recover from. But I did, even if it took me a very long time. And I gained two sisters along the way: Helen and Nina.

Which is why the next time I break down in tears, Helen is the one that I call. "I can't do it," I sob to her. "I can't marry Kimo."

———

Even though it's two in the morning, Helen comes straight over. She's wearing her pajamas, and she has a grumpy Thad in tow, but she leaves him on the couch and comes into my bedroom to talk me through it.

"What's going on, Matilda?" Her eyes search mine worriedly. "Did something happen with Kimo?"

"No." I let out a sobbing hiccup. "He's perfect. The best man that has ever lived, and I'll always love him. But he needs to be in Hawai'i and I need to be here, so we can't be together."

Helen's tired, beautiful angel face creases into a frown. "I thought that was all decided? You've broken your lease and forwarded your mail."

"But I'll be leaving!" I gesture around my room wildly, to all the packed boxes and bare walls. "I'm not the one who leaves. I'm the one who gets left behind. And now I finally have people here who love me, and I'm going to abandon that? I must have been crazy to think I could."

"Matilda." Helen pulls me into a tight, bracing hug. "This is just life, you know? We were all bound to move on at some point. Get married. Have babies. Move for our work. Whatever it was, it wasn't possible to keep everyone together forever."

I stifle another sob. "Maybe you can all move to Hawai'i? I'm rich now. I'll pay for it!"

Helen laughs quietly. "We'll come to visit. And you'll come here to visit. And we'll do video calls and Nina will send you all her gifs, and we'll find a way to stay in touch."

"That won't work." I shake my head decisively. "We'll drift apart. Everything will be different."

"Everything *will* be different, but that doesn't mean it'll be bad. It will just be . . . different. And it might be a little awkward sometimes, but we'll push through it. You don't leave behind the people that you love. You carry them with you, wherever you go."

After a moment's pause, I pull back, making a face at her. "That's so cheesy."

Helen laughs, wiping at my eyes with her palm. "Well, I hate to break it to you, but love is cheesy. It's scary and it's cheesy. It's—casu martzu."

I frown at her. "What the hell is that?"

"It's that cheese with the live maggots in it. It was the scariest cheese I could think of."

At my aghast look, Helen laughs, then shows me a picture of it on her phone. Truly horrific stuff. Then that turns into looking at pictures of Hawai'i and planning when Helen will be able to come visit, until we remember that it's almost three in the morning now and we snuggle in together to fall asleep on the bed. "What about Thad?" I ask on a yawn.

"Guaranteed he's already asleep on the couch," Helen tells me with a fond roll of her eyes. "That man can fall asleep anywhere. I guess it comes from sleeping in weird hotels and in his car and whatnot while he's bounty hunting."

I'm usually not much of a snuggler, but tonight I'm so happy Helen is here with me. "Will you still send me videos of maggot cheese when I'm in Hawai'i?"

She leans her head on my shoulder. "Just try and stop me."

Chapter Forty-Seven

I feel better about everything, mostly, until I'm standing in the airport, all of my bags checked, ready to go through security. Kimo and his family have gone ahead of me to the Big Island so they can get the kids set up for school and so I could tie up all my loose ends here in Chicago, so I'll be flying alone. But Helen, Nina, Thad, and Grady have come to see me off, each bearing a small gift. Nina gives me a pair of extra-thick socks. "Just in case you get too cold on the plane."

Thad gives me a copy of *Old Yeller*, since I "like books about dogs so much."

Grady gives me a keychain with the symbol for the women's bathroom, along with a wink. "So you won't get confused and go in the wrong one next time."

Last but not least is Helen, who gives me a T-shirt with a Pizookie on it. "Every Tuesday night," she reminds me with tears in her eyes. "It's still a requirement, even if you're in a different state."

I hug each of them in turn, hearing Grady and Thad *oof* in surprise when I get to them—they're not as used to my trademark Matilda tight-armed hug as the other two. With Helen and then Nina, I linger just a little bit longer. The men are tolerable, but these are the two I'll really miss. My sisters.

"Am I making a huge mistake?" I ask Nina. I'm not really worried anymore, but I want to hear from at least one more person that I'm not completely crazy for moving out of the continental United States for a man I didn't even know three months ago. And I also need someone to help me assuage this terrible guilt that I'm feeling. Helen will be fine on her own, especially now that she has Thad, but what about sweet little Nina? Who will protect her from all the ogling men of the world and her weird, overbearing uncle?

"No," Nina tells me simply, "but if you are, you can always come back. And we'll be here."

For the first time in my life, I'll be the one doing the leaving. I've never been on this end of things. It helps, a little, to know just how hard it is to leave behind the people you love. Almost as hard as it is to be the one left behind.

It also helps to know that Kimo's promised I can come back to visit Chicago as much as I want, and Helen and Thad are already planning a trip to come out and see us. Maybe we can persuade Nina and Grady to come along, too.

And it helps even more to know that Kimo will be waiting for me on the other side.

"I guess this is it," I say once I've released Nina from my death grip. I survey the group of them and am surprised to feel tears stinging my eyes. *Again*. What a baby I've turned into all of a sudden! "Try not to get murdered without me."

Helen and Nina come in for one last hug. "We love you, Matilda," Helen tells me.

I sniff. "Enough of the mushy stuff." But after a beat, I can't help but add, "I love you, too."

Then without looking back again, I march myself into the security line. No more looking back. It's time to look forward.

Once I'm settled on the plane, I take out the card that Kimo made me promise to wait to read until now. My inner cynic can't help but worry that it's a confession of murder or some other awful thing, now that I've already upended my life and can't turn back.

Instead, I find it is something quite different.

.   .   .

Mattie,

I can't believe I get to bring you home and keep you. Thank you for being willing to give up your life in Chicago for me. The hard part is over now. I'll take care of the rest. I got you, baby. I can't wait to start our forever.

Love,
Kimo

My heart is doing that thing again, where it feels too big for my body. I hug the card to my chest and can't help but grin at the woman sitting next to me. "I'm going home," I tell her.

For the first time, I'm going home.

———

I try to keep that sense of happy calm with me as I get off my flight at the Kona Airport, but I'm not a zen person by nature. Love hasn't "fixed" me or made me any different from who I've always been. I'll still have grouchy days, and I'll always be just a little too blunt and get irritated by the often stupid things that people do.

I'm supposed to be making this great journey home to the man I love, but I have a hard time sleeping on the flight, and my seatmate accidentally spills a bit of her coffee on my lap. I still get knocked in the head when someone opens the overhead compartment too early and their bag falls out right on top of me. People disregard the clearly stated rules of the plane and try to push their way to be the first off, and their flagrant self-interest makes me grind my teeth in irritation. I lose Grady's keychain somewhere between my seat and the bathroom, ironically enough, and the line is so long for the women's bathroom in the terminal that I'm afraid Kimo will think I didn't get off the plane. I would text him, but my phone died somewhere over the Pacific Ocean and the outlet in my seat wasn't working, so I couldn't charge it again.

In the bathroom, I splash my face and try to ease some of my building anxiety, but I'm in a new, unfamiliar place, all on my own, and I'm a little terrified. It doesn't help when I leave the secured area and can't see Kimo anywhere. What if he got the times mixed up? What if I misunderstood where we were supposed to meet?

There's some gigantic family blocking my view, all of them excitedly searching for someone in the crowd as they hold up huge signs that prevent me from seeing if Kimo is standing somewhere further back. How inconsiderate. Who brings this many people to an airport, anyway?

Irritated, I start to push my way past them, when I hear someone shouting my name. "Matilda!"

Blinking in surprise, I turn to see Nalani and Makoa breaking away from the giant family group. They each take me by an arm, jostling me as they argue over who gets to lead me to the car. "She wants to sit by me!" Nalani insists, though Makoa seems to feel like it's his turn.

Then I spot Aunty Kapono, standing off to the side. Now that I look more closely, I realize that many of these people seem to bear a strong resemblance to her. I also see that the signs they're holding say *my* name.

"Kimo was trying to get hold of you," Aunty Kapono explains to me as I get closer. "He thought he might get better reception by the parking lot. Oh, there he is—Kimo!"

My heart instantly warms at the sight of Kimo jogging toward me, grinning as big of a smile can get as his flip-flops smack along the floor. He picks me up and swings me around, oblivious to my slightly bruised forehead and coffee-stained pants. The moment I see him, I become oblivious to those minor irritations, too. I'm back with Kimo again. Everything is going to be all right.

"Mattie." He sighs my name like he, too, has been twisted up into a big ball of anxiety until this moment. "I couldn't find you. But you're here."

"I'm here," I say easily, like I didn't just have one of the most miserable flights of my life. It's over now. No looking back, only forward. Leaning into him, I whisper, "Who are all these people, and why are they here?"

I feel him smiling against my ear. "Remember my big invasive Hawaiian family? Well, now they're *your* big invasive Hawaiian family, too. I asked them to give you some space, but they couldn't wait to meet you."

My family? These people are here for *me*? I look around in wonder, taking in the smiling, happy faces of the crowd, their eagerness to meet me, and their willingness to take in a total stranger and accept me as their own.

Maybe there will come a time when it begins to feel like it's too much, when that kind of easy, open love becomes smothering.

But for now? For now, I've been waiting my whole life for this.

I link my fingers through Kimo's, grinning at him as I pull him toward the group—our family, our future, our home. "What are we waiting for . . . ?"

Epilogue

(Seven months later)

Nina

It's Tuesday night—Tuesday afternoon in Hawai'i—and Helen and I sit patiently with our take-home Pizookie in front of us, waiting for Matilda to join the video call. Thad is out doing bounty hunting stuff, and Grady caught a cold, so it's just the three of us tonight—the OG ex-nun club.

That means half a Pizookie for me, if Helen and I split things evenly. I already know I'll be lying about that in the food diary I give to my aunt at the end of the week. Even though it's only a small sin, I feel my stomach churning at the thought.

But I won't focus on that now. I'm too excited to see Matilda. She's been busy with the kids' school stuff for the past couple weeks, so she's missed our regular Tuesday meetings. I'm sure their PTA was not ready for Matilda when she arrived, but she's already managed to run two major fundraisers that have doubled the amount of money going toward art and aftercare programs, on top of the work she's been doing to get her founda-tion off the ground.

"Should we try again?" I start to suggest to Helen, when all at once the screen switches and Matilda peers in at us from the other side.

"Sorry I'm late! I was trying to find a quiet room. Kimo's cousins from Oahu showed up unannounced, so he's trying to get a barbecue going, and Makoa's practicing his drums upstairs. Hopefully we'll get some peace here in the bedroom."

Despite all this, Matilda is grinning. She looks frazzled but happy by all the craziness surrounding her. Her hair has grown out quite a bit since the last time we saw her in person, and even though it's March and still freezing (at least, here in Chicago), her usually dark blonde hair has brightened with the warm, sun-kissed streaks that come from spending lots of time outside.

I can't help but smile in response to her obvious, contagious happiness. Matilda was always a beautiful woman, but there was something stern and foreboding about her before. She looks softer now, more approachable—though there's no doubt it's a hundred-percent Matilda when she opens her mouth again.

"Oh, *дерьмо*, that's my vibrator." She tosses something off the bed that we couldn't see anyway.

I feel myself blushing, and I can tell Helen is stifling a laugh, though she quickly changes the subject. "Matilda, we've missed you! What's new? Anything exciting?"

Matilda rolls her eyes. "You won't believe the idiots I have to deal with down at Makoa's school. They're making my life a nightmare—"

The door opens in the background and Kimo enters, seemingly oblivious to the video call—or at least, I assume so, since he immediately rips off his shirt and throws it onto the bed. My eyes widen. "Uh, Matilda . . . ?" I say in warning as he shucks off his pants, leaving him in only his briefs.

Matilda glances behind her, then does a double take. "Kimo! I'm on a video call."

"With who?" Completely unabashed about his partial nudity, Kimo gets closer to the screen, squinting at us before grinning in recognition. "Oh, hey, ladies! Good to see you! That's right, it's Tuesday."

He's grinning at us so easily that I feel guilty at my instinct to avert my gaze, seeing as he's standing in front of us in only his underpants. (Another thing I won't be writing about in my sin journal this week.) "Hi, Kimo!" I do my best to wave and smile, reminding myself that he's not wearing less clothing than if he were in his bathing suit. Even though it's his underwear. And he's standing in his bedroom. Where there was just a vibrator on the bed.

Don't be weird, I tell myself vehemently. *It's fine. Everything is* fine.

Luckily, from somewhere in the Kapono household, a dog barks. "Kimo, you let the dog in!" Matilda scolds.

"Whoops! Come here, Comet . . ." With that, Kimo disappears offscreen.

Helen looks at me with wide eyes, and I'm relieved to find I'm not the only one taken aback by the sheer chaos of this call. "Matilda—did you get a dog?" she asks.

We exchange a quick, amused glance. The last time we had a video chat, Matilda was adamant that no way, never, under no circumstances, would she ever allow Kimo to get the dog he and the kids had been begging for.

Now Matilda's thunderous gaze suggests that "never" ended up only being about two weeks or less. "It's not my dog, it's Kimo's dog."

"Don't listen to her!" Kimo calls from offscreen. "She loves him more than any of us. She bought him a doggie coat—"

Matilda stands up and disappears from view, though we can hear the sound of a door being shut, *firmly*. When she sits back down, her glare dares either one of us to challenge her. "It gets cold at night and I didn't want the dog to get sick. That's all."

I refrain from exchanging another look with Helen, even though I'd bet my whole sugar allowance for a week that she's also fighting a smile.

"Enough about me—my life is obviously in shambles right now." Matilda waves her hands dramatically, though it sounds more like her old bark than actual bite. "What's new with the two of you?"

Helen shrugs. "Not much here. Just getting ready for a weekend trip. We'll go back to Boston for Easter with my parents. Thad has a plan to finally win over my mom so"—she holds up her crossed fingers—"thoughts and prayers, please! He'll need all the luck he can get."

It's hard for me to imagine anyone not liking Thad. I knew from the moment Helen showed me the picture she'd taken of him at the library and told me about the "Red Unicorn" that he was going to be the one for her. And he's so in love with her he can barely think straight. I actually saw him walk into a wall once because he was so distracted by staring at her.

I knew Kimo was the one for Matilda, too, the first time she brought him to book club. Well, the first time he *made it* to book club, that is. It was the way he looked at her, like he'd found something rare and precious.

Then again, I tend to be a bit of a romantic. Uncle Aaron says I need to set more realistic expectations. There are some people, I suppose, who get big epic love stories, and others who would probably do better with quiet companionship.

I think you can probably guess which category I'm in.

"What about you, Nina?" Helen asks me, pulling me back into the conversation. "Any special Easter plans?"

I'll be spending most of the day either helping with the cooking and cleaning, or minding my younger cousins. I've learned not to say things like that too often, though, because of those looks that Matilda and Helen always exchange when I do, thinking I don't notice. But I do. There's not a lot I don't notice. It's one of the benefits of being quiet and forgettable. I *see* things, even things that other people don't mean for me to see.

"Just time with family," I say vaguely, hoping that will be enough to throw them off the scent.

"What about Grady? Will he be alone for Easter?" Matilda worries out loud. I can tell from the look on her face that she doesn't like the thought of anyone being on their own.

For the first time, it strikes me that *she* has probably often been on her own these past few years, since Helen and I both usually spend holidays with our families. The thought honestly never crossed my mind before, but now that it has, I feel sick with guilt. She must have been so lonely. She never said she would be on her own, but I should have guessed it— knowing how proud Matilda is, *was*, and how much she hated asking for help. If I'd been a better friend, I would have anticipated it. I don't know that inviting her to spend the holidays with *my* family would have been much fun for her, but at least she wouldn't have been alone.

There's no point in spiraling about it now, though, I remind myself firmly. Matilda isn't on her own anymore. I'm so glad that she has Kimo, and that his entire family seems to have adopted her.

Helen frowns, too, at Matilda's question, and I can tell that she's going through a similar thought process. "I don't know . . . I'll have to check. Maybe he can tag along to Boston?"

"Tell him Kimo will buy him a plane ticket to come out here if he wants to spend Easter in Hawai'i. You, too, Nina."

I smile at the invitation, even though I know there's no way my uncle would ever allow it. "Thanks anyway, but we'll be busy here." I steel myself for what I have to say next, knowing it will be inviting a lot of scrutiny. But I've put off this conversation for as long as I can. "We're getting ready for a move, actually."

Seeing the alarm mirrored on Helen's and Matilda's faces, I hasten to add, "It's only temporary, for a few months in the spring. My cousin has been chosen to be the lead contestant on a new reality show."

I can tell that both women are surprised by this information. I haven't told them much about my family, beyond vague references to my aunt and uncle. I don't know if they even know that my cousin Harmony exists. They certainly don't know about how ambitious she is, and how certain she is that this is God's answer to her desire for the kind of platform that will let her launch her ministry so she can be the next Paula White or Lisa Bevere. She's so certain about this being the right path that even my uncle agreed to go along with it, even though it *is* television and Hollywood "always finds a way to mock the true believers."

I can tell Helen is trying her best not to look like she's thrown by this information, though her eyebrows are a dead giveaway. They're up almost to the top of her forehead. And she's blinking way too much. "That's . . . okay. Wow. What's the show?"

"It's called *Mountain Man*," I explain in as measured a voice as I can— as though I, too, don't find all of this to be completely bananas crazy. "I think it's new." I say *think* because I'm not really sure, since we can't watch unapproved television. At the very least, it's never crossed my radar before.

Matilda doesn't bother hiding her confusion—she is giving one of her typical exaggerated frowns directly into the camera. "So what—it's a bunch of lumberjacks vying for love?"

"Something like that," I say vaguely. So far as I know, that's true.

"That could be exciting." Helen does her best to sound supportive, giving my arm a little squeeze. "And you'll get to go somewhere new for a few months? I'll miss you, of course, but maybe you'll at least get to go somewhere cool."

I shrug. It's not like I have much of a say in it regardless, and knowing my family, I'll mostly be there to help watch after my younger cousins, not experience a new, unique culture or see new places. But again, I don't want to see the worried, furtively exchanged glances between my friends, so I do my best to smile. "I'm not sure, actually. It's some place in Tennessee. I think it's called Green Valley . . . ?"

The End

Acknowledgments

The idea of a writer alone at her desk, scribbling on her own, is a romantic one, but alas, it is not an accurate reflection of how writing really works. In *Nun Too Soon*, I forgot to include an acknowledgements section, but I do want to thank all the people whose collaboration and help made that novel possible. Thank you to Penny Reid, Fiona Fischer, and Brooke Nowiski for helping me to fine-tune the vision for that story and bring it to life. Thank you to my editors, Nicole McCurdy and Briana Ozor, for their invaluable feedback. Both of you have such incredible attention to detail and helped the story and characters have so much more sharpness and precision. Thank you also to ReGina Kaye for proofreading! Thank you to the musicians and creators whose content helped me keep my inspiration going. (Special shout-out to the score for *P.S. I Love You*, which became my soundtrack for writing.)

Thank you to my husband and son for giving me the space to write. Thanks also to my husband for being a handsome ginger and to my son for being so excited to see Mama's books when they come in the mail.

Thank you to everyone who helped me with this second book, as well —basically all the same from above, only this time the *Last Christmas* score helped me hear Matilda's heart. I had so much fun writing Matilda and Kimo's story, and I'm so thankful to everyone who has read this book. I still can't believe people are actually reading these stories and these characters; it is something I will never take for granted.

For this second book, I would also like to thank the people whose perspectives were essential in bringing Kimo and his family to life. Thank you most especially to Leilani Dong for answering my questions about Hawaiian culture. Your insights were so valuable and important; any mistakes that were made in the writing are my own. Leilani also directed me toward some important criticism that is necessary for understanding just how rich and complex Hawaiian culture is. I've tried to honor that in my writing, but with fiction there's always much that ultimately needs to be left off the page in service to the story, as well as certain aspects of the culture I didn't feel comfortable attempting to express as a non-Hawaiian, so I encourage any readers who are interested to do their own research into this vibrant, powerful community. Included here is a list of resources that were most useful to me:

- *Native Men Remade: Gender and Nation in Contemporary Hawai'i* by Ty P. Kāwika Tengan, Duke University Press, 2008.
- "What Pacific Islanders Want You To Know." *BuzzFeed Video*, 2017.
- "Aquaman Star Jason Momoa's Personal Guide to Hawaii - Going Places." *Condé Nast Traveller*, 2024.
- "We Are Mauna Kea." *Jason Momoa*, 2020.
- "20 Easy Ways to Speak Mo' Bettah Pidgin Today" by Anna Severson, *Hawai'i Life*, 2016.
- Various articles from *Hawai'i Magazine.*
- Many writings of Megan Kamalei Kakimoto, including "Our Hawaiian stories are not meant to be easy for you': Megan Kamalei Kakimoto on telling her ancestral tales"; "Megan Kamaei Kakimoto on the Many Ways to Tell a Hawaiian Story" ; and *Every Drop Is A Man's Nightmare*
- Hula by Jasmin Iolani Hakes, HarperCollins, 2023.
- "The Destruction of the Hawaiian Male" by Keone Nunes and Scott Whitney, *Honolulu*, 1994.
- *Finding 'Ohana*, Netflix, 2021.

About the Author

Lissa Sharpe is a mom, a wife, a teacher, a PhD, and an award-winning writer. She has written plays, screenplays, teleplays, short stories, songs, and now for the very first time, a romance novel. When she isn't having mental arguments with her characters, she is hanging out in the American South with her husband, son, and golden lab.

Find Lissa Sharpe online:
Facebook - https://www.facebook.com/profile.php?id=100095127281327
Twitter - https://twitter.com/AuthorLissaS
Instagram - https://www.instagram.com/lissasharpeauthor/
Pinterest - https://pin.it/1n38Ml7Vy
Website - lissasharpeauthor.wordpress.com
gmail- lissasharpeauthor@gmail.com
Newsletter: http://eepurl.com/iwYxdA

Find Smartypants Romance online:
Website: www.smartypantsromance.com
Facebook: www.facebook.com/smartypantsromance/
Goodreads: www.goodreads.com/smartypantsromance
Twitter: @smartypantsrom
Instagram: @smartypantsromance

Also by Lissa Sharpe

Bad Habit Book Club
Nun Too Soon, Book #1
Nun the Wiser, Book #2

As Elizabeth Gilliland:
<u>What Happened on Box Hill</u>
<u>The Portraits of Pemberley</u>
<u>Sly Jane Fairfax</u>
<u>Dear Prudent Elinor</u>

As E. Gilliland
<u>Come One, Come All</u>
<u>Round and Round We Go</u>

Also by Smartypants Romance

<u>The Teachers' Lounge Series</u>

<u>Passing Notes by Nora Everly (#1)</u>

<u>Band Together by Piper Sheldon (#2)</u>

<u>Ex Marks the Spot by Hazel James (#3)</u>

<u>Past Tents by Stacy Travis (#4)</u>

<u>The Best Medicine by Krysta Dearson (#5)</u>

<u>Story of Us Collection</u>

My Story of Us: Zach by Chris Brinkley (#1)

My Story of Us: Thomas by Chris Brinkley (#2)

My Story of Us: Grayson by Chris Brinkley (#3)

<u>Seduction in the City</u>

<u>Cipher Security Series</u>

<u>Code of Conduct by April White (#1)</u>

<u>Code of Honor by April White (#2)</u>

<u>Code of Matrimony by April White (#2.5)</u>

<u>Code of Ethics by April White (#3)</u>

<u>Cipher Office Series</u>

<u>Weight Expectations by M.E. Carter (#1)</u>

<u>Sticking to the Script by Stella Weaver (#2)</u>

<u>Cutie and the Beast by M.E. Carter (#3)</u>

<u>Weights of Wrath by M.E. Carter (#4)</u>

<u>Common Threads Series</u>

<u>Mad About Ewe by Susannah Nix (#1)</u>

<u>Give Love a Chai by Nanxi Wen (#2)</u>

<u>Key Change by Heidi Hutchinson (#3)</u>

<u>Not Since Ewe by Susannah Nix (#4)</u>

<u>Lost Track by Heidi Hutchinson (#5)</u>

<u>Ewe Complete Me by Susannah Nix (#6)</u>

<u>Meet Your Matcha by Nanxi Wen (#7)</u>

<u>All Mixed Up by Heidi Hutchinson (#8)</u>

<u>Write or Wrong by Heidi Hutchinson (#9)</u>

<u>Bad Habit Book Club Series</u>

<u>Nun Too Soon by Lissa Sharpe (#1)</u>

<u>Nun the Wiser by Lissa Sharpe (#2)</u>

<u>Educated Romance</u>

<u>Work For It Series</u>

<u>Street Smart by Aly Stiles (#1)</u>

<u>Heart Smart by Emma Lee Jayne (#2)</u>

<u>Book Smart by Amanda Pennington (#3)</u>

<u>Smart Mouth by Emma Lee Jayne (#4)</u>

<u>Play Smart by Aly Stiles (#5)</u>

<u>Look Smart by Aly Stiles (#6)</u>

<u>Smart Move by Amanda Pennington (#7)</u>

<u>Stage Smart by Aly Stiles (#8)</u>

<u>Lessons Learned Series</u>

<u>Under Pressure by Allie Winters (#1)</u>

<u>Not Fooling Anyone by Allie Winters (#2)</u>

<u>Can't Fight It by Allie Winters (#3)</u>

<u>The Vinyl Frontier by Lola West (#4)</u>

<u>Out of this World</u>

<u>London Ladies Embroidery Series</u>

<u>Neanderthal Seeks Duchess by Laney Hatcher (#1)</u>

<u>Well Acquainted by Laney Hatcher (#2)</u>

<u>Love Matched by Laney Hatcher (#3)</u>

<u>Wolf Brothers Series</u>